LIFE SUPPORT

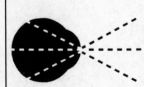

This Large Print Book carries the
Seal of Approval of N.A.V.H.

GRACE MEDICAL

LIFE SUPPORT

CANDACE CALVERT

THORNDIKE PRESS

A part of Gale, Cengage Learning

GALE
CENGAGE Learning·

Farmington Hills, Mich • San Francisco • New York • Waterville, Maine
Meriden, Conn • Mason, Ohio • Chicago

GALE
CENGAGE Learning®

Copyright © 2014 by Candace Calvert.
Scripture is taken from the Holy Bible, *New International Version®*.
NIV®. Copyright © 1973, 1978, 1984, 2011 by Biblica, Inc.™ Used by permission of Zondervan. All rights reserved worldwide.
www.zondervan.com.
Thorndike Press, a part of Gale, Cengage Learning.

LIBRARY OF CONGRESS CATALOGING-IN-PUBLICATION DATA

Calvert, Candace, 1950–
    Life support / by Candace Calvert. — Large print edition.
        pages ; cm. — (Thorndike Press large print clean reads) (Grace medical ;
    #3)
    ISBN 978-1-4104-6941-0 (hardcover) — ISBN 1-4104-6941-7 (hardcover)
    1. Nurses—Fiction. 2. Physicians' assistants—Fiction. 3. Brothers and
sisters—Fiction. 4. Mentally ill—Fiction. 5. Hurricanes—Fiction. 6. Large type
books. I. Title.
PS3603.A4463L54 2014b
813'.6—dc23   2014005549

Published in 2014 by arrangement with Tyndale House Publishers, Inc.

Printed in Mexico
1 2 3 4 5 6 7 18 17 16 15 14

For Dub and Carolyn Helm.
Yours is a true love story.

ACKNOWLEDGMENTS

Heartfelt appreciation to:

Literary agent Natasha Kern — you are forever a blessing.

The entire Tyndale House publishing team, especially editors Jan Stob and Sarah Mason and copy editor Erin Smith. (Patting my heart.) It's an honor to partner with you all.

Nancy Herriman — talented author, dear friend, longtime critique partner. I can't imagine doing this without you, pal. Let's keep rolling!

Kathy — for your gracious gift of help in creating the character of Jessica Barclay.

Jeannie Campbell (The Character Therapist) — for giving my characters some "couch time." Your expertise was beyond helpful.

Donna Weyd — for sharing your very real hurricane accounts, helping to create my fictional storm.

7

Reader Kristin Kertes — for stepping up with a new, perfect title: *Life Support.* Thank you!

Cousin Carolyn Helm — for allowing your feisty, real-life Hannah Leigh to sashay through this story. You both rock!

My husband and family — your loving encouragement lifts my heart, always.

And finally, to my dear readers — connecting with you is such a blessing. Thank you for inviting me into your homes, your hearts. You're the reason I write.

I would hurry to my place of shelter,
far from the tempest and storm.

PSALM 55:8

1

"Heart rate's climbed to 148," Lauren Barclay warned, her words blending with a monitor alarm in dark harmony. The clatter of resuscitation equipment being hustled into place by fellow ER nurses snuffed out the rest of her report. A strangled gasp from the head of the gurney validated Lauren's concerns: this man was failing in the painful struggle to fill his lungs. Her stomach knotted. They couldn't lose him. Not the brother of one of their team.

Please . . .

"O_2 saturation is tanking, Doctor." She grabbed the hissing suction catheter and wedged closer, determined to get the physician's attention. Her eyes watered at a sudden whiff of iodine and alcohol. "His skin's really gray."

"I see that, Lauren — I'm not blind." The physician pulled the fiber-optic scope from his patient's mouth, growling with frustration. "Suction! Clear his airway."

"Got it." Lauren moved in quickly, a respiratory therapist behind her with the Ambu bag. She slid the catheter between the unconscious man's lips, struck again by the familiarity of his features: dark hair and lashes, that hint of olive in his complexion despite his pallor. She'd have known he was Eli Landry's older brother even without seeing the medical record. Andrew Landry, thirty-six years old, had suffered a traumatic brain injury twenty-some years ago — a boating accident and near drowning that left him comatose on a ventilator for many months afterward. And severely disabled since. He was a man who should have been remarkably handsome, vital — embracing a hopeful, successful life — but was instead gaunt, withered, almost helpless. And dying?

Lauren glanced at his half-closed lids, the stray curl clinging to his clammy forehead. She'd never actually seen Andrew before today, but his tragic history was well known in Houston because his father —

"Hyperventilate him," the doctor ordered as a respiratory therapist slid a mask over the man's face. "And restrain those arms if you need to. Arm — he only has the use of the left one." He pulled off dark-framed glasses and wiped them with the hem of his scrub top, watching as the therapist began to squeeze the bag to assist respirations. "He's going to quit breathing. If I can't get this tube in, I'll have no choice but to trach him."

The physician ran a gloved finger over a thickened, pearly scar on his patient's throat, uttering something that sounded like "Why me?" He met Lauren's gaze at last. "Look, I'm sorry for snapping at you." Despite the air-conditioning, the young man's thinning hairline and forehead glistened with perspiration. Nervous sweat. It spread across the neckline and chest of his green scrub top, as if the stifling June humidity had slammed through the doors of Houston Grace Hospital along with the rushing ambulance gurney. "It's just that —"

"He's Eli's brother," Lauren finished in a raw whisper, the physician assistant's name never failing to cause her discomfort.

"And Judge Julien Landry's oldest son." The doctor lowered his voice. "Eli and his father have been at odds about Andrew for months. Everyone knows that. I need to be in the middle of that battle like I need a hurricane to flatten my house."

"I hear you." Lauren's gaze darted toward

the hallway that led to the ambulance bay. The Caribbean was brewing a trio of tropical storms. She'd almost prefer that over what might happen here today. Things were tough enough without added conflict. She'd moved back to Houston — accepted a position in this ER — to keep a protective eye on her younger sister, Jessica. The twenty-one-year-old was making reckless choices, and if she didn't straighten up, her job at Houston Grace was at risk. As was her acceptance into nursing school in the fall . . . *and even her life?* No. Lauren refused to believe Jess's problems were that serious. Unfortunately, there was one thing she couldn't deny: Eli Landry was part of the whole mess.

"Okay, then." The doctor signaled to the respiratory therapist that he was going to attempt another intubation. He glanced at the clock, then turned to Lauren. "What time is Eli due in the urgent care?"

"Not till four, unless he's heard —"

There were voices outside the code room doors. A woman, their emergency department manager. The other voice was much deeper.

"Is that . . . ?" The physician's gaze moved to the doorway, and the room went strangely quiet except for the *whoosh-burp* of the

14

plastic mask bucking against its seal over Andrew Landry's face.

"Oh no." The words slipped out before Lauren could stop them. "He's here."

Eli Landry shoved the code room doors open, telling himself the same thing he always did: he was prepared for whatever he'd find. After years of trying, he still hadn't convinced himself.

"Eli . . ."

The ER doctor, Mike Duhain, walked toward him. Sweating — always a bad sign.

"Mike." Eli looked at the heart monitor: tachycardic but regular. Only then did he allow his gaze to move to his brother's face, partially obscured by a translucent green resuscitation mask. *Alive.* He released the breath he'd been holding. "What's going on with Drew?"

"The care home told the medics he was breathing hard last night, sleepy today. Had a shaking episode. He arrived here with severe respiratory compromise and hypoxemia." Mike glanced toward the monitors as an alarm sounded. "Oxygen saturation's 89 percent even with the high-flow bag assist."

"Fever?" Eli noticed for the first time that Lauren Barclay was in the room. Pink scrubs, honey-colored hair rebelling against the summer humidity. Only concern for his brother could have provided enough distraction to make him miss such a staggering sight.

"His temp was 104.2," she reported, moving to the computer a few feet from where they stood. She managed to avoid Eli's eyes — a skill she'd perfected since her return to Houston. Right now, he was grateful. The last thing Eli wanted — besides for his brother's heartbeat to suddenly flatline — was to see disapproval in Lauren's eyes. Had she heard what was going on with his family?

"We sent blood to the lab and they're drawing for arterial gases now," Mike continued. "X-ray is coming for a portable chest; I hear coarse crackles throughout. I've made a couple of attempts to tube him. I was about to try again with a smaller —"

"You won't get a tube in," Eli interrupted. "His trachea's a mess. There's scarring and stenosis. Every med student and rookie paramedic in the county has used my brother for *practice.*"

He knew he'd spit out the last word and reminded himself that Mike Duhain was a skilled doctor and a more-than-decent guy. He was also providing physician support for

Eli's shift in the adjacent urgent care department. It would be an unwelcome role reversal for a PA to direct a board-certified emergency department physician. And unethical because this was a family member, but . . .

"Drew had that first trach after the accident," Eli explained further, "and then an emergency crike during a drug reaction three years ago — multiple traumatic attempts to get that tube in. More scarring. And he's had fractured ribs, sternum, and a contused spleen when some cowboy first responder couldn't tell he didn't need cardiac compressions." Eli's gut roiled. "My brother has been through way too much."

Mike swiped at his forehead. "I hear you. But he's in serious trouble right now." His eyes met Eli's, the meaning crystal clear: *What do you expect from me?*

Eli glanced at Drew with a sigh. "This is almost always pneumonia. Complicated by his asthma. He's had some close calls the past two years. Ended up on a ventilator with ARDS last Christmas. There were heart-rhythm problems related to that." Saying it out loud ripped a scab off things he wanted to forget: machines, tubes, shrilling alarms, sleepless nights. And his mother's tearful midnight request for the Landrys' pastor.

"I've put in a call to his pulmonologist," Mike assured. "But right now . . ."

"If it's early enough," Eli suggested, risking a wish that it really was, "you might turn this around with BiPAP. It worked last time. Took a while, but it worked. Drew's record will show the effective antibiotics." He glanced toward his brother again as monitor alarms briefly sounded.

"Good. We'll try that." Mike gave an order to a second respiratory therapist, then turned back to Eli and lowered his voice. "The care home sent a copy of Andrew's advance medical directive. It looks recent. And it says he's a full code. No restrictions."

Eli's pulse quickened; it was time to do this. Past time. "That's wrong. We're revising it. It should say 'no artificial life support.' " *No more painful interventions.*

"You mean . . . do not resuscitate?"

"No ventilator, no cardiac compressions. No defibrillation," Eli confirmed, remembering his long conversation with his mother last week. He'd left the paperwork with her. "Comfort care. That's what we want. If it comes to that."

The silence in the room was broken only by the *squeeze-whoosh* of the Ambu bag helping Drew to breathe. Lauren's fingers hovered over the computer keyboard.

"This is something new?" Mike asked, observably wary.

New? Eli had a sick urge to laugh . . . or scream. Slam his fist into the wall and shout loud enough for God himself to hear. Did that huge dented scar on his brother's head look *new*? Did it seem anywhere near possible that he'd tossed a football around even once in the last twenty years? Could they begin to imagine how many times he'd been poked, prodded, choked, and tied down? Eli's heart cramped at the truth: he could hardly remember a moment in his life when their family tragedy wasn't reflected in his mother's sad eyes.

"Yes," he confirmed, aware of Lauren's gaze. "It's a new medical directive. I'll make sure the paperwork gets —"

"Hold on." Mike's wariness morphed into an expression of visceral discomfort. He took a few steps away, indicating that Eli should follow, and dropped his voice to a whisper. "I had a phone call from the chief of staff."

Ah . . . no surprise. Eli heard the gargle from aggressive suctioning of his brother's scarred airway. "Let me guess — after he was contacted by Judge Landry?"

"It was made clear that your father is still responsible for all decisions in Andrew's care. He alone. Not your mother. Or anyone else." The physician's grimace could sell antacids. "Your father apparently mentioned a restraining order. Against *you.*"

"Threat. Not fact." Eli's jaw tensed. They might as well string the Landrys' dirty laundry through the halls of Houston Grace. Post photos to Facebook. "Look, Mike, no one wants Drew to pull out of this more than I do. *No one.* Anybody who says otherwise is way off base. But I can't stand by and watch my brother suffer, only to end up on the kind of 'life support' that means no life at all. If Drew can't beat it this time, or the next time or the next, I want to promise him some peace. I need to do that much."

"I get that. I do. And I respect you, Eli. You know that. I feel for your situation. But my hands are tied." Mike shook his head. "I think it's best that you step away now. I'll do everything I can to get your brother stabilized and up to the ICU."

Eli glanced toward Drew; his brother's face was now covered by a BiPAP mask. "Give me a minute?"

"Of course."

Eli walked to the head of the gurney and

rested his hand on Drew's shoulder, gave it a squeeze. "I'm here, Champ." A deep ache replaced his anger. He closed his eyes for a moment, remembering his brother's laugh. Hoping against the odds that he'd hear it again.

As he turned away, Lauren Barclay's eyes met his for an unexpected instant. Her expression was a cloudy mix of concern and . . . *judgment*? He didn't need that now.

Eli sought Mike's gaze. "If you try to tube him again, call me. Let me at least talk him through it. It helps if he hears my voice." His heart gave a dull thud. "We're a team that way. The first time we did it, I was eleven years old."

Eli walked from the room, aware of the whispers and covert glances. He didn't care. This was about his brother. He couldn't let Drew suffer. Wouldn't. And if it came down to a battle with their father . . . Well, that storm had been brewing for a long time.

2

"Another speck of humidity and I swear I'm going to shave my head." Lauren peered across the hospital picnic table at ER tech Varina Viette — Vee for short — while trying to lift her heavy hair away from her neck. There wasn't a merciful wisp of a breeze, and more clouds were gathering. Combined with the incessant *honk, screech, whoosh* of multilevel freeways, the atmosphere felt nearly as unsettling as that squall in the code room.

Lauren frowned, then drew in a breath scented by damp asphalt. "You were right," she told Vee. "Even with these trees we'd be better off having our sandwiches down in the cafeteria. Or maybe inside the blood bank fridge. It's forty-six degrees in there."

"Blood bank?" Vee shook her head, sending a mane of micro braids swinging against her mocha skin. "Now I *know* you're more interested in escape than trying my muffulettas." Her delicate lisp disappeared into a paper napkin as she dabbed her lips. "Thanks bunches, Barclay. I thought my cooking and general awesomeness were the big draws that made you finally agree to take a break from that madhouse."

"The food was great." Lauren glanced appreciatively at the last remaining olive-and-salami morsels of the Cajun sandwich. "And you *are* awesome." She smiled. It was true. Vee was a big positive in Lauren's mixed bag of feelings about returning home. She'd never met anyone quite like her. Wise far beyond her twenty-one years, she had a quiet strength and an aura of peace that, frankly, Lauren envied. It seemed so unlikely, since Vee's childhood had included major upheaval.

"I don't blame you for wanting to escape." Vee's eyes lost their teasing gleam. "It was rough in there with Eli and his brother. I've seen Drew before. First at Kingwood Medical Center about two years ago, when I was doing my tech training. He was still living at home then, using private duty nurses; they moved him into the first care home after that long hospitalization last December." She sighed. "He was here in the ER during Easter week, right before you were hired. I could tell then that he'd deteriorated. So sad."

"Yes," Lauren agreed. She'd seen the medical record. Andrew Landry had spent the majority of his time in bed during the last six months but apparently could still speak limited words. The brain injury had left him with a child's cognitive ability, but subsequent infections and cardiorespiratory events continued to rob him of even that small blessing. Lauren thought of the moment before Eli swept out of the code room. When their eyes met briefly, what had she seen there? He was so hard to read. Lauren wouldn't let herself imagine the pain she'd feel if it were Jessica on that gurney.

She tamped down a prickle of anxiety — she hadn't talked with her sister today. Jess was scheduled to start her night shift as a registration clerk in a few hours.

"He keeps things so private," Lauren said finally. "Eli, I mean."

"He tries." Vee touched the small silver cross at the hollow of her throat. "That Easter visit turned into a circus. The ER doc questioned Drew's full code status, and Judge Landry started shouting about doctors playing God, then about the sanctity of life itself. Eli tried to settle him down and his father unleashed on him, too. He actually accused Eli of wishing his brother harm.

Can you imagine?"

Lauren thought of what she'd overheard in the code room about a restraining order. Obviously there were still problems.

Vee sighed. "Poor Mrs. Landry ended up on a gurney with a panic attack. I felt so sorry for her. I think I patted her hand about two hundred times."

"Awful." Lauren clucked her tongue, knowing her own mother would rather die than create a public scene. Even worse if it were her daughters causing embarrassment to the family. She glanced toward the doors to the ER, glad to see no ambulances in the parking area. And no crowd of incoming patients, only a young boy using a cell phone near the doors. "You'd think a federal judge would be more discreet."

Vee was quiet for a moment, sliding one of her braids between her fingers. "I suppose he thought he was protecting Drew, saving him even. You don't stop to think about something like that. You react." She let go of the braid, met Lauren's gaze. "It's more like instinct. Right?"

"I guess." Protecting Jess had been a priority for as long as Lauren could remember. From that first moment she stood on tiptoe, in her *I'm the Big Sister* T-shirt, peering through the nursery window at her tiny, premature sister. Lauren wasn't sure if her role was an instinct born of that moment or something assigned by her parents. But it had stuck, and during the past year or so, the protection duty had required running interference between her sister and Eli Landry — a friendship her parents blamed for Jess's bouts of reckless behavior.

In truth, it was far from the first time Jess had been irresponsible and moody. And not unusual for their parents to blame it on the dubious influence of friends, it turned into a dizzying cycle since Jess tended to treat relationships the way their dad handled the TV remote. For whatever reason, Eli Landry seemed currently offscreen in the friend queue. Lauren was grateful to have him at a distance. The man never failed to rattle her. Eating Cajun sandwiches in the blood bank was far more palatable.

"So . . ." Lauren found a mustard-free spot on her napkin and patted her perspiring forehead. As if signaled, the dense and darkening sky rumbled with thunder, then belched a sticky breeze. "My mother —" she made her voice impressively dramatic — "the *official* Houston weather center volunteer, is convinced those tropical storms aren't a problem. She and Dad would never have flown off to Colorado otherwise —

regardless of my aunt's gallbladder surgery." She glanced at the sky. "What do you think?"

" 'Get a kit. Make a plan. Be informed.' " Vee recited the familiar disaster mantra.

"You sound like Mom. I'm surprised she doesn't have that slogan embroidered on a pillow. Along with her decorative wall of radar maps and forty framed photos of my great-great-grandmother, the hurricane hero."

"Hero?"

"Jess calls her that; she was named after her. Our great-great-grandmother was living in Galveston during the hurricane of 1900. We've heard the stories since we were babies. Folks launching mattresses from second-story windows, Grandmother Jessica tying her children to a tree with ropes . . . It was horrific, of course. Anyone who survived that disaster *was* heroic. But Jess likes to push Mom's buttons, tells her she ought to spend less time conducting tours through the weather museum and more time practicing knots." Lauren fanned herself with the crumpled napkin. "But then I'll bet no one can top the Barclay stash of D batteries, peanut butter, dry shampoo, and —" She stopped. "Oh, Vee, I'm sorry. I'm an idiot."

"Why? What do you mean?"

Lauren winced. "You lived through a cat-5 — lost everything — and I sit here making jokes about my parents' overkill storm tactics. I should snag some of that cache of duct tape for my big mouth." She didn't deserve Vee's gracious smile.

"First of all, I didn't lose everything. Not the most important things. And maybe your mother is kind of overkill sometimes, but being prepared is a good thing. We can't know what's coming." Vee's fingers found the cross again. "You just made me think of something my auntie Odette would say."

Lauren smiled. Vee's oft-quoted great-aunt had passed away in January at age ninety-three. She'd gone peacefully in her sleep after preparing a gigantic feast of red beans, dirty rice, and crab cakes. The meal had been a treat for staff, patients, and families of Mimaw's Nest, the residential care home run by several members of the Viette family — all evacuees from Hurricane Katrina. Located west of Houston, near Katy, Mimaw's cared for about fourteen residents, most of them long-term and very happy to be there. The home had recently undergone some staffing challenges, and Lauren was helping out when she could. "What would Odette say?"

Vee tipped her head as she tried to recall. "Talking about storms, she'd say something like, 'You're either in one, fixin' to go into one, comin' out the other side a one, or you're *causin'* one.' " Vee clucked her tongue. "Then she'd point that crooked finger and ask, 'Which are *you*?' "

Me?

"Ah . . ." Lauren realized she'd shredded her napkin. She dropped it onto the waxed paper from her sandwich. There was no valid reason a folksy Odette-ism should make her uncomfortable. There was no storm here, weather or otherwise.

"I'm due back inside." Vee tapped her watch. "You still have ten minutes." She glanced at the young boy walking past them, still talking on his cell phone. "Let me help you with the trash."

"No thanks. It's the least I can do. You made the sandwich." Lauren smiled, pulling her lip gloss from her purse. "And you kept me from going into seclusion in the blood closet."

Vee rolled her eyes. "You're right. You owe me."

As Vee left, Lauren checked her own watch. She did have a few more minutes, and she'd take them. Maybe send Jessica a quick text. Thankfully, this day seemed to

29

be moving away from chaos; every sign pointed in that direction. Andrew Landry had stabilized and wasn't going to need that hotly contested advance directive — at least not on Lauren's watch. In fact, his mother had called to say that since the judge was a little "under the weather" and things had improved significantly with Drew, they'd visit tomorrow instead. The ER staff had high-fived each other.

Lauren pulled out her cell phone. In a short while, Drew would be in the ICU, and Eli would put on his white coat and disappear into the adjacent department to start seeing his own patients. That alone would make things considerably better. Then Jess would arrive for her assigned shift, and Lauren would have a chance to make sure everything was okay before heading home herself. The fickle weather would clear. No hurricanes; no need for dry shampoo, stockpiled batteries, or lashing anyone to a tree. No more Landry drama or —

"Excuse me, ma'am."

"Oh . . . hi." Lauren glanced up, surprised to see the youngster appear out of nowhere. Maybe eight years old, wearing an oversize Texans football jersey and a frayed ball cap pulled low over raisin-dark eyes. The boy who'd walked by with the cell phone. "Did you need something?"

"I didn't ask the door code to get back inside the ER."

"The doors aren't locked." Lauren glanced toward the main entrance. "They're automatic. Push the button next to them."

"Not those doors." The boy turned to point toward the employee entrance, and Lauren was surprised to see a rainbow painted on his cheek. Festive neon colors, heart-shaped clouds — totally at odds with everything else about him. "There. That door," he explained. "That's the one we went in. I didn't think I could use my phone in there. So I came outside."

"But . . ." Thunder rumbled as if to underscore Lauren's confusion. It was compounded by the strangest sense that she recognized this kid. "That door is for employees only."

"My dad works here — I'm with him."

And I'm stupid. The features were so obvious. Lauren's neck prickled.

"No problem," the child said with a shrug. "If you don't know the code, I can probably get someone to let me in from the lobby or —"

"I know the door code. I'll take you inside." Lauren managed a smile. "I'm Lauren. And you're . . . ?"

31

"Emma Marie Landry."

Eli's daughter.

He'd managed to rattle Lauren again.

3

How could Lauren have missed that they were father and child? She'd paused near the door to the code room, helpless to stop herself from taking a peek inside. A trio of Landrys . . .

Emma had pulled off her cap, revealing hair the same rich loamy shade as her dad's and uncle's. It was short, worn in careless thatches like it had been styled by a leaf blower. Her smile was a picket fence of baby and adult teeth, but her chin and features were decidedly feminine. Her brown eyes were fringed with lashes so lush that Lauren wondered how she could have ever mistaken the child for a boy. Regardless, she and Eli were so alike right this moment, even in their posture as they stood beside Drew's gurney. Hips cocked a bit to one side, shoulders rounded — the much larger set now in a starched white coat, the girl's in that faded team jersey. Both had their hands clasped behind their backs. The gurney's safety rail had been lowered so that —

Oh . . . Lauren's breath snagged as Eli lifted his daughter to reach her unconscious uncle. Emma hesitated for a brief second as if figuring out how to deal with the oxygen mask, tubing, and web of electrical wires. Then she stretched forward and pressed a kiss on Drew's pale cheek. One little arm snaked across his hospital gown to hug him as she burrowed her pixie face closer, whispering in earnest. Lauren's throat tightened. In this child's entire life, she couldn't have known her uncle to be much more than what he was right now. Yet her love for him was so beautifully apparent.

"No fairy-tale ending there." Gayle Garner, the department's ever-bustling nurse manager, made a rare stop beside Lauren. She hoisted a coffee mug in both hands, her prominent eyes sweeping the code room scene. "Tough thing to learn when you're only eight. Or even forty-eight."

"Yes," Lauren agreed. She didn't know Gayle's exact age but suspected the manager was thinking of her own situation: a husband out of work for more than a year due to injury, no disability insurance or compensation. But plenty of medical bills. Gayle never complained, but the extra shifts had to be taking a toll; she looked tired, thinner, and there was an increasingly anxious look in her eyes. Nevertheless, she was probably the best team leader Lauren had ever worked with. Professional, hands-on, firm but fair. And kind. She'd been especially understanding regarding Jess.

"Well then . . ." Gayle switched her coffee cup to one hand in order to check her watch. Her fingers trembled slightly, reminding Lauren to be mindful of her own caffeine intake. "Your sister's coming on shift at seven?"

"Right." Lauren felt that frisson of anxiety again. Besides the administration, only two other people in the hospital knew Jess had tested positive on a random drug test last fall. Gayle was one of them; she'd gone to bat for Jess and had been instrumental in keeping Jess from being suspended. It was a blessing Lauren would never forget. "I'm leaving; she's coming — like ships passing in the night," she added, hoping her smile looked casual. Why wasn't Jess returning calls? "We're both staying at our parents' place right now. But working opposite shifts, we sometimes miss each other. She'll be here."

"Good. There was a sick call, so ER

registration will be short-staffed tonight. Friday night and a full moon — you know we'll be swamped. I'll count on Jessica to take up some slack." Gayle smiled warmly. "When she stays on task, she works like *two* people. A lot like her big sister."

"Nnnurse!" An alcohol-slurred shout rose from behind a curtained gurney. "I'm gonna need that bedpan again. And this yellow IV bag looks like it's runnin' low. . . . Yooo-hoo, Nurse!"

"That's me." Lauren smiled. "And that other me, too. Good thing I have four hands."

"Careful," Gayle teased, already on her way back toward the desk. "I'll clone you."

Lauren glanced at the scene in the code room one last time. *"No fairy-tale . . ."* Not even close. On all counts. Eli was the other person who knew about Jess's drug test. Jess had begged him to speak up for her. Lauren had too, asking him to at least vouch for her sister's character. But unlike Gayle Garner, he'd done nothing whatsoever to help. Far from it — he'd even suggested that Jess's emotional instability put her at risk for substance abuse. Their parents had been furious. Lauren still was. Who needed enemies with friends like that?

■ ■ ■ ■

"Look." Emma's lips curved into that innocent and incredulous smile that never failed to make Eli's heart turn to mush. "Do you see it? A rainbow. Right there on Uncle Drew's cheek."

Eli's gaze moved reluctantly to where she was pointing. Emma was right. Her enthusiastic "uncle snunkle" — a silly variation on the word *snuggle* she'd invented at age two — had left a faint imprint of a rainbow on his brother's cheek. Like one of those admission hand stamps. As if Drew had taken his only niece to the circus or Disney World. Among the innumerable things he'd never do.

The low-oxygen alarm sounded briefly to prove that painful truth. Eli adjusted the finger sensor, glanced at the cardiac monitor. Mike had made good on that promise: though catastrophically brain-injured, Eli's brother was basically stable. The irony was cruel.

"I remember all those things you told me about rainbows." Emma's expression was serious again. "About light being made up of every color, and raindrops are like that glass prism I have in my window at Grams's house. And when the white light goes into the prism, it gets afflicted —"

"Refracted." Eli smiled. "Refracted and then reflected back. Science."

"And angels." The smile came back, sweetly parrying. She glanced at the cardiac monitor, then around the room. Her shoulders rose and fell in a sigh. "Are Grams and Yonner coming to pick me up?"

Yonner — Your Honor. For the first time, her loving nickname for his father rankled, making Eli recall the conversation with Mike right here in this room. That phone call from the chief of staff, who'd been contacted by the Honorable Judge Julien Landry. "No," he told his daughter, hating that his tone sounded sharp. He took a breath. "You can stay here and sit in my office while I work. I'll get you paper and pencils and a grilled cheese sandwich from the cafeteria."

"Are you and Yonner mad at each other again?"

Eli couldn't remember a time when they *weren't* at odds. Or when his father had been anything other than completely disappointed in him. For being a father but not a husband, for joining the Army, and then for deciding against law school to become a physician assistant. *And for not being my brother?*

"No," Eli answered finally. "We're not mad."

Emma rested her cheek against Drew's arm. It was dotted with bruises from failed needle sticks, the muscles contracted from the one-sided paralysis caused by his brain injury. "I haven't been staying with Yonner and Grams so much anymore. Are you keeping me away from their house because of the fire? Grams said it was an accident."

"She explained that to me too."

"Oh, good." Emma nodded, concern in her eyes. "We didn't want you to worry."

Worry? Eli wanted to tell his daughter that even if he didn't buy into her angel theory of rainbows, he wanted to believe her grandmother was right. That it had been a careless moment, a cigar left burning in the kitchen during one of the judge's frequent bouts of insomnia. The last thing Eli wanted to accept was that his father was drinking again. Heavily enough to impair his mental faculties, endanger his health, and threaten the safety of his family. Including Emma.

If that was the case, it meant that Judge Landry's ability to make decisions could also be impaired. Like his insistence on denying his oldest son mercy. Eli wasn't going to let that happen.

■ ■ ■ ■

"I really appreciate your help," Lauren told Vee as they closed the doors to ICU and began walking back toward the emergency department. She swiped at a wavy tendril of hair that had escaped her haphazard ponytail, a last failed attempt to control the humidity's havoc. "Even with respiratory therapy taking their things, pushing Drew's bed with all that equipment was more than I could handle."

"No problem. Did you notice the rainbow?"

Lauren's brows scrunched. "It's raining?"

"No. That rainbow smudge on the side of Drew's face. At first I thought it was a bruise from the intubation attempts or the BiPAP mask." Vee smiled. "It rubbed onto him from Emma's cheek. They did face painting at her summer camp; Eli was picking her up when he got the call about his brother. She's a sweet kid. We talked for a while, and . . ." Vee sounded hesitant. "I think I'm going to approach Eli about moving his brother to Mimaw's Nest when he's ready for discharge."

"Wha . . . ?" Lauren stopped walking. Then moved aside to accommodate a nurse pushing a wheelchair with a labor patient panting and rubbing circles on her belly. "Why?"

"Because," Vee explained, "it's clear the Landrys have been moving Drew from place to place over the last few months. None of the facilities they've tried meet their approval. At least not for long." She clucked her tongue. "Emma said it's been like 'The Story of the Three Bears,' with Goldilocks and the porridge: 'Too hot, too cold . . .' "

"Hmm." Lauren thought of the Viettes' quaint refurbished home about thirty minutes' drive from here. Licensed and quite adequately equipped, it had surprising charm too. Porch rockers, overstuffed chairs, music, warm laughter — less that said "care home" and so much more that breathed "loving care." She shook her head. "And you think you can satisfy those picky people?"

"I think that sweet girl's uncle deserves some stability and plenty of TLC. It's crucial to his quality of life." Vee's eyes teased. "And besides, Mimaw's porridge is *just right.*"

They started walking again, Lauren taking a peek at her watch. It was 7:10. Her shift was nearly over. Jess would be in the ER registration office.

"It sounds like Judge Landry makes the final decisions," Vee continued. "So I don't know if anything will come of my suggesting our care home. But I thought I should clear it with you first. We really need your help right now, Lauren, and I wouldn't do anything that would make you uncomfortable."

"Uncomfortable?"

"Because Eli would come there sometimes. And you've had some issues with him because of your sis—"

"It's fine," Lauren insisted, cutting her off. She wrestled with a wave of regret; she shouldn't have confided even what little she had to Vee. Her parents would hate that she had. "I don't have a problem with Eli. And my sister has been doing fine. Great, in fact."

But when Lauren stopped by the registration office five minutes later, Jess hadn't shown up for her shift.

"How may I help you today, Ms. Grafton?" Eli stepped into the urgent care exam room, immediately discovering a part of his patient's problem: she was in police custody. A young officer leaning a shoulder against the wall straightened his posture at Eli's glance. He was a few inches taller than Eli,

42

with sandy-blond hair and an earnest expression. Though Eli had seen him around the hospital before, they'd never met officially. Eli returned the man's nod, then took a good look at his patient.

The twenty-six-year-old woman, barefoot and dressed in green shorts and a purple bikini top, sat on the exam table with her face buried in her hands. A long tumble of red hair made Eli think of Emma's DVD of *The Little Mermaid.* Her thighs looked painfully sunburned.

"Darcee?" Eli stepped closer. "I'm Eli Landry, a physician assistant here in urgent care. What brings you in today?"

Her head jerked up "What brings me in?" Her scratchy voice gave way to a cackle of laughter as she pointed to the officer. "*That* guy! That's what brought me in today. So much for your finely tuned observation skills, Doc."

"PA," he clarified, knowing it was pointless to correct her. Though his white coat was clearly labeled with his name followed by *PA-C,* certified physician assistant, many patients continued to refer to him as "Doctor." Some because they were uncomfortable using his name, most out of habit, and this woman likely because she couldn't remember what he'd said. Eli was sure he'd caught a whiff of alcohol on her breath. He squinted, taking a better look at the woman's face: attractive and basically clean, but badly sunburned — blisters, dry lips.

Before he could question her further, Darcee Grafton groaned, stretched out on the exam table, and flung a freckled arm across her eyes. Almost immediately she began to snore.

"Well." Eli turned to the policeman, read his name tag. "What can you tell me, Officer Holt?"

"Fletcher Holt." The young man offered Eli a firm handshake. "Got a call about a woman making a scene at Hermann Park. Dancing in the reflecting pool. Singing at the top of her lungs since early this morning. You can hear that her voice is strained. One of the park employees said she'd been there yesterday, too. He alleges that when he suggested she go along home, she made some . . . inappropriate advances toward him."

"No one was there with her?"

"No report of that. And no purse or ID. But she had that pill bottle tucked into a six-pack of Shiner beer." He pointed to the metal cart next to the exam table. "There."

Eli reached for the bottle, sensing he'd be turning this case over to the ER physician next door. The triage nurse had missed this one. Sunburn Eli could handle, even mild intoxication, but if there was a possibility of an overdose . . . "It's Lamictal. Empty. And —" he checked the date one more time to be sure — "she probably ran out more than a week ago. That could explain a lot. It's a seizure medication. But it's one of the drugs that's been found to be effective for patients with certain psychiatric disorders."

"As a mood stabilizer?" Holt cleared his throat. "I've been doing some research lately."

"Yes. It prevents rapid cycling from manic episodes — possibly what you saw today — into serious depression." Eli glanced at the sleeping woman. "She's under arrest?"

"No. But I may have implied that to her." Holt's expression was one of undeniable compassion. "You can see how badly she's sunburned. There were still five beers in that carton, and she only blew a .02 on my Breathalyzer. But I thought she needed a medical check. Maybe a psych eval. I didn't think she'd stick around for the paramedics, so . . ."

"Got it." Eli nodded. "I agree. Her vital signs are fairly normal, but she needs a thorough exam. Labs with toxicology and a Lamictal level, neuro workup, minor burn care, IV fluids. And that psych eval. I'll consult with the ER physician, see if he wants me to start here or send her —"

"Excuse me." Lauren Barclay poked her head into the room. She did a double take when she caught sight of the officer, offered him a tense smile. "Hey, Fletcher." Then her blue eyes met Eli's. "I need to speak with you."

"Sure." Eli wondered briefly about her connection to Fletcher Holt. "I'll be just a moment here."

"Now," Lauren insisted, her expression flooding with anxiety. "Please. It's important."

4

"Have you heard from Jess today?" Lauren tried to keep her voice calm, but it sounded breathless even to her own ears. Partly from worry, partly from being forced to have this conversation with Eli. Right now, she wasn't sure which was worse. "She hasn't shown up for work. She was scheduled to start at seven."

"What time is it?" Eli checked his watch, dark brows furrowing. The angle of his jaw and the half-lidded eyes — even the twitch of his lips — couldn't have been more like Drew's and Emma's. "It's barely seven thirty. *Late* is Jessica's middle name."

Lauren stiffened. "You didn't answer my question." She struggled to keep her voice low outside the exam room. In the office directly across, Emma sat hunched over Eli's desk. "Have you heard from her? Seen her? That's all I want to know."

"No." Eli's gaze held Lauren's for an

uncomfortably long moment. "Not since the last time we worked together. I'm guessing you haven't heard from her either."

"Not today. I've called and texted — nothing back." Lauren thought she heard singing, maybe alternating with crying, coming from the exam room they'd left. And then Fletcher's steady voice. "Look," she continued, "I'm worried. I've been after Jess to get that car serviced; the tires aren't good and she drives around on fumes half the time. Too fast *all* the time. I'm sure you know that."

"What I know is that the kind of help your sister needs isn't offered at Jiffy Lube. I believe I've tried to discuss that with you. More than once."

"Don't," Lauren warned, barely holding back a glare. "Don't start with that lecture. I didn't come over here for your personal opinions. They don't help, and I don't have time to waste." Her throat tightened. "For all I know my sister is lying in a ditch somewhere."

"Or dancing in a park."

"What?" Lauren gave in to the urge and glared. "Never mind. I shouldn't have bothered you. Clearly you don't care." She took a step away.

"Hey, wait." Eli glanced at his office, his

daughter. "It's not that I can't understand your concerns. Obviously I have family problems of my own. But we both know this isn't that unusual for Jessica." He raised his palms. "I won't shove my opinions down your throat; I'm just saying that I hate to see you get so upset by —"

"There you are!" Gayle Garner fanned herself with a clipboard as she strode forward. "So warm in here — goodness." She nodded at Eli, then turned her attention to Lauren. "Of course we're all glad to see Jessica, but it would have made things a lot less chaotic if I'd known ahead of time that she was going to be late."

"She's here?" Lauren's legs weakened with relief. *Thank you, God.*

"Just arrived. I'd had the clerk pull someone from the main admitting office to cover. And we put out a call for a night shift replacement. All unnecessary as it turned out." Her brows rose, making her eyes seem almost cartoon enormous. "Jessica tells me that she asked you to let the department know she'd be late."

"I . . ." Lauren felt Eli stir beside her.

"She said you probably forgot," Gayle added.

"I must have." Lauren's stomach churned. "I'm really sorry."

"Well —" Gayle hugged the clipboard to her chest — "no harm done. This time." She sighed. "It's been a hectic day. For all of us."

"Yes, ma'am," Eli agreed.

Gayle gave a short laugh. "And I've volunteered to stay over and help for a few extra hours. Some folks don't know how to say no."

Eli cleared his throat. "I've noticed that."

When Lauren arrived outside the ER registration office, Jess was holding court with her coworkers as if nothing of importance could have happened without her anyway. Ambulances would be put on hold, fibrillating hearts suspended, a bleeding artery magically stanched. Certainly her older sister's concern and acute embarrassment were of no consequence. A mix of irritation and relief washed over Lauren. Would it always be this way?

Jess's willowy arms punctuated the air as she talked, corn-silk hair brushing her shoulders. She was smiling, observably giddy, acting as if right this moment everything was perfect in her world. Like in *Camelot,* the old film that had been Jess's favorite as a child. She watched it over and over, wearing a plastic, jewel-encrusted dollar-store crown. Dancing and singing along with King Arthur's words about his kingdom. *" 'In short, there's simply not a more congenial spot for happily ever aftering . . .' "*

"We need to talk," Lauren interrupted. "Can you break away for a minute, please?"

"No problem." Jess tossed a megawatt smile at the clerk who'd volunteered to take over when she was a no-show. "Back in a flash, ladies. Y'all don't start the party without me. Hear?"

Party? Lauren hid her grimace and led the way toward the hospital exit, using the time and space to remind herself that there had been no actual disaster. She'd come home to make a difference in her sister's life, which involved patience. Understanding and misunderstandings, too.

"I can't be away long," Jess told her once they were standing outside the hospital doors. "I was a teeny bit late to work. It wouldn't be right to take an early break, so —"

"But it was all right to push the blame onto me?"

"Um . . ."

There was a long rumble of thunder in the distance, and Lauren realized that it was raining — hard. Bouncing up from the parking lot, sheeting from the roof overhead.

51

She noticed, too, that her sister's hair was damp. It clung to the curve of her jaw, suggesting she'd been caught in the downpour at some point. The sodden strands, combined with gray eyes, soot-dark lashes, and those high, hollow cheekbones, made her look hungry and vulnerable, like a child seeking shelter from a cruel storm. *Ah, Jess.*

"You told the department manager that you left a message with me," Lauren continued, more gently this time. "But I haven't talked to you all day. Your bedroom door was closed when I left this morning. You didn't return any of my calls or texts."

"Oops." Jess aimed a finger at her temple, fired an imaginary bullet. "Screwed up again. I'm sorry. Really. Time got away from me. I pulled an all-nighter studying and then scrambled to get to class. After all that, I needed to get the kinks out, so I drove down to Galveston Island and ran the beach. I couldn't stop. It felt so perfect — the clouds, wind . . . except for that evil sun." She frowned and pressed her trigger finger to her cheek, making a white imprint on the blush pink. "Word to the wise: don't trust SPF 30 or cloud cover. Anyway, I ran, built a sand castle, hooked up with some great folks . . . It was an awesome day!" She swept a golden thatch away from her face, the stunning gray eyes teasing. "You'll love this: I even went to the storm memorial, tried to see if that woman in the sculpture really looks like Great-Great-Grandma. I snapped a photo, and —" Her smile faltered. She reached for Lauren's hand. "Don't hate me, Lolo."

"Of course I don't," Lauren said quickly, disarmed by the silly nickname, Jess's first name for her big sister. "But you put me in a bad light with Gayle. You made me look irresponsible, Jess. I don't think there's anything worse than that. If you'd answered my texts, I would have relayed a message to —"

"I'd do it for you," Jess blurted, a sudden edge in her voice. She let go of Lauren's hand. "My sister's keeper. We're supposed to be a team. If you asked me, I'd cover for you."

"But I wouldn't ask that. Not for a lie. Ever."

Lauren wanted to flatten her palms over her ears as Eli's words rumbled like menacing thunder. *The kind of help your sister needs isn't offered at Jiffy Lube.* He was wrong about Jess. She was high-spirited, rebellious, spoiled probably. She needed guidance, not clinical intervention. How many times had their parents said that? And despite today, things had been measurably better these past weeks.

"I heard Eli's brother was in the ER," Jess said, skillfully changing the subject.

"In the ICU now. He was pretty sick."

"And Eli took a stand, I'll bet."

"What do you mean?"

"Protecting his brother's rights. Drew's right not to be tied down, force-fed . . . become a puppet on strings for people who have his 'best interests' in mind."

An interest like saving his life?

"You agree with Eli?" Lauren asked before she could stop herself.

"I'm only saying . . ." Jess tossed her a pointed look. "I know what it feels like to have people trying to pull the strings in your life. That's all."

Eli looked up from the exam room computer, watching as Jessica attempted to get registration information from Darcee Grafton.

"You're sunburned too." Darcee flicked her long red hair over the shoulder of her hospital gown as she studied Jessica's face. "Let me guess: you're an actress. Probably a model with that height." Her voice was still raspy and hoarse. "Yeah, that's it. A model with an upcoming gig for one of those 'artsy' layouts." Her IV tubing dangled as she raised her hands to make quote marks with her fingers. "*Artsy* meaning no pesky tan lines allowed, so —"

"The beach," Jessica corrected after a sidelong glance at Eli. "At Galveston Island. Sunscreen fail. That's all."

All? Eli thought of Lauren's anxiety, the blame she'd accepted to spare her sister. Sunscreen fail wasn't the half of it.

"Yeah, well . . ." Darcee's laugh ended in a groan. "Looks like we were on the same adventure quest, but you did better than me, girlfriend. I got blistered. And arrested, I guess." She peered toward the doorway. "Good-lookin' cop around here somewhere. Apparently it's a crime to enjoy yourself in this town. A girl can't dance and sing without —"

"Jessica," Eli interrupted, deciding it was time to spare her. "Are you finished there?"

"Almost." Her gray eyes met his for an instant. "Is there an emergency contact, Ms. Grafton?"

"No. Nobody I'd want knowing my business." The patient tossed a coy smile Eli's way. "But you can give our hunky doc here my number, in case he —"

"Nobody at the home phone?"

"Look —" Darcee glanced at the bag of

IV fluids — "how soon is this going to be done? This stupid hospital visit wasn't part of my plans, you know?"

"I'm sure that's true." Eli stepped away from the computer, hearing the squeak of Holt's gun belt as he moved into the doorway. "But let's get those fluids finished. I need to have a look at your lab tests."

"Fluids, tests, cop cars? What's with you people? I have an innocent beer, a little fun at the park. There's nothing illegal about that. I know my rights."

"Easy, miss." Fletcher stepped into the room. "These folks are only trying to help." His gaze moved to Jessica, obvious concern in his expression.

"That's right." Eli took a few steps closer, trying to catch Jessica's attention to indicate she should move away in case the young woman became belligerent. "You'll feel better when you're more hydrated and those burns are soothed."

"Can't stay. I was on my way to Walmart to pick up my pills and some diapers . . ." Darcee's eyes widened. She slid to the edge of the table, cursing as the IV tubing pulled taut. "What time is it? Is it night? Did I — ?"

"Easy." Fletcher managed to sound gentle despite the imposing uniform.

"Darcee . . ." Eli nudged Jessica aside. "Let me help."

"No! You can't keep me here. I have to go." Darcee hopped down from the table, swore again, grabbed at the IV tubing.

"Don't do that," Eli warned. "Wait —"

She yanked the needle from her arm. Blood sprayed.

"Stop!" Fletcher bolted toward her.

"Bring me some gauze pads," Eli shouted to Jessica as he tried to capture his patient's flailing arm.

"My baby!" Darcee fought, flinging more blood as Eli and Fletcher worked to restrain her. Then her knees gave way, the raspy voice dissolving into guttural sobs. "I went out to get the medicine. And diapers . . . I can't remember for sure, but I think she's there at the house. All day. My poor little baby — alone."

5

"Thanks," Eli told Lauren as she set the cafeteria tray on his desk. "I wondered what happened to Emma's dinner."

"Delivered to our department by mistake." Lauren noticed how tired Eli looked, his white coat draped over the back of his chair, scrubs rumpled. A few strands of hair had strayed across his forehead. She tapped the plastic lid covering the plate. "Grilled cheese, curly sweet potato fries, fruit smoothie. All inspected by hungry vultures in ER. It's a miracle I got it away." Lauren glanced toward the door. "Where is your daughter?"

"Uh . . . checking on something." Eli sighed, his shoulders stooping slightly. "This was nice of you. To bring her dinner by."

"I was on my way home. To my parents' place, actually; I'm house-sitting for a few weeks." An unexpected wave of guilt prodded. "I shouldn't have laid into you earlier.

About Jess. You didn't deserve that after what you've had to deal with today." She glanced down, noticed his coat again. There were speckles of dried blood on the collar. "Anyway, I'm sorry."

"You were worried. Even I can understand that."

But you'd do more than worry. You'd take a stand — isn't that what Jess said?

"She was in Galveston," Eli added. "I overheard her tell a patient." His lips quirked in a grim smile. "Your sister does have that tendency to run toward the sand."

Lauren's stomach sank. Eli was thinking of that awful time, a little more than a year ago, when he and Jess argued and she ran off. Disappeared for days. After filling a prescription for sleeping pills. Lauren had never been so frightened in her life. The stress caused her father to have a small stroke. She'd been weak with relief when Eli finally found Jess in Corpus Christi and brought her home. And then, when things had mostly settled down, Jess's stubborn insistence on "space" sent Lauren packing to Austin.

"You know Officer Holt?" Eli asked, making Lauren think he was as eager as she to change the subject.

"Since we were kids. He's our neighbor.

Or was. The Holts lived four doors down from my parents. They moved to California last fall — job transfer." Lauren glanced toward the exam rooms. "Was that woman under arrest?"

"No. It was a psych problem." His lips pressed together. "Off her meds. There was some concern she'd left her daughter alone at home, but thankfully, it wasn't so. The baby was with a neighbor."

"Oh, cool!" Emma Landry chirped, appearing in the doorway. She glanced at Lauren, then back to her father. "Did you ask her, Dad?"

"No. I —"

"Ask me what?" Lauren couldn't imagine.

Eli shook his head. "It's noth—"

"Shrek," Emma blurted. "Our dog. Dad picked him up at the groomer on his way to get me at camp. Then we had to come here because of Uncle Drew. Shrek's downstairs at the loading dock. Everyone's being really nice; Vee even gave me a hospital blanket — oops." She pressed her fingers to her lips. Chipped nail polish, each one a different color. "I probably shouldn't tell you about the blanket. Anyway, he has water, too. And a place to lie down. But we're worried because of the thunder."

Eli tossed Lauren a sheepish look. "Our

dog's a coward."

"We wondered if you could take him home with you." Emma's nose perked with appreciation as she caught a whiff of the cafeteria tray. "Just till Dad's shift is over. That's only a couple of hours from now. Shrek would be no problem."

"I think that's too much to ask, Emma." Eli lifted the cover from his daughter's dinner. The salty-rich aroma of melted cheddar and fries wafted. "It isn't right to impose."

"Only for a few hours?" Lauren watched as Emma poked her small finger through the vortex of a curly fry. "I'm watching my folks' dog. And Hannah Leigh's . . ." She decided there was no way she could explain that her parents' shih tzu was under the care of a canine therapist. "She's sort of sensitive."

"*Everyone* likes Shrek," Emma assured her with a decisive nod. "They'll get along *famously.* Really."

"It's okay." Eli must've read the doubt in Lauren's eyes. "I'll get some surgical cotton and plug his ears."

"No. It's fine." Lauren smiled at Emma, already wondering how she'd entice Hannah into the guest bedroom. How could she disappoint this child? "I can handle two dogs for a few hours. No problem."

Now Eli looked doubtful. "You're driving that Volkswagen Beetle?"

"Daaaad, it'll work. Shrek will fit."

Fit?

"He's a Newfie," Eli explained. "A Newfoundland. And he's big even for that."

"Shrek's on a diet," Emma promised, rainbow fingers hefting her grilled cheese.

Lauren fought an image of Bigfoot. She'd just had her lime-green Bug detailed. "How big?"

"One sixty-two," Eli admitted. "Or was. I have no idea what he's eaten down in the loading dock. We cautioned them, but the old boy's a hard-core beggar."

"Which isn't so good with his diabetes," Emma said. "But don't worry; he had his insulin shot this morning. You won't need to do that."

Insulin?

"And he'll be fine with the weather noise." Eli poked a straw through the lid of Emma's smoothie. "As long as he's inside, distracted. Sometimes I pull my old ski headband over his ears. His hearing is hypersensitive."

"Yes." Emma took a sip from her straw. "Because he's blind."

Two hours later, Shrek was asleep on the

Barclays' family room floor. With Pamela Barclay's pink satin sleep turban on his head. And a bath towel under his chin for the flood of drool. Somehow Eli had failed to include that particular affliction along with diabetes, thunderphobia, blindness, and hip arthritis bad enough that it required a team of three to boost the hairy black behemoth into the passenger seat of her Bug. A seat now slick with doggy saliva. Lauren was certain she'd swallowed some fur. Still . . .

"You are sweet. I can't deny that." She glanced down at the black dog, stretched out and snoring on the pink carpet — "Sunset Cloud," her mother insisted, a shade that harmonized with the whole weather theme that had overtaken their family room. Lauren hugged her knees on the fog-gray couch, eyes sweeping the modest space, a full-blown tribute to her mother's postcollege stint as weather girl for a tiny TV station in Sugar Land. It had been the only stretch of time in the city's history without a tornado, flash flood, impressive hail, or even record heat. That an emergency appendectomy sidelined Pamela from the career-making devastation of Hurricane Alicia was an often-repeated lament. Lauren let her gaze skim the whitewashed wood paneling and move to the glass cases holding her mother's collection of antique weather devices: marine compass, rain gauges, copper hygrometer, barometers, the beautiful liquid-filled glass Galileo thermometer, and six weather vanes. Another five were installed on the Barclays' aging roof: a horse, a rooster, an eagle, a mermaid . . . and a huge winged pig. The perfect family mascot, Jess liked to chide.

"Easy, big guy," Lauren soothed as Shrek's head rose in response to the sound of tree branches slapping the window. Lightning lit the sky, making the limbs stand out in sharp relief. Thunder rolled. Lauren reached down to adjust the dog's turban, letting her fingers linger on his silky ears, reminding herself that the TV news had reported no imminent danger to the US coastline from the tropical storms brewing in the Caribbean. She thought of what she'd told Vee at dinner: her parents would never have left home if they thought a hurricane was coming. Carl Barclay's insurance company protected hundreds of homes in their community, and his wife's smiling face appeared seasonally in his TV ads, offering weather statistics and a checklist for disaster preparedness. *Get a kit. Make a plan. Be informed.*

"We're fine," she told the dog as thunder

rumbled again. "It's been a long day, but —" A yawn escaped. She was tired, wrung out from the toll of her workday, the conflict surrounding Drew Landry, worry over Jess, and the discomfort that always came when she had to deal with Eli. She shivered but told herself it was the weather, fatigue. What happened between them, that one confusing moment more than a year ago, had been an emotional reaction to the stress of Jess's disappearance. A mistake Lauren regretted. Time and distance — 165 miles between Houston and Austin — had blurred the memory.

Lauren's cell phone rang in her lap. Eli.

"I'm sorry; it's taking a little longer than I figured." His voice sounded muffled as if he were whispering or being buffeted by wind. Maybe both. "I had to stop by my folks' place to pick up some of Emma's things. She usually stays overnight when I work, but . . ."

Lauren wondered if his unfinished statement was from a bad phone connection or because he didn't want to explain his reasons for not letting his daughter stay with her grandparents. She recalled the conversation in the code room: that threatened restraining order to keep Eli from interfering with his brother's care. "You're at your parents' house now?"

"Yes. Used my key, in and out. Everyone's asleep. I've got Emma's backpack and I'm on my way to the car. It's a distance to the parking pad."

"Ah." Lauren wasn't about to let on that she'd heard descriptions of that home in prestigious River Oaks — and seen photos. Her mother had toured the Landry gardens during a charity event last fall. Despite Pamela's disapproval of their son, she'd been more than effusive about Julien and Anita Cruz Landry's sumptuous New Orleans–style estate. She'd covertly snapped phone pics: blurry glimpses of banana and magnolia trees, ferns, and magnificent rose gardens. She'd also captured a small film clip of the towering brick house with its black shutters, ironwork balconies, and window boxes . . . ending with a zoom shot of the Landry gateposts topped by daunting sculptured lions.

Stone lions and flying pigs . . . Lauren shook her head. Different down to the yard art.

"I'm leaving for your folks' place in a couple of minutes," Eli told her. "Emma's asleep in the backseat, so I'll just run in and grab Shrek. If that's still okay. Sorry. I'm keeping you from bed."

"I'm not tired," Lauren fibbed. "It's better if you pick him up. I put my parents' dog in the guest room . . ." She touched a finger to the tender nip on her forearm, slathered in the antibiotic ointment her mother kept with a stash of dog treats and cutesy distraction toys. A sort of Hannah preparedness kit. True to form, the shih tzu had been a reluctant hostess. Even now Lauren could hear her toenails shredding the bedroom door down the hall. She'd have to repaint before her parents' return. "I'll be awake, no problem."

"Great. Thanks." Eli's voice puffed as he walked. "I hope the thunder wasn't an issue."

"No." She smiled at the ridiculous pink turban on his dog. "We're pretty well prepared for storms around here." Lauren's gaze moved to the wall of weather maps that had decorated their home for as long as she could remember. Huge, neon-color depictions of famous storms: Agnes, Hugo, Andrew, Ivan, Katrina, Rita, Sandy . . . Swaths of blue, turquoise, green, yellow, orange, and gigantic buzz-saw whorls of red. The same colors painted on Emma's cheek today. Lauren's mouth sagged open as the thought struck her: *My first rainbows were hurricanes.*

"Okay then, I'll be there in —" Eli's voice broke away.

"Eli?"

"Gotta go."

The security lights flicked on in the distance, then the porch light, illuminating the dark brick of the house.

"Eli?"

His mother's voice, frightened. This had been a stupid decision. He hadn't wanted to scare her, only to avoid a confrontation with his father. He should have taken the risk and rung the bell.

"Eli? Is it you? Darling, please . . ." Her voice was smothered by a gust of humid wind.

"I'm coming." Eli glanced at his darkened car, sighed, and began jogging back up the graveled path, once again setting off the string of motion lights that lit the towering boxwood hedges in stingy glimpses, just enough that he could move forward without tripping. He'd reassure his mother, then get away before his father could —

"Hold it there. Right there!" There was a thud of heavy footfalls, scattering gravel, a garbled curse. Then a motion light illuminating his father's angry face. A dark blur, the glint of steel, and — Eli's blood ran cold — the unmistakable sound of a shotgun being racked.

"No, Dad, it's me. It's —" Eli dropped to the ground, covered his head.

The blast was deafening.

6

"You sure you're okay?" Fletcher asked again, raising his voice over the squawk of his radio. The last remaining officer, besides him, had managed to stop an ambulance from being dispatched. It could have been the SWAT team. The neighbors had made a panicky flurry of calls regarding the sound of gunfire; recent burglaries had folks on edge. Maybe over the edge, considering the current incident. He met Eli Landry's gaze, saw the red-blue flicker of the patrol car's strobes reflected in the man's eyes. "No injury?"

"No. I'm fine."

Even twenty minutes after the incident, Eli's face was gray, shiny with sweat. No wonder — it wasn't every day a man's father mistook him for a burglar. And it wasn't anywhere near routine for Fletcher to have to question a federal judge. The truth was, he'd made the acquaintance of more members of this family than he cared to today.

"I wish you'd come inside, dear," Anita Landry called out, stepping through the huge double doors again. Her fingers trembled as she swept dark hair off her forehead. "I've fixed Emma some lemonade. Come have some — you too, Officer."

"Thank you, ma'am, but no," Fletcher told her, catching the expression on her son's face that said even a medicinal shot of bourbon wouldn't tempt him inside. "I'm almost finished here and need to be going."

"Me too." Eli glanced past his mother and into the foyer. "I'll need Emma."

Mrs. Landry's hand rose to the collar of her robe. "It's so late. The judge thinks it's better that she stay with —"

"No." Eli cut her off. His jaw muscles bunched. "She's coming home."

"I . . ." Even in the shadows, the woman's shimmer of tears was visible. "I'm so sorry about this accident, darling. The misunderstanding. I wish you'd called us. I wish . . ." She stepped onto the porch, took her son's hand.

"It's okay, Mom." Eli dipped his head to kiss her cheek. "No harm done. You're right; it's my fault."

"Excuse me." Fletcher took a few discreet steps away, motioning to the other officer

71

that he could go. When he turned back, Mrs. Landry had gone.

"We're finished here?" Eli asked.

"Unless you have something else to add."

"No." Eli dragged his fingers through his hair, sighed. "There's nothing else."

Fletcher tapped his notebook. "Judge Landry heard you leaving the porch. He brandished his weapon thinking he'd frighten a fleeing burglar, stumbled, and it accidentally discharged."

"Right."

Fletcher caught his gaze. "No injuries."

Eli smiled grimly and inspected his palms. "Some road rash when I pitched myself down on the gravel. I'll take that to the alternative."

Fletcher nodded and broached the dicey but necessary subject for the second time that night. "And no reason to think that your father would want to harm you."

Eli glanced toward the door, then met Fletcher's gaze. "Look. I did a dumb thing by going into the house without calling first. You heard what my mother said. My father wasn't feeling well and was half-asleep when he ran out here. My fault." His cell phone buzzed with a text, and he read it with a grimace. "I'm screwing up everyone's night. I was supposed to pick up my dog. Lauren

72

Barclay's watching him."

"Maybe I can help with that."

"Fletcher." Lauren stood in the doorway, stunned for a moment. Then her heart climbed toward her throat. "Is something wrong? Is it Jess?"

"No, no," he assured her. "She's fine. I dropped by the hospital and had coffee with her a couple of hours ago." A corner of his mouth tweaked upward in the same crooked smile he'd sported since grade school. "Took her one of those desserts she likes, from the place down on South Shepherd — you know."

"Yes, I do," Lauren said, hiding an amused smile. This flak-jacketed, gun-toting police officer didn't want to say out loud that he'd gone into an establishment called Sugarbaby's to order a chocolate, buttercream-filled cupcake known as the Dippity Doo Dah. For the neighbor girl he'd been in love with all of his life. It was as obvious as the badge on his chest. To everyone but Jess. "Well then," she said, looking past him and toward the street. "If everything's fine, what brings you by at this hour?"

"I'm here to take a dog off your hands."

"Shrek?" Lauren's confusion was accompanied by an unexpected sense of disappointment. "But — oh, sorry. Where are my manners? C'mon in."

Fletcher settled onto a kitchen chair while Lauren tiptoed down the hall far enough to hear that things were quiet behind the weather room door. She'd slipped the turban off Shrek when the thunder quit, and he'd been sleeping ever since. When she got back to the kitchen, Hannah Leigh was in Fletcher's lap. The shih tzu was a wriggling and glossy jumble of black-and-white, with chocolate eyes, a comical and endearing un-derbite, and a "capricious temperament" — Pamela Barclay's timeworn euphemism for "Watch your fingers, y'all." The dog thera-pist had outed her on that one during their first session.

"Be careful," Lauren warned, tapping her Band-Aid. "Your girl's in a mood."

"Nothing new about that." Fletcher's smile crinkled the corners of his blue eyes, and Lauren noticed the small scar high on his cheekbone. Pale now and shaped almost like the crescent moon in the July sky the night he'd tried to launch himself from the Barclays' roof. Wearing his astronaut suit and some shuttle wings he'd fashioned from coat hangers and Hefty bags. All on a dare from Jessica, the beguiling child princess in a plastic crown who waited on the ground to egg him on. Fortunately he snagged a wing on the mermaid weather vane, causing him to merely whip-lash over the edge of the roof rather than plunge to the driveway below. Despite his cardboard helmet, Fletcher smacked his head against the stucco hard enough to incur thirteen stitches, a concussion . . . and 75 percent of the blame. Jess was miffed that she'd been faulted at all and refused to speak to him the rest of the summer. Lauren sighed. Fletcher Holt was far too familiar with the phrase *"Your girl's in a mood."*

"I ran into Eli Landry," he explained as Hannah circled in his lap, finding the most comfortable spot. "For the second time today. He'd been waylaid by circumstances, so I offered to pick up his dog. I said I'd drop Shrek off on my way back to the station. His daughter was tired and he wanted to get her home."

"Oh." There it was again, that strange sense of disappointment. It made no sense. The only time Lauren had ever been alone with Eli turned into one of her biggest regrets. She should be relieved to avoid him tonight. "You mean you saw Eli again when you took the cupcake to Jess."

"Uh . . ." Fletcher hesitated, then nodded as if he'd decided something. "It will be public record. We were dispatched to Judge Landry's estate less than an hour ago — shots fired."

"What?" Lauren's heart stalled. She thought of Emma Landry's sweet pixie face, the happy rainbow on her cheek. "What happened?"

"An accident," Fletcher explained, lifting his fingers from Hannah's ear at her warning growl. "Apparently Eli didn't call before arriving at the house because it was late and he didn't want to wake his parents. He used his key. Judge Landry woke up, heard him leaving the porch. There have been some burglaries in that community. So the judge grabbed his shotgun and —"

"Oh, dear God." Lauren pressed a hand to her chest. "He shot —"

"Accidentally discharged the weapon," Fletcher clarified. "Stumbled in the dark. The judge said he never intended to fire, that he racked the round to scare a would-be intruder. I don't condone it, but I have to admit that sound is a powerful deterrent. Anyhow, Eli supports the judge's account of the incident, and — hey!" He pulled his arm away as Hannah attempted to sink her teeth into his sleeve.

"Sorry. Here." Lauren snatched a treat from the table, distracting the dog. She wished there were a simple way to allay her own uneasiness. "Emma saw all of that?"

"Nope. Sound asleep." Fletcher shook his head as the shih tzu jumped from his lap with an indignant snort. "I'll take Shrek home and it's all good."

Lauren made herself smile. *All good.* If only that were true.

"His brother," Eli told the night shift RN assigned to Drew's care. He repositioned himself — with a scrunch of Styrofoam — in the fuzzy pink beanbag chair next to Emma's trundle bed. "I'm Andrew's brother, Elijah Landry," he clarified, trying to keep his voice low.

"Ah, yes." There was a harsh sound on the other end of the phone, insistent, like a suction catheter. "He's resting better; the sedative is helping. Temperature's down to 100. He's still on oxygen, of course. Just a mask now, not that positive pressure machine they started in the ER."

"What's his saturation?"

"His oxygen percentage is up to 94. We normally like to see 95 to 100, but with your brother's history —"

"I know," Eli interrupted. "I know his history. And I understand the normals. I'm a PA. I run the urgent care downstairs."

There was a silence. "Oh. I'm sorry, Mr. Landry. I didn't put it together."

"That's okay." He tried not to imagine what else she'd put together, heard from the hospital grapevine.

"The monitor is showing a sinus rhythm between 88 and 92. The doctor's ordered cefepime and vancomycin; blood cultures are pending. Do you want me to read off his last set of vitals? Pull up labs?"

"No." Eli glanced toward Emma, her face softly lit by the glow of a Little Mermaid table lamp. One hand was curled against her cheek, fingertips touching the smudged remains of her rainbow face painting. She'd left most of it on Drew's cheek. "I don't need to know his labs — any of that." He closed his eyes for a moment, willing the ache to subside. "Has he tried to say anything?"

"No. Other than some grunts." The nurse's voice was gentle. "I couldn't get him to squeeze my hand, but he followed me with his gaze. I'm sure of that."

"Could I talk with him for a minute?"

"As I told you . . ." A monitor dinged somewhere in the distance. "He isn't verbal, Mr. Landry. Right now his eyes aren't even —"

"Put the phone to his ear. Please."

There was a rustle, the gentle hiss of misted oxygen. And then a rattle that was his brother's breathing.

"It's me," Eli told him. "Your brother . . . Trouble," he added, using Drew's old affectionate heckle: *"Here comes Trouble."* Still apt, he supposed. Some things never changed. "I love you, Champ. I'll see you at breakfast. Pancakes, blueberry syrup, and —" He heard a phlegmatic cough. A painful wheeze.

"I should suction him," the nurse advised, coming back onto the phone. "Was there anything else?"

"No. Thanks. That's all."

Eli disconnected from the call and sat there for a long moment, listening to a duet of snores: Emma's small puff and Shrek's deeper exhalations, accompanied by the occasional yip and vigorous paddling of the Newfoundland's legs. A blind dog with bad hips giving rabbits an Olympian chase. As much a reality as Drew eating his favorite breakfast in the morning.

Or rainbows being painted by angels . . .

Eli's gaze moved to the wall above Emma's head, to the cross she'd hung there using a thumbtack from his office and a piece of fishing line. It was made from leaves she'd braided together on Palm Sunday, a

service she'd attended with her grandparents. Eli had been working. He volunteered to do that most Sundays now. Because those shifts were always busy and
often short-staffed. And because . . . Eli
closed his eyes. Because he and God were
parting ways. It was the one thing he
couldn't explain to Emma, couldn't seem
to find the words for. Santa Claus, the
Easter bunny, the tooth fairy — she'd asked,
and he'd answered with the truth. He'd
tried to do the same with his scientific
explanation of rainbows. But God? Deny
God's faithfulness, his mercy . . . take that
from her? How did he do that? *How do I call
my doubts a truth?*

He'd accepted too many brutal truths.
Drew's brain injury — that effective loss of
his one true friend. His mother's crippling
grief and his father's disappointment in
every choice Eli made afterward. Since then,
he'd seen comrades die in war despite
desperate efforts to save them. He'd had a
woman he thought he loved leave him, and
even worse . . . Eli leaned forward to touch
Emma's hair. He'd had to accept that she
also chose to abandon their beautiful child
with never a backward glance. His doubts
about God were a culmination of all that, a
slow and inevitable erosion of faith. Like a

80

seawall giving way to season after season of merciless storms.

And then there was tonight. Eli fought a wave of nausea, recalling bits and pieces of what still seemed so surreal. His mother's voice up the long pathway. His jog toward her in the darkness. Then the sounds of footfalls coming his way. His father's face lit against the hedges, that angry shout. The shotgun racking. And Eli's own desperate attempt to identify himself.

I did that, didn't I? He knew it was me . . . right?

The judge had been adamant in his insistence that he'd believed there was an intruder. He'd been completely lucid when giving a statement to the police, even cited Governor Perry's 2007 signing of the castle doctrine and stand-your-ground law, with specific numbers and each subsection. If he'd been drinking, there was no overt evidence. No slurred words or bloodshot eyes. And no apology to Eli either, but that wasn't surprising. His mother, on the other hand, had apologized to everyone. Lemonade with apologies.

Eli's pulse quickened as his cell phone rang in his pocket. It was his mother.

"No, Mom," he assured as he stepped over Shrek and moved toward the door in the darkness. "I wasn't asleep. In fact, I was going to call you. Is Dad still awake?"

"No, dear. Fast asleep. He hasn't slept much the last few nights and wasn't feeling well most of today. Then with what happened with Drew and tonight —" Her voice cracked. "I'm so sorry, Son. You're sure you're all right?"

"Fine. But . . . when you said he hasn't been sleeping and wasn't well today, what do you mean exactly?" Eli held his breath. She knew what he was asking. She'd be torn between defending her husband and . . . *protecting me? Did he know it was me?*

"Restless, that's all," she explained. "You know the judge; being on sabbatical doesn't stop him from debating every issue at the club, the homeowners' association, or on the TV news."

"Is the 12-gauge back in the study? Closed up in the gun case?" *Cases,* plural. Julien Landry's study was lined with them — custom-made in mahogany, illuminated by halogen lights, and complete with a built-in valuables safe and an electronic humidor for guests' cigars. He owned dozens of guns: bird guns and rifles — one of which was a prized gift from a former vice president. The judge had pistols, too. . . . "Does he still keep that handgun in his bedside table?"

"No. It's put away. They're all put away in the cases in his study." Was there a quaver in her voice? "They're locked. I checked. Twice."

Twice . . . Eli flattened his palm on the hallway wall, shut his eyes as his weight sagged against it. Since when had his mother ever checked anything to do with guns? Though she'd hosted countless gun club members, firearms were a foreign language to Anita Landry. Still, she'd stood alongside her husband tonight and corroborated his story. It was a believable one; his father had made it clear he was prepared to take up arms in defense of his castle. Except tonight the intruder was Eli. A night Judge Landry had been sleepless and "under the weather."

"Mom . . ." Eli told himself that he had to press further. Had to say it. *Emma was with me tonight. My mother is sleeping in that house.* "I think you should hide the key to the gun cases."

Eli waited through a stretch of silence, knowing his mother's response could provide an answer to questions that had been turning his life upside down. Questions about his father's drinking, his mother's level of concern. In his entire life, Eli had never seen her take a stand against his

father. Anita Landry wouldn't hear of it.
But —

"Mom? Did you hear me? I think you
should hide that key." He glanced back
toward the glow of Emma's bedside lamp.

"I did," his mother said finally. The tears
in her voice tore at Eli's heart. "I hid the
key in my Bible. Just for now. I love you,
Son. Your father loves you too. He does."

7

What is that?

Lauren bolted upright in bed, her heart pounding. The sound was real, not a dream. Shrill, earsplitting, insistent. She slid from bed, mind tumbling. Her gaze jerked to the bedside clock: 5:20. Not yet dawn. The sound continued, relentless, as she headed toward the hallway. It wasn't the security alarm; she hadn't set it. The smoke detector? *A fire? Oh, please* . . . No smoke. But there was barking, too. All of it coming from the weather room. Lauren stumbled forward, her confusion compounding. What was happening?

She lurched through the doorway and nearly tripped trying to dodge a frenzied Hannah Leigh. She recovered her balance and slapped her hands over her ears, temples pounding at the cruel screech. "What's going on?" she yelled, frantically scanning the room for the source of —

"Hurricane!" a voice shouted behind her. Lauren whipped around.

"It's the hurricane warning," Jess explained, cupping her hands around her mouth. "And it's turned up way too loud."

Lauren looked toward the windows, struggling to understand. "There's a hurricane?"

"No. There's a loony mother." Jess managed a deadpan expression despite her boisterous shout. "Here, let me . . ." She hurried to the desk against the far wall, tapped one of several devices beside the computer. The horrendous screeching stopped. And miracle of miracles, Hannah's barking ended too. Without a bribe.

"Yep," Jess reported, scanning the device. "A tropical depression has been upgraded to Tropical Storm Eloise, moving at twenty-two miles an hour in a westerly direction into the Gulf of Mexico." Her lips twisted in a wry smile. "Want to toss a coin for first dibs on the dry shampoo?"

"I can't believe this." Lauren groaned, knees weak with relief at the end of the chaos. She pointed to the jumble of monitoring equipment beside her parents' computer. "Where on earth — ?"

"eBay." Jess dropped onto the couch, rubbing the side of her neck. "Our mother's a freak."

"Well, thanks for stopping that. I think I was close to a coronary." Lauren joined her, noticing the dark circles under her sister's eyes and how sharply her collarbone protruded at the opening of her blouse. She thought of Fletcher's cupcake, wondered if Jess had secretly given it away. Then she caught sight of the multiple Band-Aids on her sister's feet. Blisters, no doubt. How many hours had she run? It was far from the first time Jess had done something like that. "You're home early."

"Census was low. I volunteered to go home and save the department a few bucks; administration will like that. I have to score points where I can." Jess's eyes met Lauren's. "I am sorry about earlier. Gayle's on me about everything. I knew she'd make a federal case over my being late."

"I doubt that. She's always been on your side."

"Sure . . ." Jess yawned, grabbed a pillow appliquéd with rain clouds, and stretched out her long frame. She wedged her head against Lauren's hip.

"It's true. Gayle's your biggest ally at Houston Grace." Lauren brushed her fingers tentatively over the corn-silk hair, realizing the rarity of the moment: Hannah sleeping peacefully at her feet and her troubled sister snuggled against her. It was almost Camelot. "No," she corrected, "I'm your biggest ally, Jess. You can count on me . . . always."

"Mmm." Jess's lids fluttered, her lips parting in submission to sleep. She looked no older than Emma Landry.

Thank you, God, for this unexpected moment.

Lauren glanced toward the window, where the sky was beginning to lighten. Even without the rude awakening, she'd have had to get up soon anyway for her Saturday shift. And she had some prep to do for the hospital's disaster committee meeting; hurricane season always prompted a system-wide refresher. Because of her training as a peer counselor, Lauren was teamed with social services. She'd render support if hospital staff suffered any effects of emotional stress during a disaster scenario.

Disaster . . .

Lauren thought of the incident at the Landry estate. Though Eli would be the first to deny it, his day qualified him as a poster child for stress. She gazed down at her sister. Despite Lauren's worries, Jess was whole, healthy, and home. Regardless of a few obvious quirks — evidenced by her mother's weather devices — the Barclay family was intact and devoted to each other. And Lauren and her parents were on the same page, the same exact *line* on that particular page, when it came to helping Jess. It was a blessing.

Eli couldn't say the same. His brother was far from healthy, his daughter had no mother, and — the very real possibility stunned her — his father could have shot him last night. If eBay sold an early-warning system for family tragedy, Eli Landry could be completely deaf by now.

Drew's nose itched. Real bad. But every time he tried to get his good hand up there to —

Hey, it wasn't tied down now. It was shaky, but he made his fingers walk over the stubbly part of his face, find that plastic thing stuck in his nose, and —

"Easy, Champ. That's your oxygen." His brother's face slid into view; he was smiling the way he always did. But his eyes were real shiny like he might cry. "You're waking up. I like that." He eased Drew's hand back down to his side. Then gave his shoulder a squeeze. His brother had strong hands. "Does your nose itch?"

Duh . . . Drew wanted to say it out loud. The way that made Eli laugh. But his tongue was stuck. So he nodded yes instead. His brother always knew what he needed.

"There." Eli finished scratching Drew's nose and put the oxygen tube back. "Now hang on — I'm going to wipe your lips with one of those wet sponge things. Your mouth looks like the time we sneaked those boxes of Jell-O pudding and ate 'em dry. Remember that?" His eyebrows bunched up like he was worried. "You know who I am, right?"

"D . . . uh," Drew whispered, pretty sure he might also be spitting stuff. "Trr-rouble." He smiled, choked a little when a laugh came out, then raised his good hand for a knuckle bump. His chest hurt, and something taped on his arm pinched, but he didn't really care. It didn't matter. His brother was here. "You're . . . Trouble."

"Right." Eli smiled again, bumped his knuckles against Drew's. "That's me. Okay, good. Now that we're clear on that, let's fix those lips."

Drew closed his eyes. He heard his brother talking, felt the sponge on his mouth . . . the tube in his nose . . . He couldn't keep his eyes open. Sleepy . . . so sleepy. There was that squeeze on his shoulder again. He opened his eyes.

"I'm going to let you rest now, Champ. You're in the hospital. But I'm going to look at a new place for you to stay. It's got a goofy name: Mimaw's. Like we called our grandma in Baton Rouge. It sounds like a good place. More like being at . . ." Eli stopped what he was saying, made a face like he had a stomachache. "Anyhow, I'm going to go look at this place today. It has musical instruments. A baseball diamond, kites, and chickens. Real chickens. Emma and Shrek can visit any day, all day if we want. And —"

"Pan . . . cakes?"

"With blueberry syrup. I already asked."

Drew smiled and closed his eyes. His brother always knew what he needed.

Lauren gazed at the hospital cafeteria's ceiling-high windows and the French doors leading to the courtyard patio. "I was hoping we could eat dinner outside. Eating in here always feels like being on call." She discreetly pointed her half-eaten veggie wrap toward a woman at the next table. The gout patient, one beefy leg propped on a chair, had been staring daggers at them for a full fifteen minutes. Obviously resentful of her continuing wait for treatment in the ER. And that the staff was allowed meals at all.

"Her choice." Vee's braids swayed with the shake of her head. "Urgent care was happy to take her two hours ago if she didn't have issues about being examined by 'only a PA.' " She glanced to where Eli sat at the table closest to the patio doors, hunched alone over his own meal. "I would have preferred the courtyard myself, except that they're moving all the tables and chairs under cover with this crazy wind." As if to prove her point, a janitor outside leaned a folded patio umbrella against a stack of chairs.

"Eloise." Lauren stifled a yawn with her napkin. "Upgraded from a depression to a tropical storm around 5 a.m. — scared me half to death." She smiled at the confusion on Vee's face. "My mother has this evil weather-alert gizmo; if Jess hadn't known how to turn it off, my ears would have bled. Thank heaven she left her shift a couple of hours early."

"I heard she did." Vee's brows pinched for a moment. "Uh . . . did she mention anything about problems here last night?"

Lauren pushed her wrap aside. "Problems?"

"Well, you know that Gayle stayed over for a few hours?"

"Yes." Lauren got an uncomfortable feeling. "So?"

"One of the clerks said the night staff was

upset because Jessica 'disappeared' from the department. Never told anyone she was leaving. Someone apparently complained to Gayle. You know Gayle; she's not one to fly off the handle or jump to any conclusions."

"I don't know what you mean. What conclusions?" Lauren remembered Jess's words: *"Gayle's always on me."*

"Two employee lockers were broken into last night. One in the admissions office and one up on the second floor. Money taken. And a phone. So —" Vee turned to look as a gust of wind rattled the courtyard doors.

"But no one would think that Jess would do something like that. Gayle didn't suspect her, did she?"

"No. Security talked to everyone. It sounds like Gayle did her best to stop any finger-pointing. But apparently she did have a talk with Jessica about taking an unauthorized break." Vee's expression was kind. "I'm not surprised your sister took the chance to leave early after all that. Plus, I guess she was limping all night."

"Blisters from running. Nothing serious. But . . . do you know . . . ?" Lauren saw Eli gathering up his things at the far table. "Did Jess say where she'd gone when she left the ER?"

"The second floor. To see how a patient

was doing. I guess she'd been worried about her. Someone Eli saw in the urgent care yesterday — the young woman who was dancing in the reflecting pool at Hermann Park."

"Right. I saw her for a minute. Fletcher Holt brought her in." Lauren tried to recall if there had ever been a time Jess had worried enough to follow up on a hospital patient.

"She was admitted to treat her dehydration," Vee continued. "Social services was arranging for a psych eval. Plus, child protective services got involved because of some issues with her baby."

"Code green, second floor," the PA system blared. "Code green. Security, please report to the second floor."

"Green?" Lauren squinted at the overhead speaker. "Isn't that — ?"

"Patient elopement," Vee confirmed. "A patient's gone AWOL."

"Advise all personnel: code green," the voice shrilled again. "Twenty-six-year-old female. Five feet eight inches, 130 pounds, long red hair. Last seen near the east stairwell, second —"

"What's . . . ?" Something moved in Lauren's peripheral vision. In the tallest garden window. A hurtling flash of white.

And . . . "Oh, dear God — no!"

She leaped to her feet just as Vee shrieked and the entire cafeteria erupted in horrified screams.

"Look! Oh no, did you see that?"

"Someone fell — that girl fell right out of the sky!"

8

"Clear them away!" Eli shouted against the wind. Several security guards struggled to keep eager looky-loos from spilling out of the cafeteria — and raising cell phones. "Staff's running a gurney down. Make room." A siren yelped in the parking lot. He gripped his phone, continuing his conversation with the ER. "Right. A rescue scoop, too. And an extrication neck brace. No, she's not responsive. Make sure surgery's alerted. Find the neurosurgeon."

"It's . . . her." Lauren's pupils were huge against the blue of her eyes; she hunched over the victim, attempting to stabilize her neck, hands wrist-deep in the tangle of red hair. Blood had wicked onto the chest pocket of her scrubs, a crimson bloom against the faded pink fabric. "She's your patient from yesterday."

"Darcee." The shock hit Eli again. "We admitted her for IV hydration and —"

"Unhhh," their patient groaned. Blood bubbled from her nostrils with the effort, sending a wine-colored rivulet to pool in the pale hollow at the base of her neck. Her breath came in shallow grunts, lips going gray.

Get that stretcher here. . . . "How's her pulse?"

"Thready," Vee reported, fingers pressed against the side of the woman's neck. The wind whipped braids against her face as she glanced down. "I count 104."

"I think this stack of furniture lessened her impact with the ground a little. Hopefully." Lauren scanned the flattened tangle of aluminum, canvas, and plastic beneath Darcee's bowed torso. "Broke her fall."

"And probably her spine." Eli glanced up as a trio of police officers arrived at the gate that connected with the parking lot. Fletcher Holt was one of them. This world was shrinking way too fast. "I'd be surprised if there isn't a hunk of that chair embedded in her back."

Lauren paled. A gust of wind tossed her hair as she brushed her thumb across the unconscious woman's cheek, lips moving as if murmuring a prayer.

"Here!" Eli waved his arm overhead, beckoning to the arriving ER team. "We're over here!"

Eli helped the nurses and techs with the extrication collar and supervised as Darcee was loaded, protecting her spine, onto the gurney. Then he jogged alongside Lauren and Vee as they hustled through the cafeteria. Maybe Lauren's prayer had helped: apparently a neurosurgeon had just finished a case in the OR, and both a thoracic and general surgeon were standing by. Darcee would have the best chance that medicine provided. A skilled healing machine. But . . .

Once again, the shock sent him reeling. He'd treated her for sunburn only yesterday, fielded her caustic sarcasm and her embarrassing attempts to flirt with him. He'd cleared her medically — with the concurrence of the ER physician — and arranged for intervention with what Eli was certain was an ongoing psychiatric problem. Even so, she'd been lucid. And despite her initial objections, quite cooperative once the safety of her baby was assured. But somehow she'd still ended up in a fatal plummet from the second floor of this hospital.

Fatal. He was sure of it, even now. Darcee Grafton's last dance would be that public spectacle in Hermann Park. Her skull's impact against the courtyard pavement wasn't much different from the crush of that boat hull against his brother's head. It might take days, weeks, or even painful years for Darcee to finally succumb, but in the interim she'd never be a mother to her baby. Never be the same daughter, sister . . .

He helped them guide the gurney around a corner, slowing only for a moment before continuing full speed toward the ER. Lauren still had that stricken look on her face. It occurred to Eli that he'd never asked her about those stormy hours with Shrek. Or if Fletcher had said anything about what happened at his folks' house last night.

They slowed for one last turn, then started down the hospital's long back corridor; from here it would be a frenzied race to the ER. They were still well within a trauma victim's survivable golden hour. If Eli were subject to hope, he'd pin jaded optimism on that — time. At least it was on Darcee's side. In the meantime, he'd hold on to the only bright spot in his day: the Champ was hungry for pancakes.

"I can't talk now." Gayle stepped outside the busy trauma room, whispering into her cell phone. She glanced toward the team inside: ER physician, two surgeons, techs manning a portable X-ray machine. The young redhead was being intubated. "I'm sorry, Leo. But we have a trauma case. A bad one."

"Yeah, well —" her husband's voice competed with a background belch of ESPN, boxing probably — "it's no picnic here, either. Spent all day arguing with state disability clowns. And trying to decide if I should flush those worthless anti-inflammatory pills down the toilet or drag myself to my quack doctor's office and shove that bottle —"

"I'm sorry, sweetheart," Gayle interrupted, leaning against the wall as her pulse did one of its too-frequent skip-skip-thuds. The coffee. She couldn't keep up the pace without caffeine. Especially when she was always so tired. She'd almost fallen asleep at the wheel when she finally left the hospital last night. "I'll try to catch one of our new staff orthopods, pick his brain about some better meds."

"Pick his pocket while you're at it."

"Right." She played along, wishing her husband's quip were a sign that somewhere beneath his pain and battered pride there was still a spark of the fun-loving man she'd married twenty-three years ago. Gayle wasn't sure she'd even recognize him anymore. But these days grim jokes were better than violent blowups, fueled by —

"Beer," Leo added against a volley of thuds and shouts from the TV. "Pick some up on your way home. We're running low."

"You look like you're not feeling well." Lauren was being polite; Gayle had looked haggard from the moment she arrived today. "Are you okay?"

"Fine, thanks. A little tired." Gayle offered a smile at odds with the continuing anxiety in her eyes. "I worked those extra hours last evening and then I had trouble sleeping."

Because of my sister? Surely Gayle didn't think Jess was responsible for the locker thefts.

"Fill me in on Darcee Grafton." The manager shifted her gaze. And their conversation.

"Glasgow Coma Scale around 8 or 9. She localized pain, made purposeful movement. No neck injury, amazingly." Lauren caught a glimpse of Eli's white coat at the doorway; he'd gone back to his patients in the urgent care but clearly felt connected to this case. "I got a large-bore IV in. Her saline lock from her admission was still intact. After a couple liters of fluids, blood pressure's holding around 102 systolic. Heart rate's in the low 100s." Lauren took a few steps toward the gurney, glanced at the Foley bag near the floor. "Gross blood in her urine; they're thinking a contused kidney and probably comminuted breaks of her right lower leg and heel. Maybe compression of the lumbar spine, too." She saw Gayle wince and suspected she was thinking of her husband's debilitating back injury.

"Belly?"

"Nothing obvious there, but we're cross-matching blood. Vee and I are going with her to CT; the neurosurgeon wants to see the brain results right away. Brain, chest, belly, pelvis, legs . . . working our way down." Lauren sighed. It was surreal that this young woman had been an inpatient when she sustained these horrific injuries. "Do they have any idea how this happened?"

"The police are still up there." Gayle's wide eyes glanced toward the ceiling. "She'd been waiting for a visit from DFPS about her baby. We can't know if there is any connection between that and whatever reason it was she climbed those stairs to the roof. Thank goodness this portion of the building is only two stories."

"Yes." Lauren battled a wave of queasiness at the thought of this woman plunging from one of Houston Grace's six-story towers. Past multiple floors of windows, horrified patients, and staff. "She had a cell phone. One of the officers found it in the courtyard. Maybe she went up to the roof thinking she'd make a call from there. But got too close to the edge and was thrown off-balance by a gust." Lauren needed that to be true. She couldn't bear to even imagine that this beautiful young woman, only a few years older than Jess, could have deliberately — "It had to be an accident."

"It doesn't matter." The shadows beneath Gayle's eyes seemed somehow darker. "The hospital is liable, regardless. Fortunately Eli addressed her mental health issues and made certain that her admission orders provided for a workup. But still . . . the hospital will be subject to scrutiny for legal blame. We'll all be looked at." She shook her head. "I've had more than enough of that sort of trouble in the past twenty-four hours."

My sister? Is that what you mean?

"I'm leaving early," Gayle added. "I've arranged for Marjorie from the ICU to come in and cover the next two hours."

Lauren tried to hide her surprise. The manager never left early.

"My husband . . ." Sadness flickered across Gayle's face. "I'm needed at home."

■ ■ ■ ■

"I'm almost finished here. Except for the coffee. Thanks, Lauren." Fletcher raised his nearly empty Styrofoam cup. "Fuel to power me through till midnight." He stole a glance down the corridor toward the ER registration office, telling himself he was only hanging around for the coffee.

"Jess should be here any minute. She's working a twelve-hour night shift."

"Yeah?" He hoped there was a shrug in his voice despite the warmth creeping upward from his uniform collar. "Guess that's best with her school."

Lauren turned as Eli Landry strode up the corridor. He stopped beside them.

Fletcher returned the PA's nod. "Any news on Darcee?"

"I just spoke with one of the surgeons. They evacuated a clot from her brain, removed a piece of the skull to allow for swelling." Landry's gaze moved to Lauren. "She'll be in a drug-induced coma for now. Numbers don't look too bad all around. One kidney's pretty battered — touch and go on that. Surprisingly, the spine is intact. The leg fractures will require open reduction . . . later."

Something in his expression said they shouldn't bet good money on "later" ever coming. Fletcher thought of how Darcee had looked in that park only yesterday, dancing barefoot, singing, oblivious to the blistering sunburn and to the stares of people around her. He'd recognized that off-kilter mix of joy and defiance and had thought immediately of —

"Lauren!" Jess raced toward them, hair flying. "Is it true?" She lurched to a stop, grabbing the sleeve of her sister's scrub jacket, her expression anxious. "Did Darcee Grafton fall from the roof? Is she going to — ?"

"She's in surgery," Fletcher assured her in a rush, not even caring that he was the least qualified to say anything medical. He only wanted to fix that pain in her eyes. He set his coffee cup on the safety rail so he could reach out, but she moved.

"Surgery?" Jess's hands rose to her mouth. "Oh no, it's true."

"Hold on, sweetie." Lauren tried to put her arm around her sister's shoulders, but she stiffened and pulled away.

"Don't." Jessica's voice choked. "Don't try to tell me it's okay. One of the janitors said he was there in the cafeteria when it happened. He saw it. *Heard it.* He said that

—" Jessica's chin began to shake. "He said her head hit like someone dropped a watermelon."

"Tell her about the surgery," Fletcher said to Landry.

"She's still in the OR," Landry explained. "There was a skull fracture with bleeding; they drained it and left an opening to allow for swelling. She has a kidney injury. And fractures of her right leg —" his gaze moved to Lauren for a moment — "that will be repaired later, when she's more stable. Meanwhile, they watch and wait. Her sedatives will be backed off at intervals to check for improvements in her neurological status, and —"

"I talked to her," Jessica blurted, tears welling. "Last night. I went up to the second floor to ask the nurses how she was doing. But when I passed Darcee's room, she called out to me. She wanted me to sit with her. In the dark — I could barely see her. She told me all about her baby. How much she loves her." The tears spilled over. "Did she jump off the roof? Everyone's saying that." Jessica sagged in on herself. Fletcher and Lauren reached out their arms at the same instant. But —

"Eli," Jessica cried, stumbling forward to fling her arms around him. "I don't understand . . . Why would she . . . ?" Her words dissolved in a sob, muffled as her face burrowed into the shoulder of his white coat. "Tell me she didn't do that. Please."

"Hey . . . ," Landry whispered, making an awkward attempt to both comfort her and disentangle himself. "We don't know what happened. We might not ever know," he added, causing Jessica to groan. "I didn't mean . . . Hey . . ." He shot Lauren a help-me look.

"Here, Jess." Lauren moved forward and took hold of her sister's hand. "Let's go sit down a few minutes. Eli has patients to see. And Fletcher —"

"I'm gone," Fletcher said quickly, not at all proud of his envy. It was clear Landry would rather be anywhere else. While Fletcher was standing here useless. He might as well be invisible.

"Thank you, Fletcher. For . . ." Lauren's eyes met his. "For being here."

"No problem. We'll need a statement from Jessica. For the investigation." A too-familiar sense of disappointment filled him. "I'll have someone else do that."

9

The blessing in working twelve-hour shifts was that it meant four days a week off. The curse was that working twelve hours in the ER was insane. The only thing worse was taking Hannah Leigh to the dog park.

"Yes, Mom," Lauren assured, trying to both grip the cell phone and prevent the growling shih tzu from twining her leash around the park bench enough to strangle herself. "I'm doing exactly what the therapist said. Giving Hannah the opportunity to socialize, but protecting her from aggressive encounters." She grimaced as the dog made a sound like something from *The Exorcist*. "I think she's really enjoying herself."

"Good. I'm glad the rain stopped so that you could get outside. Of course we're tracking the next two storms on my phone's weather app. And — oh, here, your father wants to ask you something, dear."

"Lauren?"

"Yes, Daddy." Lauren waved her hand to warn away a child on a petting mission.

"The . . . roof," her father said, sounding suspiciously like he was chewing. His idea of travel was more like fork-hopping; last night he'd sent a pic of something drowning in Hatch chile sauce. "Did you have any more problems with rain leaks?"

"Not too bad." Lauren couldn't count the number of homeowners' claims her father's company had handled over the years or how many roofs he'd had repaired after Houston-area storms. He prided himself on protecting his clients. Yet the Barclay roof was original, nearly thirty years old — at this point probably only attached to the house by the mounting screws on the five gaudy weather vanes. It had begun to leak earlier this year. "I put some of Mom's Tupperware in the usual spots. I needed the roaster pan, too. I guess there's a new drip in Jess's room. I heard her pushing her bed across the floor this morning, grumbling that her comforter was wet."

"Jessica's room? Hold on — I'm putting you on speakerphone. There."

"How is your sister?" Her mother's voice held that pinch of worry she always tried to hide. "Is she eating?"

"She's fine. There's plenty of fruit and

snacks. And I'm baking those casseroles you froze. We work opposite shifts, you know. So we don't actually sit down together much. But the food's disappearing." Lauren left out the fact that she'd poked through the garbage after Jess went to bed this morning. Like some pathetic food detective. There were still some damp coffee grounds in her shoe, but at least Lauren hadn't uncovered any uneaten food tucked into empty milk cartons. It wouldn't be the first time she'd seen that.

"We're so glad you're staying at the house while we're away," her father said. "She's been getting to work all right?"

"Yep. Every day." *Late. AWOL. And now a crime suspect . . .* "School, too."

"And there haven't been any problems with —" her mother's tone morphed into something very much like Hannah's growl — *"that man?"*

"None." Lauren wished the sudden image hadn't popped into her head: Jess flinging herself into Eli Landry's arms. If her parents knew, they'd be on the next plane home. In their minds, Eli was far more of a threat than a hurricane.

There was a duet of parental sighs.

"Good," her father said. "We need to ensure that it stays that way. At least with

Jessica moving back home we have more control over the company she keeps. That apartment was a bad idea from the beginning. Her financial glitch was a blessing in disguise."

"You too, Lauren," her mother chimed in. "You've been a blessing to your sister since the day she was born. You're her guardian angel."

For some reason, Lauren thought of Fletcher. In those coat-hanger-and-Hefty-bag wings.

"I should really let you go now," she told them, noticing Hannah's attempts to chew through her leash. "Take all the time you need to help Aunt Gwen. But have some fun too. Don't worry about things here. Hannah Leigh, Jess, the house . . . I've got it all covered. Really."

"We're grateful, Lauren," her father said. "You can't know how much we count on you."

She did. Enough to call her back from Austin.

"Got to go now," she told them. "Hannah and I have some mingling yet to do."

Fat chance. As Lauren disconnected, she lolled her head back against the bench. In the distance, dozens of happy dogs in all shapes and sizes played together, yipping and chasing balls within the confines of the dog park. She and Hannah weren't going in; this was close enough. The little dog had begun growling and lunging the moment she'd spotted a German shepherd from the window of the Beetle. Lauren wasn't about to spend a precious day off acting as a referee or exchanging rabies-immunization data with some incensed dog owner.

She pulled her lip gloss from her purse and took a sniff before applying it, the berry scent carrying her back to those selfish, carefree months in Austin. When she had time to imagine her own future. Not only her sister's. A reprieve from her parents' expectations . . . But that time was gone now. Lauren had come home to Houston willingly. This really wasn't so bad.

She drew a slow breath of humid air and let her gaze sweep this small green slice of Buffalo Bayou. It was Lauren's favorite park, with premiere greenbelts spanning ten miles of a historic waterway that wound through several suburban communities from South Katy to West Houston, toward downtown. Then eventually into the city's ship channel and one of the nation's busiest ports. She loved that the bayou provided a lush, watery escape smack in the midst of a huge cosmopolitan city. Glass and steel soothed by nature. The tangled roots of massive and stately trees sank into muddy banks, flanking sunflowers, bottlebrush, dogwoods, sea oats . . . and dozens more species that Lauren had learned on school field trips and promptly forgotten.

There were plenty of creatures, too. Birds, like the slowly winging blue herons, high-nesting osprey, hawks, and beautiful wood ducks that always made Lauren think of God holding a paint palette. Bats, butterflies, dragonflies, turtles, snakes, the occasional bayou alligator, and —

Lauren jumped, then laughed at herself as Hannah rested her head on her shoe with a squeaky yawn. She took a risk and bent low to scratch the dog's soft ear, sighed, and let her gaze travel again.

Not far away was the Galleria, the amazing mall that housed two major hotels, a twenty-thousand-square-foot glass-domed indoor ice-skating rink known as Polar Ice, financial towers, dozens of restaurants, and impressive retail shopping that included the likes of Neiman Marcus, Nordstrom, Saks Fifth Avenue, and Macy's. Lauren didn't know if the downturn in the economy had made a dent in the mall's boasted twenty-six million visitors a year, but they'd certainly had Jess's business — part of the cumulative shopping binges responsible for the "financial glitch" that moved her sister back home. And eventually led to the grumpy bed-moving racket that Lauren had to endure this morning.

Sleeplessness, forgetting to eat, spending binges, and exercising to the point of injury. Were these highs warning of another dangerous low to come? Was it going to happen again?

No, Lauren wasn't going to start worrying about that. Not right now. She might have moved back to a bustling, diverse global city of six million people, but right now, right here, there wasn't any evidence of that beyond a glimpse of the skyline. Nothing that hinted of oil, aerospace, universities, shipping, rodeo . . . or, thank heaven, rush-hour traffic jams. Buffalo Bayou was providing the peaceful, quiet oasis that Lauren needed. She'd claimed a shady spot, and before the summer heat drove her to find air-conditioning, she was going to sit here and —

"Lauren!"

Oh no.

Emma Landry bounded toward her, waving. Followed by Shrek. And Eli.

She shortened Hannah's leash, pasted on a smile.

"Oh!" Emma squealed, delight in her eyes as she caught sight of the black-and-white ball of fur. "Is that Hannah Leigh?"

"Yes." Lauren raised her hand like a traffic cop. "You shouldn't get too close. I'm afraid her manners aren't always —" Hannah strained the leash, a low rumbling in her throat.

"Stay back," Eli cautioned, giving a small tug on Shrek's leash; the dog obediently sat. "Not all dogs are like Shrek."

"But Hannah Leigh knows him," Emma insisted, lacing her hands on top of her head as she peered with obvious curiosity at the dog. She'd pulled a lavender tulle skirt on over her cutoff jeans, and its sequins glittered in the sun. "She's Shrek's friend. Maybe she doesn't recognize him because her hair is in her eyes."

"They never met," Lauren confessed. Embarrassment warmed her face. "I put them in separate rooms. Because —"

"She has a problem with her manners." Eli's lips twitched. "I've been accused of that myself. More than a few times."

The big dog gave a weary sigh and one last wag of his tail, then lay down. Emma plunked onto the grass beside him, draping an arm over his neck. The pair looked every bit like *Peter Pan*'s Wendy and her nurse dog — minus its frilly cap. Lauren wondered what Eli would think if he knew Shrek had worn her mother's pink sleep turban.

"We've been at Grams and Yonner's," Emma explained, pointing over her shoulder. "Their house is over there. Not far." Her eyes sparkled like the sequins. "Close enough for alligators. But I haven't spotted any yet."

"Emma had camp today," Eli explained, sitting down to become a second bookend to the already-dozing Newfoundland. He leaned forward, wrapping his arms around his legs, a tanned and athletically muscular expanse from khaki shorts to sports sandals. "Her grandmother wanted to see her. 'Yonner' is what the kid here calls my father."

Lauren caught his barely discernible frown. Then thought of the accident at the Landry home a few days ago. Alligators might be anticlimactic.

"Yonner is short for Your Honor," Emma explained, waggling her fingers tentatively at Hannah. "He's a judge."

Eli's frown went from subtle to obvious.

Lauren couldn't imagine what it might feel like to have a father threaten you with a court order. She gave a discreet tug on Hannah's leash and was relieved when the dog finally lay back down. "Camp? What kind of camp?"

"Vacation Bible school. And I'm also going to a summer theater workshop." She grinned. "I'm going to audition for *Annie.*"

Eli shook his head. "The reason for her interesting hairstyle."

"I chopped it off," Emma explained. "With Grams's kitchen shears. Had to. Long hair is bunchy under a wig. Itchy. And too hot." She widened her eyes, looking like the perfect casting choice for the hopeful singing orphan. "Houston's the hottest place on earth. I couldn't be born somewhere like Colorado . . . or Alaska?" Something wistful flickered across her pixie face. "My mother was an actress. In Paris. She was very devoted to her career. It's why she left us."

Lauren's breath caught. The look on Eli's face made it worse.

"We should go," he said abruptly, glancing at his watch. He rose to his feet. "I've got to be at the hospital by —"

"But the dog park," Emma interrupted. "We promised Shrek he could see his friends."

"It's hot." Eli dragged his hand across his forehead to prove it. "Look at that dog. He's not built for hot."

"There's a shade cover. And a splash pad. Ten minutes, that's all. *Pleeease?*" Emma pressed a hand over her heart. "I think he has a sweetheart down there."

"Aagh." Eli closed his eyes and let out a sigh. "Ten minutes. No more. Check the time on your phone. Or I'll have to come down there and get you."

The two of them — the sprite and the patient, lumbering dog — headed across the grass to the dog park. Lauren watched, thinking ten minutes would be an interminable lifetime. She'd come here seeking peace and respite from her worries. Eli Landry offered neither.

"She's . . ." Lauren's stomach did an unexpected dip as Eli's dark eyes met hers. "Adorable. I heard you had a daughter. But . . ." Why on earth had she almost mentioned Jess? The last thing she needed was another argument. "I didn't know much about her."

"I don't share much. Even with your sister, if that's what you're implying."

"I wasn't," Lauren denied. "Regardless, Emma is wonderful."

"Yes — and better than I deserve." Eli's expression showed a rare vulnerability. "Much better."

An awkward stretch of silence made Lauren wish she were suffering her mother's hurricane-warning alarm instead.

"So . . ." Eli glanced at Hannah. "Bad manners?"

"She's seeing a therapist," Lauren told him for no reason that made sense. Except that she needed to fill the time. "Hannah Leigh is a shih tzu. And they're prone to small dog syndrome. That means she has issues around the concept of 'leader of the pack,' confusing her role with her human owners'. Which makes her snappish and . . ."

Eli's expression made Lauren want to crawl into a hole. "You're saying that this little fluff dog is running your household."

"My parents' household," Lauren corrected, feeling her hackles rise. She needed to make it clear: this wasn't about her. "I'm house-sitting."

"You're policing Jessica."

She stared. "That's ridiculous."

"C'mon, Lauren. It's the reason you came back from Austin." Eli's voice was calm, matter-of-fact. "It wasn't because you wanted to see me again."

"I . . ." Lauren struggled for words, refusing to give in to the memory: the feeling of being held in this man's arms. *Lord, please . . . don't do this to me.* "My sister is nearly twenty-two years old," she said finally, grateful for a surge of anger that boosted her to her feet. She planted her hands on her hips. Hannah's growl began to rumble. "Jess starts nursing school in the fall. She's doing fine. She doesn't need me to —"

"Keep track of what time she comes in? Who she sees? Lie for her when she's late for work?" Eli shook his head. "I'll bet you even keep notes on her food intake."

"What? You're so off base. With all of that." Lauren glanced away. There was no way he could see the coffee grounds in her shoe. She needed to get out of here.

"Look," Eli continued, the accusing tone waning. "I admire that you want to help your sister. But surely, as a professional, you can understand that your family's enabling —"

"Enabling?" Lauren took a step toward him, felt Hannah brush her ankle as she followed. "You're actually going to tell me that *we're* to blame for my sister's problems? Her family?" She pointed her finger. "*You* were the reason Jess ran away last year. She wouldn't have needed those sleeping pills if she hadn't been upset by your unsolicited, so-called friendly advice. Trying to convince her she needed therapy or medication. Can you even imagine how that felt? How hurtful it was?" Lauren's finger began to shake. She willed it to steady. "My father had a stroke as a result of your interference, Eli. A *stroke*."

"Lauren, hey —"

"Don't," she warned, somehow close enough now that her finger brushed the front of his shirt. She was vaguely aware of Shrek lumbering their way off leash, Emma following a good distance behind. "Don't say you 'admire' that I'm trying to help my sister. Not when you're the guy who wouldn't do a thing to help her during that drug-screening situation. You *knew* it was a prescription medicine. You could have confirmed that. Vouched for her." Her finger connected with his chest in a jab. "Jess's job was at risk. A *real* friend would have —"

"Shrek, back."

"Hannah — no!"

There was a bellowing bark, a high-pitched response, then a deep yelp.

"Hannah, let go of his ear!" Lauren pleaded, frantic. "Eli, Emma, stay back. She'll bite. Let me find something to distract her. I have toys, treats, and — oh no!"

Another fit of growling, a blur of black-and-white, then . . .

Laughing. Eli and then Emma joining in. "Good boy, Shrek."

Lauren stared, incredulous.

Hannah was flat on her back — completely subdued by a blind dog's enormous black paw planted square in the center of her chest. Shrek's brows perked as he gazed calmly toward the sound of his master's voice.

"I can't believe it," Lauren breathed.

Eli shrugged. "Leader of the pack."

10

"I think this was a good choice," Eli told Vee Viette, meaning it.

He sank into one of several overstuffed chintz armchairs and gazed with appreciation around the wood-paneled great room of Mimaw's Nest. Beamed ceilings, white cotton curtains topped by ruffles of red-and white-checked fabric, above a hardwood floor stenciled to look like braided rugs — real ones would have been skid hazards. A staggering number of collector's plates covered the walls — Hummels to Elvis — along with a few festive Mardi Gras masks. Dominating the far wall was a huge color portrait of a beaming African American woman. The late great Auntie Odette, he'd been told.

All in all, the room was a colorful mix of what Eli's mother would call "tacky comfortable," but most of all welcoming — down to the huge rawhide bone Shrek was happily gnawing on the wide front porch. Very welcoming. Starting with the air itself, which smelled of pancakes, hash browns, and plates of steaming boudin sausage. The room hummed with a blend of music, distant laughter, and the frequent clucking of chickens through the screen door. Chickens, Elvis. And nothing obviously "medical" — uniforms included.

The staff, mostly Vee's extended family, came to work dressed as they would be at home: jeans, T-shirts, overalls, or shirts with the tails tied up over hippie-print skirts. Some added hats, scarves, and funky jewelry that would never fly at the hospital but were sure to coax a smile or laugh from even the most challenged residents.

A group that now included Eli's brother. Drew had moved in last night. His first comment had been *"Wow — cool."*

"We're so glad your family is willing to share Drew with us." Vee nudged a basket of still-warm beignets his way. "I wasn't sure it would happen."

Eli had been surprised himself. The judge never took his suggestions for Drew. But when he'd presented the idea of Mimaw's — sitting in the Landry study, flanked by those gun cases — his father had been unusually reserved. Not distracted or sullen. Simply accepting. He'd let Eli explain what he knew about this place, allowed his wife to ask most of the questions. Including those about medical supervision, equipment, and staff training. The judge made a general statement about Drew's medical paperwork but didn't mention the advance directive. No threats. Or thinly veiled implications that Eli wanted anything other than to ensure his brother's comfort and safety. He hadn't even complained that the facility's location, acreage off the highway west of Houston, was a longer drive for visitors. And medical transport.

It had all seemed surreal, even ideal. Until the thought occurred to Eli — around two o'clock this morning, jolting him awake — that his father's strange acquiescence might have been a sort of apology to his wife. For deliberately shooting at her younger son.

He swallowed, glancing to where one of the staff was helping an elderly resident strap on one of those washboard musical instruments, encouraging the man to rub his shriveled hand against the ribs of the metal vest along with the Cajun music. He was a quick study.

"And thank goodness," Vee continued, "your brother was released before the next storm moves in. We've got rain coming

125

again — maybe winds. Francis's picking up strength. We tend to keep track."

"Yes." Eli still had trouble accepting what he'd heard about this young woman. Not only that she'd survived Hurricane Katrina, but that she and her older cousin had sought shelter in one of the temporary sites that spawned media horror stories. He didn't want to imagine what a twelve-year-old girl might have endured. It seemed a miracle that this peaceful haven could have been founded by evacuees from that disaster. Eli glanced at the ceiling. "No problems with the roof after that wind from Eloise?"

"No." Vee smiled. "We tend to check those things, too." Then her brows pinched. "I inquired at the hospital today about that girl from the urgent care who fell off the roof. No change in her neuro status."

"I checked too. Her vital signs are stable, and the injured kidney is functioning normally." Eli decided to spare her his real opinion: that none of those things mattered if Darcee was brain-dead.

He glanced away for a moment as the caregiver began to sing along with the resident's exuberant washboard strums. Another collection on the wall caught Eli's eye, one he hadn't noticed before: dozens of crosses, all sizes and shapes, colors and materials. He thought of Emma's Palm Sunday cross. She'd already pinned it up in Drew's new room.

"A lot of people were in that cafeteria." Vee's amber eyes captured his. "It was an awful thing to see. Dodie, the EKG tech, said she's had some nightmares. I'm glad Lauren's going to have that support meeting."

"Right." In the chapel. He'd heard about it. Apparently Lauren was also teaming with social services to do some one-on-one peer counseling, to assess staff for signs of traumatic stress. He'd tell her she could skip him. Not that they would be speaking after the big dogfight yesterday — theirs, not Shrek and Hannah Leigh's. Fortunately he and Lauren worked in different departments. Avoiding each other wouldn't be a problem.

"It looks like all of Drew's medicines were delivered." Eli weakened and reached for a sugary beignet. "The nurses said he's been swallowing the pills okay. He needs to have the head of his bed raised to do that. Drew's had some trouble with choking since he's been in bed more."

"No worries; he'll be fine," Vee assured. "And I think you'll notice that your brother won't be in bed as much here." She smiled,

127

her head nodding to the washboard music. "We've got great chairs and even better encouragement."

Eli wished there were hope for more. But he knew better. "Did you say all of your staff are family members?"

"Most of them. You met Renee and Eulalie and Florine. And Isaac and Uncle Henrie." She smiled with obvious pride. "There are a few more Viettes. And some Fruge cousins that help with building maintenance. But we've been short one registered nurse the past three months. Some of the Houston Grace staff have been filling in." She met Eli's gaze directly, abandoning her musical head nod. "One of the nurses is Lauren Barclay. She's due here in about an hour."

"What am I up to? Emptying rainwater from a roaster pan," Lauren answered, dropping down onto the weather room couch with her cell phone. "And poaching chicken breasts for Hannah Leigh. She won't eat dog food. What's happening in Austin?"

"Same old, same old . . ." There wasn't a speck of complaint in Kate Callison's voice. "Wes wants me to ride along with the horse-mounted team today. Be the designated nurse in spurs and chaps." Kate's laugh was

128

half purr. She deserved joy; it had been a long time coming. "I don't think that man would notice if I showed up at the church in search-and-rescue gear instead of a wedding dress. It's all he thinks about."

"Except for you." There was no denying Lauren's twinge of envy. Kate had found her happy ending. While Lauren found . . . a shoe full of coffee grounds. In her continuing role as her sister's keeper, which Jess welcomed like a hill of Texas fire ants.

"How's that dicey situation with your sister and —" Kate's voice hinted at melodrama — "the dark and dangerous PA?"

Lauren's stomach shivered for no reason she could explain. "Eli's out of the picture for the most part. But we all work together. I'm keeping an eye on everything."

"That sounds like you. Hey, we heard about your patient. The woman who fell from the roof. It was in the Grace Medical management bulletin as a prompt for a system-wide safety assessment. Horrible thing. Were you involved in any of that?"

"I helped on scene. She landed on the patio right outside the cafeteria — full of visitors and staff. I'm sure you can imagine how it affected people." Lauren thought of Jess, how distraught she was even without witnessing the incident. "I'll be doing some peer counseling for the staff. And helping with the annual disaster plan update, of course."

"Speaking of that, our weather reports keep mentioning those tropical storms. I don't have to worry about you getting caught in a hurricane, do I?"

"No. That's common news coverage this time of year. Besides, my mother wouldn't allow it, not when she's not here to direct things." Lauren glanced at the rainbow of storm maps and the plethora of weather gizmos. "Our only weather challenge is this pathetic sieve that's masquerading as my parents' roof. I'm running out of Tupperware bowls."

"Ha! Oops — better run. Wes's truck just pulled up. Stay safe, pal."

"Always. You too, Kate."

Lauren disconnected and was about to slip the phone in her pocket when she saw she'd missed a text from Vee. About thirty minutes ago. Probably came in when she was watching the dog-training DVD. She'd had to turn the TV volume up in order to hear it over Hannah's growling critique. She tapped to open the message:

Drew Landry @ Mimaw's. Eli here too.

"Great," Lauren groaned aloud. Apparently there was no place she could go to escape him. Not work, not Mimaw's, not even her Buffalo Bayou.

She walked toward the kitchen, yesterday's encounter prodding once again. Eli had seemed as wary as she'd been about their chance meeting at the dog park. If Emma hadn't been there, Lauren had no doubt they would have pretended not to notice each other. They'd been doing that, avoiding each other like two repelling magnets, since the day she'd begun work at Houston Grace. It was easier than she'd imagined — minimal professional contact required because they worked in separate departments and almost no personal interaction at all since he'd dropped down on Jess's revolving list of buddies.

She poured fresh coffee into her cup, added a generous splash of almond milk, then carried it to the kitchen table. She set it next to her open Bible, a safe distance from the vintage orange Tupperware Servalier bowl positioned under a ceiling drip. She was going to leave the bowl there even if the latest weather report promised sun.

Lauren chuckled, thinking of Emma Landry and the way she'd burst into an exuberant *Annie* song as she left the park. " '*The sun'll come out tomorrow. . . .' "*

That such a hopeful and sunny child could be the daughter of "the dark and dangerous PA" seemed impossible. They were so different. Lauren frowned as she recalled what the little girl had said about her mother: she was an actress in Paris, and it was the reason she'd left them. The innocent revelation clearly bothered Eli. By his own admission, he didn't share much about his daughter. That much seemed true; Jess rarely mentioned her, had insisted Eli's wife was dead when her parents pressed for information about the older man who was a single father — and the Landry family black sheep. Lauren suspected it was a combination of all those things that made Jess strike up a friendship with him in the first place. Another way to rebel against her parents. She'd waved him like a red cape under a bull's nose. And Lauren, as always, had been the appointed fixer.

She'd made a point of attending a few of the Grace Hospital softball games — Jess and Eli were both on the team. But instead of an arrogant and entitled "player" exerting undue influence — her parents' claim — Lauren's first impression of Eli had been much different. Good-looking, obviously, but quiet, more interested in the game than

132

in socializing. In truth, he and Jess didn't interact all that much. Still, Eli had engaged Lauren in conversation a few times, once even suggesting she join the group for pizza afterward. The spontaneous invitation had made her uncomfortable. She wasn't sure if it was because she saw something in his eyes that hinted at interest in her . . . or because she could imagine herself being okay with that.

Considering the whole situation, it was unnerving at best. She decided to back off and told her parents she didn't think there was anything to worry about. Only a few weeks later, Jess had filled the prescription and run away.

Lauren took a sip of her coffee, attempting to wash down the too-familiar swirl of guilt. She should have done more to discourage the friendship, especially when it became clear that Eli's unwelcome counsel was upsetting Jess. That kind of friction always sent her into a tailspin.

Lauren squeezed her eyes shut against the memory of her sister's disappearance that spring break, her parents' frantic worry. Her first instinct had been to call Fletcher, but he'd been on that Hawaiian anniversary cruise with his parents. And then she'd seen Jessica's Facebook posts about needing to get away, along with those photos of beaches in Corpus Christi. So she'd raced there alone, crazy to save her sister and not knowing Eli was on his way too. When she met up with him, she'd raged against his intrusion into Jess's life. Blamed him for her disappearance. She'd made Eli a target for every frustration, every moment of anger and anguish she'd felt in a lifetime of protecting Jess. All the while terrified — more than Lauren had been in her entire life — that her sister was dead, gone forever.

She'd screamed at Eli, told him she hated him. He'd taken it all, offering nothing in his defense.

Then Lauren had dissolved, sagging to her knees and sobbing. For the first time ever she'd lost hope, exhausted from trying to remain strong and responsible. Sick at heart of it all, she'd wished someone could just take over, make things okay.

Eli had reached down and helped her stand again. For a brief moment he'd hugged her close, then stepped back and looked her squarely in the eye, promising he'd find her sister. Which, thank God, he did.

And then, back in Houston, somehow she'd ended up in his arms again. Where, so unexpectedly, they'd shared that kiss . . .

Lauren's phone chimed in her pocket. The alarm she'd set:

Jess. Anatomy & Physiology 1 PM

It was a recurring weekly reminder, one of several alarms she put in place in the event that Jess overslept or forgot she had class. This was her sister's final required course in pre-nursing. A last milestone to ensure Jess's acceptance into the degree program in the fall — a foothold on her future. Lauren had promised her parents she'd help that happen.

"You're policing Jessica."

"I'm not," Lauren hissed aloud, hating that Eli's words had drifted back. She stood, gritting her teeth. It was time to get ready for her shift at Mimaw's. She'd take care of Drew Landry if she was asked to; Vee was right that he could use some stability and TLC. But that didn't mean Lauren had to put up with his brother's off-base opinions about her family. Or be constantly reminded of her mistake that night he brought Jess home.

"Jessica!" Fletcher slowed his open Jeep, pulling to the curb in front of the Barclay house. He cupped his hands around his mouth. "What are you . . . ? Hey, hold on there!"

Jessica halted her ladder climb, twisting her torso to peer his way. She leaned back, raised her arm to wave.

"Watch out!" The top of the fifteen-foot aluminum ladder lost contact with the stucco and wobbled sideways, jolting Jessica like a clown act. She pitched forward, arms hugging the ladder, her slender frame in baggy jeans and a gauzy tunic not enough ballast for even a kitchen step stool. She yelped, flattening her palms against the house.

"Don't move!" Fletcher vaulted from the Jeep and jogged toward her, trying not to imagine her hurtling to the ground.

"I'm perfectly fine now," she shouted down to him, wind whipping her hair as, miraculously, the ladder steadied against the wall. She smiled, her beauty making his breath catch. "No worries, neighbor."

"Come down," Fletcher croaked. He cleared his throat, told himself he shouldn't be thinking what he was: that he wanted her down here, safe — in his arms. He watched as Jessica swept her hair away from her face, giving the pale strands one last stubborn tug, the way she had for as long as he could remember. "It's way too early to string Christmas lights around your mother's flying pig. Why are you up there?"

"Trying to keep from drowning in my sleep." Jessica descended the last several rungs, then dropped light as dandelion fluff to the lawn. She walked toward Fletcher, brushing her hands together. Her lips pouted. "Bad enough to have to move back home without a roof leak over my bed."

"For sure." Fletcher tore his gaze away from her mouth and glanced at the ladder. Beyond that, there was no sign of repair equipment. He had a feeling this woman was about to talk him onto a roof again. "What were you fixing it with? Bubble gum?"

She sighed. "I haven't thought that far. I . . ." The look in her eyes tore at Fletcher's heart. Exactly like the night the neighborhood bully set fire to her Halloween candy bag. "Hard to think at all. It's been that kind of week."

It's been that way too long, Jessica. The need to fold her into his arms, comfort her, was a physical pain. Would it ever happen? If he dared to tell her how he felt, right now . . . "What's going on?"

"Everything. Always." Jessica frowned. "My boss . . . She's out to get me."

Gayle used a trembling fingertip to pat concealer over a darkening bruise on her cheekbone. It was a two-step process: first a greenish liquid that looked like melted pistachio ice cream, then one in a shade lighter than her skin tone. A simple fix, the woman at CVS had promised. But nearly impossible in the flickering fluorescent light of this little-used bathroom near the hospital's basement mail room. Gayle stared at her reflection, blinking back tears she couldn't let fall. Calling in sick had been out of the question; she needed to be at work. So much depended on it.

In five minutes, she'd done as much as she could and headed down the corridor to the elevator. She squared her shoulders and managed to return the smiles of the two engineers loading supplies onto a cart, no doubt related to the second-floor project: welding extra height to the roof railing. Business as usual, Gayle told herself as she pushed the elevator button. It would be the same for her today, despite —

"Hi, Gayle. Oh, my goodness . . ." The dietician stepped back in the elevator to make room, concern in her expression. Her eyes swept over Gayle's face. "What on earth happened?"

"A fender bender," Gayle offered quickly, wishing she'd taken longer with the makeup. Wishing so much more. *Oh, Leo . . . why?* "A little accident on my way home from work yesterday. I'm fine, really."

11

"Come in," Eli told her, after glancing sideways at his brother. "You've never seen the Champ awake."

"That's right. I . . ." Lauren was stunned. Drew Landry was in bed, propped up by several pillows and tucked under one of Auntie Odette's flamboyant crocheted afghans, this one in Mardi Gras colors of purple, green, and gold. He wore a set of padded headphones, his long-lashed eyes closed and the fingers of one hand tapping as he nodded to the music. His hair was freshly combed and his lips curved in a smile. Drew looked nothing at all like the pale, critically ill man who'd struggled to breathe in the ER. "This is amazing," Lauren said simply.

"Yes." Eli held her gaze for a moment before reaching over to nudge his brother's shoulder. "Company, pal."

Drew fumbled to pull the earphones away,

then grinned at Lauren, his heavy-lidded eyes nearly identical to his brother's. Except for a delighted sparkle, which Drew's held in abundance. "Uh . . . hi."

"Hello, Drew."

"This is Lauren," Eli explained as she stepped close to the bed, skirting the slumbering Shrek at the last moment.

"Yeah . . . Laurr-en." Drew's voice was a halting monotone. But there was an innocent eagerness in his expression, undeniable warmth that matched the look in his eyes. "Like . . . my room?"

"I do," she said, shaking the hand he offered. The other, paralyzed like his leg, was encased in a splint to prevent further contracture. She glanced at the wall beside the bed and saw what had to be a gift from Emma: a huge rainbow drawn with colored markers and embellished with dozens of shiny foil stickers. A faded and dry Palm Sunday cross was taped to the high point of its arch. On a table beside a blobbing orange lava lamp were framed photos. Judge Landry and his wife. Drew in a wheelchair, wearing a Santa hat and holding a toddler-age Emma. And what looked like the enlargement of an old snapshot: two young boys in swim trunks, carrying fishing gear. *Eli and Drew, before . . .* Lauren had an

141

uncomfortable sense that she was snooping. "And you have music, too," she added, pointing at the headphones.

"My . . . favorite." Drew's smile widened as he extended them toward her. "Lissssten."

She tilted her head against one of the earphones and heard familiar strains of a popular contemporary Christian group. "Casting Crowns," Lauren said, surprised.

"Emma's pick." Eli's expression gave no clue whether or not he approved. "She's taken charge of getting him settled. Although —" his lips quirked — "she keeps taking his pillows away. She said it's not healthy for him to have so many. I have no clue where she got that idea."

"No . . . clue." Drew's grin morphed into a wide yawn.

"You need some sleep, Champ." Eli leaned close, gave his shoulder a squeeze. The tenderness on his face made Lauren's heart cramp. "I'm going to talk with Lauren. Maybe see what's for dinner too. I'll be back. Don't worry."

"Okay." Drew's eyes teased. "There . . . goes . . . Trouble."

"Right."

Lauren stepped outside the room, Eli following.

"Trouble?" she asked as they walked down the hallway.

Eli shook his head. "My nickname. He's always called me that."

"Ah." She made no effort to hide her smile.

"Drew's medicines have all arrived." Eli wondered if Lauren suspected he was using this as an excuse to follow along, talk with her. His dog had dropped hers flat yesterday. After she'd laid into him because of things he'd said about her family. He wished he'd kept his mouth shut, that none of it had happened. At least not that way. Maybe this place could provide the neutral ground he needed to . . . *what?* What was it that he wanted, anyway?

"I checked your brother's medicines as soon as I arrived," Lauren told him, sweeping her hand to indicate the individual medicine cubbyholes built into the wood-paneled wall of what had once been a butler's pantry in the old house. Several more photos of Auntie Odette hung on the adjoining walls. Along with a framed Rockwell print of a boy preparing a spoonful of tonic for his sick dog. "Were there any special instructions?"

"He's had some problems with swallow-

ing pills. So his head needs to be elevated."
Eli noticed that Lauren had dressed the way
the Viette family did: an embroidered peasant shirt over jeans, a string of pink beads
and matching hoop earrings. She'd tied her
hair back with one of those bright, wrinkled
scarves that looked like a kid's potato-stamp
project. She looked beautiful. And unusually relaxed. Almost like she could be in a
video for that old song Drew used to sing,
"Don't Worry, Be Happy."

"Was there anything else?" she asked,
making Eli realize he was staring.

"No. Drew does pretty well if he's propped
up." Eli shook his head. "I need to tell
Emma to stop taking those pillows away."

"Sounds like it won't be a problem then."

It sounded like Lauren was dismissing
him. But she met Eli's gaze instead, compassion in her eyes. "I'm glad he's doing so
well. It must be a huge relief."

"It is." Eli's throat tightened; he hadn't
known how much he needed to tell someone
that. "I never know what will happen," he
heard himself say. "All these years, I nev—"

"Nurse!"

A young woman, her eyes frantic, burst
through the door to the medication room.
"Please, we need help. Poppy . . . my
grandpa's on the floor. I don't think he's

144

breathing!"

"We're coming — tell someone to call 911," Lauren instructed. "Eli, grab the kit." She pointed toward something that looked like a big picnic hamper. "I've got the AED." Pulling the automated defibrillator box from where it hung below the Norman Rockwell print, she took off running. "Show me where Poppy is."

"I'm right behind you," Eli shouted, snatching up the basket and hustling toward the hallway. There was no time to think, only a strange sense of mismatch that the emergency was accompanied by distant strains of zydeco music instead of "code blue" paging. And today Lauren was in charge.

"Here!" Vee beckoned from the threshold of the great room. "I called 911." She led the way with Lauren following and Eli right behind.

He dropped to his knees beside the unconscious victim sprawled on his back. Then recognized him: the man who'd been learning to play the washboard. The sheet of corrugated tin was still strapped to his chest.

"He was f-fine," the granddaughter insisted, her voice choked by tears. "Showing me his music. And then he kind of choked, and his eyes rolled back."

One of the gathered Viette clan eased her into a chair.

"Not breathing," Lauren reported. "We need —"

"Have it," Eli answered, amazed to find an Ambu bag in the wooden hamper. Along with exam gloves, portable suction, a small assortment of emergency drugs. "I'll give him a few breaths while —"

"I'm getting this washboard off of him. And his shirt," Vee said, reading Eli's mind.

"AED's ready when we are," Lauren reported, already pulling the adhesive pads from the automated defibrillator. "The paramedics won't be long, but we can at least get things going." Her eyes found Eli's for a split second. "Poppy's recovering from a cerebral bleed. And he's a full code."

"Understood," Eli told her, knowing Lauren had no professional responsibility to explain that to him. He slid the rescue mask over Poppy's mouth and nose, thanked Vee for attaching the oxygen tubing, and gave the man a few squeezed breaths.

"Analyzing," the ever-calm mechanical voice of the AED reported, flashing a yellow warning light. *"No one should touch the patient."*

Distant sirens joined the granddaughter's sobs and gentle murmurs of comfort from the Viettes.

Eli leaned close to Lauren, both of them staring at the digital screen on the defibrillator. There was no heart tracing like at the hospital, simply —

The orange warning light flashed. *"Shock advised. Stay clear of patient. Press the orange button now."*

V-fib. Eli reached out the same instant as Lauren.

"Oh, I —"

"Go ahead," he told her, leaning back. "Sorry . . . reflex."

"Everybody stay clear!" Lauren punched the button and Poppy's body jerked in response to the electricity. The granddaughter gasped. A siren yelped from the parking lot. Eli realized he was holding his breath.

"It's analyzing again," Vee whispered, holding the cross on her necklace between her fingertips.

The orange light flashed. *"Shock advised. Stay clear of patient."*

Eli pressed the button as he heard someone praying aloud in the background. He glanced that way, saw that Shrek was lying at the feet of Poppy's granddaughter.

"Shock delivered," the machine reported. There was a moment's silence, then, *"It is*

safe to touch the patient."

Vee's breath escaped. "Please . . ."

Eli reached for the Ambu bag.

Lauren pressed two fingers against their patient's throat to check for a pulse. "I feel it. There's something there . . . It's slow; let me count —"

"Medics coming through!" someone shouted, and in mere seconds they were surrounded by rescuers. First responders from Katy: fire, paramedics, police. Starched and formal uniforms blending with the folksy rainbow that was the Mimaw's staff. There was a metallic *squeak-rattle* of a stretcher moving through the doors, soft thudding of boots against the painted-rug hardwood floors, squawking of radios, and the beeps of monitors.

". . . collapsed in front of his granddaughter, no apparent warning," Lauren was telling one of the medics. "We —" she glanced at Eli — "found he wasn't breathing. Gave some rescue breaths, got him on the AED. It delivered two shocks." Her cheeks were flushed, her voice a little breathless. "I found a carotid pulse just as you arrived."

"The IV's in," one of the medics reported from his kneeling position on the floor.

"Hand me that atropine. Monitor still the same?"

"Bradycardia . . . at thirty-seven," his partner confirmed. There was a whoosh as he squeezed the Ambu bag to deliver another breath. "Still no respiratory effort. We'll get him tubed in the rig."

Tubed. Headed for a ventilator . . .

Eli thought of Drew in his bed a short walk down the hallway. He hoped he had those earphones on. And that his music — the Crown band or whatever it was called — was turned way up loud. What had just happened here was something he never wanted Drew to suffer through again.

"Thanks for the help." Lauren watched as Eli repacked the emergency equipment. "It was a lot to grab by myself. The emergency kit is heavier than it looks."

Eli's lips curved toward a smile. "It looks like a picnic hamper. My Baton Rouge grandmother had one exactly like it. But she knew what to pack it with: crawfish sandwiches, mango salad, deviled eggs, and the best praline cheesecake you've ever tasted. Not a single surgical glove or suction catheter."

"That basket fits with the whole not-icky-medical thing they have going here," Lauren countered, totally disarmed by Eli's rare smile. It almost hinted at the sparkle she'd seen in his brother's eyes. "Less white coat and rubbing alcohol. More music, laugh therapy, and home cooking. Every day is casual Friday at Mimaw's." She plucked at her embroidered blouse, nudged a beaded earring, and felt it swing against her neck. "You didn't notice?"

The smile stayed put. "I noticed."

"Anyway . . ." Lauren hoped her face didn't look as pink as it suddenly felt. "I like what the Viettes are doing. And I really did appreciate your help with Poppy. It was the first time I've had to deal with a code blue here."

Eli was quiet for a moment, as if fitting a new package of oxygen tubing into the basket took all his concentration. When he looked up, any trace of the smile was gone. "Back there with Poppy, you made a point of telling me he was a full code."

"I guess . . . it was a reflex," she said, using his earlier word. "It felt like we were at the hospital, and . . ." Lauren hated the way Eli was looking at her.

He closed his eyes for a moment. "After my conversation with Mike that day Drew was in the code room . . . you thought I was going to question what you were doing.

That I'd even ask you to pull out Poppy's advance directive, start arguing with his family. You thought you needed to defend the poor man from —"

"Whoa." Lauren raised her palm. "Where's that coming from? You're wrong, Eli. I was thinking out loud, that's all." She looked toward the hallway, lowered her voice. "But yes, unless we've been instructed otherwise, we'll call 911 and start some basic emergency care."

"Including defibrillation." Eli glanced at the still-open box of the AED.

"Yes. You know as well as I do that automated defibrillators are a standard in first aid now. I'm sure there are several at the Galleria mall. Our policy here is to do whatever we can to help until first responders arrive. Every employee is trained in CPR. We follow the health care directive provided by each patient. Or legal guardian." She expected to see that look in Eli's eyes.

"Including the existing instructions for my brother."

"Including Drew's," Lauren said as gently as possible. She'd read his advance directive twice. Judge Landry's signature looked like it had been written in a broad-tip permanent marker. Or his own blood. "I'm sure the

Viettes gave you copies of their policies."

"Yes." Eli exhaled slowly. "I suppose I thought that with this casual, 'home-style' atmosphere . . ."

"We might play God?" The words slipped out before she could stop them.

His gaze hardened. "You think *God* wants my brother tied to a bed on mechanical life support? You think that's mercy?"

"I think . . ." Lauren's stomach churned. "I can't do this conversation."

"Right." He closed the top of the emergency basket. "We can't talk about my brother, your sister, your dog — or your God. What's left?"

"I don't know."

"Me either."

Lauren watched Eli leave, an empty feeling washing over her. It was an ebb she'd felt plenty of times after the adrenaline rush of handling an emergency situation. But this time it seemed like more than that. Maybe it had something to do with the way Eli had smiled at her only moments ago, when he teased about the picnic basket. And that look in his eyes when he said he'd noticed how she was dressed. One good moment. Hopeful, even. Like feeling Poppy's heartbeat against her fingers. But now . . .

"What's left?"

Lauren didn't know if there was anything safe to talk about — or if they should try at all. She knew only one thing for sure, now more than ever: their objectives were completely opposite. She was working to ensure her sister's future; Eli was determined to direct his brother's death. They couldn't be more different if they were Hannah Leigh and Shrek.

12

"Heaven," Vee sighed as she adjusted the massage controls on the pedicure chair. She bobbed her head to strains of reggae music, then turned toward Lauren with a blissful expression. "I'm grateful your daddy has such lovely connections in the business community — and that you dawdled on using that Christmas gift certificate." Her smile spread. "Until after you met me."

"Me too." Lauren smiled back at her; she couldn't agree more. And wasn't about to spoil it by mentioning that she'd been far too busy doing damage control with her sister to even consider any "me" time. But the stars had aligned today. Vee wasn't working until three, and Lauren was free until the staff gathering in the chapel, that support meeting she'd arranged for people affected by the Darcee Grafton incident. Meanwhile . . .

Lauren wiggled her toes over the bubble

jets, breathing in the scent of soaps, essential oils, and nail products, then glanced outside. Montrose was one of her favorite areas of Houston: tree-lined streets with historic, renovated — sometimes garishly painted — mansions, cottages, and bungalows. Dubbed alternately "the heart of Houston" and "the strangest neighborhood east of the Pecos," it had also been lauded as one of the ten great neighborhoods in America a few years back. It was pedestrian friendly and boasted a defiantly eccentric mix of junk shops and vintage clothing stores, coffeehouses and tattoo parlors, along with fine restaurants, galleries, and top Houston tourist attractions like the Menil Collection art museum, the University of St. Thomas, and the Rothko Chapel. Plus great little eateries like Barnaby's Cafe, Brasil, and the West Alabama Ice House. . . . Lauren's stomach rumbled at the thought. The Montrose district was an amazing mix for sure. And was close to River Oaks. She found herself wondering if Eli liked to walk these quirky streets as well.

"And so," Vee said, hauling Lauren back to pedicure status, "it's unanimous; the party's on. Sunday. Unless you need us to change the date. Because it wouldn't be a party without you. But let me know now, girl —" she grinned — "because I'm about to have these toes painted purple, green, and gold."

"Mardi Gras in June?" Lauren chided, reaching for her icy tumbler of sweet tea. "You're almost as late as I am using this gift certificate."

Vee shrugged. "No one wanted to tackle it after Auntie passed. Mardi Gras was always her party. Right down to the plastic baby in the king cake. Don't get me started on Uncle Henrie swallowing it one year; we thought he'd bought himself an esophagoscopy." She offered a thumbs-up to a woman wobbling by with cotton threaded between her freshly lacquered toes. Then turned to Lauren again. "Truthfully, no one had the heart to do a party so soon after losing Auntie. But now we think it will be fun, a way to honor her. She'd love that. And it's a celebration, too: Poppy's pacemaker, having you on staff, passing our licensing inspection with flying colors, and Drew Landry getting up in a chair. Plus there's Tropical Storm Francis fizzling out . . . and our eleven new baby chicks . . ."

"Chicks?" Lauren laughed, set the tea back down. "You *so* want a party."

"You bet." Vee stretched a micro braid across her chin. "You'll be there? Sunday, after church?"

"Definitely." Lauren smiled. "But if we're eating gumbo, you'll have to crank up the AC or we'll all sweat to death. And I don't play the kazoo. Remember that." She laughed again, raising her hand to meet her friend's in a hearty high five.

Vee lifted her feet from the water as one of the spa staff readied a towel. "Shall we meet up for dinner at the hospital?"

"Sure. You'll be at the chapel gathering?"

"Gonna try my best," Vee promised. "Though I'm thinking I'll be running back and forth between the ER and urgent care tonight. Thank goodness Eli is more merciful than the other PAs."

"Right." Lauren sighed. *Merciful?*

It had been two days since Lauren and Eli knelt over Poppy, then exchanged those tense words in the medicine room. They'd passed each other in the Houston Grace hallways with barely a nod. It was probably better that way. But when Lauren heard about Drew's recent accomplishments — the chair and even tossing a Nerf ball with one of the Viette cousins — she *so* wanted to tell Eli how wonderful she thought it was. And more. She wished she could tell him that Drew's improvement was a sign of hope. That despite Eli's bitter doubts about mercy, God did promise it.

"Your God." That's what he said. As if Eli had no connection to him. How did you explain the promise of hope to someone like that?

"Hope and a future . . ." Lauren believed in that promise, always had. It was the only thing that had held her together this past year. During Jess's disappearance, her father's stroke, those confusing moments with Eli afterward. And all the months Lauren stayed away in Austin to give her sister a chance to succeed on her own. She'd chewed her fingernails but faithfully reminded herself to let God handle it. She'd tried to find the peace promised in that; it was her consistent prayer. But lately Lauren couldn't shake the awful feeling that . . .

She wasn't getting it right.

"It would really help me out, Doug," Gayle told the physician. "Leo's miserable, and he's got this stoic pride that's butting up against his good sense these days." She shook her head, dizzy for a moment as her heart did a double somersault. "I love that big guy, but without the steering wheel of an 18-wheeler in his hands, he's floundering like a bear on roller skates."

"Surely Leo's physician is giving him pain meds."

"Anti-inflammatories. They're not working. And he's trying to gut it out because he thinks if the record shows he's not better, he'll get passed over for jobs. It's been more than a year now." Gayle tilted her head a little, hoping the doctor didn't see her bruises. This was humiliating enough. "Leo's attacking physical therapy like a demon, but I can tell he's suffering. The pain keeps him awake. I thought if I could convince him to take one Percocet at bedtime . . ."

"I'm sorry," the doctor told her, visibly uncomfortable. "I'd like to help you out. And I do understand. My father has disk disease; he's being seen in a pain management clinic now. Mom's had a lot to deal with." He met her gaze. "I'm your gynecologist, Gayle. I've known you for a long time. I feel for what's going on with your husband. I know it affects you. But writing a prescription for narcotics would be unethical. I'm sure you can understand that."

She couldn't. This doctor was her last hope. She wanted to scream that to him, drop to her knees and beg. Tell him she was afraid her husband's sanity depended on that triplicate narcotic script. Maybe her own life depended on it. . . .

"Of course I understand, Doug. No problem."

The physician's brows drew together. "You look thin, Gayle. I'm concerned. Make an appointment; I think we need to run some tests. Repeat that thyroid panel. I want to be sure everything's okay."

"First spare minute I get. Promise." She forced a smile, murmured something about giving regards to his wife, and walked away.

Sweat beaded on Gayle's forehead. She'd have to check her makeup. And try to think of someone else she could ask.

She stopped walking, peered toward the ICU. "Jessica?"

"Oh . . . hi, Gayle." Jessica Barclay stepped from the alcove outside the ICU doors. Her expression said she'd rather have gone unnoticed.

"You're not working today." It was a statement, not a question; Gayle had reviewed the schedule, of course. The young woman's appearance confirmed it: baggy jeans, faded burgundy hoodie topping a long ribbed tee. Too much clothing for a June day in Houston. Flip-flops, oversize sunglasses perched atop uncombed hair, not an ounce of makeup. And still so incredibly lovely. Something only the very young could pull off. Gayle was surprised by a stab of envy, then more so by the match-strike of anger that immediately followed. "What are you doing up here?"

"I wanted to check on a patient." Jessica's expression was wary, guarded.

"It's immediate family only in the ICU."

"I know that." Jessica scraped her teeth across her lower lip. "I thought maybe I could catch one of the nurses, find out how Darcee Grafton is doing."

"I see." Gayle crossed her arms. "I don't think I need to remind you about privacy laws."

"No . . ." Jessica was quiet for a moment, then glanced at the ICU doors. She muttered something under her breath. "You don't need to remind me. The same way you don't need to tell me where I can be and what I can do on my day off." Her eyes narrowed a fraction. "You know?"

"What I know," Gayle countered, "is that — day off or not — it's a bad idea for you to be wandering around the hospital. Considering the recent security problems."

Jessica's beautifully young face went pale, pupils dilating. Gayle waited for a rush of satisfaction that didn't come. *What am I doing?*

"I'm only thinking of your best interests,"

she added more gently.

"Right." Jessica pulled her glasses from the top of her head. "I hear that a lot."

"Well . . ." Gayle's anger gave way to shame. "I could find out for you," she offered, stopping herself from touching Jessica's arm. "If you'll wait right here, I'll go in and —"

"Don't bother." Jessica slid the dark glasses in place, then shoved her hands in the pockets of her hoodie. "Thanks. But it really doesn't matter anyway. I guess I'll see you tomorrow. In the ER."

"Yes."

Gayle watched as Jessica walked to the stairwell and disappeared through the door. She told herself that despite handling it poorly, she was right. There had been several instances of theft in past months. Three more than regular staff were even aware of; security had briefed management. Supervisors were expected to watch carefully. If Jessica Barclay was seen wandering around the hospital in areas unrelated to her work, it could generate suspicion.

Flowers. Mom's hands smelled like flowers. They were soft. And busy. All the time.

"There, Drew. Isn't that better?" She rubbed lotion onto his bad hand, moving his fingers back and forth like those people from therapy. Only Mom sang while she did that: " *'You are my sunshine, my only sunshine . . .'* " And then she'd hide a kiss in his hand. Every time. She'd kiss his hand, then fold his fingers around it. Tell him to hold on tight. She didn't care that he couldn't; she just liked to do it anyway. Like she was doing right now. "And here's a good-night kiss to save for later, darling."

"O . . . kay." Drew smiled at her, breathed in the flowers.

Dad stood. "I'll have another look around. Poke into the nooks and crannies. Talk with the staff. I want to be sure they know his needs. I'm still not happy with the fact that this place is almost twenty miles from the Houston hospitals. And more like a dude ranch than a care facility. But on the whole, barring problems, I'd say it could pass muster."

Mustard. Dad talked about it a lot. Like it bothered him. You could tell by his face. Sort of mad. And sad sometimes. Even when he was smiling. He didn't sit very long. He liked to move around, look at things. Now he was holding the fishing pole picture. Champ and Trouble . . .

"I'll bring more photos, Drew. You need new ones."

Dad liked to tell him what he needed.

"I'll bring that picture of you and me at the space center. With Neil Armstrong." Dad walked back to Drew's bed. "I arranged for you to meet a famous astronaut, Son. Do you remember?"

His dad always asked that: *"Do you remember?"* It was his favorite question. But Drew didn't remember those things. He mostly remembered his brother, Emma, Shrek, his favorite breakfast, words to his favorite songs . . . a lot of good things. The really good things were easy to remember.

"Well, well, you're having a nice visit, Mr. Drew." The lady came in, the one with the big white flower in her hair. Florine. The same lady who closed her eyes, raised her hands, and sang to Drew's music. "I promised you we'd try the iPad today. Remember?"

He smiled at her. "Yeah. Remember."

"You don't have class today?"

"I wasn't feeling well. My throat's kind of scratchy. I keep feeling too hot, maybe feverish." Jess swallowed with a lackluster grimace, then glanced across the hospital parking lot. Her desire to escape couldn't have been any more obvious if it were tattooed on her forehead. "Thought I should stay

164

home," she explained. "Try to fight it off."

"Ah . . ." Lauren watched her sister sweep back her hair; her nails were chewed to the quick. "Gayle said she ran into you upstairs."

"Gayle?" Jess's brows pinched. "What did she say? Did she accuse me of something?"

Accuse you?

"Nothing," Lauren assured her. "Really. She only said she was surprised to see you here on your day off." *I am too.*

"What's with Gayle, anyway? Doesn't she have something better to do than follow people around? I only wanted to find out about a patient in the ICU. Darcee Grafton. That's all I wanted." Sudden tears rose in Jess's eyes. "Is it some kind of crime to check on a patient?"

"No. Oh, sweetie . . . Of course it isn't. It's only natural you'd want to; you met Darcee. And talked to her the night before the . . . the accident. You care. That's the kind of person you are." Lauren ached to put her arms around her sister. But Jess's moodiness had her second-guessing every instinct these days. In truth, *most* days, for more than a year. She hated feeling that way. Was it a crime to hug your sister? "What happened to Darcee has affected a lot of the staff," she added, tentative. "It's why I'm leading a staff gathering this afternoon. I think it will help. We can talk about what happened with Darcee. Support each other."

"No." Jess hugged her arms around herself. "I won't come."

Lauren took a slow breath. "I wasn't suggesting —"

"Yes, you were. You want me in that pathetic group huddle, taking part and grateful, while every one of them talks about *feelings.* And then takes bets on whether it was the wind that knocked Darcee off the roof or if she was crazy and flat out *jumped.*" Jess prodded a finger toward Lauren. "You think if I agree to come to the hospital chapel, I'll take the next logical step and wade back into church again. Then maybe flop myself down on the couch of that 'amazing' Christian therapist Fletcher keeps hinting about." She frowned. "Subtle as a patrol car siren."

"Fletcher?" Lauren's brows rose.

"Forget it. All I know is that I don't need to sing 'Kumbaya' with the Houston Grace staff to understand why that girl went off the hospital roof. It's pretty obvious. A bunch of folks with good intentions *chased* her off." Jess slid her sunglasses over her eyes. "Maybe God cheered them on."

"Jess . . ." Lauren took a slow breath. There was no point in taking this further. Better to change the subject entirely. "I think there are some Ricola lozenges in Mom's medicine cabinet. There's plenty of juice. You do look a little flushed, but I'm really not surprised. It's ninety degrees and ugly humid, and here you are in those jeans and *two* layers of long sleeves. It doesn't make sense when you have all of those cotton shorts and T-shirts, a whole rainbow of tank tops, and —"

"Now you're the fashion police? Just what I need. Gayle telling me what I can't do on my day off and my sister dictating what I should and shouldn't wear." She hitched her purse over her shoulder, lips tense. "What are y'all trying to do? Shove me off a roof too?"

13

Gayle sneaked a discreet glance at her watch before returning her attention to the small circle of staff gathered in the chapel. She still had time to catch the podiatrist when he came out of bunion surgery. He was new to the Houston Grace staff, and they'd chatted several times in the cafeteria. He'd had back surgery himself and might be empathetic enough to write a prescription for a few pills to tide Leo over. If that didn't pan out, Gayle didn't know what she'd do. Leo's patience was long gone.

She blotted her damp palms against her scrub top and watched as Lauren encouraged the group to share their concerns regarding the tragedy with Darcee Grafton.

"I'd never seen anything like that," the hospital dietitian admitted. "It seems impossible it could happen outside the cafeteria, so near my office. I guess it's unrealistic to work in a hospital and expect to be insulated from tragedy. But still . . ."

"I know what you mean," one of the housekeepers agreed. "I can't tell you how many delivery room floors I've mopped down. But seeing Ernie and Hal hosing off our patio after the poor girl fell . . . I've eaten in that cafeteria for seventeen years. Never miss Taco Thursday. But now I'm packin' a sack lunch."

"Rita?" Lauren nodded at one of the ER registration clerks, compassion in her expression. "You signed Darcee in the day she arrived in our department."

"Yes." The clerk twisted the hem of her cardigan, eyes wide behind her bifocals. "She reminded me of my youngest daughter; Holly's had some troubles. Emotionally. Depression, they say. And when I heard that girl jumped off the —"

"We don't know it was intentional," one of the second-floor nurses blurted. "People shouldn't jump to that conclusion." She groaned, obviously regretting her choice of verbs. "I mean we don't know for sure."

"I'm sorry," the clerk apologized. "You're right. I only meant that it made me worry about my daughter."

"Of course." There was a sudden pained look on Lauren's face. "It's only natural, normal, to personalize an incident like this.

Some of us witnessed the tragedy firsthand. A few provided care for this patient before it happened. Many only heard about the incident later. Regardless, the chances are that we're all affected in some way by what happened that day."

"I agree," Gayle heard herself say. When Lauren nodded encouragement, she continued. "That's why we're here. I appreciate this opportunity to support each other. I think it's helpful that social services provided those brochures with information about coping with traumatic stress. I encourage you each to take one. We all have worries."

Lauren sighed.

"And . . ." Gayle resisted the urge to check her watch again; if she didn't catch the doctor when he left surgery, she'd have to look in the physician parking lot. He drove a Lexus SUV. "I have no doubt that some of our staff feel deeply affected by what happened. In fact, today one of my registration staff was concerned enough to drive to the hospital and check on this patient." Gayle saw Lauren's brow furrow, told herself she wasn't breaching privacy or pointing any fingers; she was simply helping her staff. Making certain they understood the symptoms of stress. Everyone needed to hear this.

"This employee was here — up on the second floor. *On her day off.*"

Lauren caught Gayle's gaze, anxiety in her blue eyes.

"Anyway," Gayle finished, "I only wanted to say that I'm proud to work alongside you all. You're dedicated and caring. No better team exists. If there's anything I can do to help you with this situation or anything else, please let me know." She glanced at her watch, felt her pulse quicken. "I'm afraid I need to get to an appointment. Thank you, Lauren. This was good of you."

Lauren cleared her throat. "No problem."

"I'm sorry," Eli apologized, certain that the older woman — tall and slender with graying auburn hair — had to be Darcee Grafton's mother. He glanced toward the bed. The trauma patient was nearly hidden beneath a plastic-and-wire web of machinery. "I didn't know she had a visitor."

"It's all right." The woman set a small book on the bedside table and walked forward, extending her hand. "I'm Marsha Grafton. Darcee's mother."

"Elijah Landry — Eli," he told her. "I'm a physician assistant in the urgent care. I examined your daughter when she was brought in."

171

"By the police."

"Only as a courtesy," Eli reassured. Something in Marsha's expression said an arrest wouldn't have been a surprise.

"She was dancing." Marsha glanced at her daughter.

"Yes."

From her tone, Eli had a strong sense that this was history repeating itself. He had a sudden urge to run from the ICU before this mother calmly informed him that she was certain her daughter had jumped from the roof. Because she'd attempted suicide a dozen times before. Instead, she turned back to Eli with what could only be a proud smile.

"Darcee's creative," she told him. "From forever back. She finger-painted with the Sunday gravy, tattooed her sleeping grandmother with permanent markers, wrote a gossip column about the neighborhood." She clucked her tongue. "Not well received. Her father and I called Darcee our Energizer Bunny; she never ran out of ideas. Or zeal. When she was a child, she charmed the pants off everyone. When she got older, it started to worry us." Marsha's expression grew more wistful. "Her friends made plans. College, careers . . . family. Darcee seemed detached from all of that. She got angry, resentful, alarmingly irresponsible, then depressed. That was the worst. People call it 'the blues,' but that's not enough. Not even the right color. It's so much darker. More like black." Marsha drew a slow breath. "To see your child in those depths is like the world before there was light."

"She was on medicine," Eli said gently. "For bipolar disorder."

"Several medicines over the past few years. This last one — the one that's also used for seizures — has been the best. It evens things out. When she takes it. That's the problem, *taking* it. Darcee thinks medicine dulls her creativity, 'snuffs her spark.' She's a dance teacher; there's a waiting list for her classes. She performs in local theater, paints. Sells her work. A lot of it — she's very talented." Marsha shook her head. "But she always thinks she could do better. Be more. She misses the creative high she feels when her mood would swing her that way."

Eli thought of Darcee on that rooftop. A two-story, lethal high.

"It's a frustrating, elusive illness . . . and it destroyed Darcee's marriage," Marsha continued. "But I've seen her taking huge strides forward since, long stretches of time where I almost forget how bad things can

173

get. She's been happy, enjoying her life, her daughter, friends. And now this happens. . . ."

Eli wished he could offer this woman hope that her daughter would survive fully intact, but he didn't believe it was there. Not after Drew. These days he would settle for simple mercy, and even that seemed impossible to find.

"But," Marsha added, certainty in her expression, "there was a small response today when they lightened the sedation. It only looked like flinches to me, but the doctor called it an 'appropriate response to stimuli' that hints at brain recovery. I'm hanging on to that. My sister was diagnosed bipolar years ago, and she's living a full and satisfying life — she's a research biologist for St. Jude Children's Hospital." Marsha's smile lit her face, making the resemblance to Darcee even more obvious. "I may not be a scientist or a dancer or an artist, but I'm a stubborn woman with big faith. That's my 'spark.' And I believe to the depths of my soul that all things are possible."

"Well . . ." Eli couldn't think of anything to say, so he offered his hand to say goodbye.

"Thank you." Marsha surprised him with a warm hug. "Thank you for caring about my little girl. I'm going to keep you in my prayers, Elijah Landry. You and your family."

My family. This poor woman had no idea that there weren't prayers strong enough to fix any of this. Eli took one last glance at Darcee, then beat a hasty retreat from the ICU.

He'd made it to the second-floor stairwell when his phone buzzed with a text. Eli pulled it from his coat pocket, certain the urgent care staff was getting antsy for his return.

Impossible . . . He stared, read the message a second time. And grinned.

"I was bummed I couldn't get to the chapel," Vee told Lauren, drizzling salsa over her remaining nachos. "That new ortho resident thinks every cast has to be a masterpiece. Michelangelo carved *David* faster. With less mess; I have plaster in my hair." She nibbled at a tortilla chip. "How was it — the staff gathering?"

"Good." Lauren glanced toward the doors to the patio, thinking of what the housekeeper had said about not wanting to eat in the cafeteria anymore. There were definitely fewer people at the tables. "Social services sent the brochures about coping with stress.

And the chaplain stopped by. There were maybe a dozen people from several departments."

"Gayle thought it was a good idea."

"Hmm." Lauren bit her lip before she could say what she thought of Gayle's idea to reveal Jess's visit to the second floor. Granted, Gayle hadn't used her sister's name, but the registration clerk would know who she meant. The remark had surprised Lauren; it felt out of character and insensitive. Jess had come to the hospital on her day off because she was worried about a patient. She didn't need to be pointed out as an example of traumatic stress.

"I heard Darcee showed some appropriate responses when they backed her off sedation this morning."

"Yes. Her mother was there. With the baby. She got permission to bring her in for a little while. She's fourteen months." Lauren sighed, thinking of Emma Landry and her uncle. How did you explain something like that to a child? "Darcee's response was only to painful stimuli, but at least that's something."

"A beginning. Hope." Vee smiled. "I saw the mother in the chapel on my way down —" She stopped. "Excuse me a second." She pulled out her cell phone and scanned the screen. Then frowned.

"Something wrong?"

"It was Bella. You know her — the tech who works per diem. Her wallet is missing. Security's on it."

"Not another —" Lauren's heart stalled. "Where was Bella working? Which floor?"

"Second."

Lauren fought a wave of nausea, remembering Gayle's reference to Jess's visit.

"Bella said she left it in the break room. She ran back to get it, and it was gone."

She wasn't going to ask. There was no reason to worry about — "How long ago was that?"

"Sounds like only a few minutes ago."

"Oh . . ." The rush of relief made Lauren dizzy. "Poor Bella. Awful feeling."

"I'm betting it turns up." Vee gathered up her trash and stood. "I love Bella. But she always makes me think of something my auntie would say: 'That girl would lose her head if it wasn't glued on permanent.' " She rolled her eyes. "I'm going back a few minutes early. I need to check the vacation schedule."

"I'll probably stop by the ER on my way out. See you there."

Vee tossed her a mock salute and headed off.

Lauren glanced toward the patio, then leaned back in her chair and closed her eyes.

Rotten timing. Jess had always had an unlucky habit of being in the wrong place at the wrong time. Thank heaven the wallet had gone missing hours after she left the hospital. Gayle had all but announced over the PA system that Jess was hanging around. Someone certainly would have recalled that she "disappeared" the night Darcee Grafton was admitted and that there'd been a theft on the second floor then, too. Lauren remembered the tears in her sister's eyes the times she'd talked about the young trauma victim. And her defense of that visit to the ICU today: *Is it some kind of crime to check on a patient?*

No. Caring was not a crime. And Lauren wasn't about to let anyone imply —

"Hi."

Lauren's eyes snapped open. "Oh . . ."

Eli's lips quirked very slightly. "With your eyes closed like that, I thought maybe I should check for a pulse. Or get you some caffeine."

14

"Did you need something?" Lauren asked Eli. She looked wary — blue eyes filled with suspicion, a flush high on her cheeks. Obviously she was a million miles from trusting Eli. With anything. And not too keen on conversation, either.

"I was coming out of the ICU, and I got a text message," he explained. "I thought you might like to see it."

"A text?" Lauren's wariness morphed into confusion.

"Here." He sat down and pulled the phone from his jacket. "I didn't believe it at first, but . . ." Eli opened the message, held it out for Lauren to see. His chest warmed at her incredulous and delighted smile.

" 'Hi brother. Ate pancakes. Love u.' " Lauren pressed a hand to her throat. "It's from Drew."

Their eyes met. He nodded, not trusting his voice.

"But how did he do that?"

"I called to ask. One of the staff, Florine, helped him use an iPad. Big font, one thumb — it took a while. She even set up that e-mail address for him."

" 'Champ Landry.' " Lauren smiled. "I saw that."

"We've tried a laptop before, hit or miss. He'd get bored or frustrated. But he did do it. Until this last year . . . It's been a rough year."

"Drew seems to like staying with the Viettes. How did you decide on their place?"

Eli gave a short laugh. "It was weird. I've never had any real input regarding my brother's care, and to tell you the truth, I didn't have a clue how to choose a care home. I talked to Vee, visited the place once. Our grandmother in Baton Rouge — Dad's mother — was named Marie. We called her Mimaw. I think I picked the Viettes' place for the name. And the promise of those pancakes." He shook his head, still baffled. "But yeah, he seems to like it there."

"And you . . . got a text message."

Eli decided Lauren's smile should be bottled. "Yes, and — oh, I forgot. When I talked to Florine, she said something about a party on Sunday. And Drew really wants me to be there. Do you know anything about that?"

"It's a Mardi Gras party." Lauren raised her palm. "I know, I know. Long story, but it was postponed. Now the Viettes have an itch to do it. I've heard rumors of gumbo and costumes and king cake. If Poppy's discharged from the hospital in time, I have no doubt he'll be playing the washboard." Her expression clouded. "Anyway, yes, Sunday."

"Okay. Thanks."

She'd glanced away, the beautiful smile erased. Eli would bet she was thinking about the tense words they'd shared during Poppy's resuscitation. She'd assumed he would question the order, make some judgment about the elderly man's right to aggressive medical intervention. He had no intention of doing that. This wasn't about Poppy, Darcee Grafton, or some long-range moral agenda. This was about Drew — only him. It was about his brother never spending another Christmas the way he had last year. But no one got it. Lauren included. Still, Eli was glad he'd shown her Drew's text; he'd needed that smile.

"Are you going?" he heard himself ask.

"Yes," Lauren said, gathering up the napkins and a few stray bits of lettuce. "Jess is at home, sick. I'd better go see if she needs anything."

"I meant the party. Will you be there?"

When she met his gaze, Eli realized he was holding his breath.

"Yes, I'll be there."

"Just sleepy. It's the cold medicine," Jess mumbled, squinting at Lauren from the weather room couch. The room's only meager light came from the TV, its audio muted now. The window shutters had been closed tight as if the world wasn't welcome inside.

It wasn't a good sign; Jess had holed up in her apartment for days before she took off for Corpus Christi with those sleeping pills. But this time she was sick with a sore throat. So . . .

"You know. That awful stuff Mom buys in a gallon jug from Costco." Jess pulled her legs up, hugging her knees, long thermal shirtsleeves around plaid flannel pj bottoms. A Band-Aid fell from her bare foot to the pink carpet. "The stuff always makes me groggy."

And slurred? Was her voice slurred? Had she been drinking? No, there wasn't any liquor in the house. The Barclays didn't drink. But . . . Dad kept a bottle of brandy up high on the pantry shelf, dutifully trotting it out at Christmas and setting it alongside the Corsicana fruitcake. In case guests wanted a little "ho-ho-ho" in their eggnog. Lauren hoped she was wrong, but her sister's bleary eyes looked less like Costco and more like a few jiggers of Santa's belly laugh.

"How's the throat?" she asked, sinking onto the ottoman; Hannah Leigh had a firm stake on the comfy armchair. "Any better?"

Jess shrugged, swept her fingers through her tousled hair. "I'll live."

And keep your job? Pass that class? Have even a chance at getting into nursing school?

Lauren gritted her teeth against a familiar snarl of worry and exasperation. As strongly as she'd wanted to wrap her arms around Jess in that parking lot today, she now had an urge to switch off the TV, fling open the shutters, take her sister by the shoulders, and shake her. Tell Jess *she* was the reason Lauren had put her own life on hold. It was *her* inability to get herself together that made their mother a hovering wreck and their father a stroke victim.

"Did you hear anything about Darcee?" Jess hugged a pillow to her chest. Her expression was solemn, eyes as droopy-sad as Eeyore's.

"She's showing small signs of improvement." Jess hadn't even asked about their aunt in Colorado, and yet she seemed compelled to check on this near stranger. "They lightened her sedation to do neuro checks, and Darcee showed some appropriate response."

"To what?"

"Pain. There are ways to test that," Lauren explained. "Things like applying pressure to a fingernail, squeezing the top of the shoulder. Not enough to injure, but strong enough to cause a groan, a grimace, make the patient open her eyes or try to pull away. Darcee has bone fractures, so caring for her — moving her as needed — has to hurt. She's started reacting to that, too. It's another positive sign." Lauren sighed. "Harsh as it sounds, showing a response to pain is important."

Jess hugged the pillow closer. "So pain . . . is good."

"I'm not sure I'd go that far, but sometimes it's a reason for hope."

"Hmm." Jess sat quietly for a few moments, her gaze on the silenced TV. A weather segment. The eager young reporter wore a polka-dot blouse and a brilliant smile, her arms swooping in muted mime across a rainbow-color map of the Gulf of Mexico.

"Well . . ." Jess stood, swaying slightly as she hitched up the low-slung pajama bottoms. "I'm going to bed. Work tomorrow." She pointed toward the TV, polka dots moving frantically over the rainbow. "Glorietta is approaching hurricane status. But don't wake me up unless she's at least a cat-2. And our roof caves in."

"Deal." Lauren stopped herself from asking if Jess had eaten anything. Then on impulse caught her hand as she limped by. "Hey . . . I put a new tube of Neosporin in the bathroom for those blisters. And . . ." She smiled at her sister, gave her fingers a warm squeeze. "I love you, kiddo."

"Me too." Jess's lips curved in a rueful smile. She slid her hand away. "Careful, Lolo. You don't want to catch what I've got."

"I'd risk it. Sleep tight."

Lauren watched her sister leave, trying to remember the last time Jess looked happy. Truly happy. Not the giddy I've-been-running-the-beach high from last week. Or that giggling, gleeful unveiling of her one-woman all-night apartment-painting project last year: garish pink and lavender kitchen cabinets. None of that showed soul-deep happiness. None of it erased Lauren's continuing worry. But at least Jess had shown no dangerous signs of depression since Lauren had come home from Austin. Not like before.

Lauren's phone buzzed with a text: Vee.

Bella forgot wallet in lavatory. Good thing head glued on permanent.

Lauren sighed, grateful that drama was squelched. Now, if only . . .

She headed into the hallway and glanced at Jess's closed door before walking to the kitchen. Then opened the pantry door, pulled the dangling chain for the lightbulb, and scooted the stepladder into place. She climbed high enough to reach the top shelf. Felt around the Christmas candles, searching for that seasonal bottle of ho-ho-ho.

It was there.

She pulled it down.

Dusty. And as full as it had been last Christmas.

Lauren's breath escaped in a whoosh. Her sister was okay. She'd make up her school-work; she always did. Tomorrow she'd be at Houston Grace. Maybe Jess wasn't completely happy yet, but still . . .

Lauren hopped down from the ladder and snagged a box of cinnamon grahams. *Happy* was a relative term. It's not like she had a big claim on happiness herself. She slid a cracker from the package and bit in, sugar and crumbs speckling her chin. Then she squinted in the dim-lit pantry, trying to think of the few people she knew who were truly happy. Her parents, married thirty years next fall. Kate Callison in Austin, soon to be a bride. Even Vee Viette, who, despite her struggles, seemed so very much at peace. That had to feel good. Lauren smiled, thinking of Emma Landry. Even at her tender age, she looked pretty happy hugging that blind bear of a dog, singing her heart out about the hope of tomorrow . . . and sharing rainbows with her beloved uncle, who, just today, sent that impossible text:

. . . Ate pancakes. Love u.

Maybe that was it: true happiness boiled down to . . . love.

After all, it was one of God's greatest commandments: "Love one another." Yet it was the one almost everyone botched. On all levels: families, neighbors, communities, churches, governments, nations. One glimpse at the TV news proved that. There should be a storm map for the global breakdown of love. Commandment or not, it was complicated, frustrating, hard. Especially romantic love; Lauren doubted she'd ever figure that one out. Really *feel* it. Though maybe, just for a moment —

She inhaled a speck of cinnamon and coughed, stunned at what she'd been thinking. Remembering. Those confusing, pulse-quickening moments with Eli. When she'd gone to find him after Jessica was safely home. Gone to thank him. And then broken down again in the wake of such incredible relief. She'd found comfort, safety in his strong arms. He'd offered tender words that completely surprised her. Almost as much as his kiss.

"He loves it when I do this." Emma drew her Little Mermaid hairbrush gently over Shrek's broad, furry forehead. His brows lifted alternately over his sightless brown eyes, tongue lolling in drooly bliss. "If Shrek was a cat instead of a dog, I bet he'd purr."

Eli smiled, thinking he might purr himself. This was the closest he came to pure happiness. This hour before Emma's bedtime when work, carpools, last-minute forgot-the-milk treks to the grocery store, dinner dishes, and bath time had all been accomplished. And the family room was a minefield of books, LEGOs . . . and that remnant of a giant soap bubble still glistening on top of the darkened TV. This precious time when his pajama-clad daughter smelled of shampoo and her delighted chatter gave way to reluctant yawns.

"Here," she said, moving a book so she could join him on the couch. "Dip your head down here a minute, Daddy." She raised the hairbrush. "I'll show you how this feels to Shrek."

"Okay," he obliged, glad their Newfie was on flea control.

"Now, hold still." Emma stroked the brush over Eli's forehead, brow, snagged the soft bristles across the stubble of his jaw. Then she moved the brush slowly upward again. "How's that?"

"Great." He peered at her, one eye closed to avoid a corneal abrasion. "Lucky, spoiled-rotten hound."

"Yes, he is. Because we love him." Emma sighed, lowering the doll brush. Her expression took on a seriousness he recognized. The look that preceded questions about her mother or a problem or a painful slight at school.

"Parrish Donnelly's dog got put to sleep," she told him. "Oscar. The little dachshund they dress up in that foam hot dog bun for Halloween." Her brows bunched. "I don't know why they call it 'sleep.' The vet gave

Oscar a shot so he'd die. Mr. Donnelly took him there on purpose. For that."

Ah, no. He didn't want to have this conversation. Not yet. "Was Oscar really sick?"

"Old, I guess. Not eating good." Emma shrugged as she buried her thumbs in the brush bristles. "They told Parrish it was because they loved Oscar. And didn't want him to suffer anymore."

Eli cleared his throat. An ache was choking him senseless. "It's hard when you see someone you love suffering," he tried to explain. "Sometimes you have to make decisions you don't want to. Because in the end it's . . . kinder." It sounded ludicrous out loud. And saying it to his innocent child made Eli feel old himself.

Emma stared at him for an endless moment, unblinking. Then she ran the soft brush bristles against Eli's arm. Her eyes brimmed with tears and she glanced down, turning the brush over in her hands. "Shrek is old. I don't know if being blind and having diabetes means he's really sick. But I see him every day, Daddy. I don't see any suffering. He's happy. He loves to eat. He loves it when I brush him. He wags his tail all the time, and —"

"Hey, hey. Hold on." Eli tucked his fingers under her tiny chin, desperate to ease her fears. "Listen, sweetie, Shrek is fine. Don't worry. Of course he's happy. He's loved by the most amazing little girl in the whole wide world. Who wouldn't be happy about that?"

"He'll stay here with us, no matter what?"

Shrek was seven; Emma was eight. The life span of a Newfoundland dog was . . . Eli wasn't going to do the math, wouldn't let himself imagine a worst-case scenario. Right now he only saw his daughter's hopeful eyes. "No matter what. Cross my heart."

"I love you, Daddy!" She flung her arms around his neck and snuggled close. "Shrek and you and me, Grams, Yonner, and Uncle Drew — we're a family team. The best team ever!"

Drew . . . my parents . . . Eli's heart gave a dull thud and he hugged his daughter closer, inhaling the sweetness of her. "You betcha, punkin. I love you too. Big-time."

"Oh!" She leaned away, tears gone and eyes lighting. "Parrish invited me for a sleepover on Sunday. She wants me to bring Shrek. It's okay with her parents." Emma's expression was far wiser than her years. "Parrish needs us, Daddy. She misses Oscar. She's my best friend and I don't want her to suffer. Is it okay if I go?"

He wasn't sure his chest could contain

the rush of pride. "Of course it is. We'll load up Shrek and maybe stop at Hank's Ice Cream. Buy Parrish's favorite. I'll get you there, Emma. No problem."

"But what will *you* do, without me here?"

"Sunday? I'm working at Houston Grace. And after that, I'm going to a party."

She shot him a dubious look. "You're not a party guy, Dad."

He laughed. "I'm making an exception this time," he explained, remembering Drew's request that he attend. Lauren planned to be there too. Unexpected warmth flooded through him, triggering a memory of how she'd felt in his arms all those long months ago. Eli smiled, pointed to the hairbrush in his daughter's lap. "Sometimes a party is almost as nice as having your head brushed."

Emma giggled. He joined her. Shrek added a deep woof.

Mardi Gras in June. It didn't make sense, but not many things in Eli's life ever had. Why start now?

15

There was a ladder pushed up against the side of Mimaw's. With a man on it. One of the burly Fruge cousins, wearing work overalls, boots, and a chin-deep layer of glimmering gold, green, and purple beads. His party mask rested atop his head, feathers lifted by the late-afternoon breeze. Lauren chuckled, watching in disbelief. Somehow he was able to hammer at the roof's fascia board while dancing in place to the lively music spilling through the screen door below.

"Cyril," she called out, hands cupping her mouth, "wouldn't it be safer to dance inside, with two feet flat on the floor?"

"Ha!" He turned and grinned at her, feathers rising like an exotic bayou bird. "I'm guessing you never danced to swamp pop music, then. No such thing as two feet flat down anywhere, not when you're doin' the Cajun jig."

"Swamp . . . ?" Lauren raised her hands in surrender. "Got me on that."

"I'll show you, once I get this board tight." He glanced at the sky. "Doesn't look like much now, but that third storm's building out there. I'm praying it's not so but can't help feeling Glorietta's fixin' to flirt with Houston. That means wind and water. And we're not far enough away to be spared."

She looked over her shoulder, certain she felt a raindrop on her cheek even though the sky was fairly clear. "I saw shovels and wheelbarrows in the parking lot. And that dump truck."

"Yes, ma'am." Cyril nodded. "I believe God listens to every prayer, but I don't expect him to fill the sandbags."

Lauren had a sudden thought of her mother's weather alarm system. Had Jess turned the volume down or completely off?

She waved to Cyril. "See you inside."

"You bet. Wouldn't miss Odette's party." He pointed toward a plastic tub on the porch. "Don't forget your bling."

Lauren grabbed a necklace and opened the door to find festivities in full force, despite the fact that several partygoers' dancing skills were hampered by canes, walkers, and wheelchairs. One wheelchair held a young woman with two leg casts and a halo brace bolted to her skull. Lauren waved to her and she grinned back, then tooted her kazoo.

The air smelled of gumbo — chicken, smoky sausage, shrimp, tomatoes, peppers, garlic — spicy and pungent, but there was a bakery scent too, yeasty and sticky-sweet like frosting. The king cake, Lauren would bet. She stood in the doorway, trying to take it all in. The Viettes had done an amazing job turning the homey great room into Mimaw's version of the French Quarter in New Orleans, featuring a huge vinyl mural complete with brick walls and triple-story ironwork balconies, street signs, and even the gaudy likeness of costumed dancers and musicians. Green, purple, and gold streamers hung from the overhead beams. An elegant sequined mask was affixed to Auntie Odette's smiling portrait.

To say that there was music was an understatement.

The hardwood floor thrummed from speakers offering blues and jazz — saxophone, trumpet, piano — alternating with an upbeat blend of accordion and washboard: zydeco. More than enough to make any able foot tap, even on a ladder. And they were indeed tapping and clapping along. Staff, family members, and all fourteen residents — even their one bedridden gentleman, on a padded gurney now — were gathered together, most in masks, all wearing beads, and every one of them smiling.

"You're here!" Vee arrived alongside Lauren. Her braids glittered with Mardi Gras beads. "Did you see that we got everybody here?"

"I'm stunned — it's great."

They walked farther into the room, and Vee smiled and pointed discreetly. "Even the Champ is partying."

It was true. Drew Landry was in a wheelchair, and though his weight shifted a little toward his weak side, he was wearing multiple strands of beads and a grin on his face.

"What's that thing he's waving? That plastic deal that lights up when it flaps?" Lauren asked.

"A noisemaker. My idea." Vee smiled like she'd invented penicillin. "Three plastic hands that make this great clapping sound when you shake it. Solves that pesky problem of having one uncooperative arm when you want to clap along with the music."

"It sure does." Lauren thought of Jess, wishing there were as easy a way to make her smile. At least she was at work tonight, not holed up in the weather room.

Weather . . .

"I saw Cyril on the ladder," she told Vee. "And the dump truck with the sand."

"Precautions. Auntie chose this site because it's not in the mapped floodplain and it sits high. But the roads getting in and out can be a problem. We've had to stay put a few times in bad storms. Not for long."

Lauren glanced toward the window. "Cyril said he has a feeling Glorietta will head this way."

"I tend to trust his feelings. He's had some up-close experience. Like most of my family."

Hurricane Katrina. Even the name chilled Lauren. And she'd only watched it on TV.

"I hope Cyril's wrong," Vee added. "And I'm praying."

"But you can't expect God to fill the sandbags. Cyril's words."

"My cousin the philosopher. He's right. You need to be prepared. And sometimes that means stepping up . . . even if it's the hardest thing you've ever done." Something that looked like sadness flickered across Vee's face.

Before Lauren could say anything, Vee's radiant smile was back. She bobbed her head to the washboard-and-accordion beat. "You gotta love that look on Drew's face."

"The clapper's a big hit."

"Right, but —" Vee nudged Lauren and glanced toward the door — "that smile's for his brother."

"He's here?" She turned to look.

Cyril must have caught Eli at the door, because he wore a trio of bead strings around his neck, a complete style clash with the pale striped shirt, jeans, and running shoes — all of it so different from the white coat and scrubs he wore at Houston Grace. His hair looked damp. Rain maybe, or more likely he'd showered after leaving the hospital. But even beyond the beads and casual clothes, he seemed more than a little out of his element. His dark eyes were serious as he scanned the room, taking in the decorations and the crowd.

Oh, dear . . . Lauren's stomach did a foolish somersault as their eyes met.

Eli caught Lauren's gaze, relieved there was finally someone he recognized. Everyone else seemed to be hidden behind feathers and masks, but she looked everyday normal.

Normal? No, not even close to that. She looked . . . *amazing*. Long hair in loose waves around her shoulders, a simple blue T-shirt that fit like it was made for her, khaki shorts, tanned and athletic legs, sandals. He swallowed, glad she'd looked away. Enough staring; time to remember why he came. He stepped farther into Mimaw's transformed great room, planning how he'd get through the crowd to the hallway, toward his brother's room.

"He's over there." Somehow Lauren was beside him. Hand on his arm, fingers warm even through his sleeve. "In the wheelchair," she continued, pointing. "Somebody talked him into a mask, looks like." Her smile bloomed. "He's been waiting for you."

Right this moment, Eli knew the feeling.

"Great," he told her, wishing she hadn't taken her hand away. He watched as a fellow resident leaned down to say something to his brother. Drew lifted his hand in a thumbs-up. "I can't believe it. It's been so long since he's shown an interest . . ." Eli's voice threatened to break. "This is great."

"I think so too." The compassion in Lauren's voice was audible, even over the strains of saxophone and piano. And as warm as her fleeting touch. "Go on. Make his day."

Eli caught hold of her hand without thinking. "Come with me."

"I . . ." Her fingers moved inside his. The incredible blue eyes looked hesitant, uncertain.

He wished there were some way to erase

their complicated history but knew he was as much a fool now as he'd been that spring Jessica ran away. Any moment, Lauren would pull her hand from his, and —

"Okay. Let's go," she told him, leaving her hand right where it was. "Your Champ's waiting, and I really need to see that kind of happy today."

Gayle hesitated outside the door to ER registration, trying to calm the anxiety that rose without warning these days. She probably had a virus; she'd run a fever last night and slept poorly, awakening over and over drenched in sweat with her heart pounding. But while exhausting, the hours of insomnia helped her to finally formulate a plan, accept what she had to do. Things couldn't go on this way. She and Leo were both suffering. The future looked like a gaping black hole. Right or wrong, there was no other choice.

"Where's Jessica?" Gayle glanced around the registration office.

"On her break." One of the clerks nudged a half-eaten Butterfinger candy bar behind a stack of forms. "You need help with something?"

"An ER patient has some additional insurance information. A card she forgot to provide. Mrs. Adele Humphries. Jessica registered her."

"No problem; I'll go talk with the patient." The clerk tapped her computer screen. "Humphries . . . still in room six?"

"Yes, but this patient asked for Jessica specifically. I need her to do this. Mrs. Humphries is elderly and anxious," she explained, irritated that she had to. "Jessica reminds her of her granddaughter."

"Well . . . okay then." The clerk shrugged. "She's due back from her break in —"

"No!" Gayle snapped. She crossed her arms to still a vicious rush of chills. "Where is she right now?"

Both clerks stopped typing and stared. "Staff lounge," they said in unison.

"Thank you." Gayle gave a curt nod. "I'll get her myself."

"You think," Lauren whispered, pointing at the tiny plastic baby in Eli's palm, "the fix was in for your brother to get the king cake prize?"

"I had a strong hunch." Eli nudged the toy. "Especially when Vee handed me the slice and said, 'Y'all be careful and cut that piece up *reeeal* small. Might be something special to find in there.' "

Lauren laughed at his imitation, close to

perfect minus the micro braids. Actually, right this moment everything felt close to perfect. Drew's frosting-sticky smile and gold paper crown, the tender and protective look on Eli's face as he watched him clap, the laughter in this room mixing with hearty praise from guests enjoying second helpings of gumbo. And mostly . . . Lauren sighed. What felt most close to perfect was her rare absence of worry.

"Loook!" Drew's clapper flapped, lighting like captured fireflies. He pointed it toward the dancers.

"That's right." Eli leaned down closer to the wheelchair. "It's a Cajun jig. Here . . ." He knelt, waggled his brother's laced sneaker side to side. "See if you can dance that foot around a little, Champ."

Lauren's throat tightened and she glanced away toward the dance floor. It was true: the "swamp pop" music had ramped up, and Cyril and Vee, Florine, and the family member of a resident were out there kicking up their heels. Literally it seemed. Feet sort of springing up and down, hands clasped with arms seesawing back and forth. The dancers were bouncing and moving along . . . kind of half Irish clog, a quarter Texas two-step, and maybe a dash of German polka. With twirls and hip bumps and —

"Let's go," Eli said to her, pushing the king cake prize into his pocket.

"Go where?"

"There." He pointed to the growing crowd of feathers, beads, and thumping shoes in the middle of the room. "To dance."

"What? No way. I'm adding swamp dancing to kazoo playing on the list of things I don't do. But you go ahead. I'll wait right here."

"Nice try, but no cigar." Eli pointed at the wheelchair.

Drew smiled up at them, purple sugar on his cheek, crown tipped over one brow. His shoe tapped ever so slightly against the metal footrest. He pointed the green plastic hands at his brother.

"C'mon." Eli held his hand out to Lauren. "By royal command of the Mardi Gras king."

"You're doing great," Eli assured Lauren, mesmerized by a wavy tendril bouncing over her forehead. Her brows pinched as she struggled to mimic the other dancers and follow the push-pull motion of his lead. This was probably an idiotic idea; he was beyond rusty himself. The last time he'd danced the

Cajun jig was with his toddler daughter in his arms. "Don't be so serious," he said over a crescendo of washboard and kazoo. "This isn't a disaster drill."

"Oh yeah?" She grabbed tighter to his hands, casting a wary eye toward the festooned ceiling. Her flushed cheeks showed a faint sheen of perspiration. "I'm not sure if that ominous rumble is Glorietta blowing in or my heart pounding in my ears. This is more Zumba than jig."

"Cajun cardio." He smiled, glad she couldn't know his pulse was faster too and it had everything to do with the feel of her hands in his. "You haven't seen anything yet," Eli told her, raising her hand high and guiding her into a twirl.

Lauren looked panicked, but she moved into the turn gracefully, anticipating the second twirl, laughing at a third, and —

"Hip-to-hip spin," he announced, pulling her close enough that their sides touched. "And this step . . ." He lifted Lauren's hand high, then captured her closely in both arms, leading her into a slow backward spin. She felt incredible against him — berry-scented warmth, softness, and —

"Good going." Cyril grinned, shuffling close with Vee. "The 'sweetheart.' "

"What?" Lauren's eyes widened. "No.

We're just —"

"The dance step," Eli explained quickly. "It's called the 'sweetheart.' "

"I get it." Her flush deepened. The music ended and she stepped away, sweeping stubborn tendrils of hair from her damp forehead. "Well," she said, avoiding his eyes, "I guess I survived the Cajun experience."

"Right." Eli already missed holding her. His arms felt oddly awkward, dangling empty at his sides. "Thanks for being a good sport."

"No problem." She took a half step sideways to accommodate a couple leaving the floor, then lifted her gaze to his at last. The flush was still there. She shrugged, a smile teasing her lips. "Might have been worse. You could have asked me to bite the heads off a platter of boiled crawfish." She laughed at the immediate insulted pinch of his brows.

"Great." Eli shook his head. "I guess I'm flattered then."

"No, really." Lauren touched his arm. "The dance wasn't that bad. And if it made our Mardi Gras king happy . . ." She glanced toward Drew's wheelchair and gasped. "He's having trouble breathing."

16

"What on earth?" Gayle's eyes widened as she brushed through the exam room curtain. Mrs. Humphries was sound asleep on the ER gurney, and — "What are you doing there?"

"Uh . . ." Jessica Barclay drew her hand back from the plastic patient-belongings bag perched atop the bedside stand. "Getting that insurance information. You sent me in here, remember?"

"Of course I do. But you know full well that you can't go poking around in a patient's personal property."

"She told me to find her coin purse."

"Mrs. Humphries is *asleep.*" Gayle gestured toward the elderly woman beneath a double layer of cotton blankets. "I would think you could recognize snoring when you hear it."

"Excuse me." The clinical coordinator slipped through the curtain, taking in the scene with an expression of concern. "Is there a problem?"

"Apparently." Gayle shook her head. "Maybe you can explain to our clerk that policy prohibits staff from handling a patient's personal belongings. Especially when that patient is sedated." She frowned, her frustration underscored by a wave of dizziness. "I do *not* need this today!"

"Huh . . . what? What's wrong?" Mrs. Humphries's eyes jerked open, and she struggled to sit up.

"It's okay, dear," the clinical coordinator assured, hurrying to her side.

Jessica stood frozen in place, the lovely eyes narrowed to mere slits.

"Get back to your desk, Jessica," Gayle ordered. "Now."

Gayle snatched the curtain aside and strode away, aware that several staff members were staring. She took a deep breath, told herself to get a cup of decaf and calm down.

Her cell phone buzzed in her pocket. Gayle retrieved it, grinding her teeth together at the sight of her husband's ID. She made a beeline toward the corridor before answering.

"Leo . . ."

"Been listening to the news?"

"No. I'm working."

"TV's saying that storm's got her sights set on Houston later this week," he reported with a grim laugh. "Howard next door said he bought himself some plywood and plastic tarps." Leo snorted. "I told him I was stocking up too. On beer and Jack Daniel's. Who gives a rip if my feet get wet when I'm crippled up with a bum back and my whole life's gone to —"

"I did it, Leo," Gayle broke in. "I got the pills."

Drew wasn't dizzy anymore. The breathing treatment made a fizzing sound, like Mountain Dew bubbles, only louder. And even if the plastic mask smelled bad and tasted bad against his lips, it did help him get more air. That's what his brother always said: *"Gotta take the bitter with the sweet, Champ."* Drew would rather skip bitter and have blueberry pancakes. But he was better now. Not having enough air made him dizzy, like when you dive down too deep in the water. And you don't think you're going to make it back up to the top.

Drew touched his tongue, just a little, against the plastic, then looked up at the lady with blue eyes — Lauren. Her hand was soft and cool on his forehead.

"He doesn't feel feverish," she said, looking at his brother. "And his respiratory rate's down to 22. Pulse ox is 96 percent."

"Asthma. This is his typical mild attack. The nebulized albuterol does a good job if we catch it early. The wheezes are all but gone now." Eli bent low, gave Drew's shoulder a squeeze.

Even with the oxygen clip on his finger, Drew could hold the plastic clapper; he was glad they let him take it back to his room. With the baby toy from the cake. And his crown.

"You feel better, Champ?"

Drew shook the plastic hands enough to make them light up.

"We'll take that as a yes, then." His brother smiled at him. At Lauren, too.

"A lot of excitement today." She petted Drew's hair like his mother did. He wondered if she was a mom; she seemed like one. "He looks tired. Maybe if we put his music on . . ."

His earphones, his music. On and going now. With songs about heaven, lambs, love, glory . . . rainbows. Drew looked up at the drawing on the wall, at all the colors Emma had drawn just for him. And at the cross she made out of leaves. Then, even though it was hard to keep his eyes open, Drew looked at his brother and Lauren. Maybe they'd dance again. Or eat cake. He didn't know. Drew was just glad he could get enough air now. And that he had music that made him know he was someone special. No matter who he was, what he did . . . or couldn't do. And he was glad his brother didn't look worried anymore. Eli was smiling at Lauren. Like the bitter was gone. And he'd found the sweet part.

"No wheezing; breathing slow and easy. Sound asleep with that clapper in his hand," Eli reported, the tenderness in his expression touching Lauren. He glanced around the empty great room — residents and families gone, a few staff members putting away the food in the kitchen. The Cajun music had been replaced with gospel, turned way down low. Odette smiled at them from her portrait, sans mask. "Barely five and they roll up the sidewalks at the Nest."

"Mm-hmm. Wild bunch." Lauren noticed Eli's shirt was untucked, his hair rumpled. A toss-up whether it was from the Cajun jig or being his brother's keeper. "I tried to get them to let me help with the cleanup, but Vee kicked me out of the kitchen." His eyes met hers and her heart hitched. "Are you going to stick around?"

"Probably. Emma's at a sleepover." Eli scraped his fingers along his jaw. "She and Shrek are trying to cheer up a friend. So I don't have a curfew. I've seen enough of Drew's asthma to know this isn't a bad one. The staff seems . . ."

"They can handle it. Florine and Renee will be on duty tonight. They'll be checking him frequently," Lauren assured him. She stopped herself from saying they'd call 911 if things got worse. "He has the nebulizer and plenty of albuterol doses."

"I'll probably still stay for a while . . ." Eli covered a yawn. "Excuse me. Cajun cardio. I'm out of shape, I guess."

Lauren remembered the feel of his arms and felt her face flush. Out of shape? Not even close.

"Anyway," Eli continued, "maybe I'll go grab some coffee while the staff gets everyone settled." His brows rose. "Come with me. I know a great little place."

"No. I shouldn't."

"Why not?" He obviously wasn't going to let her brush him off that fast. "It's coffee. Not a platter of crawfish. Promise."

Could Eli promise he wouldn't confuse her again? That she wouldn't revisit the regret and sleepless nights?

"I have things I need to do at the house,"

she told him, praying he wouldn't ask faster than she could come up with a plausible excuse. "Hannah. And getting things ready in case the storm really does hit. And —"

"Your cell phone is chiming."

"I heard it," Lauren acknowledged, planning her exit.

"Aren't you going to check it?"

"Right." She felt his eyes on her as she fished the phone from her pocket and silenced the insistent alarm. Read her stupid mistake:

Jess. Physiology Lab

She'd set the reminder for the wrong time. And swore she heard Eli's accusing whisper in her head: *You're enabling . . .*

"Everything okay?"

"Perfect."

She was surprised by a memory of her humiliating search for the bottle of brandy. How she'd stood in the pantry eating that cinnamon cracker and wondering how it would feel to be truly happy. Not certain she ever would be — even accepting that. And in an instant Lauren was angry. It was coffee, for goodness' sake! Not happily ever after. *Coffee.* What was wrong with that? She'd cooked Hannah Leigh two chicken breasts, painted over the scratch marks on the guest room door, and put Tupperware bowls under every drip spot just in case. Jess was safe and secure at work, and —

"I can't tempt you?" Eli asked one last time.

"I need to return a jacket for Jess. I have it in the car."

"We could do that on the way, no problem — I'm a free man tonight."

Breathe.

"Could that coffee include something chocolate?"

Eli smiled. "Of course."

17

"Summer in Houston . . . You can drink the air." Eli raised his voice as two METRO-Rail trains — separated by a cement-lined ribbon of water — passed each other in a rush over streets inlaid with red brick. Past palm trees, restaurants, upscale shops, and world-class museums. They sped like sleek glass-and-metal caterpillars, following some seven miles of electric wires north to University of Houston–Downtown and south to Rice University and Reliant Park. "Your sister couldn't have bought that whatever-it-was at the Galleria mall? I could have waited facedown on the ice-skating rink."

"It was a jacket," Lauren laughed, grateful for the tease in Eli's voice. And more grateful that he hadn't pressed for details. It was a ridiculous, six-hundred-dollar jacket bought nearly four months ago, tags intact, never worn. One of seven in Jess's closet, according to Lauren's last covert count. Jess had promised their parents she'd return them all and lessen her credit card debt, in exchange for their gracious free room and board. The ending return date for this purchase was coming up fast, so Lauren was getting the job done. "And you, Eli," she added, sitting down beside him on a Main Street Square bench near rows of animated fountains, "are a good sport."

"I'm practicing." He shrugged, his handsome face glistening with equal parts perspiration and fountain spray. "I have a daughter. I'm guessing I'll be dragged to malls, expected to whip out the plastic, then tote packages like a dutiful llama. Hopefully that's a few years off yet."

"Hopefully." Lauren smiled at a sudden image of little Emma twirling in a prom dress. She drew in a breath of air city-scented by asphalt, car exhaust, and faint whiffs of an enticing mix of Tex-Mex and curry. Her stomach rumbled. "I'm holding you to that dessert. You think we can make it back to your car without IV fluids?"

"No problem." Eli blinked up at the towering glass skyscrapers that reflected the sun like a kid terrorizing an insect with a magnifying glass. "But I'm thinking our coffee should be *iced.*"

Lauren raised her hand. "I second that."

■ ■ ■ ■

"The building's a hundred years old," Eli
said as Lauren gazed around the downtown
coffeehouse, Ben's Beans. Once a historic
but decaying print shop, it had been renovated a few years back; Eli had watched it
come along. The still-narrow space —
wedged between a law office and the House
of Blues — had been on Houston "best of"
lists more than once. It was definitely one
of his favorites. Always busy, but Southern
friendly, colorful, and cozy despite the
crowd. Cement floors, potted plants, ware-
house lights and fans hanging from the high
ceiling, a veritable herd of leather couches,
red lacquered walls boasting contemporary
art, and huge chalkboards announcing both
menus and live entertainment.

"The owner, Ben, is originally from Loui-
siana and proud of his Cajun roots," Eli
added, breathing in the aroma of his freshly
brewed and mercifully iced coffee. "He's an
anesthesiologist."

"Really?"

Eli tried not to stare as Lauren's tongue
caught a dark crumb at the corner of her
mouth. She'd finally chosen a cherry-
chocolate scone over the cake balls, and by

the look on her face, it was a big hit. Smiling, he read the words stenciled on the wall behind her: *Harmony, Happiness.*

"An anesthesiologist. That seems strange somehow," she mused. "I mean, his day job is putting folks to sleep, and here it's all about caffeine. I think Gayle Garner is the biggest consumer in Houston." There was the smallest hint of a wince in her voice as if she knew that he knew . . . this was all nervous small talk.

"Yeah, good point." He was willing to agree to anything as long as she didn't bolt. Being with Lauren, away from the hospital and the care home, almost felt like a fresh start. Maybe it could be. As long as he steered the conversation away from everything they butted heads over. Or his monumental mistakes. He'd keep things simple, light. He pointed to Lauren's plate. "The scone is Emma's favorite too."

Lauren stilled the fork. "It must be hard raising a daughter alone."

So much for simple.

"My parents have been a big help. My mother, especially. Diapers, formula, colic . . . You could have written everything I knew about babies on the head of a pin." Eli saw the inevitable question in her eyes.

"Emma's mother left not long after she was born."

"And then . . . I heard that your wife passed away?"

My wife? Jessica would have assumed he'd been married, of course. He'd told her next to nothing. Never discussed that part of his life with anyone. And sure wasn't comfortable doing it now. "Yes, Trina died. When Emma was nine months old. I was still in the Army. She was killed in a motorcycle accident. On the French coast."

"I'm sorry."

He was too. About that and about so many other things. Including the way he'd messed things up with Lauren. He'd been a fool. And was kidding himself that there was any hope of —

"I admire that," she said, surprising him by reaching across to touch his hand. "How hard you work at being a good father to Emma. And how you are with Drew. Even though he can't say a lot, it's there in his eyes: your brother loves you, Eli."

He struggled to find the right words . . . any words.

"But still . . ." A smile tugged Lauren's lips as she slid her hand away. "You've got a long way to go to make up for that hip-to-hip spin. And the dog slobber on the passenger seat of my Beetle." She pointed her fork at him, eyes teasing. "Although this scone's a great start."

"If chocolate could really do it, make it all good, I'd melt that Hershey bar down and shoot it directly into a vein. Trust me, Fletcher." Jessica's frown gave way to a grim smile. "Sorry. That was supposed to come out, 'I appreciate the offer, Sir Knight. But not right now.' "

"No problem," he told her, setting the candy down on the hood of his patrol car. "Save it for later." Fletcher saw Jessica's shoulders sag in a deep sigh. "Rough shift?"

"You could say that." She leaned against the patrol car's fender, gazed out across the hospital parking lot. The deepening sunset tinted her hair with splashes of color like the fairy-tale drawings she'd make on his driveway using those fat pieces of chalk she carried in an old Folgers can. "I wish I could just beam myself out of here. You know?"

He watched the pink light turn her eyes from gray to lavender. And wished he could do something to make their sadness go away. *Please, Lord. Tell me how to do that.* "Another run-in with that manager, Gayle?"

She closed her eyes for a moment. "A lot

of stuff. I won't bore you."

He wanted to say that never once — not since the first spring day when she met his family's moving van, barefoot in that princess costume — had Jessica Barclay come even close to boring him. Worrying him, absolutely. Making him crazy, giving him a concussion . . . The words slipped out before he could stop himself. "I saw Angela at church. She wants to meet you. I think you'd have a lot in common."

Jessica peered sideways. "I'd have a lot in common with a religious shrink?"

"Counselor. But that's not all she is. Angela's funny; she's a runner like you; she volunteers with dog rescue —"

"So take *her* a chocolate bar. Marry her. She sounds perfect." She folded her arms tightly against her chest.

"Jess . . ."

She turned and met his gaze fully, eyes stormy gray again. "I didn't like it when Eli lectured me about my 'problems,' and I don't like it any better coming from you. You're supposed to be my safe place, Fletcher."

Keeping her safe was what he'd always tried to do. It still killed him that he'd been in Hawaii with his folks when she ran away that spring. . . .

Jessica checked her watch. "My break's almost over, and if I don't get back in there, Gayle's going to chew my behind for no good reason. *Again.*" She reached for the chocolate bar, offered Fletcher what looked too much like a Band-Aid smile. "This will hit the spot later. Thank you."

"Sure."

He watched Jessica walk back toward the hospital doors, fairly certain she was faking her interest in the candy bar. He wasn't convinced that she'd been telling the whole truth about her manager either. What was going on there?

"He looks comfortable," Lauren whispered as Eli slipped off the borrowed stethoscope and set it on Drew's bedside table.

"No wheezes. Upper airway's nice and clear." He glanced toward the iPod dock sitting beside the framed photo of the young Landry fishermen. Florine had removed the earphones but left Drew's music playing softly. A woman's voice, pure and gentle, singing about blessings coming through raindrops.

Eli reached out to stroke his sleeping brother's hair. The corner night-light cast a soft glow over both men's features. They could have been mistaken for twins.

"Are you going to stay?" she whispered.

"I . . ." Eli glanced her way almost as if he'd forgotten she was there. "Yes. I'll be staying for a while. But I'll walk you to your car."

She started to tell him there was no need but decided it was useless. Eli was stubborn. Still, they'd managed to get through the past several hours unscathed. No reason to rock the boat. Walk to the car, get in, and drive away. Simple . . .

But once they'd hiked down Mimaw's moonlit driveway, she had a feeling she'd made a mistake.

"I didn't think I'd parked so far away," she told him, her voice provoking several indignant clucks in the dark distance. "Out with the poultry and the sandbags." Lauren glanced back toward the building, on a gentle rise that Odette's plan had required, and saw the warm glow of lights from the windows. A staff person, likely Renee, moved in and out of view. "Quite a place."

"It is." Eli held her gaze for a moment. "That day in the ER, I didn't think this would be possible. I thought he'd end up on a ventilator in the ICU, like last Christmas." Something that looked like a physical pain came into his expression.

"That time must have been awful."

"It was." Eli shook his head. "Emma made him a Christmas stocking, wrote his name on it with glue and glitter — maybe a pound of the stuff. Shrek stepped in it and left sparkly footprints all over the house. She brought the stocking to the hospital and hung it on the pole with one of the IV pumps. I remember there was glitter on the floor, the wheels of the ventilator . . . even the restraints tied to my brother's arms." There was a noise low in his throat like he'd swallowed a groan. "She drew a Nativity scene, too, and talked a janitor into taping it on the ceiling over Drew's bed so he could see it whenever he opened his eyes, day or night. When they had to poke him with needles or shove suction catheters down the ET tube . . ."

Lauren winced.

"He kept looking at me with this fear in his eyes." Eli's voice was husky, low. "Like he expected me to make it all stop. He was begging; he couldn't understand why I was letting all of it happen. In my whole life I've never felt so blasted helpless." His dark eyes were intense. "Can you understand what I mean?"

She nodded. "I felt that way when Jess was missing. When I thought she might try to . . ." Lauren couldn't talk about this.

223

Especially not with Eli.

"I know," he said. "I saw how worried you were. I was there, remem— ?"

"I need to go," Lauren insisted, cutting him off. She stepped away, began searching her purse for her keys. "Thank you for the coffee."

"No." Eli grasped her arm. "Don't leave. We need to talk about that time. All of it. Jessica and me. And you. About . . . *us.*"

Her heart stalled.

"Please, Lauren." Eli let go of her arm. "Just talk with me?"

18

They were sitting on stacks of sandbags. Downwind from a chicken coop. The countless times Eli had imagined this moment, it had looked very different. But at least Lauren was here. Though from her expression, she was still thinking of escape. Even if that meant running him down with her car.

"I don't see the point of this," she told him, swiping at her hair in the humid breeze. Her eyes looked wary in the moonlight. "There really isn't anything we need to discuss."

"Except the elephant in the room." His stupid cliché was refuted by an immediate volley of *bawk-baaawk*s and wing flaps. This was off to a lousy start. "It's been more than a year, Lauren. You ran off to Austin before—"

"I didn't *run.*" She stiffened, lifted her chin. "Jess was trying to make a new start after all that happened that Easter. She

225

needed to feel independent and asked me to give her space."

And you wanted plenty of space too . . . between us. Because I kissed you.

"Okay," he conceded after taking a slow breath. "I get that. But those times I called to explain, you wouldn't talk to me."

"I don't see what more you could have explained, Eli. We heard it from Jess. She was feeling low; she reached out to you as a friend." Lauren's brows pinched. "There was an argument. She filled the prescription for sleeping pills and took off."

"It wasn't that simple." He regretted the word instantly.

"You think that was 'simple' for my family? We had to file a missing persons report. Ask for her dental records. My father was so sick with worry he had a stroke!"

"I'm sorry." Eli reached for her hand without thinking. "I didn't mean that. I'd change all of those things if I could. That's what I wanted to tell you those times I called. That I'm sorry." He couldn't believe she hadn't pulled her hand away. "What I meant was that the change in my friendship with Jessica happened over weeks . . . months. Not because of one isolated argument."

"That's not what she said."

Eli warned himself to be careful. This was about mending things with Lauren. Offering his opinions of her sister's psychological problems would be as welcome as a fox in that chicken coop. "I'm not going to defend myself. I've made too many mistakes to even try to do that. But the truth is, I haven't been looking for relationships, friendship or otherwise. Not with anyone. I can't afford the complications. Emma is my first priority. In truth, work is probably my second. And third."

Lauren's fingers curled under his. "And my sister —"

"Understands that. I don't think she's in a place to deal with relationships that require anything more either." He hesitated, weighing his words. "I sensed that about her from the beginning. And I wasn't surprised when she found reasons not to spend time with me. Frankly I was relieved. I had a lot going on with my family. Jessica and I hadn't had so much as a cup of coffee together in weeks before she ran off to Corpus Christi."

"But the argument . . ."

"She called me on the phone early that morning — woke me about 2 a.m. She was sort of generally angry about a lot of things. Rambling, the way she does sometimes. She insisted that I meet her for breakfast. To use me for a sounding board, I figured. I told her no. I had Emma, and I was leaving for a fishing trip that morning. She hung up on me."

"I see." Lauren's hand slid away from Eli's, but not before he saw the pain in her eyes. How could she doubt this was true? She knew Jessica's mercurial moods.

Somewhere inside, you know your sister needs help.

"My parents think Jess's problems were caused by you. That you led her on. Used her. Maybe beyond friendship."

"It wasn't like that," Eli explained. "I don't know what Jessica told you. Or what you might have heard from hospital staff. But we barely knew each other until we played on the Grace softball team. We didn't get together that many times beyond work. Group stuff, mostly. Not anything you'd call a date."

"I get what you're saying."

"No, I don't think you do," Eli continued, seeing it on her face. "She never met my folks. Or Drew. I think *you've* seen Emma more times than your sister has. I was at her apartment maybe twice. She never came to my house or . . ." He saw Lauren's teeth scrape her lower lip and decided it needed to be said. Even if she went into big-sister protective overdrive and bolted for her car. "I didn't sleep with her, Lauren. I never even came close to wanting that. She's a friend. That's all."

Lauren closed her eyes, made a sound that might have been a sigh of relief but was probably a muffled expression of disgust. He wouldn't blame her. But he couldn't leave any room for doubt.

She shifted on the sandbags, moonlight splashing her face. "I think we've come full circle. I still don't see the point of this."

"I have one." His mouth was going dry. This had to be said too. "It's true that I wasn't interested in a serious relationship. After Emma — because of her — I haven't wanted that. I wasn't looking." The breeze swept strands of hair across Lauren's cheek, and he had to stop himself from brushing them back. "And then I met you. The timing couldn't have been worse. Or the situation. Your folks launched you at me like a drone missile strike."

Her brow puckered; he wasn't going to wait long enough to interpret it.

"And then, when I'm trying to figure out how to handle that and still get to know you better — maybe even convince you I can be a decent guy — Jessica runs off." He leaned closer, urging her to understand. "I went looking for her out of genuine concern. I do care about her, Lauren. But when you arrived at the beach . . ."

"I don't think I've ever been so scared in my life."

"I saw that. I understand because of Drew. I wanted to help you. I wanted to fix it."

"You did. You found her." Lauren flinched. "I don't think we ever thanked you. Not really."

"That doesn't matter. What I'm trying to say here is that in spite of the situation, I meant the things I said to you that night. After Jessica went home with your parents and you dropped by my house. I said it all badly; I admit that. I was trying to comfort you, make you understand that you hadn't failed Jessica in any way. Then it turned into something else, and I'm sorry for that. But it's all true, everything I said: I do think you're special, Lauren. Beautiful and caring and brave."

"Eli, don't . . ."

"Don't tell the truth?"

"I mean, I don't think we should do this."

"You're wrong. I shouldn't have kissed you. I wasn't thinking; I'm sorry. But that was a year ago. This is now."

There was a long stretch of silence, punctuated here and there by distant clucks.

"I think . . . ," Lauren said, barely above a whisper, "it wasn't all your fault. I think I kissed you back. Maybe a little."

"No need to apologize."

There was a hint of a smile, the first he'd seen since the cherry-chocolate scone.

"So where do we go from here?" he breathed.

"Go?"

She might as well have hit him with a sandbag.

"I'd still like to see you," Eli explained. "I know it's sort of awkward. Because of everything that happened back then. But —"

"Awkward? That's when someone shows up with the same dress at a party . . . or when you accidentally send a text for your girlfriend to your mother." Lauren's breath escaped in a groan. "What you're talking about is *impossible.*"

She was exaggerating. She had to be. He could make this work.

"My daughter and my dog like you," Eli ventured, remembering that kiss.

"My parents hate you. I think on some levels my sister may too."

"You and my brother like the same music."

"You and my family have a painful history. There's no way they'd understand a truce, let alone . . ." Lauren's smile disappeared. "I love them. They're *my* priority."

"But . . ." Hope was slipping through Eli's fingers like sand. "I've been thinking about this, about you, for a year."

"You should probably stop."

"Please," Gayle pleaded into the phone, "don't call here anymore." She peered across the breakfast bar to where Leo lay half-asleep in the recliner in front of the TV. Her pulse began to hammer her temples. "My husband's not well. You'll disturb him. I've told you that I'll be making up those payments soon . . . as soon as I can. I'm working extra hours, but if I lose the car, I can't get there. Certainly you can understand that."

"Better check the bus schedules, Gayle. If we don't get —"

She jabbed the disconnect button and sagged back against the kitchen counter. The man was relentless. He'd actually called the hospital today, told the clerk he was her brother and there was a family emergency. And he wasn't the only creditor who'd been hounding her. It was turning into a nightmare.

She picked up the knife she'd left on the cutting board, a utility blade from the expensive German set Leo had given her for Valentine's Day — probably part of the overdue balance on their Visa card. She stared at the knife, the earlier anger receding into an empty sadness that came too often lately. When had roses, jewelry, chocolates, even simple kindness given way to kitchen tools? Somehow they'd lost all of that. And now . . . *I'm losing everything.*

"God, please," she breathed aloud, surprising herself. She couldn't remember the last time she'd even come close to a prayer. At this point, after all her mistakes, God would be as eager to hear from her as she was to see that collections thug on her front porch. There didn't seem to be any way out of this mess. But at least she'd solved one problem, even if temporarily.

Gayle glanced at the amber medication bottles, a narcotic and muscle relaxers. Those pills, with a beer chaser, were the only reason her husband wasn't in here right now complaining and criticizing or —

"Whatcha doing there?" Leo blurted, his sudden appearance causing Gayle to cringe.

"Cleaning up, that's all." She made herself smile. "I made some dinners for the rest of the week, so you'll have —"

"You look tired," he said, stepping forward and searching her face. "A lot lately. And you're too thin, babe. Bony even. Aren't you eating?"

"It's the extra shifts, I guess. And problems at work." Gayle thought of her confrontation with Jessica and felt a stab of guilt. She'd done what she had to. "I'm dealing with it." Tears rose unexpectedly.

"Hey . . . c'mere." Leo opened his arms, waited until she moved into them. "Shh," he murmured into her hair. "It's okay."

"Oh, Leo . . ." She closed her eyes, pretending it really *was* okay, that this out-of-the-blue moment could last. Continue beyond the effects of the beer and the medications she'd done the unthinkable to obtain. His embrace tightened, defensive-guard muscles gone soft with age and repeated injury but still strong — a touch that could inflict pain as easily as comfort. Still, in Gayle's whole life, this had been the safest place she'd known. If only there was a chance . . .

"I'm sorry you have to work so hard," Leo said. "I'm going to make it up to you. I'm going to make it right."

"I know." She inhaled to dispel a wave of dizziness, trying not to imagine how her husband would react if the car were repossessed. It could happen. But this brief reprieve in their ugly, ongoing scrimmage was something to be grateful for. Right now, she'd settle for that.

19

Her plants were dying.

Lauren gave the peace lily a ginger touch and watched a leaf fall onto the tabletop. So much for a top-ten-easy houseplant. She'd moved a trio of potted plants from Houston to Austin and then back again. Three homes in less than a year, and all of them were having problems adjusting. She frowned, realizing that the same thing could be said about her. Except that for Lauren, it would be four homes, now that she was sleeping at her parents' place. She'd only recently finished unpacking here.

She glanced around the one-bedroom apartment she'd chosen because she could afford it. The one she'd really wanted was in a gleaming high-rise with a view of Buffalo Bayou. Not on a nurse's salary. Still, this space was modern and light-filled, with a garden tub, maple floors, and a small tiled balcony. The balcony had made the decision easier. A room with a view. Lauren could stand — on her tiptoes, craning her neck — and catch a minuscule glimpse of Hermann Park. The park where Fletcher rescued Darcee Grafton from her painful dance. Considering where the girl was now, perhaps leaving her there would have been a better thing. In the end, saving her might prove fatal.

Her gaze moved to her laptop sitting beside the potted plant, at the page pulled up on the screen: a page discussing bipolar disorder, complete with graphics of the comedy and tragedy masks, van Gogh's *Starry Night,* and a vividly colored snapshot of a brain MRI. There was also a wrenching black-and-white photo of a woman curled up in the corner of a room. Lauren tried to tell herself it was Darcee Grafton who'd prompted this Internet search. But it wasn't the first time Lauren had held her breath while reading lists of manic symptoms: decreased need for sleep, pressured speech, racing thoughts, impaired judgment . . . irritability and hypersexuality. And the less dramatic symptoms of hypomania, often difficult to diagnose, since they could "masquerade as mere happiness."

She thought of Jess, that day she'd come late to work, giggling and giddy after running the beach for hours, blistering her feet. And how quickly she'd moved to biting sarcasm, finally to holing up in the weather room with the blinds closed. Depression, shown so graphically in that black-and-white photo, was the equally dangerous flip side of bipolar disorder. She thought of what Eli said last night about Jess's angry early morning call the day she disappeared with the sleeping pills. Though her parents hadn't given voice to their fear, Lauren had seen it in their eyes: was she planning to harm herself? They found no comfort in knowing Jess was prone to impulsive whim, that she always leaped first and asked questions later. In the past few years, they'd all lived in fear of the next what-if.

Another leaf fell from the peace lily, missed the table, and hit the floor. Lauren winced at an image of Darcee's body lying on the hospital patio. She closed her eyes, took a slow breath.

"I trust you, God. I know you're watching over my sis—"

Her phone rang on the table. An incoming call from . . .

"Eli?"

"I wondered if we could get together. Talk for a few minutes."

Lauren bit into her lower lip. "I . . . I'm

238

busy taking care of some things. Over at my place."

"I'm near there, maybe a mile or so from your apartment complex."

Her eyes widened. "But how did you know . . . ?"

"You mentioned where you lived a few weeks back. Then last night you said something about being there today. So I took a chance. Hoped I might catch you."

"Where are you exactly?"

"At a Starbucks."

"I don't know, Eli . . ." Lauren's pulse quickened. She didn't want to see him, did she? "Talk about what?"

"Last night . . . I don't think I handled it right. I thought if you'd let me come to your apartment . . . Or maybe you could come here, if that's more comfortable for —"

"I'm in the back building. Upstairs. Apartment 715."

"Looks like I should be grateful." Eli stepped back in from the balcony. "You could have changed your mind and dropped one of those potted plants on my head." He was lucky she'd asked him up at all; this time he had to get it right. She handed him a cold bottled tea. Snapple raspberry. "My favorite — thanks."

"There's not much here." Lauren moved to the table and closed her laptop. "No food. Only the tea . . . and plants that have seen better days. I've been staying at my folks' place for almost two weeks now. In the Fairwinds subdivision, near —" She glanced away. "I'm sure you've been to the house."

There it was again: the elephant in the room, even seven stories up. It was time to send that animal to someone else's circus. "Once. And only in the driveway." Eli shook his head. "My chance of being welcomed in by your folks wasn't too good. I got the feeling all that hardware on the roof was more threat than decoration." He saw Lauren start to smile.

"Don't ask Fletcher Holt about that." Her eyes warmed as they often did when she mentioned the police officer's name. "Long story."

"I've seen him at the hospital a lot. Not always in uniform." Eli watched as she sank onto the brick-colored corduroy couch, tucked up her legs. He considered things for a moment, then settled on the ottoman in front of her. "You said you were neighbors. Guess it makes sense Holt would come by to see you."

"He's in love with Jess."

Relief washed over him. *Jessica, not Lauren.*

"I mean, that's what I think," she clarified. "He's never admitted it to me. Or to her, as far as I know. But I recognize it. I always do." She grabbed a pillow and hugged it to her chest. "All Jess's life it's been like that — people being drawn to her. She was beautiful even as a child. But it was more than that. It was like she was . . . magical. That's how it felt to me when I was a kid. Even when she aggravated me the most, I still knew she was special. Shiny, almost . . . and impossible to hold on to. Like a shooting star." Lauren shrugged. "I'm not explaining it right. But I think Fletcher's always been attracted to my sister. A year before the Holts moved to Houston, they lost a younger daughter, hit by a car. She was only three."

Eli winced.

"I think having Jess tagging along was good for Fletcher — for all of them, maybe," Lauren continued. "But it's easy to see that his feelings are much deeper now."

"Makes sense." Eli wished he could tell Lauren to look in the mirror if she wanted to see special. To recognize the "shiny" in her own beautiful eyes, see herself the way he did right now.

241

"He seems like a decent guy," Eli added. "And he went out of his way to help me that night when you had Shrek."

"He did." Lauren stretched her legs to the floor and leaned forward, closing the distance between them. "When Emma was asleep in the car at your parents' house. And your father accidentally shot that gun."

"Yeah." Great. The circus had come to the elephant. "It's complicated with my father and me. Because of Drew. And a lot of other things, including Emma." His daughter's name slipped out before he could stop it.

"Emma?"

"I wasn't married to her mother," Eli told her, knowing it had to be said at some point. "We met in Germany when I was in the service. Things moved faster than they should have. I was crazy about her — maybe just crazy, now that I look back at it. But Trina wasn't interested in a serious relationship. She was . . ." The words *shooting star* came to mind. "She was always looking for a new adventure, the next 'perfect taste of life,' she'd say. Maybe an acting career someday. A relationship didn't fit into that. And a baby . . ." Eli shook his head. "I'd say I made a stupid mistake, but my daughter is *no mistake*. I'll never let anyone say that."

242

Lauren nodded, encouraging him.

"Trina wanted to end the pregnancy," Eli continued, words he hadn't said aloud in nearly a decade. "I'd never given much thought to having a child, but knowing there *was* one and that Trina might . . . She wouldn't consider marrying me. She'd made an appointment at a clinic. I had to stop it." Eli saw Lauren's brows draw together. "My father called in a favor, flew over in a senator's jet. He offered her a choice: a messy lawsuit to claim my paternal rights or a check big enough to fund years of 'perfect tastes.' All she had to do was have the baby and sign away her rights. She did. . . . And then Landry money put her on that motorcycle in France."

"Eli . . ." Lauren touched his hand. "Emma doesn't know?"

"That her mother didn't leave us for her 'art'?" He heard the old bitterness in his voice and wished he'd never brought this up. It wasn't what he came here for. "No. Emma knows that Trina died in an accident, but none of the rest of it. Someday she'll ask. Maybe I'll figure out an answer by then. Meanwhile, I just —"

"Love her," Lauren finished, barely above a whisper.

"As best I can."

"I see that." Her fingers brushed the back of his hand.

Eli stayed quiet, acutely aware of Lauren's touch. He didn't want to say or do anything that would cause her to move away. But . . .

"I don't know why I told you all of that," he said finally. "Except maybe it explains why I hadn't been diving into any complicated relationships. Very few of any kind," he amended, knowing he was treading a fine line. "I haven't even been much of a friend, I guess." He told himself he might as well say what he'd come here to say; there was nothing to lose at this point.

"I wanted to apologize for last night," he started, not at all encouraged by the fact that she'd slid back on the couch. Then reached for the pillow again like it was some kind of shield. "When I asked you where we go from here, it sounded like I assumed you wanted that too."

"And that I'd risk upsetting my family." Lauren's grip on the pillow looked far too much like she wanted to hurl it at his head.

"I don't see it that way."

"I know you don't. But it's *all* I see, Eli."

But it wasn't really true. Lauren saw so much more now.

She hugged the pillow close, thoughts

reeling from all he'd told her. How he'd fought for Emma and quite obviously felt partly responsible for her mother's death. *Complicated* didn't begin to describe that. Or what Lauren was feeling either.

"I came back home," she explained, "because my parents were worried sick about Jess. The financial problems, her health, and that issue with the drug test." Eli's dark eyes met hers; he knew how she felt about his unwillingness to help in that situation. "I've always looked out for my sister. My parents count on that. It's what I do."

"Even if Jessica fights you every inch of the way?" Eli bridged his fingers. "And takes unfair advantage of your generosity?"

"I don't see it that way." Lauren bit back a groan, hating that she'd parroted his words. And that with his next breath, he'd probably start talking about "enabling." *Please, don't —*

"I think . . ." Eli hesitated as if he was being careful. "We want to jump in, do everything we can to fix it when we see someone hurting. It's human and an even stronger instinct for us because we're medical people. Give us electricity, drugs . . . a fiberglass cast, and we'll patch it up, make it good. But when it's personal, someone we care for, it gets harder." His eyes met Lauren's.

"I've tried most of my life to fix my brother. I know now that it's not going to happen. I've faced that."

"I'm not trying to fix Jess. If that's what you're implying. She doesn't need to be fixed. She's just —"

"A shooting star. I got that." Eli glanced at his watch. "And I need to get going." He stood.

But I don't want you to.

Lauren pushed the pillow aside, scrambled to her feet. She followed him, confusion swirling. He was right; he should go. She was crazy to want him to stay. He was wrong about Jess. And Lauren was right that it was impossible for a relationship with Eli to go anywhere, but —

"Thanks for the tea." He turned toward her as he reached the door. There was an unsettling blend of warmth and regret in his eyes. "And for not bombing me with a potted plant."

"Sure." She smiled, too aware that he was close enough to . . . "I meant what I said last night. At the coffeehouse. That I admire what you're doing with your daughter. Even more now after what you've told me. She's lucky to have you, Eli."

"She might not agree after tonight if I can't make her look like that girl in *Pirates*

246

of the Caribbean — Elizabeth something."
Eli shook his head. "Swords I get, and I can
row a boat, no problem. But women's
makeup is a complete mystery." He laughed
at Lauren's confusion. "Kids Day — boat
races tonight."

She choked on a laugh, imagining him
fumbling with all those girlie things.
"Where?"

"Buffalo Bayou. I need to have her there
by six thirty. Mom rented the costume and
planned to come with us. But she's down
with a migraine now, so . . ."

"You'll need lipstick or gloss, eye shadow,
and blush. Really subtle; she's only eight,"
Lauren advised, making a list in her head.
"Maybe some eyebrow pencil to make a
beauty mark. A temporary tattoo would be
cute. And glitter. Lots of glitter . . ."

"Not happening." Eli held up his palms.
"I wasn't going to hang around the Wal-
greens makeup counter. I bought the first
lipstick I saw and jammed out of there."

"I'll do it."

"What?" He lowered his hands. "You'll
come?"

"We'll meet there."

His brows scrunched. "Right — that
'awkward' thing."

Heat crept up Lauren's neck. "I'm helping your daughter, not dating her father. *Awkward* doesn't factor in."

Eli's lips twitched. "I wouldn't count on that."

"Meaning?" She wished her heart would stop doing what it was doing.

"She wants Shrek to be a pirate too."

20

"Can't you find someplace better to be on your evening off?" Jessica glanced from the visitors' table toward the hospital doors, heaving a melodramatic sigh. "If I had a choice, I'd be . . ."

"Where?" Fletcher was struck once again that this intelligent, quick-witted woman could be so clueless. For so ridiculously long. He didn't take a leap off her roof because he wanted to fly. "Where would you be if you had a choice?"

Her expression turned wistful, then impossible to read. He told himself he was the clueless one. And a fool to be here.

"The beach, I guess." Jessica sank her fingers into her hair and slid them through, frowning as she reached the ends. "You know how I am about the ocean. It suits me. More than that — the ocean is like me."

Beautiful, restless, always changing . . . unpredictable, risky . . .

"Probably not a good idea to go to the coast anyway," Fletcher told her. "Not with Glorietta heading our way in a couple of days. The Gulf's battening down the hatches."

"Oooh, I love it when you talk sailor!" Jessica pressed her fingers to her heart and fluttered her lashes.

"Quit it. I'm serious." Fletcher feigned irritation, trying to ignore the heat flooding into his face. "Police, fire, rescue . . . all services are prepared for the worst-case scenario. Hospitals, too; Lauren's on the Grace Medical response team. I'm sure you know that."

"What I *know* is that my worst-case scenario is having Gayle Garner breathe down my neck." Jessica bit at the edge of a fingernail. "It's like a stroke of mercy that she didn't pick up any overtime tonight. If I didn't know for sure that God doesn't give two hoots about me, I'd say it was a miracle." She caught the expression on his face and frowned. "Don't do it, Fletcher."

"Do what?" He knew full well what she meant.

"Go all 'Jesus loves you' on me," she explained. "You know better."

"Right." He knew *much* better. And wouldn't give up hope that someday she would too. Now wasn't the time to push, but Fletcher allowed himself a short memory of a towheaded girl sitting next to him in Sunday school. Not that she wasn't as unpredictable as a shore-bound hurricane even back then. "What's the deal with this nurse manager anyway? Why is she giving you a hard time?"

"I don't know. Probably the Lauren factor."

He raised his brows.

She tossed him a wry smile. "Don't pretend you don't see it. Or agree with it. I've heard it all my life: Lauren's smarter, kinder, harder working, better mannered. And far holier, Lord knows." Something close to sadness flickered across her face. "Boy, does he know. I do my best to remind him every day. Disappointing God. It's my strength."

Jessica . . . It was all Fletcher could do not to move close, take her in his arms. "I don't agree," he ventured. "With any of that. And I think there's a lot more to your strength than you even realize."

She stared at him for a long moment, then wrinkled her nose. "Too serious, neighbor boy. I like it better when you stick to sailor —"

"Excuse me," a woman interrupted, arriv-

251

ing at their table. She was carrying a plastic drinking cup crammed with garden roses, and her shoulder sagged with the weight of a bulging Kroger market tote. An adolescent boy wearing earbuds stood beside her. By their facial features, Fletcher guessed they were mother and son. The woman looked at Jessica's name tag. "Where do I go to find the security office?"

"Basement. Is there a problem, ma'am?"

Fletcher glanced toward the parking lot, aware of the bulk of his off-duty weapon at his waist. But there was no trouble that he could see.

"Not a serious problem," the woman answered. "As far as I know. We're here to visit my mother. She was admitted from the ER up to the fifth floor. Today I got a call from the hospital pharmacy asking about Mom's medicines. In the rush, with the ambulance waiting outside, I just scooped up everything from her medicine cabinet. I knew they'd want to see her prescriptions. But I never know which is which." She shrugged. "I guess there were some old, outdated medicines. Mom asked that they be disposed of. It's hospital policy, they said, to send them to the pharmacy. A request was made. But . . . it seems the pharmacy never received some of them them."

"Security's involved?" Fletcher asked, though it was none of his business. Still, it sounded suspicious.

"We brought everything," the woman repeated. "Cleaned out her medicine cabinet. Her pills, Dad's — he passed two years ago — anything that was there. Mom said there were some pain pills and muscle relaxers in there too. 'Controlled substances,' security told us. That's the problem: they've gone missing."

Fletcher caught the change in Jessica's expression, her posture.

"Oh," she said, offering a tight smile. "What a nuisance. I'm sorry you have to deal with all this. I work at the ER registration desk. What's your mother's name?"

"Adele. Adele Humphries."

Fletcher heard Jessica's breath catch.

"I hope Mrs. Humphries is getting better," she said, rubbing her hands together.

"She is." The woman smiled warmly. "And please know we're completely happy with her care in your emergency department."

"Thank you. I'll pass that along."

"Yes, do that, please, and —" The woman pressed the roses into her son's hands and began digging through her tote. "Ah, here it is." She presented Jessica with a ziplock bag. "Pecan brittle. I make it myself — light on the salt, but plenty of butter. Paula Deen's recipe with my own twist. You tell the staff that our family appreciates all they do to help so many folks." She patted Jessica's shoulder. "God bless you, dear."

"Uh . . . sure. Thank you."

Fletcher watched them walk away, thinking of what Jessica had said a few minutes back: *"If I didn't know for sure that God doesn't give two hoots about me . . ."* A blessing and pecan brittle. He smiled. That beat sailor talk any day. But when Jessica turned his way, her expression looked angry and . . . anxious, too?

"Great," she grumbled, gathering her things. "Just what we need. Security poking around our department again. Crazy Gayle pointing fingers." She shoved the pecan brittle into her purse. "Those narcotics are probably still in that old woman's medicine cabinet. Or maybe she threw them out years ago and forgot. She could hardly speak she was so sedated."

"You talked with her?"

"I registered her when she arrived. And then . . ." The look returned, nervousness tinged with anger. Exactly like the Barclays' shih tzu before she growled and snapped.

"Gayle called me away from my dinner to go talk with Mrs. Humphries again. About her insurance. Gayle made a huge deal about how it had to be *me.* The patient didn't want anyone else. Then after all that, she barges in and —" Jessica stopped short. "Never mind. I need to get back."

"I'll walk you to the door," Fletcher offered, trying to quiet his investigative curiosity. What had the nurse manager done that Jessica decided not to reveal?

"Parrish thinks I look even better than Elizabeth Swann," Emma gushed, checking to be sure the water splashes hadn't damaged the temporary tattoos on her forearm. Waning light cast a rosy sheen over the glittering pink skull and a glow-in-the-dark rainbow. She grinned at Lauren, her eyes almost as bright as her gold hoop earring. "And she thinks it's way beyond cool that you and Dad got dressed up."

"Yes, well . . ." Lauren peered sideways at Eli. "Way beyond sneaky, too, since these costumes were a complete surprise to me." She glanced down at the frilly peasant blouse, making her plumed hat tip forward.

"Good thing you and Grams are almost the same size."

Lauren heard Eli's low chuckle. It was also

a good thing that Anita Landry — obviously a great sport — had modest taste. No corset vest, plunging neckline, or side-slit skirt with thigh-high boots. It could have been much, much worse. She bit back a laugh; Eli couldn't say the same. His costume was labeled "pirate scalawag," and the laced shirtfront gaped dangerously over his broad chest. That he'd acquiesced to the earring, bandanna, and Lauren's generously penciled mustache was proof positive of how much he loved his little daughter.

"Anyway," Emma concluded, reaching down to adjust Shrek's eye patch, "Parrish says you're probably the best mother in the world."

Lauren's heart tugged. "Tell her thank you, but I'm not a mom. I've had practice, though. With my sister. Jess liked to dress up as a princess," she clarified, certain Eli was thinking that she was guilty of mothering her sister still. "So I'd help her with her crown and the play makeup. All that." She smiled at Emma. "I liked helping you today."

There was a chorus of childish pirate whoops from a picnic table a few yards away, followed by a crescendo of *yo ho*s from distant speakers blasting a continuous loop of Disney's "A Pirate's Life for Me."

Someone shouted Emma's name. Shrek whined and nudged his big head against his mistress's hip.

"Daddy? Please," she begged, pressing her palms together. "Mrs. Donnelly's taking videos, and Parrish wants to film Shrek doing that cute trick. He could be the star. And I'll sing my *Annie* song. And then maybe we'll go viral on YouTube, and —"

"No YouTube." Eli touched the tip of his plastic sword to Emma's sleeve. "And it's getting dark, so stay right there at the Donnellys' table, where I can see you, pirate girl." His smile stretched his penciled mustache. "Back here in twenty minutes. Or you and that fuzzy varmint will be walkin' the plank — argh!"

"You're crazy, Daddy," she giggled, giving him a quick hug. "Thanks!"

They watched her trot away with the loyal Newfoundland close behind. Eli swept off his bandanna and earring, sighed. "Kids — impossible to keep up. She's making an old man of me."

Lauren smiled, thinking nothing could be further from the truth. Eli had never looked so . . . She shook her head, nearly laughing aloud as her grandmother's corny word came to mind. *Dashing.* It was the costume, probably. The pirate shirt over faded jeans, hair tousled from the bandanna, a healthy glow from rowing that boat, and those sleepy eyes.

"Bottle of rum?" He lifted a dripping can of Dr Pepper from the cooler as they settled into beach chairs.

"No thanks." Her skin prickled as he rocked his chair and scooted it closer until they were scant inches apart. "I should be careful with that stuff. Have to be able to drive myself home."

"Right." His eyes held hers for a long moment, and Lauren was certain he was thinking what she was. In any other scenario — with any other woman — Eli would insist upon providing that ride home. Except that this wasn't a date. Even if everything seemed to be conspiring to make it look that way. Maybe even feel that way . . .

"It's beautiful here." Lauren shifted her gaze toward the tree-lined bayou shore and the glittering Houston skyline beyond. She took a slow breath, inhaling the earthy scents of slow-moving water, tree moss, native grasses and flowers, blending with the tangy-sweet and smoky aroma of someone's barbecue. A trio of fireflies blinked, disappearing and reappearing magically along the shoreline, the original model for Disney's electronic twinkles in their Pirates of the

Caribbean ride. Here and there on the darkening expanse of lawn, children in layered glow necklaces competed boisterously with the courting insects. "Emma had so much fun. I'm glad I came along."

"I am too." Eli stayed silent for a few seconds. "Was being with me uncomfortable for you?"

"No."

"Then I'm glad about that, too." He was quiet again, new fireflies choreographing the beats of silence. "I wish I could change it all."

She turned to look at him, shadowed now in dimming light. The *yo ho* chorus and childish squeals blended in the distance. "Change what?"

"The way things happened. With your sister . . . you and me."

"You can't." He couldn't change that any more than he could change what happened with Emma's mother. Or his brother. "But I wish it was possible too."

"Because of your sister running away. The effect it had on your family."

"Yes, that." Lauren's heart thudded in her ears. Truth beating a merciless drum. "And because I wish all of that didn't make things so complicated now. Between us."

"Wait . . . hold on." Eli shifted in his chair,

his knee brushing hers. He leaned forward, searched her face. "There's an 'us'?"

Lauren managed a chuckle despite her anxious sense of free fall. "You sound like I did when I saw this ridiculous costume." She saw the question repeated in his expression. "Yes, I guess so," she heard herself say. "Even if it feels as scary as walking that plank, I think there is an 'us.' Like it or not."

"Ah . . . okay then." Eli feigned a grimace. "But don't worry; even after that huge show of interest, I'm not going to ask where we go from here. Not this time." His tone sobered. "Promise."

"Good. I don't have an answer." Her heart stalled as he gently took hold of her hand.

"That's okay. We'll figure something out. Take it really slow. We both have things, other people, to consider." His thumb brushed over her fingers. "But you're important to me, Lauren. Too important for me to mess it up this time. Please believe me."

"I'll try."

"No pressure. Like right now. I'm not going to try to kiss you. Even though I want to — a lot."

Her eyes widened.

"Only being honest." He smiled. "So, deal?"

"Deal."

"Great." Eli raised her hand, touched his warm lips to her palm.

"Hey," she protested despite a dizzying rush. "That was a kiss. You said you weren't going to do that. You totally cheated."

Eli shrugged, a Jack Sparrow smirk on his face. "Pirate."

21

Lauren checked her clock in the pale morning light, not sure what had awakened her so early. Probably the rain pelting her bedroom window or Hannah snoring from the spot she'd commandeered at the foot of the twin bed. Or maybe . . . Lauren reached up to stifle a yawn, then stopped, staring in confusion at a black smudge in the center of her palm. What — ?

Oh yes. That artfully penciled pirate mustache and . . . Eli's kiss.

A bit of the smudge had survived her hand washing; the memory was just as indelible.

She scooted up in bed, felt Hannah stir, and saw one sleepy eye open in the tousle of black-and-white fur. The dog's chin rested on the light comforter well within toe-nipping range, and she generally woke up cranky. Lauren might as well be sleeping in a minefield. But right now she didn't really care. She just wanted to remember last night. All of it: the exuberant crowd of kids in the park, Shrek with his eye patch, Emma's delighted giggles, and that sun on Eli's shoulders as he rowed their boat down the bayou. Lauren's pulse quickened as a collage of memories continued: distant music, lazy looping fireflies in the deepening dusk, and then the hopeful timbre of Eli's voice.

"Wait . . . hold on. . . . There's an 'us'?"

Us. Her stomach quivered.

She'd told him yes. And he'd said they'd take it all slowly, because *". . . you're important to me."*

Lauren stared at the brow pencil on her palm. Proof that she'd finally accepted that Eli Landry was important to her too. Despite her confusion, after running to Austin to avoid it, she could no longer deny her feelings. Feelings she still didn't fully understand, but that included respect for his work at the hospital and for his beautiful devotion to Drew and Emma. And maybe even for Eli's stubborn, opinionated courage. Courage that too often pitted him against others. Coworkers, his parents, certainly hers, many times against Lauren herself . . . and God, too?

She glanced at her well-worn study Bible on the bedside stand. She knew very little about Eli's faith, other than his doubts about God's mercy when it came to his brother's tragic life. But for Lauren, absolutely, the *us* in any serious relationship would have to include God. She had no idea how that might play out with Eli. A huge reason for taking it slow.

She brushed her thumb across the smudge on her palm. Eli had admitted it too, that there were other things to consider. And people. Like —

Hannah lifted her head and stared at the doorway. Lauren leaned forward. Then she heard it, even over the drumming rain. It was coming from down the hallway and was probably what had awakened her in the first place: the unmistakable sound of crying.

Jess.

Hannah's indignant growl did nothing to deter Lauren as she kicked off the covers and padded down the hall to her sister's room, worry crowding in. What could have happened?

"Jess?" Lauren pulled her hand from the doorknob, made herself knock first. "Are you okay in there?"

"Go away."

"It sounds like you're crying."

"It sounds like *you're* butting in."

Touché. Lauren reached for the knob

again; she'd learned to find hope in her sister's hostility. It was pathetic, but tears and dark silence scared Lauren far more. She tested the knob. Not locked. "I'm coming in, Jess."

"Suit yourself."

A welcome mat in sisterspeak.

But there was raw misery in Jess's eyes.

"Stupid roof." She inspected the ceiling, her glare seeming to include far more than the growing water stain, then hugged her arms around herself. "Stupid storm."

Lauren settled on the edge of the bed, reminding herself that taking it slowly was just as important here, too. "Guess it rained all night."

"I don't think it's ever going to stop." Jess's red-rimmed eyes connected with Lauren's. "There comes a time when you run out of Tupperware."

"Bad shift at work?"

"Maybe I'm just tired of it, you know? All of it."

Please, God . . . Lauren pushed down an all-too-familiar fear. Jess wasn't being doomsday. Everyone got tired of work.

"Security's on that witch hunt again," Jess explained with a frown. "Pretty soon we'll have to use the buddy system to go to the bathroom so no one gets accused of thievery."

Lauren welcomed a wave of relief; this she could handle. "Was there another complaint — valuables missing?"

"Um . . ." Jess glanced down, picked at a thread on her comforter. "Not sure. But no doubt Gayle will sniff around like a bloodhound this morning." She yanked the thread, hard. "And we all know who her favorite target is."

"Jess, I know you think that, but —"

"Don't! You'll never sell me that load of —" She drew a deep breath. "You don't get it. How could you possibly?"

"I want to. Let me try." Lauren took hold of her sister's hand. "Please."

"Sometimes . . ." Tears brimmed in Jess's eyes. "It feels like I'm outside. Not really part of anything. Not at work. Or even —" She stopped, swiped at her eyes. "Never mind."

"Tell me what's wrong. Tell me what I can do."

"To fix it — fix me?"

Eli's words whispered in her head. *"We want to jump in, do everything we can to fix it when we see someone hurting. . . ."*

"Thanks, but I'm not a roof leak." Jess gave Lauren's fingers a squeeze, her shoul-

266

ders relaxing with a sigh. "You're like Fletcher. Too serious. It was just a bad shift. I'll get over it."

"You're sure? Nothing I can do?"

"Nope. Except keep Gayle out of my hair. And maybe wash your hands." She pointed at Lauren's palm. "Yuck. Is that mascara?"

"Uh . . . brow pencil."

"Seriously?" Jess examined Lauren's warming face. "I'd say that's the last thing you need."

"Parrish thinks she's pretty."

Eli hid his smile as he dropped Emma's French toast onto the flower-doodled plastic plate she'd made in kindergarten. Shrek's tail thumped against his knee. Two years on insulin and the old boy still begged for syrup-laden scraps. Now *there* was proof of hope.

"Do you?" Emma continued.

Eli threw a dish towel over his shoulder and reached for the jar of applesauce before heading to the table. "Do I what?"

"Oh, puh-leeeeze," his daughter groaned, inspecting the pirate tattoos she'd managed to keep in place despite her bath. "Lauren. Do you think she's pretty?" Her smile was decidedly impish. "You don't have to say it out loud, Daddy. You could just do a thumbs-up or thumbs-down like on Face-book."

He halted, plate in one hand and jar in the other. "Excuse me?"

"I know, I know. Don't worry. I don't have a Facebook account. I only heard about that thumbs thing. But do you *like* her?"

Eli blamed sudden warmth on the heated plate in his hand. "Sure. She's nice. And you are going to be nice and hungry if you don't stop asking questions and start eating. Grab this applesauce, would ya?" He set the plate of cinnamon-scented triangles in front of her, slid the butter dish closer. Then let curiosity get the best of him. "How 'bout you? Do you like Lauren?"

Emma raised a thumb. Then grinned and raised the other. "The other one's for Shrek. He likes her too."

"Okay," Eli said, realizing he'd been holding his breath. "That's settled. Now let's —"

He stopped short as his cell phone buzzed against the tabletop. An incoming call from Mimaw's Nest.

"Elijah Landry," he answered, motioning for Emma to get started with her breakfast.

"I'm sorry to bother you so early," Florine apologized. "I believe things will be fine, but we're treating Drew for an asthma flare-up. I know you asked to be notified. I suspect the change in weather may have triggered it; rain's really coming down out here. And that wind's kicking up."

"He's getting the usual dose in his nebulizer?" Eli saw Emma's fork droop.

"Yes, sir. And we have the steroid mix if we need it; I'll let you know on that. I took a good listen to his chest. Only wheezes."

"No fever?" He tried to reassure Emma with a look, but she left her chair and skittered to his side.

"Temp's normal. And . . ." There was a small chuckle of amusement. "Your brother's already reaching for his breakfast tray — pancakes."

"Good." Eli's breath escaped in relief. "That's a positive sign. Tell him I'll stop in before work." He smiled as Emma tugged at his shirt. "And tell him his favorite niece sends a kiss — her dog, too."

"I'll do that, Mr. Landry. Please check those road reports. We're getting a bit of standing water. That means some of the low-water crossings could be a problem."

"Will do. Thanks for the reminder." Eli said good-bye, then reached down to ruffle his daughter's hair. "Don't worry. Drew's okay. Sometimes the weather stirs up his asthma. You know the drill: nebulizer treat-

ment, get him all propped up on pillows."
He feigned a frown. "When they can find
his pillows, that is. Someone seems to be
stealing them away and hiding them. Do
you have any idea who that might be?"

"Um . . ." Emma glanced down.

"Hey." He tucked a finger under her chin,
raising her face. "You're not in trouble. I'm
only teas—" Eli stopped, concerned as her
expression became even more pained.
"What's wrong, punkin?"

"Nothing." She shrugged. "Only it's better if there aren't pillows. I heard that. It's
safer."

"Safer?" he asked, trying to understand.
"You've seen what we do. Use the pillows
to help Drew sit up straighter. Keep him
from leaning to his paralyzed side when he's
having breathing trouble. You've seen that
hundreds of times." A thought occurred to
him: Parrish had a new baby brother. "Are
you thinking about babies? That it's not safe
for babies to sleep with pillows?"

Emma's eyes filled with tears.

"What?" Eli sat down and pulled her close
to his chair, dismayed to see she'd begun to
tremble. "What is it, honey?"

"I don't want Uncle Drew to die. He's
not too old . . . he still eats, and —" a tear
slid down her face — "he's not suffering,

270

Daddy. I don't want it to be like with Parrish's dog. I don't want anyone to do that to him." She covered her face with her hands, sobbing. "Please . . ."

"Wait, Emma . . . hey." Eli slid from his chair to his knees in front of her, his heart stalling at her pain. He gently pulled her hands away so he could search her sweet face. "I don't understand what you're saying, honey. No one's doing anything bad to Drew. Where did you get that idea?" He waited. Saw doubt in her eyes. "Emma, tell me."

"Yonner," she whispered. "He said some people . . . might think it's better for Uncle Drew to die than to be like he is." Her chin quivered, causing her teeth to chatter together.

Eli's stomach lurched.

"Yonner was so mad, Daddy. He didn't know I was listening, but I heard him telling Grams that . . . someone . . . might think it was okay to put a pillow over Uncle Drew's face and smother him."

No . . .

"Emma." Eli grasped her shoulders, blood pounding in his temples. "Who? Who was that 'someone' your grandfather said might want to hurt Drew?"

"I didn't believe it . . ." She choked on a

271

sob. "I don't, but —"

"Who?"

"Yonner said you, Daddy."

22

"Someone stole medications from a patient?" Lauren kept her voice low as a registration clerk passed by the triage office.

"Our patient — maybe one of our ER staff. Or so the nervous whispers go." Vee grimaced. "Mrs. Humphries was here for *hours.* Apparently she arrived with a grocery bag filled to the top with old meds. Hers, her late husband's, everything they could find. From laxatives to foot cream to hair ball tablets to —"

"Hair ball?"

"Her cat's prescription." Vee frowned. "And there were narcotics, too. Pain medication and some muscle relaxers, I guess. There's the real problem. They were missing from the bag. The reason for Gayle's current twitchiness."

"I'm not sure even something like this could explain our manager lately. I'm concerned frankly."

Vee pulled a braid between her fingers. "You mean how thin she looks? How kind of jumpy she's been?"

"Exactly. And short-tempered the last couple of weeks." Lauren wondered if her last point reflected Jess's complaints more than her own observations. No. It might have contributed, but Gayle was definitely not Gayle these days. "It's not like her."

"Agreed." There was empathy in Vee's expression. "I can only imagine how hard it would be to have a husband injured and hurting. To have a two-paycheck family shrink to one. She has to be under a lot of pressure. Maybe we should try to find a day we can take her out to lunch or . . . treat her to a pedicure. I'll bet she'd love that place in Montrose. Something to help her unwind."

"Good idea." Lauren couldn't help but think of Jess's distress this morning, her remark about security being on a witch hunt. She'd said she wasn't sure about the reason. "What day was that patient here in the ER?"

"Sunday. The day of our Mardi Gras party. So you weren't here. And neither was I." Vee shook her head. "Once the word got around about those missing drugs, all the staff started doing head counts."

Lauren tensed. Jess had been here that evening. "But can security be certain the medicines went missing from the ER?"

"A pharmacy tech came down to pick up the outdated medicines for disposal, and the narcotics weren't there. Someone said the hair ball tablets were gone too."

Lauren tried to smile but found it impossible as she recalled her sister's words: *"And we all know who her favorite target is."* But Jess was wrong about Gayle. Stressed or not, the nurse manager didn't have it in for her.

"When you said that about 'head counts' . . . you haven't heard anything official, have you?" Lauren ventured. "I mean, is management trying to trace all the staff who came into contact with Mrs. . . . uh . . . ?"

"Humphries. I don't know for sure about head counts, but Gayle and the director were looking over the staff schedules this morning. One of the other techs said he overheard some talk. He said he'd bet good money there's going to be a random drug test tomorrow — maybe even today."

"Today? You mean our ER staff?"

"I have no idea," Vee assured her. "I only know my tech friend shouldn't be so reckless with his money since there's no way he

275

could know for sure. They don't exactly pre-announce those things." She tossed Lauren a teasing smile. "But I did tell him he should go easy on hair ball tablets just in case."

Lauren faked a smile — successfully this time. At this rate she could go pro soon. She told herself there was no reason to worry. Even though . . . *Jess is working today. And tomorrow.*

"Despite our differences . . . ," Eli started, stealing a glance at his mother. He'd asked that she be spared this uncomfortable exchange. No surprise, His Honor ruled otherwise. "I'm hoping you'll understand my concern . . . sir."

Julien Landry nodded very slightly — a move, he'd once explained to Eli, that was calculated to show he was listening yet didn't necessarily agree. Important for a judge.

Eli reminded himself to keep his temper in check. To be respectful. Regardless. He took a slow breath, inhaling the room's familiar scents: leather, wood polish, tobacco . . . and gun oil. Reaching for his coffee cup, he noticed the small sugared cookie his mother had tucked on the saucer beside it. A Pepperidge Farm gingerbread man.

Emma's favorite. It seemed ridiculously innocent in this room. "It involves Emma," he continued. "I know how much you love her. And how important she is to both of you."

"Of course she is. Your point, Elijah? Unless we're to infer that you intend to hold our grandchild hostage. More than you already are."

"Julien, darling . . . don't, please."

"It's all right, Mom."

It wasn't. But certainly something Eli expected. His father always went on the offense; even his image in this room conveyed that. The leather club chair, taller by far than the two Eli and his mother occupied. The way the illumination from the gun cases settled on his silver-streaked, inky head of hair and his still-muscular shoulders. But it was the wood-paneled wall behind him that spoke the loudest, said this was a man who commanded respect. Photo after photo, artfully framed and spotlighted, of Julien Landry with a staggering array of VIPs. In his life, Eli had seen countless jaws drop over the framed photographs of George W. Bush, Dick Cheney, Justice Scalia, the Reverend Billy Graham, astronaut Neil Armstrong, Dallas Cowboys' Jerry Jones and Troy Aikman . . . right on to Willie Nelson and George Strait.

Connected was Julien Landry's middle name. Except when it came to Eli.

"I'll rephrase my question." His father reached for his coffee. There was no cookie on his saucer. A small crack in his Wall of Fame. "Why are you here?"

"Emma overheard you talking with Mom," Eli explained, his gaze still lingering on the massive painting in the center of all those vanity photos: a revered Texas artist's rendering of his grinning father, Drew hoisted high on his shoulders. With Anita Landry half a pace behind, holding her younger son's hand. A family portrait inspired by a photo taken on a South Padre Island beach. A warm, happy scene snapped by a senator's wife . . . less than a mile from where the hull of that skiff caved Andrew Landry's head in. And changed their lives forever.

Eli reminded himself to stick to the facts. Emotion would be a failure here. It always was. "She's upset, sir. Emma heard you say that I want to harm her uncle."

His mother paled.

"I'm sure I don't know what you mean," the judge countered, setting his cup down.

"I mean . . ." Eli fought to stay calm despite a heartbreaking image of his daughter's eyes. "She's hiding pillows at the care

278

home. Because she's afraid I might hold one of them over my brother's face. To smother him in some kind of delusional mercy killing."

"Oh no. Jesus, please . . . ," Eli's mother prayed, closing her eyes.

His father shifted in his chair. "Emma must have misunder—"

"You said that!" Eli spit out, despite all his good intentions. Protecting his child was the only thing that mattered now. "You were angry, and blasting away at me was all you cared about. Emma was simply . . . collateral damage." He held his father's gaze, sickened by a sudden memory of that shotgun racking in his parents' driveway. The only thing worse was the anguished look on his mother's face right now. Eli's anger fizzled; her sadness was like spit-dampened fingers on a candle flame. "You're hurting my daughter."

The grandfather clock ticked, underscoring a long silence. And then his father cleared his throat.

"I'm sorry." The judge's posture slumped very slightly, and a look of genuine remorse came into his dark eyes. "And you're right. Despite our differences, I *do* understand your concern. That shouldn't have happened."

His father's phrasing of the apology wasn't lost on Eli: it *"shouldn't have happened."* Not that he was wrong to say it. Still, Anita Landry's grateful expression said it was an answer to prayer. Eli would let it go.

"I believe you mean that, sir. Thank you."

"Good. You bring Emma by, then." His father's shoulders squared again. "And I'll explain —"

"No," Eli interrupted quickly. "I mean, that's not necessary. I got her calmed down; she's okay now." He glanced at his watch. "I need to get to the hospital."

In minutes Eli was on his way back down the rain-drenched driveway. Carrying the Pepperidge Farm package his mother insisted he take for Emma. And still disturbed by his father's addition to that apology — his instruction to bring Emma here so he could explain. Even now, Eli's gut reacted to the idea in the same way it had to that shotgun blast in this very driveway. It made him physically sick.

The sky rumbled and he glanced up at the dark, foreboding clouds. The air was warm and oppressively muggy, too many signs that a big storm was coming. He was glad Emma and Shrek had been invited to the Donnellys' for another sleepover, that he'd checked on Drew before the rain caused road detours. And he was especially grateful no weather glitch had stopped him from handling *this,* here. With his father. Eli had done what he had to do. Now he could go on to work. Lauren would be there. A reason to start feeling good about today.

The first big splashes of rain caught him before he could get the car door open. Then, when he reached to get the seat belt out of the way, the sack of cookies escaped his grip and dropped into a puddle. Lightning split the sky as he retrieved it. Thunder followed within a heartbeat.

Just as Eli slipped the key into the ignition, it finally came to him — the reason his father's apologetic offer to "explain" hit him on such a visceral level. It had nothing to do with his lifelong frustration over the judge's need to control. Or his father's probably alcohol-induced rant about Eli's intentions toward his brother. Or even that Emma had been an innocent casualty in that shameful moment.

The truth was much harder to deal with than his father's venomous lie. Eli had never told Emma how he felt about Drew's advance directive — how strongly opposed he was to seeing her uncle in the pain and helplessness they'd witnessed last Christmas. He'd never told her that the very thought of it hurt like a physical wound. How could he burden Emma with any of that? His sweet, faith-filled child, who was certain that rainbows were painted by angels, who sang about sunny tomorrows . . . and who couldn't understand why her best friend's dog had to be euthanized.

How would Eli even begin to explain?

"The weather makes it worse." The woman pressed her fingertips to her cheekbone, nearly endangering an eye with her jeweled acrylic nails. She nodded at Lauren. "I always tell my Herbie, 'Who needs all those storm maps on TV? I've got a fail-safe barometer in my sinuses.' " Her fingers straddled her nose, tapping both cheeks as if she were testing a melon. "Glorietta's headed to Houston. Says so right here in my face. Mark my words, darlin'. Better be prepared."

" 'Get a kit. Make a plan. Be informed,' " Lauren quoted. Then, for some reason, she thought of Jess's rebuke this morning. *I'm not a roof leak.*

"I'll be examined when the clinic opens?" The woman pulled a handful of tissues from the box on the triage desk, reached for her purse. "By the urgent care doctor?"

"You'll be examined by a PA-C," Lauren clarified. "A certified —"

"Physician assistant. Oh, I know what that is, dear. Herbie and I prefer them to MDs, to tell you the truth. The PAs and nurse practitioners seem to take more time and explain things better. Anyway, that's our opinion."

"I'm glad you feel that way." Lauren glanced at the clock. "The urgent care will open in a few minutes. And the PA you'll be seeing today is actually the man in charge of that department. His name is Eli Landry." Her heartbeat kicked up a notch, as finely tuned as this woman's sinuses. "He's experienced, very skilled, and —"

"Thank you."

Eli leaned in the doorway, his stethoscope settled over the shoulders of his white coat.

"Oh, hello." Lauren made a hasty introduction, hoping neither of them noticed the telltale color in her face. "Mrs. Barrow, PA Landry . . ."

"Nice to meet you," he offered, nodding politely at his patient. Then his gaze connected with Lauren's, the dark eyes warm. "Thanks again; I'll do my best to live up to your expectations."

"I'm sure of that."

Eli's parting smile was professional and courteous. With the smallest hint of pirate.

23

"Darcee Grafton's awake." Lauren hunched over the triage desk, keeping her voice low as she spoke into the phone. But this wasn't a privacy violation; the media would be reporting it soon enough. "I knew you'd want to know."

"That depends on what 'awake' means." Jess's voice sounded far too sleepy for someone due at work in less than an hour. "If it means her brain's mangled like Eli's brother's, then I *don't* want to know."

Was Jess's voice just sleepy . . . or slurred? "I haven't been to the ICU. I ran into Darcee's mother. In the chapel." Lauren expected her sister's immediate sigh. "She told me that her daughter regained consciousness sometime during the night. Recognized her and asked about the baby." Her throat tightened, remembering. The mother had been on her knees in the chapel, grateful tears running down her cheeks. "It sounds very hopeful. Enough that they're going ahead with plans to surgically repair her leg fractures."

"Right. Gotta be able to walk to the roof again." Jess's laugh was closer to a groan. "Kidding. But hey . . ." Her voice sounded more plaintive. "Did the mother say anything about that?"

"About what?" Lauren wished she hadn't bothered to call. This conversation was as unsettling as today's weather.

"I meant, did Darcee say if the wind knocked her off that roof or if — ?"

"No," Lauren interrupted. "Look, I can't really talk now. I thought you might want to know she's conscious. Since you'd seemed concerned." *Enough to leave your desk and wander upstairs without telling anyone . . . to go back there on your day off . . .*

"Okay. No problem." Jess yawned. "Go. Do what you gotta do."

"You're still coming in to work, right?"

"Why wouldn't I?"

Because there might be a drug test. Lauren was nearly overwhelmed by an urge to say it aloud.

"I don't know . . . You sound tired."

Another grim laugh. "I dare you to sleep with the Tupperware water torture in your room. But I'll be there. Can't give crazy

Gayle another reason to draw a bull's-eye on my behind or . . ." Jess hesitated. "Is something else going on I should know about? Besides our redheaded Lazarus?"

"No . . . not really."

"Good. See you later."

Lauren said good-bye, disconnected. Then sat there, sickened by the implications of her urge to tell Jess about the rumored drug test. Hospital gossip, completely unfounded. No good could come from helping to spread it. So why had she been tempted to do exactly that? Because she suddenly agreed with Jessica that Gayle Garner would un-justly accuse her? Or . . .

Because I think it's possible my sister stole those drugs?

"I'd heard she regained consciousness," Eli told Marsha Grafton as they stepped aside to let the ICU nurse do her assessment. "And I wanted to come and see for myself." He glanced back at the young woman. She was still bruised and swollen and encumbered by monitoring equipment, but her eyes were open and she was speaking. Halt-ingly, with a voice hoarse from the recently removed endotracheal tube, but intelligible and coherent. Maybe it wasn't so much that

Eli *wanted* to see it as he *needed* to. After Drew.

"The neurosurgeon said it's because the medications helped the swelling to go down." Mrs. Grafton's eyes shone over the top of her granddaughter's hair — the same auburn shade as her own. "And because of the power of prayer. Did you know that she prayed with me? Darcee's neurosurgeon — she prayed with me right there in the waiting room, minutes before they wheeled my daughter into surgery. I never expected that. I'm so grateful. For all of you. For everything."

Eli swallowed, turning his head to watch as the nurse inspected her patient's surgical dressing, then moistened Darcee's lips with a swab. How many prayers had his mother sent heavenward for Drew in these past decades? Didn't that count? Or was it Eli's doubts about God that caused things to go so sour for his brother — for their whole family — this past year? Maybe God simply picked and chose randomly, and the Landrys just plain lost out.

"I know how hard it is," Eli heard himself say. "My older brother suffered a traumatic brain injury."

"Oh, my." Marsha's brows pinched. "I'm so sorry to hear that. Recently?"

"A long time ago. He was almost fourteen at the time. It was a boating accident. A head injury and near drowning." There was compassion in her eyes. For him, too, now. Eli wished he'd never brought it up. "I'm very glad that your daughter's showing such progress, Mrs. Grafton."

"Thank you." She pressed a kiss to her granddaughter's head. "Did your brother — ?"

"He's severely disabled. We've found a good care home not far from here." He glanced toward the door, wanting nothing more than to escape. "So . . ."

"I won't keep you." Marsha stepped close, patted Eli's shoulder. She'd hugged him last time; he had no doubt she'd do it again if there weren't a baby in her arms. "I know you're busy. I really appreciate your coming up here." Her eyes searched his almost as if she could see right into his heart. "What's your brother's name?"

"Andrew — Drew."

"I'll be praying for Drew. And his younger brother, too." Her caring smile was a hug in itself. "Oh. I meant to ask you. Do you work with a woman named Jessica?"

"There's a clerk by that name. In the ER registration office. Jessica Barclay."

"Would my daughter have met her?"

"Yes," Eli confirmed, remembering the two of them in the urgent care. And Jessica's distress when she heard about the fall from the roof. "They did meet. Why do you ask?"

"Darcee mentioned her. They were testing her memory of things that happened right before the fall. One of the few people she could recall was a woman named Jessica. Your clerk must have made a strong impression."

"It's no problem, really," Lauren assured Eli as she restrained the one-year-old boy on the gurney. She pinned the baby's chubby face gently between her palms as Eli applied a last layer of surgical glue to the moon-shaped laceration on the tiny chin. "I'm caught up in triage, so I had the time to help over here."

"Great . . . thanks," he murmured, head down and intent on the wound repair. The perspiring tot heaved a sigh, his eyelids finally drooping in exhaustion.

An urgent care tech hustled by, offering Lauren a grateful look; they were short-staffed today.

"Plus," she added, fairly certain Eli was only half-listening, "I'm pretty close to a championship belt in toddler wrestling. This could do it for me. I'll be able to go professional and stop working these cruel twelve-hour shifts. Thanks."

"Right. Sure . . ." Eli's head popped up. "What?"

Lauren smiled. "Not important. All finished?"

"Yes. I think that's going to do it nicely." He stripped off his surgical gloves, dropped them on the equipment stand. "Drool- and apple juice–proof, minimal scar."

"You did a great job." Lauren's heart tugged as Eli tenderly touched a fingertip to a damp curl clinging to the sleeping child's forehead.

"And fortunately he's not too traumatized," he observed with a sigh. "Mom and Dad are out in the waiting room. Parents can hear their baby's cry through closed doors — even over our newsworthy storms." Eli shook his head. "Emma stepped on a piece of fireworks debris when she was four. Tiny foot, huge blisters. Hearing her cry tore me up. And I was a combat medic."

"Completely different when it's personal."

"I'm learning that." Eli reached for his stethoscope, resettling it around his neck. "We haven't had a chance to talk. About last night."

"Mmm . . . no." She was unprepared for

her knees to weaken.

"I wanted to call you this morning, but things got a little complicated. Family stuff I had to take care of. I should probably warn you: that sort of thing isn't unusual. The Landrys could operate a fourth ring with Ringling Brothers, Barnum and Bailey."

My family would be hawking peanuts and tent insurance.

"It's not a problem. Not calling me, I mean," she said, self-conscious. "Really. I —"

"Lauren, there you are!" Gayle Garner strode toward them, exasperation on her face. "I expected to find you in the triage office."

"Is there a patient ready for me?" Lauren was surprised by the manager's appearance: hair escaping from a careless ponytail, no makeup. No shower, either, from that unpleasant whiff. "I'm sorry. The clerks said they'd let me know. Eli needed a hand here, and —"

"There's no patient waiting," Gayle interrupted. "I'm short on time. It's urgent that I talk with you. About your sister."

Lauren's pulse picked up. "What do you mean? Was there an accident?"

"No. It's not that. I need to talk with you

about something personal. Before she arrives for work." Gayle swiped at her forehead, eyes anxious. "Of course, I expected to find you in your office."

The child on the gurney awakened and began to fuss.

"I'll finish up here," Eli interjected. "My fault for pulling her away, Gayle." He met Lauren's gaze, concern in his expression. "Thanks for your help."

"No problem," she managed, sudden dread choking her voice. Something "personal" about Jess?

Lauren checked in with the ER clerks, then used the short trek back to the triage office to take a breath, say a silent prayer.

"Close the door," Gayle instructed as Lauren entered the office. "There's enough gossip going around already."

Lauren settled into her desk chair, regretting the closed door. The air was too close and the nurse manager's scrub top was damp with perspiration.

"I felt I should warn you about a situation," Gayle began. "The fact is, I simply can't look the other way. Not this time."

"Warn me? This has something to do with Jess?"

"Everything to do with her, I'm afraid." Gayle pressed a hand against her abdomen.

"Last Sunday your sister was seen at an ER patient's bedside going through a bag of personal belongings."

"I . . . I don't believe that. Who said — ?"

"Me." Gayle squirmed in the chair, rubbed her stomach. "I'm the one who saw her, Lauren. I confronted your sister on the spot. Obviously she didn't tell you. The patient's name is Adele Humphries. She was medicated, asleep. And Jessica had no business going through her things."

"This is about those missing drugs? You're accusing her?" Lauren leaned forward, heart starting to pound in her ears. "You reported my sister to security?"

"I haven't yet. But . . ." Gayle squeezed her eyes shut for an instant. "I have no choice. She was there. The drugs are missing."

Lord, please . . .

"You're mistaken," Lauren insisted. "There's some other explanation. Jess wouldn't —"

"Please, spare me. I'm tired of hearing people defend your sister's behavior." Gayle rose to her feet, trembling. "Arriving late, conning other staff into doing her work, disappearing. Making excuses. And always that . . . that *attitude.*"

"Gayle, wait . . ." Lauren struggled for

words, horrified the other staff would hear. And concerned by Gayle's increasingly ill appearance. "Please . . ."

"Please what? Look the other way? Because she's your sister? Because —" Gayle retched, clutched her stomach, her face going pale.

"Gayle! Here, let me —" Lauren leaped from her chair, catching the manager under her arms as her legs began to buckle. She eased her down to the floor, alarmed when the woman's eyes rolled back. "Stay with me . . . please." Lauren pressed her fingers against Gayle's throat. *Rapid pulse but breathing . . .* "It's okay. Be still now. I'll get help."

"I'm so . . . sick . . . ," Gayle moaned, then began gagging again.

"Help!" Lauren reached up for the door handle, yanked the door open, and shouted again. "Need help in here!"

Jess burst through the doorway, stopped cold, staring at Gayle on the floor. "Oh, my — what's wrong?"

"Get Eli!"

24

"I'm not signing in as a patient, Eli." Gayle gripped the Styrofoam cup of Gatorade, trying to control her trembling. "This is humiliating enough. Turning the nurses' lounge into a sickroom . . ." She grimaced at the sight of the plastic bag on the chair beside hers. Her clothes. She could smell them from here. "I really thought this stomach flu had simmered down. Obviously I was wrong. But I don't need you to fuss over me."

"I'd feel better if we had you on an exam table," Eli countered, reaching for her wrist.

"No. I won't take up your time and Lauren's any longer. Or keep my staff out of their lounge. This is all so unnecessary." She connected with Lauren's gaze. "Help me convince him?"

Lauren's silence said the obvious: Gayle was lucky she hadn't left her on the floor, stepped over her, and walked the other way.

Gayle had taken things too far in that triage office. She'd been needlessly harsh about Jessica.

"Your heart rate's still above a hundred," Eli confirmed, glancing at his watch. "I think it might be good to have some labs drawn. Make sure your electrolytes aren't out of range. I've discussed it with the ER physician and —"

Gayle squeezed her eyes shut. They'd all be talking about her now. That's the last thing she needed. "Look, I'm sorry I made a scene. And a revolting mess. But this isn't serious. It's not a heart attack or a stroke; it's the tail end of the stomach flu. I got light-headed in the triage office from retching. That's all. I didn't completely pass out." She captured Lauren's gaze. "Tell him I didn't."

"Pretty close."

"But I didn't. And . . ." Gayle pumped the flex straw in her Gatorade, making it squeak against the lid. "I've kept three cups of this stuff down without vomiting. And no more diarrhea."

"You've had a fever with this illness?" Eli still looked unconvinced.

"Never over 101. Garden-variety virus. It just got the best of me today."

Eli scratched his chin. "We could give you

a liter of IV fluids, Gayle. As a little insurance."

"No. I don't need that. Give me a chance to wash my face, gargle some hospital mouthwash, and I'm good to go. Right home to bed." She traced a finger over the breast pocket of her borrowed scrub top. "Promise."

"Your doctor . . ." Eli tipped his head, still scrutinizing her. "He's following your enlarged thyroid?"

"And ordering appropriate meds." *Which I'll refill when I can afford the co-pays.*

"We can't force you to stay for an exam. But I'd better not see you here at work tomorrow."

"You won't."

Eli nodded. "Your husband's on his way?"

"Yes, sir." Gayle smiled. *Loaded on Percocet and Valium? Sure Leo's coming.* Once these two were gone, she'd head to the parking lot.

"Thank you," she added as Eli reached for the door. "Really. I do appreciate the concern, and — Lauren, wait. I want to talk with you."

"I need to get back to triage."

"I'll only keep you a moment." Gayle expected the look on Lauren's face. Like she wasn't sure if she'd be trapped in a room with Dr. Jekyll or Mr. Hyde.

"I'll leave you ladies, then," Eli said, stepping out.

"Thank you." Gayle turned to Lauren as the door closed. "I wanted to say that I appreciate what you did. Helping me like that."

"Of course." Lauren's eyes were more than wary. "But I think you should have let Eli examine you. You seem like you're not feeling well lately. Not just today. For a while now. People are concerned."

"The staff is talking behind my back?"

"They're concerned. As in, they *care*." Lauren sighed. "Forget it. But I need to know something: are you going to take that story about my sister to security?"

"I don't see how it can be avoided." Gayle flexed the straw in her cup. "I wasn't the only witness. The p.m. coordinator heard me question her. There's probably talk already."

Lauren grimaced. "I heard the staff's going to be drug tested."

A rumor, no doubt. But then, Gayle wouldn't have been included in the planning this time. Because . . . *I'm a suspect too?* Cool sweat trickled beneath her scrub top.

"I don't know if that's true," she told Lauren finally.

"If you did, you wouldn't tell me. You think I'd warn —" Lauren stepped out of the way as the door opened inward behind her.

"Oh, excuse me." Jessica's eyes darted from Lauren to Gayle. "I didn't know you were still in here." She glanced toward the sack of soiled scrubs, nose wrinkling. "I was going to grab one of the bottled waters from the fridge."

"No problem. I'm leaving." Gayle rose slowly, grateful the dizziness was minimal. She reached for the plastic sack. "Going home. Eli's orders. I'll get out of your way."

"No need to leave on my account," Jessica said quickly. "Really."

"I insist. And I'm gone."

Gayle stepped into the hallway and closed the door behind her, relieved. She'd planned to tell Lauren she was sorry for her behavior in the triage office, apologize for letting that confusing rush of anger make her say things she regretted. But it didn't matter now. And it didn't matter, either, what Lauren would relay to her sister. Or how many rumors floated around the department today. She wouldn't be here.

"Why didn't you tell me?" Lauren leaned

against the closed door, staring at her sister. "Last night. You never once said Gayle confronted you about handling a patient's personal belongings."

Jess cracked the cap on the water, regarding Lauren as if she'd asked about her preference in dental floss. "Is that what she said?"

"*Said* is too polite a word, Jess. Gayle trapped me in my office and ranted, saying the patient was sedated, that you had no business being in the room at all. She cited problems with your work and —" Lauren made herself stop.

"And what?" Jess frowned at the label on the bottled water.

"The fact is," Lauren explained as calmly as she could, "this patient is missing medications. Percocet, I think, and some muscle relaxers. Those are all controlled substances, Jess. And Gayle's determined to put you right there at the scene."

"I guess now you'll stop saying all that stuff about her being my ally."

"That's all you have to say?" Lauren's temples began to throb. "Don't you understand? Gayle's going to say she caught you."

"Gayle Garner sent me in there," Jess spit out. "Her claim that I had no business being with Mrs. Humphries is a stinking pile of — you want to hear what really happened?"

"Please."

"I registered that patient when she arrived. Her family was there too — that daughter and the teenage grandson. I got it all done, papers signed, the works. But then a couple of hours later, Gayle pulls me out of the lounge — away from my dinner break — to go back in there and talk with that woman again. Something about another insurance card. One of the other clerks offered to do it. But *nooo,* Gayle says it has to be me." Jess jabbed her thumb against her chest, sloshing her water. "She makes this big deal about Mrs. Humphries personally requesting me. And she says nothing about her being zonked from meds. Don't you think that's all a little strange?"

"I suppose," Lauren ventured, fairly certain her sister was making her usual case that the manager had it in for her. "But were you doing what Gayle said? Going through Mrs. Humphries's belongings?"

"She told me to find her card. In a purple coin purse, she said. Inside a big bag of junk her family brought in. I swear, there was gross denture stuff and an old flea collar in that mess." Jess frowned. "I couldn't find the coin purse. I was going to set the bag on her lap and wake her up again. Make her do it. That's when Gayle walked in. She started in on me. Loud enough for the clinical coordinator to come in. And for everyone else to hear probably."

Lauren thought of the chapel staff meeting. How Gayle had made such a point of indicating that Jess had been at the hospital on her day off.

"I admit," Jess continued after taking a swig of water, "I should have told that lady she'd have to look for the card herself. I know that's what we're supposed to do. But she was groggy and *sooo* slow, and I was on my dinner break. I wanted to get it over with as quickly as possible. That's what I told security today."

Lauren's mouth sagged open. "You talked to them already?"

"Had no choice. They called me down to the office the minute I walked in." Jess smirked. "A lovely way to start the day. In the bathroom with someone watching you."

"They took a urine sample?"

"From me and a couple other people." Jess stared at Lauren. "What's wrong? You think I couldn't pass a drug test? You think maybe I really did — ?"

"No," Lauren interrupted, guilt jabbing. "I'm not thinking any of that. But why didn't you tell me about this? Last night, when you were so upset?"

"I don't know." Jess picked at the label of her water. "I guess I didn't want to worry you. Bring up the business from last fall. You know."

The positive drug test . . .

"At least the heat will be off about those other thefts now," Jess added with a sigh.

"Meaning?"

"Something else I heard first thing today: they caught a cook's son breaking into a locker in the basement last night. A teenager." She rolled her eyes. "Comes to work with his mom when she works p.m.'s so she can watch him, keep the kid out of trouble. Anyway, he admitted to all of it."

Lauren sighed, partly out of relief . . . mostly from empathy with the cook.

"So see, you can stop worrying your pretty head on that one, Lolo." Jess began to smile, her eyes teasing. "Just pinkie swear you won't rat me out to Fletcher."

"Rat . . . ?"

"I mean, the urine test won't show any drugs, but . . . it's also going to show a seriously negative chocolate level. Our man with the badge is a good pal, but I can't eat that many cupcakes. Swear you won't tell?"

"Swear." Lauren laughed as Jess linked

their fingers, then gave her a quick hug. "Your guilty secret's safe with me."

"I count on it." Jess glanced at the wall clock. "We both better get back."

"Right. And even if it might not be all over yet, I think it was good you explained things to security before Gayle did. I'm proud of you."

Jess shrugged. "I get it that you don't think she's anything but honest and fair. But . . ."

"But what?"

"If anyone asked me, I'd say it was nothing but a setup: Gayle hauling me away from my dinner and sending me into that exam room. I'd say she won't let up till she sees me fired. Those drugs probably weren't even in that bag of stuff. Maybe the grandson swiped them from her medicine cabinet. Look at that cook's son — it happens. Or —" Jess cocked a brow — "maybe it's even worse than that."

"What do you mean?"

"Between you and me, I think someone ought to make sure Gayle gets a specimen cup."

25

"Not too much damage, considering how far it fell." Eli stood in the Barclays' doorway, hefting the weather vane in his hands. "The screws are missing. Rusted, from the look of these holes. And one wing's bent. Maybe the snout, too." He looked from the metal pig to Lauren and shook his head. "I'm trying to avoid the symbolism here. Me at your door. Actually invited."

"Well . . ." Lauren shrugged, and her beautiful lips hinted at a smile. "You said you were going to be in the neighborhood."

"Emma wanted her Barbies at the sleepover," he confided, noticing that Lauren had pulled her long hair up into a casual knot with several pieces escaping to brush the skin left bare by her tank top. The strands were wavy. More coppery than gold in this light . . .

Eli was staring; he knew that. Holding a stupid flying-pig weather vane and staring like a complete fool. It occurred to him that maybe this sudden, embarrassing fascination with feminine detail was the result of carting dolls around for too many years. Dealing with hair clips, lacy socks, and Little Mermaid pillowcases. Maybe he should spend a few more hours at the gym. Up the weight on his bench press. And take that four-day marlin fishing trip with the PAs from Memorial Hospital.

"The Donnellys live a few blocks north," he continued to explain after clearing his throat. "On Tradewinds."

"I remember that from our phone conversation. Please. Come in." Lauren stepped away from the doorway, gave the hem of her running shorts a discreet tug as she walked. "You can put Wilbur over there on the hall tree." She smiled at the look on his face. "From *Charlotte's Web*. Mom bought that weather vane when I was in grade school. And this isn't the first time our 'radiant' pig has taken a dive from the family roof."

Eli couldn't stop the memory of Marsha Grafton, of what she'd confided about her daughter and Jessica. Lauren would want to know that. And he'd tell her. Eventually. Right now he didn't want to talk about the hospital. Didn't want to think about pain, tragedy, or family problems. Lauren's or his, especially. Eli only wanted *this.* The two of them together.

"Okay, then." He settled the weather vane on the oak hall tree's bench top, next to a stack of mail and an umbrella stand. Then he glanced around the cozy, wallpapered entry. Pink had to be Pamela Barclay's favorite color. "Where's your dog . . . Hannah?"

"Why?" Lauren asked, a Nike running shoe dangling from her hand. She peered at him from the adjacent kitchen. "You worried?"

"Hardly."

"She's safely tucked away in my parents' bedroom. With her Vanilla Woofer dog treats and a pile of toys. Including what's left of my new *Journal of Emergency Nursing.* We can usually tempt her to trade for something else, but . . ." Lauren wobbled toward him, attempting to wiggle her foot down into the shoe. "Orthotic — necessary evil. Anyway, Hannah Leigh's settled for a while. We're doing better, actually. I think this new training is working."

Eli stopped himself from asking who was training whom. He wasn't stepping into that one. There had been more than enough conflict for one day. Right now he was looking for something much, much different. Spending quality time with an intelligent and caring woman whose coppery hair was going rebel wild in the humidity, who somehow smelled of sun-warmed berries and —

"Ready?" Lauren asked, reaching for her keys. "Mom's weather feed says there's only a short window before the rain starts up again. It's going to be dark before too long." She cocked her head. "You came here to go for a run, remember?"

"Right."

"I'll drive us to the track." Lauren nudged Eli with her key. "Top down on the Beetle. I don't care if it's insanely windy. I need to shake this day off. It's going to take wind in my hair and then maybe thirty minutes of running." Her eyes narrowed. "Lace up your shoes, Landry. I'm warning you: I'm fast. Fletcher could never beat me to the ice cream truck. And the day I let some pirate catch me will be —"

"When pigs fly?"

Fletcher hated the sadness in Jessica's eyes and wished he hadn't come empty-handed tonight. Empty was the opposite of what he felt when he was with her. Even when she didn't seem to notice he was here.

"I asked to speak with the manager at Sugarbaby's," he explained, thinking that sitting at this visitors' table outside the Houston Grace ER was the closest they'd ever come to a date. He shifted his weight on the cement bench, his leather gun belt squeaking. "I told him that discontinuing the Dippity Doo Dah was a big mistake. He asked me if it was a crime; he had me there. I couldn't exactly threaten to shoot him if he wouldn't bake my . . . neighbor her favorite cupcake."

"It's okay." Jessica's thin shoulders rose and fell with a sigh. "I should cut back on desserts, anyway. You wouldn't like me fat."

I would love you in any shape . . . in any lifetime.

She propped her elbows on the table, sank her fingers into her hair. Her expression was impossible to read. "Don't tell anyone. I'm making an escape plan."

"Escape from where?"

"Work . . . judgment . . . my whole life as I know it."

His gut tensed. "Jessica, hey . . ."

"Don't panic, pal. I don't need a rescue team — or your holy shrink. I just need someone to ring the bell for recess. Remember? When we'd watch that big clock, hold our breaths. Listen forever for the last stinkin' tick before *brrrrrrrring* — recess!"

"You're planning an escape to play hop-scotch?"

"Fletcher, Fletcher . . ." Jessica reached across the table, patted his hand. "Why did you have to go and grow up on me? You used to be a lot more fun. Not hopscotch, silly. More like sandbox." Her eyes lit. "Galveston beach. Midnight. I'll be there. Just forty-one miles south to a perfect escape." She slid her hand away. "You should try it sometime. It would do you a world of good, serious guy."

She was right; he wasn't that boy on her roof anymore. He'd traded an astronaut suit for a gun and a badge. Grown up. Found soul-deep priorities that put fun farther down on the list. But some things would never change. "You're driving to the coast after your shift's over?"

"Not even stopping at the homestead." Her nose wrinkled. "Tupperware bowls are a major part of this escape."

"Tupperware?"

"Doesn't matter. If it rains, I want it fall-ing on my face, my hair, every inch of me, directly from the clouds —" she raised her hands high — "while I'm running barefoot in the sand. And singing, maybe . . . like one of those sirens of the sea."

311

Oh, man. Please don't do that to me.

A single squawk from Fletcher's radio — static, nothing serious — brought a cold shower of disturbing images: a woman stranded with a flat tire on an isolated stretch of road, alone on a darkened beach with men drifting down from the boardwalk bars . . .

"I see it in your eyes." Jessica's giddy expression was gone. "You're going to say something about my overprotective sister having a serious hissy fit . . . and all the annoying reports of Glorietta wiping us all off the face of the earth. You're going to —"

"Pick you up right here." Fletcher gave the tabletop a rap with his knuckles. "At 11:30 sharp. I'll bring the coffee."

"A cab?" Leo let the kitchen curtain drop and stared as Gayle closed the door behind her. "You came home in a cab? Where's the Camry?"

"Towed." She was too exhausted to lie. "I was about to pull out of my parking space, but I had to run back inside to use the bathroom." Gayle grimaced as her intestines gurgled again. She might have to make a dash for the powder room any minute. "I got back to the car and it was hoisted up like one of those ugly red groupers you and

Wally used to catch out in the Gulf. Remember? You'd —"

"Quit!" Leo lumbered forward. "You're not making sense — towed? The Camry died on you? Is that what you're saying?"

"Died?" Her laugh was as uncontrollable as her incessant heaving in that cab. She was certain the driver had cursed her in a foreign language. "That's a good one. I should have thought of that when everyone in the *entire* hospital asked me what was going on." She hugged her body against a vicious chill. "It was repossessed, Leo. Because we've missed two payments."

His jaw went rigid. "You told me you made those payments."

"Sure . . ." Tears rose without warning. "I told you a lot of things. I said what you needed to hear. Because you were hurting, worried, discouraged. Because I love you, Leo. . . . And then I kept on doing it because I was afraid that —" She watched as his fist began to grind into his palm. "I wish everything I told you was true, but . . ." She was stepping into the eye of a storm; she knew it. "We're behind on everything except the rent — and the cable bill. We can't have you miss a boxing match. So we are in a hell-deep hole because you haven't worked in thirteen months. The medical bills won't go away. Even with overtime that's costing me my sanity, I can't do it." She took a step toward him, her temples beginning to pound. "Do you hear me? I can't do this any—"

His fingers closed around her wrist like a vise.

"Leo, stop." Gayle wriggled in his grasp, nausea swirling. His hand tightened until she felt a grating pop. Her knees weakened. "You're . . . breaking it."

She struggled to free herself. He twisted her wrist again, and in desperation she raised her knee toward his groin. In an instant, his beefy hands were around her throat, cutting off her air. "Leo . . . no . . ."

"You —" His obscenity was delivered in a spray of spittle. "Try that again and you'll be sorry."

"I'm sick," Gayle whimpered, her voice raspy as she struggled for air. "Please. Let me go to the bathroom. Just let me go . . ."

He loosened his grip a fraction. "You smell sick. Go ahead, get yourself cleaned up. But first, tell me something. The truth this time." His thumb threatened her airway again. "Those pills you got for my back pain. I looked at the labels — it's not my name on those bottles. What did you do, Gayle?"

"I . . ." She withered against the pressure of her husband's stranglehold — and a sickening rush of guilt. "Okay, please . . . let me get a breath. Let me breathe, and I'll tell you what I did."

26

"You surprised me." Lauren slid the elastic hair band over her wrist, gave her head a shake. There was no point wrestling her stubborn mane in this humid breeze. She smiled at Eli, sitting beside her on the bench she'd claimed as her own way back in grammar school. "You kept up with me. Almost passed me a couple of times the first few laps of the track."

"Almost died . . . trying." Eli laughed, letting his head fall back as he drew in a deep breath of air fragrant with camphor leaves. His hair clung to his damp forehead, the mild sweat giving him a healthy and very appealing glow in the fading light. Below the beard-stubbled angle of his jaw, his throat quivered with the still-rapid beat of his pulse.

"I was born competitive." He turned and smiled, a flash of white in the deepening dusk. "Older brother and all."

"Drew's five years older?"

"Almost six. Believe me, he reminded me of that. Not in a 'you're a pest' kind of way; more like he was letting me know he was there to look after me. Older and wiser, and I should listen up."

Lauren nodded, wondering if Jess ever saw it that way. More likely she saw Lauren as the pest.

"He was good at everything," Eli continued, glancing toward the sound of childish laughter from the school playground. "Soccer, basketball, football, swimming. Scouts. And school — put me to shame there. Dad was sure he'd be adding his firstborn's name to the list of partners on the Landry Law letterhead." He shook his head. "I think I was the only person who knew what Drew really wanted to do with his life."

"What?" Lauren asked, wondering immediately if she should have. "What did he want?"

The metallic hum of summer cicadas filled a few beats of silence.

"To go to seminary." Eli chuckled. "Seriously, my brother the preacher. When I was tying Mom's dish towels around my neck for Superman capes, Drew was all fired up about Jesus, planning foreign missions in a journal he kept in the box with his baseball

317

mitt. He'd show me photos of starving kids, tell me how he was going to go to all those places someday. Save their souls. Feed their bodies. Change lives — change the world."

Lauren stared at Eli, staggered by his brother's dream. "That's why his praise music's so important to him. All these years."

"No. Only since last year. Emma asked me to load her favorites onto his iPod last Christmas when he was so sick. I should have thought of it myself a long time ago. I'm ashamed that I didn't."

"I'm glad he has it now." The streetlights blinked on through the line of camphor trees. "That look on his face . . . Drew's faith is still there, Eli."

He held her gaze. "How can we know that — *any* of that?"

Lauren reminded herself of what she'd said countless times. That any serious relationship between herself and a man would have to have God at its center. But Eli —

"Excuse me," he told her, glancing at his buzzing cell phone. Worry etched his features. "I should grab this. It's Mimaw's."

"I appreciate it, Vee." Eli glanced, phone to his ear, to where Lauren waited on the bench a few yards away. She'd pulled something from her pocket — lipstick, maybe. "I wasn't trying to trade on our friendship or get you in any kind of trouble."

"No worries," Vee reassured with that faint lisp. "I didn't think you were. But you can understand our situation here. We're bound by the law."

Bound. Eli's jaw tensed, her choice of words bringing an image of his brother tied to that ICU bed. Panicked, helpless. "I'll talk to my parents, smooth things over. How's the Champ doing tonight?"

"Coughing. But Florine said his chest sounds okay. Ate most of his dinner, and —" there was a warm chuckle — "he wanted his music played out loud so we can all hear. He was very insistent about that. Your brother's quite the evangelist."

"Maybe so." Eli thanked her again, disconnected, and walked back to Lauren. Lamplight, filtering through the tree branches, lit her face enough that he could read her concern even before she spoke.

"Is he all right?"

"Still coughing, but not worse." Eli sat down beside her, deciding to risk telling her the real problem. He wished he could keep his family battles out of their relationship, but that was as easy as putting a gag order on those cicadas. "My parents were visiting. When Dad heard Drew had an asthma flare-up this morning, he had a fit that I didn't think it was necessary to have his physician come for an assessment." He shook his head. "He read Florine the riot act for calling me and insisted the pulmonologist should have been the one to come. Apparently the words *real doctor* were mentioned several times. With malice."

"Ouch. I'm sorry, Eli."

"I'm used to it," he told her, wondering if alcohol had provided fuel for his father's tirade. He hoped his mother had been driving. He had to approach her again about that situation. "I don't really remember a time when my father approved of anything I did. Maybe before Drew's accident. I can't say for sure."

"That accident . . ." Lauren's voice was soft. "I know it involved a boat. And Drew was struck by it. But I never heard exactly how it happened."

Because Eli didn't talk about it. He took a slow breath.

"Dad bought this fishing boat. Small — fourteen-foot — aluminum. For the 'Landry men,' he said. He told us he was going to make us fishermen." Eli tried to smile. "Drew wanted to call it *Fishers of Men.* Dad stenciled the boat with *Legal Eagles.* We took it out on the Gulf for a couple of years. Lots of times. The three of us. Mom doesn't like water. She always made us count life jackets while she watched."

Lauren's blue eyes were luminous in the pale lamplight.

"She didn't want us to go out that day. The weather was changing . . ." Eli hesitated, remembering. He'd never really told the whole story to anyone. "It was one of the only times I remember her arguing with him. But she lost. We counted the life jackets and left her standing in the driveway."

"Was it stormy?"

"Not at first." Eli inhaled, swearing he smelled brine. "And we caught fish. Great catches, more than we ever had. None of us wanted to quit. Even when the water got choppy and the wind started up. Even when the other boats headed back to shore. I remember Dad said something about Landry men being tougher than that."

Lauren moved closer, slipped her hand into his.

"I was sitting up in the bow. We'd turned into the wind and I put out my arms like I was flying — like I was Superman. Clowning around like always." Eli swallowed.

"That's what you do when you're the younger brother to someone like Drew. We weren't wearing our life jackets. We never did. The boat must have hit something . . ."

Lauren pressed her other hand to her throat.

"I remember going under, swallowing water, tasting the salt. My eyes were burning, then my lungs. I was choking, screaming. I heard my father shouting to me. Then Drew called my name. More of a gargle because he was in the water then, swimming toward me. The swells were so big. The motor passed by us, my father whipping the boat around. I smelled gasoline, tasted it in the water. Then I went under. Almost blacked out. I think Drew dove down. I felt him pull at my clothes and push me up until I saw the sky. I was choking, trying to get my breath. Then I heard the boat — I saw the hull coming toward us. It all happened so fast." A groan escaped Eli's lips. "My father grabbed me, pulled me in. He called my brother's name over and over. And then he started to scream; I'd never heard him make a sound like that. That's when I saw Drew floating beside the boat. His head . . . There was so much blood."

"Eli . . ." Lauren wrapped her arms around his neck. Her voice was choked with

322

tears. "I'm sorry. . . . It's so horrible."

"Shh," he managed finally, slipping his arms around her. "Don't cry. I'm okay. Don't cry, Lauren." He hugged her tightly for a moment, then moved away so he could connect with her gaze. The caring in her eyes made his heart ache. "It was a long time ago."

"It was like . . . losing your brother."

"Yes. But I have Emma now. And I have —"

"Me," Lauren whispered, reaching up to rest her palm along his jaw. "I'm here too, Eli. Please believe that. I'm here for you. Even before you told me all of this, I saw how much you care for Drew. I see how painful it is dealing with your family issues. I understand how hard it must be to talk about it."

"I don't. Talk about it. I haven't . . . until now." Eli was very aware of her touch, that she'd closed the space between them again. Close enough to smell that elusive warm-berry scent.

"I'm glad you trust me enough." Her lips curved upward, eyes beginning to tease a little. "After all, one of us *should* be trust-worthy . . . keep solemn promises."

"Promises?" He had no clue what she meant. Only that having her this close was making him crazy.

"At the bayou. You said you weren't going to kiss me." Her thumb traced his chin, sending his pulse to jogging speed again. "And then you left a mustache print on my hand. Blamed it on being a pirate."

It was pointless to deny it; besides, Eli wasn't sure he could speak.

"So," Lauren whispered, "I'm not going to promise that I won't —" she leaned forward and touched her soft lips to his cheek — "do . . . *this.*"

She leaned away again, smiled at him. Like she knew she'd sent his heart running laps on that school track. "What are you thinking?" she asked.

"Seriously?"

"Of course." She tipped her head, the untamed waves framing her face. One tendril clung to her glossy lips. "We're telling the truth here."

"Okay, then." Eli reached out, brushed the wayward strand gently back. "I'm thinking that the flying pig must have been a sign. Or that I'm dreaming." He hooked a finger under her chin. "But mostly I'm thinking that there's room enough for two pirates on this bench." He leaned close, stopping when their lips were scant millimeters apart. "Are you on board with that?"

She smiled. "Aye, captain."

Eli chuckled low in his throat, then tipped his head to touch his lips to the corner of her mouth. Her arms moved around his back. He slid his hands toward the nape of her neck, burying his fingers in that silky mass of waves, holding her face gently between his palms. He brushed her warm skin with his thumbs. "You're so sweet, Lauren," he whispered, lips brushing hers very lightly. He moved away just enough to look into her eyes. "And this, right now, is more than worth a year of waiting."

"Yes." Lauren nodded, her beautiful lips parting.

Eli kissed her again, more thoroughly this time. Discovering, then confirming, that her lips were the source of those delicious berries after all.

"She mentioned my name?" Jessica stopped sifting sand through her fingers and stared at Fletcher in the salt-scented darkness. A slash of light from the Pleasure Pier midway above lit her hair like a tilted halo. "You're sure?"

"Darcee's mother told me." Fletcher watched Jessica hug her arms around herself. Finally feeling the chilly effects of playing cat and mouse with the rising tide, probably. She'd made good on her promise and thrown off her shoes, run barefoot through the foam. Loving every moment and taking Fletcher's breath away. "The medical staff was testing her pre-incident memory and she recalled your name."

"From the ER, probably." Jessica shifted on the sand beside him, her shoulder brushing his. "When I registered her."

"Could be."

The salty breeze carried a far-off hint of something grilled, spicy. Shrimp, maybe. Bubba Gump was up there — though it had closed two hours ago. As had the roller coaster, Ferris wheel, carousel, arcades, and every establishment that offered more than beer and pretzels. Fletcher's stomach rumbled. His luck to be a fool for a woman who made food a low priority. "But Darcee could be thinking of later that night," he added, "when you saw her upstairs in her room. That might be more likely, since you and she talked about her baby. Right?"

"Mmm . . . hmm." Her chin quivered.

"You're shivering, Jessica. Here. Take this." Fletcher pulled off his Sam Houston State jacket.

"No, I'm —"

"Don't argue. Or I'll throw you over my shoulder and haul you back to the car. Your jeans are soaked to the knees." He rested the jacket around her shoulders. She didn't look any older than the time she'd swiped his Little League jacket from the dugout.

"You're pushy," she grumbled.

"Comes with the badge." Fletcher checked the off-duty holster clipped to the waist of his pants before settling onto the sand beside her again. He glanced sideways, saw Jessica's chin snuggle below the collar of his jacket. "Better now?"

"I guess."

"Good."

Jessica was quiet for a while, her silence filled by the sounds of waves, gulls, and the occasional distant traffic on Galveston's Seawall Boulevard. A lonely mix.

"She was afraid they'd take her baby away," she said finally. The fabric of his jacket muffled her voice. "Because of her problem. That bipolar issue."

Bipolar disorder. The topic of his recent research. Fletcher said a silent prayer. "That had to be rugged. Not knowing what might happen with her daughter."

"Darcee said the worst thing about being crazy is being 'crazy.' " Jessica's hands rose from the baggy sleeves, fingers making air quotes. "Meaning that when you have a mental health issue, that's what you become

327

to people. *Crazy* is the sort of judgmental filter they see you through. Always. Before anything else. It's unfair." She sighed. "Darcee's an artist. A dancer, a painter. And a mother. She's a mother first, Fletcher. She hates that 'crazy' gets in the way of that."

There was no mistaking the emotion in Jessica's voice. Anger, empathy . . . fear?

"She had a medication bottle with her," Fletcher offered. "When I found her in the park. Medicine for bipolar disorder. She said she was on her way to get it refilled."

"The drugs make her feel sedated. Like she's looking at things through a fog. Almost like it feels when you're . . . really down, emotionally." Jessica hugged her knees. "It's like driving at night, and you can't see because there's this cloud pressing in. Dense and suffocating. Even when you turn on the defroster, open the windows, have your wipers on high speed. Even when you ram your nose toward the windshield and stare . . . you still can't see. Can't think. And then, finally, you don't really *care* anymore. I told Darcee I know how that feels."

Even in the dark, Fletcher saw tears glistening in her eyes. "I think," he ventured, "it was a blessing that Darcee had you there to listen."

"I don't know . . ." Jessica shook her head, blonde hair sifting like beach sand over the too-big shoulders of his college jacket. She swiped at her eyes. "I'm not sure I believe in blessings anymore, Fletcher. Lately, I'm not sure about much of anything."

He reached toward her without thinking, slipped an arm around her, and drew her closer to his side. "It's okay," he whispered. "I believe enough for both of us."

"I know that about you." Jessica sighed, resting her head on his shoulder.

Fletcher reminded himself to breathe.

"You know what else I don't get?" she asked, sounding exactly the way she had in grade school, when they'd lie on their backs on the Holts' fresh-mowed lawn and stare at the star-strewn summer sky.

"What don't you get?"

"That you don't give up on me. You've known me nearly forever — longer than almost everyone. I can be a royal pain. Even I see that. Maybe I do push people away. For whatever reason, eventually everyone gives up on me, Fletcher. Or wants to. Even my family, probably; I'm not kidding myself there. The fact is that I'm not even close to being a good person. But after all this time, *you're* still here. Why?"

Lord, help me now. . . . The breeze swept

strands of Jessica's hair across Fletcher's lips, fine as that spun glass on his grandmother's Christmas tree. He cleared his throat. Found the words.

"One of those things I believe is that in the truest sense . . . caring is unconditional." He'd almost said *love*. It was the right word, but Fletcher didn't trust himself with it. Not yet. "Meaning we can't earn that kind of caring, Jessica. Or be enough of a 'pain' to drive it away, either. It doesn't depend on us being good. It's bigger than that. A sort of undeserved gift, like —"

"A chocolate bar?"

He scrunched his brows. "Sure. But —"

"Sorry." Jessica's laugh warmed his cheek. "I only said that because I sensed one of your Jesus-loves-you moments brewing. C'mon, admit it, Fletcher."

He shook his head, smiled in the darkness. She'd nailed it. He'd been describing God's grace without realizing it. "Maybe."

"It's okay," Jessica assured, sliding her arm through his. She nestled, kitten-soft, against his shoulder again. "I love you anyway, neighbor."

"And I . . . will always be here."

27

"The hospital engineers are swarming." Lauren watched as the man exited the exam room, electronic notebook in hand. She double-checked the digital display on the medication pump and then glanced to where Vee knelt to take a urine sample from their patient's Foley bag. "That's the second time I've seen them in the department today."

"Getting things ready for that additional testing of the emergency generators tonight." Vee stood, tightened the cap on the specimen bottle with gloved hands. She set it on the metal table next to the woman dozing on the gurney, a middle-aged pancreatitis patient who'd found relief at last after several titrated doses of pain medication. "Cyril's doing the same thing at Mimaw's today." She stripped off her gloves. "We're on a much smaller scale, but no less determined to keep our folks safe. Those latest predictions say that storm could be on our doorsteps as early as tomorrow. Florine and I were glued to the TV until way late last night." She raised her brows. "I'll bet your mother's weather doo-dads were putting on quite the show."

"Absolutely . . . unbelievable."

In truth, Lauren hadn't even known there were changes in the storm status until she heard it at the hospital this morning. All four of the remaining weather vanes could have slid from the roof and landed on the front doorstep and she wouldn't have noticed. Not with Eli standing there kissing her one long, last time. He'd politely turned down her invitation to come in for coffee, saying he needed to go check on Drew. She had no doubt it was true. But Lauren got the feeling that Eli didn't want her to worry he might pressure her in any way . . . physically or otherwise. Maybe because of what he'd said about his relationship with Emma's mother. That it had moved too fast. She was glad Eli felt that way. His protective tenderness touched her far beyond what she'd felt in his arms.

Still, it was going to be a challenge to be physically near him and play it casual, cool. He'd be arriving at Houston Grace in less than half an hour. Thank goodness she'd be kept busy. For the first time ever, short staffing might be a blessing.

"I'm surprised," Lauren said, adjusting the pulse oximeter probe on her patient's finger, "that Gayle didn't show up for work today. Even if she promised to take a sick day, I half expected her to be here."

"Me too. It would be more like Gayle to get one of the docs to write her a script for an antinausea med. Keep on working." Vee sighed, an expression of discomfort on her face.

"What's wrong?"

"Only that . . ." Vee glanced toward the patient and stepped out of earshot regardless of the fact that the woman was snoring. Lauren followed her.

"Some of the staff are saying that Gayle went home yesterday because of that drug screening. So she wouldn't have to give a urine sample."

"Oh, please. She almost vomited on my shoes. Pretty hard to fake." Lauren thought of Jess's words yesterday: *"Someone ought to make sure Gayle gets a specimen cup."* "Who was saying that about the drug screening?"

"Some of the registration clerks."

"Yesterday?"

"I don't know." Vee frowned. "I heard it

333

this morning. When she didn't show up for work. I did my best to set them straight. Hospital staff should behave better. And Gayle certainly doesn't need that kind of talk. My heart breaks for that woman. She's had so much to bear. And yesterday was a double dose of ugly."

"The tow truck. I heard."

Vee nodded. "I told you what my auntie always said about storms. 'You're either in one, fixin' to go into one, comin' out the other side a one, or you're —' "

" '*Causin'* one,' " Lauren finished, thinking again of her talk with Jess. Her sister's speculation that Gayle sent her into Mrs. Humphries's room as a setup. Where was the truth in any of this turmoil?

She groaned. "If your auntie's right, we're gonna need a whole lot of backup generators."

That listening thing — the scope — wasn't as cold as usual on his chest. Florine rubbed it in both her hands first to warm it up. She was nice like that.

"One more deep breath, Mr. Drew."

He did his best, and she smiled at him like he'd kicked a soccer ball way down the field.

"I still don't like that cough. I'm keeping

an eye on it. I'm keeping my *other* eye on that rain." She pointed toward the window. "We've got a big storm coming. Cyril moved the chickens way up here near the house. Listen real hard tonight and you might hear them. They'll be grumbling in chicken talk." She shook her head and that big flower in her hair wiggled. "Those chickens didn't like having to move. I suspect you didn't like it much when you had to move all those times either. I understand that. I didn't like it when that big hurricane moved me out of New Orleans. But I'm glad I'm here now." She winked at him. "Otherwise I wouldn't know you, would I? There's a plan in all that, Mr. Drew. It's bigger than any kind of storm."

Florine reached toward his music pod on the table. "Let's get you set up here. You want your headphones?"

Drew shook his head no. He liked it better when she listened too.

"Let's see what we're listening to, then." The music started, and Florine's smile stretched bigger. " 'Revelation Song.' It's one of my favorites." She sang along.

Drew sang the words in his head; he knew them all even if he couldn't say them out loud. He felt the music too. Everywhere, even way down deep in his chest. It was warmer than that scope rubbed by Florine's hands. Because it was music about God. And this song talked about rainbows.

Florine pointed at Emma's drawing on the wall beside his bed. "Rainbows are God's beautiful promises after the storm. There's always going to be storms in this life. No good to grumble like a chicken. We need to hold on to that heavenly promise. All these places we move into and out of here on earth, none of them are really our home. Heaven's our only true home. I've got it on high authority that it's better than anything — even king cake." She winked at him again. "Now, how about we get that iPad out and send another note to that special brother of yours?"

"Yeah."

"Looks like we're having that coffee anyway. Without worries of your neighbors thinking you're inviting dubious men home while your parents are away." Eli smiled. "Far safer coffee."

"If you can even call this coffee. 'Safe' is a stretch." Lauren stirred powdered creamer into the Styrofoam cup. A hint of a blush said she was remembering that last kiss on her porch. He was too; if he didn't stop thinking about it, he'd never get any work done today.

"I think this stuff is actually eating my plastic spoon," Lauren added. An urgent care staffer walked by, and she took a nervous step back, widening the distance between them.

"Hey . . ." Eli connected with Lauren's gaze but stopped himself from reaching out. "It's okay. There's nothing unusual about coworkers talking over a cup of . . . toxic sludge. In fact, I've had several conversations with Vee, the triage nurse, and at least two engineers."

"I know. It's just . . ."

"I know."

As much as Eli wanted to reassure her, she was probably right. Hospital workers could sniff out a staff romance in less time than it took to jolt a fibrillating heart. "So it might be awkward if I walk over to the ER and tell the clinical coordinator I really need you in my department today."

"Extremely." Lauren chuckled. "Because *I'm* the coordinator today. Everyone's moved up a notch to fill in. Gayle stayed home sick."

"I didn't think she'd follow my advice."

"I didn't either." Lauren sighed. "Well, I need to get back to the ER. We're busy. And short-staffed. I hope you don't really need to borrow a nurse today."

"Only you," Eli admitted, pleased by Lauren's immediate smile. "No problem; we're fine in the clinic. But how about if we go get some real coffee after work? Emma's been drooling ever since I told her you had that chocolate-cherry scone at Ben's Beans. I promised I'd take her. We could come by and get you." He lowered his voice as the triage nurse passed them pushing a wheel-chair. "I have to pick her up from the Don-nellys'. So maybe around —"

"No. I mean, I don't know," Lauren said with an expression that made Eli's stomach sink. "I'm not sure tonight's good. It's Jess's day off. She might want us to do something together. And . . ."

"And she doesn't know we're seeing each other. Because you haven't told her."

"No." Lauren reached around the door-way, dumped her full coffee cup into his of-fice trash can — an obvious stall. When she faced him again, her expression looked anxious. "I'm not sure how Jess will react."

"And you won't know that until you tell her." He reminded himself, the way he had last night on the Barclay porch, that this relationship was too important to risk mess-ing up. "I know I'm going to have to work at changing your parents' opinion; I'll do my best with that. But I told you that Jessica and I have never been more than friends. It's not like you need her permission to —"

"You don't understand," Lauren insisted, cutting him off. "It's complicated with my sister."

He did understand. Far better than Lauren did — that was the problem. And there it was again, that blasted elephant. Wedging its bulk between them. He had a bad feeling that in the end this would all be about Jessica.

"She's having a rough time right now." Lauren swept her hand across her forehead, snagging a stray wisp of hair. Her beautiful blush was long gone. "She's been upset about some things. I'm not at liberty to say. But I know her, Eli. I know how sensitive she is. I have to be careful how I handle these things so I don't make it worse."

He hated that he'd just thought of that ill-tempered shih tzu. All the doggy-treat bribes and that chewed-up nursing magazine. Dancing around her sister's problems was chewing up Lauren's entire life. And breaking her heart. Eli wanted to sit her down, make her finally listen, finally accept the fact that Jessica's problems needed clinical intervention. But the truth was if he did that now, when this relationship was so new, it could mean losing Lauren. He had to wait until she trusted him more.

"Jess didn't come home after work last night," Lauren confided. "I tried to call her, but it kept going to voice mail. All sorts of awful things went through my mind. I'm sure you can imagine. Then after midnight I got a text from Fletcher. I guess she talked him into driving her to Galveston. She wanted to run the beach. With a major storm approaching. Of course, that's our Jess . . ." Lauren's voice broke. "Thank God for Fletcher Holt."

"You saw it," Fletcher told his rookie partner as he steered the patrol car into a U-turn. "Situation's changed." The computer update was more than clear; the call had taken a dangerous turn. "That domestic dispute turned out to be an ADW — the male was stabbed. Fire has first responders and an ambulance on scene. Sounds like our guys have it under control. But we're close enough. Might see what we can do to help out."

"Let's go."

In less than three minutes they joined two other PD units who were on scene, along with a Houston Fire engine and an ALS

340

ambulance — a light show of red, blue, and white strobes competing with the merciless afternoon sun.

"Looks like we'll be backing up the backup," Fletcher observed as he and his partner made their way up the driveway. He glanced at the gathered crowd being kept back by a trio of firefighters; most of the neighbors were young, several with children in their arms. All of them had that inevitable mix of horror and fascination on their faces. "Not exactly a block party."

"Not even close."

The residence was one of those too-big brick and Georgian column houses packed crayon-tight in one of the many neighborhoods that had grown like weeds in the pre-recession real estate boom. Most of them were rentals now. The lawn was brown as shredded-wheat cereal, and what few shade trees existed were still in nursery pots.

"Coming through!" a medic shouted, clearing the way for paramedics exiting onto the porch. There was an immediate buzz from the crowd of neighbors as a stretcher emerged from the open doorway: a middle-aged, burly man with close-shaved hair, face pale and sweaty under the breath-fogged oxygen mask. Blood leaked through the sheet partially covering his bare, equally pale chest. One of the paramedics held two IVs overhead as he hurried alongside.

"Butcher knife," an officer explained as Fletcher moved into the foyer. "Got a lung, medics say. I could've predicted that. Blood was bubbling like somebody salted a snail."

"You have the assailant in custody?" Fletcher's gaze moved toward officers at a doorway in the distance. A crime scene investigator passed by, laden with equipment. "The wife?"

"Yeah, we have her. There in the kitchen, not making a lot of sense. Burning up with fever. And ranting about tow trucks and Valentine's Day." The officer shook his head. "Beat up fairly bad herself and —"

"Need help in here!" an officer shouted, beckoning at the kitchen doorway.

Fletcher jogged into the kitchen, where he saw a single paramedic struggling to control the airway of a woman convulsing on the floor. Her wrists cuffed, body arched, and spine lifting away from the floor with the cruel spasms. Her eyes had rolled back, and pink froth escaped between her clenched teeth.

"Get one of the other medics in here!" Fletcher shouted to the officers as he dropped to his knees. He pulled safety gloves from his pocket, connected with the medic's gaze. "Tell me what to do."

"Help me turn her to her side." The paramedic yanked a portable suction canister from his rescue bag. "I'm going to need those cuffs off her wrists. But right now we need to keep her from choking, and — ah, there, seizure's over."

"I've got her. Go ahead." Fletcher steadied the woman's limp body as the medic slid the hissing suction catheter between her teeth. "That seizure . . . from drugs?"

"Could be several things. Drugs, fever, or a head injury. From the looks of those bruises, I'd say this battle went both ways. But I also get the feeling something else might be going on here." He pressed his fingers beneath her jaw, glanced at his watch.

"What's up?" Another medic hurried through the door as Fletcher was removing the woman's cuffs.

"Seizure. And . . . I'm not sure." The first medic's brows drew together. "Grab that oxygen. We'll need an IV, but let's get her on the monitor right away. This heart rate's so fast I can't even count it."

Fletcher slid the cuffs away, then stepped aside to give the medics room. He watched for a moment before taking a step closer again. Really studying the unconscious, battered, and blood-smeared woman for the first time. Tall, he'd guess, and painfully thin despite those shapeless gym sweats. Lank brown hair and big eyes, even half-closed. Something about her features nagged at him. Almost like he knew —

Fletcher's breath caught. "That's Gayle Garner, the emergency department manager at Houston Grace."

28

How can this be happening?

Lauren stepped close to the trauma room gurney, fighting an involuntary shudder. "I've cleared it for you in the clinic; your nurses will order any obviously necessary X-rays and labs." She watched as Eli lifted his patient's eyelid to test pupil response with his penlight. Gayle's eye. Their department manager, lying there semiconscious. And in police custody . . . for the attempted murder of her husband? It was impossible to grasp. "I made a general announcement to the waiting room," she continued. "Told them both you and the ER doc are tied up with an emergency and they should expect a delay in treatment until our on-call staff arrives. The triage nurse will advise us of anything that looks serious."

"Sounds good." Eli had stripped off the white coat long ago; there was a trace of perspiration at the neckline of his green scrubs. They'd all been running nonstop since the first Code 3 ambulance stretcher swept through the doors. "I appreciate your handling that."

He met Lauren's gaze, his expression saying he was as shaken as she was. All of Houston Grace was feeling it. Lauren didn't want to imagine the media frenzy their public information officer must be handling. She only hoped she could get a minute to warn Jess before it interrupted storm coverage on the local news.

The EKG technician peeled the electrode pads from Gayle's arms. Lauren caught a glimpse of the red marks on her wrists . . . from handcuffs.

A radiology tech pushed a portable X-ray machine through the far door, its wheels squeaking on the speckled vinyl tile floor. Chaplain services was paged overhead.

"I've ordered the initial tests," Eli continued, "and I can keep a lid on things until Mike has that chest tube in to stabilize the hemopneumothorax on . . ." He grimaced slightly. "On Mr. Garner."

A hemorrhaging lung collapse, possibly a dangerous nick to the sac around his heart . . . *because Gayle shoved a butcher knife into his chest.* Lauren pushed down a wave of nausea. What on earth led up to this tragedy?

"Her heart rate's still hovering close to 170," Lauren noted. "Isn't that unusual, even taking into account her fever?" Gayle had been given a Tylenol suppository and was lying on a cooling blanket. "Of course 104.8 is a high temp for an adult, but —"

"She's dehydrated." Eli pinched up the skin on Gayle's forearm above the site of one of her two normal saline IVs; the skin remained tented, a further sign that she was far too dry. "We saw some of that yesterday, when she nearly fainted after vomiting in your triage office. But I think it's more than can be explained away by a stomach flu." He glanced toward the cardiac monitor as an alarm sounded. Her heart rate had increased to 180 beats per minute. "Her pressure's too high for this to be only dehydration." He walked a few steps to the head of the gurney and gently grasped Gayle's neck between his fingers. Her eyelids fluttered with her barely audible moan. "She said her doc's been following her thyroid. But . . ."

Lauren's breath snagged; in her entire nursing career, she'd never seen a case of — "Thyrotoxicosis? Thyroid storm? Is that what you think?"

"It fits. The enlarged gland. Hyperactive

reflexes. That protrusion of her eyes —
we've seen it so long I expect we all thought
that was just part of her features. But I have
to consider Gayle's dramatic weight loss and
the recent shakiness she kept blaming on
coffee, lack of sleep, and all those extra
shifts. She's been working herself to death
because of her financial situation." Eli
sighed. "We were all too close to notice the
progression of symptoms. But when you
add staff complaints about Gayle's irritability, yesterday's episodes of vomiting and
diarrhea, the fever, and the seizure tonight . . . yes, I think we need to seriously
consider a diagnosis of thyroid storm. I
already ran it by Mike. He agrees."

"Gayle said she has medication for her
thyroid condition."

"Has it prescribed and took it in the past.
But taking it now? I'd guess not. She's not
coherent enough yet to give us reliable
information." Eli glanced at the monitor:
steady, regular, but rapid at 148 beats per
minute. "She's been under a lot of stress.
That's a trigger in itself. And if she stopped
her medication abruptly . . ."

"It could throw her into thyroid storm."
Lauren scraped her teeth across her lower
lip. It was rare and a true medical emergency. One that could lead to heart attack,

stroke, pulmonary edema . . . *death.*

"One of the internists is on his way down from the ICU. He's already put in a call to endocrine. If this is a storm, they won't wait for blood tests to come back. Or for a Doppler ultrasound. No time. She'll need aggressive multidrug treatment: thioamides, iodide, beta-blockers, glucocorticoids." Eli frowned as he caught a glimpse of the uniformed officer outside the trauma room door. "Our friend's in deep trouble, Lauren — on all counts."

"She *what*?" Jessica's mouth sagged open. She set Hannah's brush on the couch, stared at him. "You can't be serious, Fletcher."

"I wish I wasn't. And at this point it's still an alleged stabbing. But I wanted to swing by and tell you before you saw it on the news."

"Oh . . . right." Jessica glanced toward the darkened TV.

No TV or music on. Still in her pajamas at nearly 5 p.m. Fletcher knew it was a bad sign. Especially in the wake of Jessica's tearful episode last night. She'd closed the shutters and was sitting in near darkness with her dog on her lap — considering Hannah's tendencies, riskier than running on a storm-path beach at midnight.

"Her husband claims she attacked him with a knife," Fletcher continued. "From a set he gave her for Valentine's Day — Gayle must have said that a dozen times. It was one of the few clear things she was able to convey. They say she was pretty incoherent, even before the seizure."

"I don't get it." Jessica played with the sleeping dog's ear. "Was she drunk?"

"Don't know. Fever could account for some of the confusion, but I'm sure she'll be drug tested."

"You think drugs made Gayle turn violent? And caused her seizure?"

"No idea." Fletcher raised his hands. "I'm not even close to being a medical expert. You know that."

Jessica was quiet for a moment. She shook her head, the sleep-tossed tumble of hair brushing the shoulders of her cotton pajamas. "What I know, Fletcher, is that Gayle Garner's been acting like aliens hijacked her brain. I don't mean that as a joke. It's really sad. Everybody's been worried. I'm sorry all of this is happening to her now. But . . ." She picked up the dog brush and sighed. "Drugs might explain it."

"Th-thank . . . you." Gayle's tongue moved

across her lower lip, seeking moisture left by the sponge swab. One of her eyes had narrowed to a bruised and swollen slit; the other was struggling to focus on Lauren. "So . . . thirsty."

"I wish I could give you some water, Gayle. But it will have to wait. Maybe after they move you to the ICU." Lauren glanced at the IV bags, a much-needed fluid load. Thankfully there was no evidence of pulmonary compromise. "Your temperature's below 103 now. And the propranolol has brought your heart rate far closer to normal — thank heaven that run of a-fib didn't last."

"Mmm." Gayle reached up with a shaky hand to touch the oxygen cannula in her nostrils. There was still some dried blood on the side of her hand. After they'd collected evidence, the forensic team had given the okay to clean her up; Vee missed a spot. It could be Leo Garner's blood or maybe even Gayle's from the small finger lacerations she'd apparently sustained during that unimaginable scene in her kitchen.

Guilt prodded again. Lauren worked with this dedicated, caring woman almost every day. How could she have missed how sick she was?

"I'll check with Eli, see if we can give you

a few ice chips or —"

"Leo needed the pills," Gayle whispered suddenly, reaching out to grip Lauren's arm. "I shouldn't have lied. Shouldn't have . . . done it." Tears welled. One slid down her cheek, disappeared under the oxygen tubing. "Please . . . pray for me."

"Thanks for helping me out over here." Eli handed Vee a cup of coffee, the aroma of French roast wafting. "It's fresh. Made it myself. Lauren said the old batch melted her spoon." It seemed impossible that moment was only a few hours ago. What a nightmare of a day.

"I'm glad things finally settled down for her in the ER. Getting Gayle moved up to the ICU helped." Vee's sigh parted the steam from her coffee. "It's so hard to see Gayle like that, to take it all in. Have you heard any word about her husband's condition?"

Eli saw a tech pushing the ortho cart past them toward the ER. "Mr. Garner's in the recovery room. No damage to the vessels or pericardium. The knife was probably deflected by a rib." The gritty reality struck him again; he'd heard the officers describe the Garners' blood-spattered kitchen. "His vital signs stabilized after the second unit of blood. And the most recent X-ray shows the chest tube is doing its job."

"Good to hear." Vee took a sip of her coffee, then was quiet for a while. "Gayle looks like she's been beaten."

"Looked like that to me, too." Eli heard it was Gayle who'd placed the call to 911. Reporting domestic abuse. The stabbing likely happened afterward. Gayle's secondary exam showed she'd sustained a wrist fracture. It all fit.

"We can't really know the pain in other folks' lives. In their hearts and souls. Sometimes that troubled water's so deep all you see is the pieces of wreckage that float up top." Vee shook her head. "Families — not easy. Ever."

"I won't argue that." Eli met her gaze. "I'm sorry mine's been such a pain in the rear for yours at Mimaw's. It sounds like my father made a scene."

"We've seen worse. Having a family member in a care home is hard. I expect your father's doing what he thinks is right to protect his son. And you're doing your best for the brother you love." Her expression was far too wise for her tender age. "I try not to judge the debris floating on top."

Troubled waters. Eli thought of his conversation with Lauren. About Jessica.

A blonde woman wearing a light-blue blazer walked briskly by, casting a warm smile at Vee as she passed.

"Our on-call chaplain." Vee watched as the woman continued down the hallway toward the ER. "Angela. Have you met her?"

"I saw her outside the trauma room." He decided Vee didn't need to know that he didn't customarily make time to converse with chaplains. But then, sharp as this tech was, she'd probably already guessed that.

"She's a licensed family therapist; the hospital work is something new for her." Vee smiled. "Got to love a small world — Angela goes to the same church as the Barclays. She was hoping to get a chance to talk with Lauren once things settled down."

29

"Even though we've seen each other at church, I didn't know you were a family counselor until . . ." Lauren hesitated. She'd come to the chapel to offer that promised prayer for Gayle. Not to talk about . . . "My sister mentioned it to me."

"Jessica." Angela nodded, a spiky thatch of her short hair bobbing over her brows like a quail's plume. "I know your sister's name, but I don't think I've seen her at church yet. I'm relatively new there."

And completely gracious. Jess hadn't attended services in nearly a year.

"Fletcher mentioned Jessica to me." Angela held out a container of oatmeal raisin cookies. Grace and baked goods — the woman was firing on all cylinders. "He's been concerned about her and thought it might be a good idea if we met, talked."

Lauren decided taking a cookie wasn't a family betrayal. "I'll be honest with you,

Angela. She's not willing to do that. Not even close. Jess was fairly incensed that Fletcher talked with you at all."

"I promise you, he didn't reveal anything personal. Only that she was a member of the church and he wanted to help her."

"That sounds like Fletcher."

Lauren glanced across the small chapel toward its nondenominational altar. A chrome-and-glass podium on a raised, carpet-covered platform. No cross, no displayed Bible. The only adornment was a large piece of artwork hanging on the wall behind the platform. A painstakingly hand-crafted mosaic, donated some forty years ago by a patient who was a commercial fisherman. Recessed lighting in the chapel ceiling set off the man's handiwork, caught the jewel-bright colors of the glass: red, gold, green, purple . . . and so many shades of blue. He'd captured the ever-changing shades of the ocean — and its turbulent waves — so perfectly. A fragile boat, the men's fearful faces . . . that breathtaking moment before a miracle saved them. Jesus calming the storm.

"Fletcher is the best kind of friend," Lauren continued, turning her gaze back to the chaplain. "But Jess isn't willing to consider any kind of counseling. And my mother would be mortified if neighbors, friends, people at church thought someone in our family was under treatment for mental problems. I realize in today's world that probably sounds archaic, but . . ." Lauren looked at her lap, brushed at some crumbs.

Angela handed her a napkin, the discreet movement accompanied by a dip of her quail thatch. "I assure you I haven't said anything to anyone, Lauren. I'd never do that."

"You should know that to my mother . . . to both my parents," Lauren continued, needing to make this chaplain understand, "it would be like admitting they failed, made some awful mistake that harmed their child. Or that their faith isn't strong enough. It would be saying they don't trust God's ability to handle problems."

Angela's gentle silence was more encouraging than words. Lauren couldn't seem to stop.

"You need to understand that it feels like pointing Jess toward those things — psychotherapy, especially medications — would be giving up on her, telling her she's flawed. It feels like . . . giving up hope." Lauren swallowed against an embarrassing threat of tears. "For my parents, I mean. Maybe Fletcher doesn't get that. Maybe you don't.

But that's how it is. For them."

"I do get it, Lauren. It's not only your family who feels that way. I hear it almost every day in my practice. And I believe with all my heart that those concerns spring from love. A sincere desire to protect. Love is powerful medicine. As a believer, it helps me to remember God also created the human brain. Amazing medical advances have come from that gift and continue to come every day. Some of those advances include targeted medications. I'm sure you agree we've made great strides in the treatment of cancer, cardiac conditions, diabetes . . ."

Lauren nodded. Of course that was true. Still . . .

"Would you feel comfortable telling a diabetic patient that medications shouldn't be considered?" Angela glanced toward the hallway leading back to the ER. "Did you 'give up' on your nurse manager when you started therapies to combat her life-threatening thyroid condition?"

"Of course not." Lauren saw where this was headed. She wished she'd never come into the chapel; she could have prayed for Gayle in the Beetle on the way home. Though Angela sincerely denied it, she was as bent on painful intrusion into Jess's life as Eli was. "Those are all *medical* conditions."

"From chemical imbalances. Which are sometimes at the root of mental health issues. A reason I always encourage people to begin any evaluation process with a thorough medical workup."

"Ah." Lauren sighed, reached for her phone. "Which reminds me: I should get back to the ER. I'm in charge today."

"Of course. I didn't mean to keep you. Or intrude. Honestly. But when Fletcher and I talked today —"

"Fletcher called you?" Lauren's chest tightened. *After being with Jess last night.*

Angela smiled. "I called him. I'm trying to con him into fostering one of my rescue dogs. I told him I was coming here today. And promised to touch base with you if I could. Now I did."

"You did." Lauren dredged up a return smile. "I'm sorry, Angela. I hope I don't seem ungrateful for your concern. Or Fletcher's. My sister did have some problems. But she's doing better. I'm keeping an eye on things."

"I'm sure you are." Angela handed Lauren the box of cookies. Her business card was lying on top. "Do me a favor and take the rest of this batch to the ER team.

They've more than earned them today." She rolled her eyes. "I'd have to jog too many extra miles if they came home with me. Easier to apply them directly to my thighs."

Lauren laughed. "I hear you."

Angela extended her hand. "A pleasure, Lauren. Fletcher was right: I *do* like you."

"Ditto." Lauren clasped the chaplain's hand. "Well, I'm back to the trenches. Another hour and I get to climb into my little car and go home."

"Sounds good. Be careful — and stay dry," Angela added. "From everything I'm hearing on the news, we're in for some really rough weather."

"Well . . ." Lauren raised her voice over the drumming of rain on the hospital porch overhang. She pointed to the blue tent a few yards away in the parking lot, a newly erected structure covering a mound of neatly stacked sandbags. "Looks like the building maintenance team has joined the engineers. A duet of doom."

Vee nodded. "These storms have been teasing us for weeks, but Glorietta's looking mighty serious. They're predicting she could be a cat-1 sometime tonight."

The breeze wasn't even close to cool, but somehow Lauren felt chilled. Vee was right.

They had been teased by storms — too many lately, on all levels. The last time Lauren stood out here in the rain was the day she'd been so worried about Jess being late to work. She'd confronted Eli in the urgent care . . . where Fletcher had brought Darcee Grafton after he found her in that reflecting pool.

"Gayle doesn't have any local family. Except for her husband." Vee tugged on a braid, frowning. "It's a time when she should be able to count on her friends. I hate to think this tragedy might fuel more whispers about those missing drugs. I can hear it now: 'Poor thing. Her thyroid made her do it.' "

"Let's hope not." Lauren felt a nudge of discomfort, recalling Gayle's words in the trauma room. Something about pills and then *"I shouldn't have done it."* Gayle had been feverish still, somewhat confused. It probably meant nothing.

"I wouldn't say anything to anyone," Vee continued, "but between you and me, I was very relieved to see that her drug screen was negative. Gayle is in a world of hurt right now; she doesn't need that added to her plate."

"No." Lauren's shoulders rose and fell with a sigh. "In the trauma room, when we were alone, Gayle asked me to pray for her. She never once came to any of my chapel meetings. We never talked about faith." She shook her head. "She must have been so desperate, frightened . . . or felt completely threatened to do something that violent."

"Yes." Vee was quiet for a long moment, that familiar faraway look in her eyes. Insistent rain and the distant wail of a siren filled the silence. "In that emergency shelter in New Orleans, there was a lot of praying going on," she said finally. "I expect for a lot of those folks it might've been the first time. No lights, hot as hell itself . . . stink like you couldn't believe. The fear in the air smelled a lot worse. There was plenty to be afraid of." Vee drew a halting breath. "That storm wasn't close to the scariest part."

Lauren stayed silent. It was the first time Vee had shared details about what she'd endured when she was only twelve.

"The Viettes are a prayin' family — always have been, always will be. Nothing will change that. And those nights, when I was in that shelter with my cousin Florine, I think I prayed nonstop. Prayed I'd see my mother again. Prayed I still had a house and that my little dog Bebo had figured out how to climb onto the roof and hang on. I even prayed I could cross my legs tight enough not to have to use those filthy bathrooms in the dark." Her braids swirled with the shake of her head. "I asked the Lord to keep the crazy man sleeping next to us from firing that gun he had under his pillow. Even a kid like me knew he was tellin' everybody about it over and over — as many times as I prayed to God — because he was as scared as we were."

Lauren moved closer, wanting to say something to ease the memory but knowing there were no such words.

"It was on the third night, I think, that I learned there was something a lot worse than the nasty, fly-infested bathrooms — and having a crazy man with a gun huddled close enough that I could smell his armpits," Vee continued. "Something worse than never seeing my house again. Or even finding out my dog drowned." She swallowed. "Florine told me to stay on our cots when she went to the bathroom. The crazy man was snoring, so I said okay. But she was gone too long. I think maybe . . . I heard her screams."

Lauren's stomach twisted.

"When she came back, she said she was okay, not to worry. Told me to go to sleep. I couldn't. I heard her crying."

"Vee . . ." Lauren reached out, touched

her hand.

"I prayed harder than I'd ever prayed in my life," Vee continued, grasping Lauren's fingers. "I begged God to help us. I asked him to keep us safe — to stop that awful thing from ever happening again." She drew a slow breath. "It wasn't two hours later that the man came to us. Grabbed hold of Florine's hair, dragged her onto her knees."

"Oh, Vee, no . . ."

"I don't know how it happened, but the gun was in my hands." A tear slid down Vee's face, but she didn't flinch. "I'd never touched a gun before. But I fired it that night. I killed that man so he couldn't hurt my cousin. Then some of the other people . . . they just dragged him off somewhere. Everybody said they didn't know anything about what happened. But I knew. I still know . . ."

Lauren stretched out her arms and her friend filled the space.

"I don't know what happened with Gayle." Vee's breath warmed Lauren's ear. "But I can tell you this: I will never judge anyone. I can't. I still believe, with all my heart, that God is my strength . . . my only true shelter. And my hope, always. I will pray to him for the rest of my life. And I'll always wonder if I did the right thing that awful night." She leaned back, holding Lauren's hands, the expression on her face impossibly serene despite her tears. "Sometimes you have to take action — step up. I don't pretend to know everything, but in my heart I do know that much."

He had to catch her. *Please don't be gone.*

Eli jogged into the storm-darkened parking lot, wind in his face and rain splashing his hair and scrubs. He squinted, searched . . . There, the green VW. And a glimpse of Lauren's face between rapid swipes of wiper blades. He picked up speed, hit a puddle that drenched his pant leg.

"Lauren, hey." Eli bent low and rapped his knuckles against the fogged driver's window, rain sluicing from his hairline to his nose. The window slid down. "Caught you. Oh, sorry," he apologized, seeing the phone in her hand. "I'm interrupting."

"No," she said, beginning to smile. "I'm finished. But you're washing away. Get in."

"Definitely better," Eli admitted, settling into the bucket seat beside her. He had to be imagining that her car smelled of berries too. Music blended with the *scrunch-scrape* of the windshield wipers — a song he recognized from Emma's Christian collection. That one about blessings coming from

365

raindrops. He stared at Lauren, trying to remember what he'd come out here to say.

"Aren't you working for another hour?" she asked.

"My relief came in early. I still have to finish up some records, but . . ." Eli reached for her hand. "I don't like how we left things this morning. I wanted to say I'm not going to tell you how to handle things with your folks or Jessica . . . regarding us. I don't want seeing me to feel like some kind of added conflict. I think we've both had enough of that — still do."

Lauren nodded. Her fingers moved against his.

"Which reminds me . . ." Eli unclipped his phone from the waist of his scrubs. "Look what I found in my messages." He scrolled, then opened the text for her to see.

My music makes me smile.

"Drew. And . . . Florine." Lauren's eyes shimmered with tears. "Oh, Eli . . ."

"Hey . . ." He set the phone down, cradled her cheek in his palm. "What's wrong?"

"It's just been such an awful day. So hard."

"I agree. Gayle, her husband, the media. All of that." He traced his thumb across her tear-dampened cheek. "The only good thing for me — the only reason to smile — was you. It's sort of like you're my music." Eli grimaced. "I can't believe I said something like that. I sound like Andrew Lloyd Webber. Your fault. See what you do to me?"

"Yes." Lauren pressed a hand to her mouth, failing to hold back a giggle. "But don't stop. Please."

He smiled. Well worth making a fool of himself to see her tears gone. "I thought maybe tomorrow night I could take you out to dinner. If this storm hasn't shut things down. I want to do it right this time. Skip the hospital coffee, pirate gear, and flying pigs." He raised her hand, kissed her fingertips, and swore he saw the windshield's raindrops reflected in the blue of her eyes. "I want to spend more time with you, Lauren. I know you need to be home for your sister tonight, but —"

"I don't. Jess agreed to come in and work the night shift. Overtime pay and tomorrow off. I'd just talked to her when you walked up. She's going to try to get some sleep before coming to the hospital. Told me not to wake her up." Lauren rolled her eyes. "With her usual tact."

"So . . ." Eli's mind ticked in time with the wipers. "That means . . ."

"I'm free for dinner. I'd have to run home,

367

get out of these scrubs. Shower. I know you have Emma, so I'm game for whatever she wants. Really. Maybe Jus' Mac or Amazón Grill or even Chuck E. —"

"My house. I'll cook." Eli shook his head. "Don't get your hopes up. I can't even come close to competing with Rainbow Lodge." Lauren's brow arched, and he made a mental note that Houston's most romantic restaurant would be their official first date. "But at least we won't have to shout over shrieks from the toddler zone and sing with a giant mouse. Although I did promise Emma we'd watch *Annie* so she could practice."

Lauren's immediate grin warmed his heart. "I'll bring the popcorn."

30

"You had me at the candles," Lauren said, glancing around the cozy, contemporary family-room-and-dining combination. Several of the flames still flickered — on the breakfast bar, table, and faux mantel — in a sort of casually romantic single-father LEGOLAND ambience. They cast a golden glow against a teal-and-gray color scheme that harmonized with the Berber and Corian practicality of the space. Pumpkin orange in the couch pillows and in a few pieces of nondescript wall art were the only warm match for the flames. He'd said they'd moved in last summer; this wasn't the same house Lauren had visited after Jess ran away. She was glad — and she liked the feel of this place. Overall the look was comfortable and probably light-years from what Eli had grown up with at the Landry estate. Lauren suspected he'd consulted a decorator, but minimally — told her to do what she thought was best as long as it was kid-proof, dog-friendly, and incorporated as many of Emma's artful offerings as possible. The framed Thanksgiving turkey handprint in the kitchen proved it.

Everything pointed to the fact that this man's priority was his daughter. Eli had admitted he was protective of her when it came to relationships. And had shared very little about her with Jess. But even that was more than Lauren had shared with her sister about her new relationship with Eli. The prickle of anxiety came back. Eli didn't understand that Lauren had to be careful when it came to Jess. Do everything possible to keep her from going off the deep end again. The littlest thing could set her off. Their parents counted on Lauren to keep that from happening. She pushed aside a new, intruding memory of her conversation with the chaplain and thought instead of what Eli had said in the hospital parking lot this afternoon. That in all the troubling chaos, Lauren was his "music." Right now, she needed to hang on to that.

"The candles are a very nice touch," she told him sincerely.

"And practical. They're from our disaster kit. Emma said ladies *must* have candles." Eli smiled. "She's the only reason we had cloth dinner napkins. With rings — Emma made them for me last Christmas. Those were holly leaves with berries, in case you couldn't tell. Summer holly tonight. She said you'd be fine with that." There was pride in his voice.

"I am fine with it. And she's very thoughtful."

"Yes." Eli lifted the curly red costume wig from where it lay between them on the microsuede couch. "For a wannabe stage star who fell asleep before her big solo."

"She tried, but . . ." Lauren's skin warmed as Eli slid closer. "All that hokey pokey and backward skating with Parrish probably wore her out."

Eli had carried his pajama-clad, sleepy daughter — half-giggling, half-yawning — over his shoulder fireman-style down the hall to her bedroom. Lauren watched their tucking-in ritual from the doorway, an ache rising as his deep voice blended with Emma's sweet lilt in the Lord's Prayer. It was followed by Emma's earnest prayers for her father, Lauren, her grandparents, Uncle Drew, her mother in heaven, her best friend forever Parrish, and Shrek.

As if on cue, the big dog had given a deep, warbling sigh and fallen immediately asleep, his head resting on Emma's Little Mermaid backpack. It would be hopelessly soggy by morning.

"Thank you." Eli rubbed his knuckles very gently along Lauren's cheek. His dark eyes held hers, lids drooping slightly in the exact same way as his daughter's and brother's. Not film-star sexy, Lauren reminded herself, but Landry genes. Simple genetics that were creating complicated havoc with her pulse. Those eyes and the way his skin smelled clean and enticing too, like soap and a whiff of fresh basil.

"You were a good sport tonight," Eli told her. "I usually add some wine to that sauce if I'm cooking for adults. And I always drain the spaghetti before it's as rubbery as a tourniquet. Emma knows better than to roll a meatball under the table. I have no excuse for Shrek. Except that if I were an arthritic, blind, diabetic hound, I'd probably con a little girl into food bowling too."

Lauren laughed, grateful for a distraction from her runaway senses. "You're giving me a flashback to *Lady and the Tramp.*"

"That's me: Mr. Romance." Eli's frown wrinkled the edges of his beautiful eyes. "I wasn't kidding when I told you I've put dating on hold. I'd say I was out of practice, but I think it's more honest to say I never practiced this at all."

"You did fine. I'm touched and honored you'd share your home and your daughter with me." She gave up on stifling her foolish heartbeat. Rain drummed on the roof, blending with soft, bass-heavy jazz from speakers . . . somewhere. "Adding wine to the pasta couldn't make this more wonderful."

"You deserve more," Eli whispered, leaning close enough that Lauren could feel the warmth of his skin. "I'm going to find a way to make that hap —"

A cell phone buzzed; both of them reached for their own.

"Mine," Eli said, an apology in his expression. "I'd let it go except it's Mimaw's."

"Take it."

He stood, walked toward the kitchen, listening. Asked questions, his voice low.

Lauren glanced toward the mantel, noticing that a candle flame had burned low enough to be barely visible. Next to it was a small collection of photos, mostly of Emma. One of the frames held that old shot of Eli and his brother, the same one Drew had beside his bed at the care home. Boys with fishing poles. A carefree summer so long ago.

Lauren peeked at her own phone, knowing it could easily have been a call from Jess that interrupted them. Which she couldn't have ignored either. She sighed as it occurred to her that the hopeful music between Eli and her might forever be drowned by a collective melody of insistent ringtones.

"By way of apology," Eli offered, setting a plate of brownies on the coffee table next to the steaming mugs. "Don't worry; I didn't bake those. Dessert Gallery — thawed."

Lauren smiled. "I wasn't worried. And you don't need to apologize for the call. Is Drew okay?"

"A slight fever. Not even 100. But the cough is hanging on. Vee wanted me to know, even though —" He made himself stop; he'd wanted this evening to be free of family conflict.

"Even though what?"

"My father wants to be called first." Eli glanced toward the hallway. He'd closed the door to Emma's room but lowered his voice anyway. "Actually, he doesn't want me called at all — definitely doesn't want me to offer opinions about Drew's care or make any decisions if he gets really sick again. He thinks . . ." The words slid out before Eli could squelch them. "He told my mother I'd be capable of holding a pillow over my brother's face. Emma overheard it."

"Oh, Eli . . . *no.*"

"I think I cleared that up, short of telling her I suspect alcohol has a lot to do with her grandfather's rants. Another reason I want to be part of the decision-making process. Or at least see medical power of attorney shifted to my mother." Eli dragged his fingers along his jaw. "Try to figure out a diplomatic and low-profile way to suggest a federal judge may not be competent to make decisions." He met her gaze. "I'm sure I don't have to say that was for your ears only. And I don't blame you if you want to shove that brownie in your purse and make a run for the door."

"I'm not running. Of course I'll protect your privacy, Eli." Lauren rested her hand on his arm. "I know how it feels to be caught in the middle. Trying to respect parents' wishes, worried for your sibling, praying . . . not sure if you're doing the right thing."

"You're giving me too much credit, Lauren. I don't think I have respect for my father anymore." Saying it aloud made Eli's gut twist. "And God doesn't want to hear from me. But I'm dead sure that I'm doing the right thing for my brother." He shook his head. "It's ironic. You can't turn on the TV or radio without hearing that disaster slogan: 'Get a kit. Make a plan. Be informed.' We don't question it. We stock up on batteries and candles. But an advance medical directive that offers mercy and dignity and peace? That's too much planning, too uncomfortable to talk about. It smacks against almighty hope."

"You'll never get me to agree that God doesn't want to hear from you," Lauren told him. "I think this is exactly when he wants to. And hope is what keeps me going. The only thing lately. I need to believe that if I put things in God's hands — trust enough — it will all be okay." Her brows pinched. "I understand that for some people it feels impossible not to step in and act. Grab trouble by the throat. You're that kind of person, Eli." Her expression softened, warmth flooding into her blue eyes. "I see how much you love your brother. I know everything you're doing is because of that. I think he's blessed to have you."

"Thank you." Eli managed a short laugh. "I also got a text after that call from Vee. One of the other Houston Grace PAs, letting me know I probably wasn't going to be busted for drugs."

"Drugs?"

"That issue with the ER patient and her missing meds. Apparently the word's leaked out that no one tested positive." Eli pretended he didn't see the look of relief on her face. Jessica had been tested too.

"I wasn't worried." Lauren's chin lifted in a way he'd seen dozens of times. "Jess told me they wouldn't find anything — not even cupcake frosting. I believed her."

Eli took a slow breath. "I want to say something about that other time. Last fall, when your sister did test positive."

"What about it?" Wariness came into Lauren's eyes, making Eli wish he hadn't brought it up. But she was right; he tended to take trouble by the throat.

"I did know Jessica had a legitimate prescription for Vicodin. She told me it was for an ankle sprain she got hiking Big Bend the summer before. She also told me she'd had trouble with the ankle off and on since." He paused, making sure Lauren understood. "But the fact is, we went for a run that morning before work, the same day as the drug test. Five miles — you Barclays have gazelle blood." His brief smile faded. "Jessica wasn't having any problems with her ankle that morning. Wasn't limping when she came to work a few hours later."

"What are you saying?"

"Only that I couldn't go on record vouching that she needed medication for an ankle injury. Even if she was a friend — maybe *because* she was." He saw Lauren's brows lift. "I'm not saying your sister took that Vicodin for any other reason. I don't know that. I'm only telling you what I saw. And that I couldn't be part of the problem, condone it, if there was one. With *any* friend. Despite what you and your parents think, I didn't refuse to help Jessica because I'm some kind of insensitive jerk."

Lauren's lips curved in a trace of a smile.

"Does that smile mean you forgive me?"

"Only if you stop there."

"Deal." At some point he'd say more. Now wasn't the time.

"Good. I can't listen to another concerned opinion about my sister today. I'm going to drink this coffee and eat enough brownies to test positive for chocolate." She sighed. "Gayle's thyroid problem . . . Could it have caused skewed thinking and erratic behavior before tonight? Make her say and do things she wouldn't ordinarily? Like in her capacity as ER manager?"

"Possibly." Eli lifted his coffee, blew on its surface. "But I think the progression was slow enough that people around her accepted it, blamed it on all those extra hours she was working. I know I did. I thought Gayle seemed jumpy, a little scattered. I figured all that, including her weight loss, was from stress."

"Vee and I were going to fix it all by taking her out for lunch and a pedicure. I believed Gayle last week when she said those bruises on her face were from a minor car accident. Her husband was probably abusing her then and I didn't see it. I feel awful about that."

"I do too. I wish we'd talked Gayle into an exam yesterday. We could have stopped all of this from happening. My best guess is that she defended herself from a beating. Probably more violently than she intended because the fever and thyroid condition impaired her thinking. It may end up being her legal defense."

"She asked me to pray for her."

Eli set his coffee down. "I'd say she chose exactly the right person."

He watched as Lauren lifted the brownie at last and took a bite. Her expression said he'd made a good choice as well.

"Mmm. This is heaven," she murmured. She set it down, reaching for her napkin. "Truly perfect."

"I'm glad." He reached out to trace a fingertip along one of the loose, wavy strands framing her face. "I'm afraid my good intentions didn't pan out, even after the meatball bowling. I didn't want family issues or medical shoptalk to be part of our evening. Then I talked your ear off on both counts." Eli swept her hair back, touched her ear. "No, it's still there. And completely beautiful."

Her smile encouraged him.

"I should have said less about all those other things," Eli continued, "and a lot more about how special I think you are."

"You said I was the music in your day." Lauren's eyes met his. "No one has ever told me anything as wonderful. In my whole life."

Eli took her face in both of his hands. "Well then, be prepared. I have a plan to do that sort of thing a lot more. Starting right now . . ."

He bent low, watched her eyes flutter to a close, and kissed her lips very lightly. Then he kissed her forehead, her cheek, her eyelid, and the tip of her nose — before claiming her mouth a second time, tasting berries and chocolate.

Lauren wrapped her arms around his neck, her fingers in his hair as their kiss deepened and —

The brash ringtone made them both pull back, breathless.

"What *is* that?" Lauren asked, staring at

his phone on the table next to the brownies.

"Emergency alert," Eli groaned, hating technology like never before. "My weather app." He snatched the phone from the table. Jabbed the text, frowned as he read.

"What?" she asked, trying to see.

"Glorietta's been upgraded to a category-1 hurricane. And she's headed this way."

31

"Parrish said not to worry; she didn't invite Glorietta to her birthday party."

"Well then . . ." Eli smiled, watching his daughter add yet another rainbow sticker to her homemade card. She'd stuck an entire sheet of them on Shrek's collar. "I'm certainly relieved to hear that."

"They're planning all inside games because of the rain. Maybe even a treasure hunt." Emma's dark eyes met his. "If things get real bad, the Donnellys are going to the San Antonio grandma's. You know, in case their house gets lifted up and dropped down in Oz."

"Hey . . ." Eli set his coffee down. "We're fine, Em. No one's going to Oz. Parrish's parents are just making a plan. That's smart. Our house is a lot newer than the Donnellys', and we're not in the floodplain."

"So we stay here, even if it gets bad?"

"It won't. I'm watching the reports. And I

don't think we'll need to, but we can always go stay in River Oaks."

"With Yonner and Grams?"

"Yes." He forced a smile. His mother had called last night after Lauren left. Her sister and husband had boarded up their Gulf Shore home and were expected at the house soon. Eli finally promised if there was any doubt of safety, he and Emma would come to stay there as well. His mother didn't mention what the judge thought of that idea. Fortunately it was a very big house. "I don't think it's going to be necessary. And right now you're going to a birthday —"

"Shrek and me."

"Shrek and I."

"Oh, Daddy . . ." Emma rolled her eyes. "You're not invited. Girls only."

He laughed, touched the tip of her nose. "Right. I'll be at a hospital meeting. And then I'll pick you up from the party and we'll order Hawaiian pizza and watch movies."

"Lauren too?"

Eli's chest warmed. "I don't know."

"She probably already has a Glorietta plan."

He realized he didn't know that, either. He only knew, now more than ever, that he wanted Lauren's plans to include him. "I'll have to ask her about that."

"Good." Worry pinched Emma's expression. "When you see Uncle Drew, be sure they have a good plan there, too."

"I don't like this number. Let's try it one more time, hon."

Florine rolled the thermometer over Drew's forehead; it felt as cool as the water she kept asking him to drink. She'd added a lot of extra pillows to help him sit up high, but the water still made him choke. Coughing made his chest hurt. He tried to smile as Vee waved at him from the doorway.

"How is it this time?" she asked Florine. She'd crossed her arms and her face looked worried.

"It's been forty-five minutes since that Tylenol, and I'm still getting 101.4." Florine brushed his hair off his forehead. Her hand was as cool as water too. "And I'm hearing some crackles in the bases of his lungs now." She pinched Drew's chin gently, smiled at him. The flower in her hair was yellow today. "None of those things would really bother me if you'd chowed down on those pancakes, Mr. Drew."

He'd tried. Hard. He wanted to make her proud. But the pancakes didn't taste right today, even with blueberry syrup. It was hard to chew and still breathe.

"I'm glad the courier was able to pick up blood and sputum samples — and get back out." Vee looked toward the window. "This rain's not letting up. Cyril's sandbags won't do anything to keep the roads open."

"No. And if the doctor sees those lab results and orders an ambulance transfer to the hospital for X-rays . . ."

Vee nodded. "Are you going to call —" she smiled at Drew — "our concerned physician assistant?"

"He's planning to come visit. But I thought you might want to call him to report these vital signs. Let him know we've sent labs and tell him pretty much everything on that latest order sheet."

Vee smiling knowingly. "I should be the one to call . . . because it was made explicitly clear that *nurses* shouldn't be doing that. And I'm not a nurse."

"Yes." Florine's cool fingers brushed Drew's cheek. "And because that particular PA cares to his very soul about this special man. A beautiful kind of caring that has gone both ways for a long, long time. And *my* soul isn't about to let me interfere with that."

"I hear you." Vee raised her eyebrows. "What about that envelope the officer brought by this morning — from the court?"

"Well . . ." Florine pulled the sheet over Drew's chest, then reached for his pod and earphones. "It's like I was telling that nice officer when I was getting him a second helping of biscuits and gravy. Auntie Odette always said you've got to have your priorities straight. People come first, after God. But legal papers are *way* down the list. I'll get to that envelope. But right now . . ." Florine set the music pod on Drew's chest, straightened the cords on the earphones. He could almost hear his music already. "Right now I'm busy connecting a person *with* God. On that list of priorities, I'd say this is a glorious twofer."

"Of course I know where it is, Mom."

Lauren set her fork next to the remains of her scrambled eggs, then stretched the ancient pink phone cord taut as she walked into the pantry. The phone call had come only minutes after she'd closed her Bible, finishing her early morning quiet time. It interrupted a skin-tingling reverie about Eli. Their dinner. The candles. Those amazing kisses. And how completely special he'd made her feel. Music . . . she was his music. Lauren wanted to relive it, moment by moment. Savor it. She needed to let herself believe, even for a short while, that what she and Eli felt couldn't be affected by the problems of the real world.

"Inside the door, darling."

"I know." Lauren sighed. "It's been there for as long as I can remember."

She tugged the light string, blinking against the bulb that illuminated a sixty-inch, laminated disaster-preparedness checklist stapled to the pantry door. Two neatly penned columns: *Hurricanes* and *Tornadoes*. Lauren bit back a smile. Some years back, Jess had scrawled her own column of emergency preparations: *Twinkies, Dr Pepper,* and *Mom Repellint* — a misspelled and pubescent snit forever immortalized in permanent marker. "I'm reviewing your disaster instructions right now."

"Good." Pamela Barclay's anxious sigh wafted through the receiver. "Glorietta's expected to make landfall near Victoria late tonight. I've been frantic to get us a flight home, but the airline expects cancellations to all destinations in south Texas."

"Stay in Colorado," Lauren insisted. "Aunt Gwen still needs you. We're fine, and — Daddy, is that you? Are we on speakerphone?"

"Yes, baby. Listen, I don't want you to

worry about those roof leaks." Her father's voice was as confident and reassuring as his TV commercials. Lauren could almost see her mother hoisting her camera-ready pink umbrella. *"No need to worry when Barclay Insurance has you covered."*

"It's only a small problem with the flashing," he explained. "I'd have had it repaired already if your aunt's gallbladder hadn't hijacked us. But our old homestead is built like a fortress. Wind isn't going to be a problem."

"Thanks," Lauren murmured. No good could come from reporting that the pig had already crash-landed in the driveway. Mankind would have perished if Carl Barclay had been chosen to build the ark. "I won't worry, Daddy. Promise."

"That's my baby. And your mother has stocked the pantry with everything you could possibly need."

"Right." Lauren frowned at her mother's all-caps addendum to the disaster list. A saying she'd borrowed from a Florida coast Facebook friend:

RUN FROM WATER. HIDE FROM THE WIND

She'd drawn a neon-pink arrow from the

word *wind* to the last numerical item on the tornado list:

If necessary, take refuge in tub — guest bathroom.

"We're so proud of you, Lauren." Her mother's voice again, accompanied by a sniffle. "We know you'll watch over your sister. And our little Hannah Leigh. If it should come to it, the doggy crate is on the top shelf of the pantry, right above your head. Wear Daddy's long, quilted barbecue mitts if you have to load her up. She won't be a happy puppy. Sweet-talk her. Be sure you have plenty of Woofers for bribes. Maybe some of those bacon strips I have in the freezer. And —"

"I've got it covered, Mom." For some horrible reason, Lauren imagined herself herding Jess into that purple dog crate. Wearing barbecue mitts and risking mortal wounds. While Eli, Fletcher, and Chaplain Angela urged the process along, saying Lauren was finally doing the right thing. Her heart began to sink. "We're fine here. Really."

"We'll check in tomorrow," her parents assured. "Should I call your cell phone? When I tried this phone last night, it just rang and rang."

"Jess was sleeping before her night shift. And I . . . had a sort of date." Lauren's heart obliterated the sound of the rain on the roof. "I've started seeing someone."

"You have? That's wonderful. Did you hear that, Carl?"

"I did," her father confirmed. "Good. We'll look forward to meeting this young man when we get home."

"Yes." Her mother sighed. "It's such a relief not to have to worry about *your* choices, Lauren."

"Um . . . right."

"We'll let you go now. Love you."

"Love you back."

There was a click, call ended.

Lauren cut the pantry light and followed the phone cord back to the kitchen wall, the tether to her parents mercifully loosened. She reached for her coffee cup, took a sip as she stared through the rainy window, and thought of what she'd witnessed as she stood in the doorway of Emma's bedroom: Eli's bowed head, his voice blending with his daughter's in that most perfect of prayers. It had been a precious, natural moment. So touching that Lauren had found herself closing her eyes, breathing the familiar words along with them. It still made her hope that despite the doubts he'd voiced later, it was possible she and Eli weren't really all that different. They both placed a high priority on responsibility, at work and in their personal lives. They were both loyal to their siblings and determined to help them. Even if Lauren tended to do that through trust and hope, and Eli was more prone to jumping in with both feet.

"I've started seeing someone."

She'd said that. Done it. Taken a first step in telling her parents about Eli. Lauren glanced toward the hallway in time to catch Hannah exiting Jess's bedroom. Tonight she'd figure out a way to tell her sister about Eli too. It wasn't exactly jumping in with both feet — maybe it was only a baby step — but it was a start. She was going to be stubbornly hopeful that things would work out. For Eli and her, for Jess, Drew . . . Darcee Grafton, Gayle . . . There was always reason for hope, just like in Emma's *Annie* song. The sun *would* eventually come out. Even with Glorietta whirling like an angry red buzz saw, the roof springing leaks, and —

"Hannah Leigh," Lauren scolded, rising from her chair. "What have you got there? One of Jess's CDs?" She took a step toward the black-and-white burglar, then heard the growl and thought better of it. "Here, let's trade. . . ." Snatching the buttery remains of her toast, Lauren knelt down and waggled it in her fingers. Dog bribe. Pathetic, but it could be worse. At least this time she wasn't bargaining for a houseguest's stolen undershorts.

"Here we go. Good girl," Lauren purred. The dog's nose managed to perk with interest, despite the fact that her jaws were stretched around the small, unopened plastic package. Not a CD. "That's right, Hannah Leigh," Lauren praised as the package dropped to the floor in favor of the table scrap. "Good trade. You got that yummy toast, and I got this boring —"

What?

"Hair ball medicine?" Lauren stared at the package. Turned it over, confused. Then read the handwritten label.

Adele Humphries/for Fluffy.

32

"Uh . . . dog medicine?" Jess's teeth sank into her lower lip. Lauren swore she could hear her sister's brain ticking. "You dragged me out of bed for — ?"

"It's cat medicine." Lauren wanted to grab Jess by the shoulders, force her to make eye contact. *I want to believe you. . . .*

"So?" Jess shrugged. "Hannah's always rooting around and swiping things. You know she's a thief. So she found some old medicine under the bed or in a closet somewhere. I'm not surprised."

"Dad's allergic to cats. We never had a cat. Not one."

"Then it belonged to a neighbor . . . or a cleaning lady. What's the big deal?"

"The big deal is that this medicine is for Adele Humphries's cat. See that? Her name, right there on the label."

Jess's face paled.

"Our ER patient," Lauren continued. "It

came from that bag of medicines she had with her. The bag with the missing narcotics."

Jess finally met her gaze. "Exactly what are you accusing me of?"

Lauren felt sick. "I'm not accusing, Jess. I'm asking how a medicine belonging to Adele Humphries got into this house."

"And next you'll turn me in for stealing narcotics."

"Please sit down with me. I want to understand what happened."

"Do you? Really?"

"Yes." It wasn't true. What Lauren really wanted was to run away as fast as she could. "Of course. Please . . . sit with me."

Jess refused a cup of coffee but finally sat. Lauren scooted her chair close. She was shaking inside. "I'm listening."

"It was an accident," Jess began. "I wouldn't steal that stupid cat medicine. I may be screwed up in some ways, but I'm not coughing up hair balls. At least not yet." She gave a grim smile.

Lauren reached out, touched her sister's hand. *Please, God, help me to simply listen.*

"It was Gayle," Jess continued, biting at a ragged cuticle. "I was looking for that purple coin purse — I told you about that — and then all of a sudden I hear Gayle outside the exam room. Snarly like she's been lately. She doesn't like me, Lauren. I know you don't believe that."

"Actually, I do. After everything that's happened, I do believe she's been unfair to you."

There was gratitude in Jess's eyes.

"And then what happened?"

"I knew Gayle would jump all over me about handling patient belongings. I tried to slip them back into the bag, but she barged in too fast. I still had that stupid cat medicine in my hand." Jess grimaced. "So I shoved it in my pocket. I was wearing that long linen vest with the deep slash pockets from Neiman's; you know the one."

Lauren nodded, beginning to hope.

"I hung it up in my closet, forgot about what was in the pocket. Until all that talk started about the missing meds. I figured I should throw those cat tablets away, not take them back. Obviously I could have picked a better place than Hannah-town." Jess's eyes shone with sudden tears. "I didn't take those drugs, Lauren. I told you that before. I explained things to security — almost all of it, anyway. I took a urine test."

The tests. Eli had said that all the Houston Grace drug tests came back negative.

"What else do you want me to do to prove

it?" Jess brushed away a tear. She pointed at Lauren's Bible. "Put my hand on that book and swear I'm telling the truth? I'll do that. Right now. I'll swear —"

"No," Lauren said quickly. "You've explained enough. It's okay."

"Good." Jess shook toast crumbs off a napkin and dabbed at her eyes. "I heard that whole story about Gayle. It's awful. I feel bad for her. People are saying that thyroid storm thing probably caused all her crazy behavior — criminal behavior. So it's not a stretch to think maybe she did set me up so she could take those drugs. But I guess we'll never know."

"Maybe not."

"Well . . ." Jess stifled a yawn, stood. "This has been a real giggle fest, but one of us worked all night and needs to sleep — with her door closed. I've got class this afternoon." Her gaze met Lauren's. "Are we good?"

"We're good." Lauren rose, intending to give her sister a hug, but Jess raised her palm.

"Stay put. I'm going. Don't wake me up unless —"

"Glorietta hits and the roof caves in," Lauren finished, remembering the last time she'd said that. "Thank you for trusting me with all that, Jess. I love you."

"Love you too, Lolo." She started toward the hallway, then looked back. "By the way, where were *you* last night? The phone woke me about nine o'clock and you weren't here."

"I . . . had dinner out. So you could sleep."

"That's cool. Thanks."

"You're welcome — sweet dreams."

Lauren watched her sister disappear into her room. She told herself she wasn't a coward for not mentioning Eli. She was sparing Jess from too much at once. It had been a difficult discussion for both of them, directness they hadn't achieved in a long time. It was a good thing.

She watched the rain on the window for a few moments, sipping her coffee — hoping its warmth would soothe her remaining uneasiness. There was no reason to feel this way. She glanced at her Bible, remembering what she'd told Eli. That she needed to believe it would all turn out okay if she put things in God's hands. Lauren did believe that; letting these unsettling feelings crowd in was at odds with faith. And as potentially destructive as that angry storm out in the Gulf. She closed her eyes, took a slow breath.

I trust you, Lord. Please take these whisper-

ing doubts away. . . .

"Not on duty?" Fletcher asked, noting that Eli Landry was in khakis and a shirt instead of his usual scrubs and white coat.

"Meeting." Landry stepped aside as a gurney rattled along the ER corridor, IV bags swaying. "What brings you in?"

"Darcee Grafton. I'm trying to get some additional information regarding that fall. Not sure we're going to." Fletcher grimaced slightly, remembering the young woman's badly bruised and swollen face, her head still swathed in bandages. "She doesn't even remember being on that roof."

"Not surprising. It was a serious head injury. Frankly I didn't think she'd survive it. Odds weren't on her side."

Fletcher saw Landry's brow furrow. Probably with thoughts of his brother. He could imagine how rough that must be. "Mrs. Grafton said they're planning to take her to surgery tomorrow. To fix the leg fracture. She's hurting, groggy from the pain medications. And maybe those pills for her mood disorder."

"I don't know if they've put her back on them yet." Landry frowned. "Though not taking them is the reason she's here."

"She told Jessica that those drugs make

her feel sedated, like she's seeing things through a fog."

"And they dull her creativity . . . snuff her spark . . ." Landry nodded. "Her mother told me that."

Both their gazes darted toward the ceiling as the lights flicked off, then instantly on again.

"There are drug side effects, of course," Landry explained. "Doses can be adjusted, medications switched. There are several treatment options. But without treatment, the moods swing between manic highs and depressive lows. Both risky." He shook his head. "You found her dancing in a pool. And I'll bet you share my doubts that the wind blew her off that roof." His gaze met Fletcher's. "I think we've both seen enough to know this can be a dangerous disorder."

"Right."

They were talking about Jessica. Fletcher felt it as certainly as the bulk of the service weapon on his hip. Landry had broached the subject with her; Jessica had implied that only recently, when Fletcher tried to talk with her about counseling. It was probably the reason she'd backed away from her friendship with Eli. It made sense now. An unlikely ally, but maybe together Fletcher and Eli could —

The ambulance bay doors opened for a gurney, and the wind howled in behind it, carrying a flurry of wet leaves. A janitor moved to mop puddles of rain from the floor.

"Bad out there." Landry checked his watch. "I'd better get moving. I want to pick up Emma before this storm gets worse. There are too many low spots on the road to take chances."

"Smart. Latest reports say Glorietta's building up speed. My parents rented their place out — they're hoping to get back in a few years — so I'll be doing some drive-bys to check on the house."

"And the Barclay house."

Fletcher shrugged. "Been doing that for as long as I can remember." He was saved from saying more by Landry's buzzing phone.

"I should take this," he said, brows drawing together. "My brother's care home."

"No problem. Stay safe out there."

"You too."

Fletcher slid into his patrol car, his hair plastered to his forehead from sideways-slanting rain. He estimated at least two inches of water accumulation on the parking lot asphalt during the short time he'd been in the hospital. Several branches lay across the top of the gazebo, and a front loader had chugged by, packed to the gills with sandbags. Hard to tell right now if it would be wind or water that proved to be the biggest problem with this storm. But they'd planned and prepared for both. He'd report to dispatch and then give Jessica a quick call. She was probably awake by now. He smiled. Likely trying to deal with one of Hannah's infamous foul-weather fits.

"Holt!"

Fletcher rolled down the window and saw Landry lean low, rain pelting his face.

"A temporary . . . restraining order," he huffed over the sound of the wind. "Doesn't that have to be . . . physically served? The papers handed over in person?"

"Temporary order?"

"Yes." Despite the water sluicing down Landry's face, there was no mistaking the anger in his expression. "They can't do anything without serving you?"

"A TRO can be put into effect without notice," Fletcher explained. "Pending a court hearing. It's put in place immediately because . . ." He hesitated, certain by Landry's look that this was personal. "It's put in force when there appears to be an immediate safety risk."

Eli's barely suppressed curse proved it was

personal.

"Hey, hold on . . ." Fletcher didn't like the look in the man's eyes. He'd seen too many bad outcomes with this kind of conflict. He reached for one of his business cards, jotted his personal phone number on the back. "Take this. Give me a call later if you have more questions."

"Thanks — gotta go." Eli grabbed the card, whipped around, and took off at a jog, his boots splashing like a hunting dog after a downed duck.

Fletcher had a feeling it wasn't the last he'd hear of this.

33

"The chocolate chips were a stroke of genius." Lauren shot an appreciative look at her sister, busy manning the Barclays' ancient electric griddle. "And how on earth did you come up with the idea of crumbling bacon into the batter?"

"Easy. It's the cooked bacon Mom keeps in the freezer for Hannah. I tried to reheat the slices, but they broke. So voilà!"

"Well —" Lauren pointed her fork — "Martha Stewart has nothing on *you*. Best. Lunch. Ever."

"My pleasure." Jess's spatula flourish was made more comical by the fact that she was wearing their mother's hand-painted Wizard of Oz apron: Dorothy's house swirling through the air. With Toto strapped to the back of the Wicked Witch's bicycle. Lauren made a mental note to get the dog crate down from the pantry. Just in case.

"That's my entire foodie repertoire." Jess

shrugged. "Pancakes."

"Drew sure wouldn't have any problem with that."

Aagh . . . Lauren wanted to grab the words, drench them with syrup, and swallow them back down.

"Drew? Eli's brother?"

"Mm-hmm." Lauren scooted a chocolate chip with her fork, head down. A betraying flush crept toward her ears. "Pancakes are his favorite . . . I heard."

She felt Jess's curious stare.

"Oh yeah, at Vee's place," she said finally. "You see him there. I almost forgot."

Relief made Lauren dizzy — she'd forgotten it herself. Thoughts of Eli swept all else aside. Somehow she'd figure out a way to discuss this with Jess. At the right time. But this afternoon was too precious to risk spoiling. A rainy day, her sister in pajamas — and a rare good mood — fixing them lunch. Even if it was food Lauren would never eat ordinarily, and even though Jess was still managing to eat practically nothing herself, the point was that they were spending real time together. The Barclay sisters. Giggling, hanging out, like when they were kids. All that was missing was a nest of blankets on the weather room couch, cartoons on the TV, and a plastic crown. Lauren was surprised by an unexpected prickle of tears. "These are great, Jess. Really."

"Eat up. I made lots." She sat down, picked at a pancake, then reached for her black coffee instead. "Mom's weather station says the wind is —"

The lights flickered, eclipsed for a few seconds, then snapped back on.

"I guess that proves it," Jess continued. "Increasing winds. Rising creeks. Local flooding. We'd better bust out the candles and the hand-crank radio." She smiled. "And lash Hannah Leigh to the nearest tree."

"Which will require a double set of barbecue mitts and —" Lauren's voice rose on a laugh — "all the bacon we just ate."

Jess snorted, sloshing her coffee. "Maybe we could float her on Mom's big exercise ball. Have her keep it spinning like one of those circus dogs."

"Or maybe . . ." Lauren hunched over, blinking back tears of mirth. Right this second, she didn't care if it did flood. Up to their iffy roof. She wanted to keep laughing, freeze this silly and hopeful moment.

"Your phone. Hospital ringtone." Jess pointed. "Under your napkin."

Lauren answered, talked for a few moments, hating that Jess had begun clearing the plates. Their afternoon was disappearing.

"Problem?" her sister asked as Lauren disconnected.

"I'm on disaster call. They're short in the ICU — weather's causing problems with staffing. Folks are delayed or not coming in at all. I said I'd go in for a couple of hours." She glanced upward as the kitchen lights flickered again. "Will your class get canceled?"

"I have to check the website. As far as I know it's still a go." A look of regret flickered across her face. "Looks like the Barclay IHOP is closed for business, Lolo."

"We'll do it again. Let's count on that." Lauren rose. "I said I'd be there in fifteen minutes."

"Go." Jess waved her on. "You go ahead and get ready. I can clear these dishes."

"Thanks."

Lauren had made it to the hallway when she heard her phone ring again. She'd left it on the table. And that was the ringtone she'd assigned to —

"Phone!" Jess shouted. "It's . . . Eli?"

Oh, great . . . Lauren hustled back to the kitchen, trying to decide if it was too conspicuous to take the call privately.

"Hey, Eli," she answered, avoiding her

sister's gaze for the second time in minutes.

"Hi. Look, I'm sorry to have to ask this, but . . ." His voice sounded rushed, uncharacteristically anxious. "Are you at your folks' place?"

"Yes," she confirmed warily. Was he coming here? "Where are you?"

"On my way out to Mimaw's."

Her relief turned to concern. "Is there a problem with Drew?"

"Something like that. The roads are bad, and traffic's ugly." There were sounds of distant honking. "Emma needs to be picked up at four. That's the problem. I'm not going to make it in time. Can you do that for me . . . for her?"

"Where is Emma?" Out of the corner of her eye, Lauren saw Jess watching intently.

"At a birthday party. Parrish Donnelly's. They live close by — 873 Tradewinds. They'd keep Emma there, but now they've decided to drive to San Antonio to wait out the storm. And they want to get on the road as soon as possible. If you could pick Emma up — Shrek, too, he's there — and keep them at your folks' place until I —"

"Wait. I'm so sorry, but I won't be here, Eli. I got called in to work. And Jess has class," she added quickly, not sure if she was saying it for her sister or Eli. Her mind tumbled toward confusion. She wanted to help, but how?

"All right. Let's see . . . I could call my mother. Emma could go there — just until I get back. I don't have a choice." The sudden bitterness in his voice was drowned by another barrage of honking. "Could you drop her off?"

"Take her to River Oaks?" Lauren glanced sideways. Her sister was signaling to her. "I'm not sure. I'd have to call the hospital and let them know I'd be late."

"I can help," Jess offered, moving up beside her. "What's he need?"

"Hold on a second, Eli." Lauren pressed the phone to her chest. "His daughter's at a party a few blocks from here. She needs to get to her grandparents' house. I don't know, Jess. . . . You have class."

"There's time. Tell Eli I'll do it. Emma's met me. Here, let me have the phone. I'll tell him myself."

Lauren listened to the one-sided conversation, heart sprinting. She was afraid to let herself imagine Eli's response. Or her sister's reaction if he turned her offer down flat.

"He says yes," Jess reported, looking almost as surprised as Lauren felt. "But he thinks I should take your car. Better seat belts. He'll call his mother — I know how to get to their house. And he'll tell Emma to expect me. So all I'll need is the birthday party address and we're good to go."

Lauren took the phone back, but Eli had already disconnected. She stared at it, hating the uncomfortable sense of foreboding crowding in.

"He hung up. Sounded like he was in an awful hurry," Jess explained. "So write that address down and go get ready for work. I'll dump these dishes in the sink, throw on some clothes, and head over to pick up the kid. And the hairy beast. I'll let you handle the car detailing afterward."

"Okay." Lauren scraped her teeth across her lower lip. "You're sure about this, Jess?"

"Of course. Pancake Queen Shuttle Service." Her smile faded. "You don't trust me?"

"Sure . . . of course. Absolutely." Lauren grabbed a pencil and scratch pad off the hutch, wrote down the Donnellys' address. "There."

"Good. Just one more thing." Jessica's gray eyes met hers.

"What?"

"How long have you been dating Eli?"

Lauren's brain turned to chocolate-bacon mush. "Not long. Barely any time. How did you — ?"

"Figure it out?" Jess hitched the drooping apron up, making the Wicked Witch shimmy in flight. "That he called you just now — trusted you with his only child — would have been a major clue. Even without your lame excuse about going out last night so I could sleep. And then there was the report of his jogging into pouring rain to sit with you in your car in the hospital parking lot." Her shrug looked forced. "I have my peeps."

Lauren hated that her knees felt so ridiculously weak. It was impossible to read the look in her sister's eyes. "So . . . what do you think?"

"About you and Eli?"

"Yes."

"I *think* . . . that if you didn't bother to tell me about it, then you couldn't care less what I think."

"That's not true." Lauren battled a queasy wave of guilt. "It's just that this is so new. And I wasn't sure if —"

"If it might bother me? Because of the obvious issues I've had with Eli?"

"Yes," Lauren admitted, barely above a whisper. "All of that."

"Well . . ." Jess glanced toward the remains of their pancake lunch and was quiet for an endless moment. Then she sighed. "I guess

I'm not surprised. You're both the same type."

Lauren's brows rose.

"Pushy, parental." Her lips quirked in a bare semblance of a smile. "And don't look so worried; it's your life. I'm always telling you to butt out of mine, so I guess this makes us even."

"Jess . . ." Lauren wasn't at all certain this felt resolved. "I never meant to —"

"Go. Get out of here. You're due at work, and I have a kid and a dog to chauffeur." She shook her head. "Consider this your first hurdle because when you tell our parents you're dating Eli Landry, it's going to make Glorietta look like a kid blowing out birthday candles."

"I drove through some water, but it's still fairly dry here," Eli told Lauren, nestling the cell phone against his ear. "I think high ground topped the priority list when Odette chose this spot." He glanced at her portrait on the great room's paneled wall. There was a tiny, glittering strand of Mardi Gras tinsel clinging to the frame. "Cyril has sandbags mounded like a bunker anyway, and the generators are gassed up and ready to go. You wouldn't believe the food they cooked ahead of time — ice chests all over the kitchen. And propane cookstoves. Hurricane Katrina taught these folks some big lessons."

"Yes . . . I'm sure of that. Tough lessons."

"How is Houston Grace faring?" he asked, hating the distance between them. He wished he were holding her now. "From what I'm hearing on the news, you're harder hit in that area."

"The power keeps threatening to quit. At this point I think we have more engineers working than nursing staff. I've been assigned to both Darcee and Gayle. Talk about a storm within a storm. But emotional issues aside, they're both pretty stable physically, so that's good. If the power goes out, at least I won't have heart flutters waiting for the generators to take over ventilators. I'm glad to help, but I wish I were somewhere else."

With me. Eli heard it in her voice, a sudden warm and peaceful eddy in the tempest of his day. "I promised Emma we'd order pizza and watch movies tonight if there's still power. She asked if you could come. I have candles."

Lauren's laugh was a purr. "I know you do. That sounds good. Or you guys could come to my parents' house. I think we might have the world's largest collection of

Disney DVDs. And a closet full of Weather Channel videotapes — we'll skip those." He heard her take in a breath. "I told Jess. About us."

Eli's arm rose in a victorious fist pump. "That's great. I told you she'd handle it — she handled it okay, right?"

"I . . . guess. She said she wasn't surprised. Because we're alike. Pushy and parental."

Eli smiled. "That sounds like your sister. I appreciate her helping me with Emma." He wasn't going to let on that he still had qualms about that rushed decision. But he'd been stuck, desperate to get here. Besides, any implied distrust of her sister could distance Lauren. He didn't want that to happen. "I'd been planning to bring Emma here with me today, but then Florine called."

"Because of Drew's fever and lack of appetite."

He dragged his fingers across his chin. There was no reason not to tell her. "And because the judge has been throwing his weight around again."

"Your father?"

"He made good on his threat. Florine was served with a copy of a temporary restraining order this morning. Demanding that I have no further contact with my brother."

Eli's teeth clenched. "For his safety."

"He can do that?"

"He can — he did, without even inform-ing me. It's only in place until the court date." Eli heard Lauren take a sharp breath. "According to the papers, it's set for three days from now. But it's not like he even has a case. This could be another big bluff. And I'm calling that bluff. I'm here."

"Is the staff having issues with that?"

"There's not much they can do. I don't think Florine would, but even if someone here called the police, I doubt they'd come out. I have to think law enforcement's time is better served troubleshooting the effects of this storm. And I think Houston taxpay-ers would agree." Eli glanced up as Vee walked by towing a portable oxygen tank. "The medical transport rig wouldn't even come out because of road conditions. Drew's doc ordered a nonemergency chest X-ray."

"Do his lungs sound bad?"

Eli glanced toward the hallway to his brother's room. "Some crackles, scattered wheezes. He's had two doses of antibiotic. Breathing treatments. He's . . . he's glad I'm here with him. He trusts this staff. If my father had his way, Drew would be tied to a hospital bed by now. And I'd be banned from seeing him. I'm not going to let that happen, Lauren. I won't let him do this to me."

34

"Voluntary evacuations for people in mapped floodplains," Lauren explained after checking Gayle's medication pump. "That's all they've called for so far. It shouldn't affect the hospital. Or my parents' neighborhood, thank heaven. And my apartment is seven floors up."

"Our house isn't affected either. Though I guess that's a moot point now. Since neither of us may go back there at all. I wonder if the county jail is in the floodplain." Gayle attempted a grim smile just as the overhead lights flickered, making her bruised face look close to macabre.

"Have the police said anything?" Lauren knew better than to offer Gayle false assurances; the manager was too realistic for that. There was an officer stationed outside the ICU doors. And from what Lauren had heard, Leo Garner would be facing assault charges himself. Thankfully, he'd been transferred to Memorial Hospital — less awkward for everyone.

"I haven't heard anything specific about the charges. But then, I've 'lawyered up' — isn't that what they call it on *Law & Order*? Someone from the public defender's office. He feels there's a strong case for self-defense." She swallowed, closed her eyes. "I still can't believe I did that to my husband."

Lauren's throat tightened. There was a small hospital-issue Bible on the nightstand; chaplaincy had come by. The card left with it indicated that Angela had been the one who made contact. The cookie-toting chaplain had been busy.

"I've been a nurse for nearly twenty-five years," Gayle continued. "Can you imagine how many domestic-abuse forms I've filled out? How many times I routinely asked a patient that 'Are you safe at home' question?"

"I should have seen it." Lauren touched her hand. "Those bruises recently. And your illness — there were symptoms. I should have figured all of that out. I'm sorry, Gayle."

"No." Gayle blinked back tears, eyes still wide from her thyroid condition. "I hid it the best I could. Leo's always had problems with his temper and with alcohol. He could be sweet, too, really sweet. But losing his job did something awful to him. I tried hard to make things better. But I'd felt so sick for so long and couldn't sleep. It was like I was in this pressure cooker with no way out." She shuddered. "And then his hands were around my throat again. . . ."

Lauren winced.

"It was my Valentine's present," Gayle whispered. "That knife set."

Lauren stayed silent. As hard as it was to hear, Gayle needed to get this out.

"I can't count the number of times he's hit me. But I could take it. I'm pretty tough. I shouldn't have stabbed him." A tear slid down Gayle's cheek. "I love Leo. He's the only man I've ever loved. I should have left long ago, made him get help. I should have done something before things got so out of control. But I wanted to believe it wasn't that bad. That he'd get better — I needed to believe that, you know?"

"Yes." Lauren nodded, thoughts of Jess intruding. "I think I know what you mean."

"I'm ashamed. I've made so many mistakes."

The words slipped out before Lauren could stop them. "Yesterday after they brought you in, you asked me to pray for you. You said something about Leo needing

418

pills. And that you'd lied."

"I did." Gayle shook her head. "Why does this seem like the lesser of two evils now? I did lie. To get pain pills for Leo. He was abusing them. Some part of me knew that. But the truth was, he was easier to be around when he was high, and less dangerous than when he was drunk. Then his doctor cut him off, and every doctor I tapped to get him a prescription said no. I was desperate. So . . ."

Lauren held her breath.

"I went to a clinic down in Pearland. Gave a false name. I faked a back injury. I probably looked awful enough to be believable. I paid cash for a no-refill prescription for Valium and Percocet. I was really buying time."

Lauren swallowed. "I was afraid you were talking about those missing drugs from Mrs. Humphries." *Afraid . . . or hoping?*

"Our patient's medications? No. Don't worry. I'd never do something like that." Gayle's faint smile was rueful. "I guess that sounded completely absurd. Considering."

Lauren checked Gayle's IVs and the circulation to her casted arm, then reassured her that she had been praying for her and would continue to do so. She encouraged Gayle to let the chaplain stop by for a visit.

As Lauren was on her way back to the nurses' desk, her cell phone buzzed. Jess.

"I'm here. Coming up in the elevator."

"At the hospital?" Lauren asked, confused. "What about class?"

"Canceled. Because of the storm. I think I Jet Skied your Beetle all the way here. A lot of the streetlights are out. The highways are packed. That voluntary evacuation."

"What about — ?" Lauren stopped herself from mentioning Emma. Jess would equate that with a lack of trust. "Did you come to trade cars? You didn't have to do that."

"They want me to work a few hours in the ER, help them catch up on some paperwork. But Mrs. Grafton called too. Darcee wants to see me. So I thought I'd come up here first and — oh man, the lights are blinking in this elevator."

"Hang on. It's been happening off and on." Lauren glanced upward as the unit's lights flickered. Monitor alarms dinged in the distance. "I'll meet you at the ICU doors."

"Just a sip, Champ. You can do it."

Eli watched his brother's dry lips close around the straw, his flushed cheeks sucking inward in earnest but weak compliance.

420

An immediate cough and gag shook Drew's shoulders. He was choking on every sip of water, despite the fact that Florine had dutifully propped him on three — no, four — pillows. Eli thought of Emma's desperate attempt to hide those pillows . . . *because my father said I'd smother him.*

"Easy, Champ. Here, let me wipe your lips. If Emma were here, she'd say 'dab' your lips. You know how she is."

Eli had sent a couple of texts to her cell. And called once, but it went to voice mail. The judge had a strict policy of no cell phones at the dinner table. It was too early for dinner, but Eli had no doubt his father would hijack the phone anyway. Cut off Eli's communication with his daughter as effectively — if not legally — as he had with his brother. Eli had lied to his mother, told her that he was working a few hours at Houston Grace because of his role in disaster response. He'd told Emma the same thing so she wouldn't be caught up in this whole ugly mess. He'd done what he had to.

Right now, his priority was Drew.

"Those chickens are on the screened back porch now. Next thing, they'll be right here in the house wanting pancakes for breakfast. Better watch your plate." Eli brushed his brother's hair away from his damp forehead, feeling the fever under his fingertips. He'd ask Florine to check it again. See what time they'd given the last Tylenol — maybe add some ibuprofen. "I need you to get better, Champ. You're my big brother." His throat squeezed. "Who's gonna give me a better knuckle bump?"

Drew's eyelids flicked open. His arm stayed still, but he tried to smile. It broke Eli's heart.

He set the water cup on the table beside the framed fishing photo and lava lamp, reached for Drew's headphones. Then he remembered Florine had said Drew liked it better in the dock these days, the music playing aloud in his room. Eli switched it on. For the Champ, he'd cope with Christian music. And chickens on the porch.

"How's he doing?" Cyril, his impressive bulk in full rain gear, peered through the doorway. "Looks more peaceful now that his brother's here."

"I don't like this cough," Eli admitted, grateful once again that this family team was so dedicated to the welfare of their residents. As far as he knew, they hadn't taken action regarding Eli's presence here. Cyril would be a forbidding bouncer. "He's trying to drink fluids, though. That's good."

Cyril smiled. "And my man has his music — battery-powered. Music is good medicine too."

Music, rainbow drawing, palm-leaf cross . . . Eli was still betting on the antibiotics.

"How's it look out there?" Eli glanced toward the window, forgetting the view was obstructed by plywood covers. Cyril and his brothers had been busy.

"Chicken house is maybe six inches underwater. The gravel road has a couple small mud rivers running across it, but all that's far from the house. We're good up here. I've seen to it this roof's as watertight as a frog's —" Cyril grinned. "It's not gonna leak."

Eli smiled back at him.

"Plenty of rural roads flooded between here and the city," Cyril continued. "City crews have their hands full with local flooding in the usual spots, and the TV news says folks are moving up the I-10 pretty thick. Coming up and through from the coast, I suspect. No contraflow yet, but I'm glad I'm not drivin' in that." He shook his head. "You ask me, it's the wind that's gonna be the bogeyman in this storm. Already have a lot of power outages." The lights blinked off and on again as if to prove Cyril's point. "My guess is we'll be on generators before long now." His dark eyes connected with Eli's. "You're here. Better plan to stay. Is that little daughter of yours in a safe place?"

"She's at my folks' house in River Oaks." Eli thought he saw a hint of surprise on the big man's face. Maybe because of the upscale zip code — or the down-and-dirty family feud.

"News hasn't reported serious problems there," Cyril assured, "even with the bayou so close. Seems like most of the damage has been in neighborhoods closer to the Grace Medical complexes."

Eli frowned. The Barclays' house was roughly in that area. As well as the Donnellys'. He was glad now that Parrish's family had decided to evacuate and that Emma was with his folks — even if she'd had her cell taken away. He'd call his mother. Have her put Emma on the phone. He'd let her know there was a possibility he'd be spending the night away from home. And Eli would warn Lauren to stay at her apartment tonight. No reason to take chances.

"The Weather Channel — TOR:CON — is putting out warnings of a potential tornado risk. Gave it a value of 6. High probability over the next couple of hours."

"What? In Houston?" Eli tensed.

"Yes, sir — spawned from that landfall

424

near Victoria. Glorietta may have been downgraded from hurricane status, but she's still having one ugly hissy fit. We're too close not to feel it."

Eli pulled his phone from his pocket. "I should call my —"

The room went inky dark. Quiet except for the soft sound of Drew's music.

"That's my cue." Cyril's voice sounded as if he'd moved into the hallway already. A flashlight snapped on, illuminating his rubber wading boots. "I'll get the generators going. You and my man there . . . you sit tight."

Eli watched the flashlight disappear, then scooted his chair closer to the bed. Somehow the darkness — so much deeper with the window boarded — made the sound of Drew's breathing louder, shallower, faster. Anxious probably . . . or getting worse?

"I'm here, Champ." Eli took hold of Drew's withered and contracted hand. "I'm right here with you. The lights will be back on any minute. I promise. Remember when you read the Narnia stories to me after we had to turn the lights out? I'd hold your Scout flashlight, and you'd do all the different voices: Peter and Aslan and that evil White Witch." His throat tightened as the memories flooded back. "I'd get excited and talk too loud, and you'd tell me to put my hand over my mouth so Dad wouldn't hear. . . ."

Lauren checked the desk monitor at the nurses' station again. Darcee Grafton's numbers had changed. Blood pressure 94 over 50 — not really hypotensive, but trending downward. Heart rate 104, respirations 28. Darcee had been talking to Jess for almost ten minutes and had initially been more animated than usual, intense. That might account for the faster heart rate and breathing. Heaven knew, Jess could wear a person out. But Lauren didn't like Darcee's oxygen saturation reading: 94 percent on two liters of nasal oxygen. Whether they liked it or not, she'd break up this conversation, check Darcee's temp, listen to her heart and lungs, and —

Lauren's personal cell buzzed in her jacket pocket. Eli.

"Hey there." She glanced at the monitors again, then leaned against the desk. "How is Drew?"

"Temp's climbed some." It sounded like Eli was whispering. "I don't like the sounds in his left lung. But there's no way we'd get him transported for an X-ray now. First responders are having issues with this

426

weather. Mimaw's is on generator power."
There was the sound of a wheezing cough.
"I should see about getting him another
breathing treatment. Then I'm going to
check on Emma. But I wanted to tell you it
might be better if you and Jessica stay at
your apartment tonight. It's a much newer
building. Apparently there's a tornado risk."

Lauren had a sudden image of Jess in the
Oz apron. "I hadn't heard. We'll do that,
then. Jess got called in to work for a few
hours. But the nurse I'm covering for
should be here any minute; her husband's a
firefighter and he's bringing her in a rescue
rig. As soon as she takes over, I'll head home
and get Hannah Leigh packed up."

"Check with Fletcher before you drive
over that way. I saw him earlier and he said
he was going to keep an eye on your street.
I don't want to worry you, but Cyril said
there's already been some wind damage
around your community. And with that
warning about tor—"

"Lauren!"

Jess called frantically from Darcee's room.
There was no mistaking the panic in her
voice. "Hurry. Something's wrong — she
can't breathe!"

"Gotta go, Eli."

The moment Lauren began jogging toward the bed, the overhead lights flickered and the ICU plunged into darkness.

Ten-second delay for the backup generators — just ten. *One, two . . . God, please . . .*

35

"It . . . hurts. . . . make it . . . stop. Oh . . . God . . . Can't breathe!"

"Darcee, hang on. Easy now. I'm going to help you. We are — Jess, grab that oxygen mask, the one with the bag hanging down from it. Yes." Lauren had never seen eyes as panicky-big as her sister's. Except maybe Darcee Grafton's right this minute. "See that oxygen meter on the wall? Twist the knob to crank up the flow, make that silver ball go as high as it goes. Do it. Right now."

Lauren kept her voice as calm as possible amid the cacophony of distant alarms and hustling footfalls, the short-staffed intensive care unit scrambling to get things settled down after the power switchover. Thank heaven they had light. Dim, but there. She took the rebreather mask from Jess. "Where's the pain? What's hurting, Darcee?"

"My . . . ribs . . . my chest . . . bad. Hurts

to breathe." She pressed a hand to her chest. Her face was pale, shiny with sweat. "Can't get . . . air. I need to be up. . . . Let me out of here!"

"Easy. This will help." Lauren settled the mask over her patient's face.

"What's wrong?" Jess bit at a fingernail, eyes fixed on Darcee. "What's happening?"

"Push that red button. Right there beside the oxygen meter. That will bring extra staff," Lauren instructed, diagnoses swirling in her head. *Trauma patient with a leg injury. Pulmonary embolism, fat embolus?* Both dangerous.

The panic button began its urgent chime.

"I need to page the doctor." Lauren's gaze moved to the monitors. Blood pressure now 88 over 58, pulse 118, oxygen saturation 92 percent. "He'll want an EKG, X-rays, labs, blood gases. Help me keep her still, Jess. She's getting agitated. I can't lose those IV lines. I need your help."

Lauren brushed back the stray red strands of hair clinging to her patient's forehead, connected with her panicked eyes. "Hang in there, Darcee." The young woman gulped for air, fogging the oxygen mask. "It's going to be all right. Stay with us." *Please don't die. . . .*

430

■ ■ ■ ■

Fletcher strode toward the road crew, a headwind plastering his rain jacket against his uniform shirt; at this point, even his body armor felt wet. But at least he wasn't having to hunch over a downed tree while wielding a chain saw, like these men.

"How's it going?" he shouted over the wind and tool roar. The air smelled like sawdust, sweat, and motor oil. Wooden street barricades blinked amber light in the deepening dusk.

" 'Bout got it," one of the crew shouted back. He grinned, exposing a gold-rimmed front tooth. "Which means our crew's only twenty-seven trees behind. I'm hungry enough to eat some branches. How come no tree ever falls outside a County Line BBQ?" He glanced at the patrol car and then toward the blocked entrance to the community. "Power went out a while back. Someone need help in there?"

"No," Fletcher reassured him. "I'm not answering a dispatch call. It's my parents' neighborhood. Thought I'd do a drive-by. You know."

"For sure. My ma retired to Florida. Out of the frying pan into the fire, I tell her, far as hurricanes go. But you don't argue with Ma." He reached for a huge pair of branch loppers. "We'll be finished in about twenty." His grin glinted again. "Faster if I start eating them branches. Who knows? Beavers might be on to something."

Fletcher slid back into his car, checked the computer. No changes in the disaster-response plan. Still on voluntary evacuation, though the highway traffic was thinning some now. Numerous rescues of citizens from vehicles stranded in water . . . lots of reported wind damage to buildings, both residential and business. Even some citizen reports of isolated tornado touch-downs — suspicious but not confirmed. No looting so far. Plenty of power outages. Three hospitals on emergency power. But no storm-related fatalities, thankfully. The coastal communities had taken a much harder hit in the storm. By all predictions, the worst of Glorietta would subside before morning. Fletcher hoped that was true.

He glanced toward the downed tree. They probably would have that road cleared in twenty minutes. But there was another gate on the adjacent street, so —

His computer signaled a call: a neighbor versus neighbor complaint about stolen storm supplies? The neighborhood was a couple miles away. Fletcher sighed. He'd settle that — short of hefting wet sandbags — and swing by here again. His drive-by could wait awhile. His parents' tenants had decided to evacuate yesterday. And he'd talked with Lauren briefly; she and Jessica had been called in to work. As for the shih tzu, well . . . Fletcher smiled. Miss Hannah Leigh had the strongest sense of self-preservation he'd ever seen.

"It's good soup." Eli lowered his spoon as Vee stepped through Drew's doorway. "Gumbo?"

"Yes. My own version." She smiled. "Somehow soup always tastes better on a stormy night."

"That's true." Eli glanced at the bed. The rhythm of Drew's breathing blended with the chug and hum of the power generator. "Our Mimaw made andouille-shrimp soup on rainy nights. We'd camp out with sleeping bags on her screened porch and eat the soup out of coffee mugs. One time Drew said whoever got the most shrimp in his cup was a winner. I had eleven and a half pieces. He had nine. It was the first time I ever beat him at anything. He teased me that the prize was helping Mimaw wash the dishes. Then he gave me his favorite baseball." Eli shook his head. "I'd forgotten that until just now."

"Memories taste better on stormy nights too."

"Maybe so." Eli took a slow breath. "I wanted to say I appreciate that you all didn't give me a hard time for showing up here today. Because of that restraining order. Your whole family has been nothing but kind to Drew and to me. I don't want to get any of you in trouble."

"We know that. And we see how much you care about your brother, how he feels about you. It's not something we want to get in the way of." She raised her brows. "But for the record, Florine did report your being here to an officer. A sheriff's deputy, Marcel Fruge."

"Fruge . . . like Cyril?"

"His older brother — two years on the force. We're hugely proud of him." She shrugged. "Marcel says he's sorry, but unless you start throwing furniture around, this storm has him pretty much tied up."

A lump rose in Eli's throat. "I promise not to do that."

"We figured."

She glanced toward the dimly lit hallway as a wheelchair passed by. The young woman with the halo brace, being pushed by her mother. "We also wanted to let you know that if you want to bunk down on the couches in the great room, we have plenty of sheets and blankets. Or we're fine with bringing a cot in here."

"I haven't been listening to the TV weather. Are the nearby roads flooded?"

"Pretty much. At least enough that the first responders said it's doubtful they could get in here." She glanced at Drew. "Florine checked. Just in case."

Eli's heart stalled. He didn't want that anyway . . . right? He didn't want to start that awful journey toward the misery of last Christmas. It was at the bottom of the whole mess with his father.

"Well, think about it," Vee told him. "We'll set you up with anything you need." She clucked her tongue. "Regular pajama party goin' on here tonight. Poppy's granddaughter. Debra's mom. The cousins bunking in the loft. Chickens on the porch." She winked. "All we're missing is your darling Emma and her big lug of a dog."

"Yes." Eli chuckled, missing her. He'd gotten no answer when he called the house — they'd probably been at the dinner table by then. "I was just going to try calling her again."

"A fat embolus," Lauren told Jess, standing

435

back as three physicians, the EKG tech, and two oncoming ICU nurses jockeyed for position beside Darcee's bed. "That's the working diagnosis at this point. Set loose from her leg fracture to her lung. They're still ruling out a blood clot, though."

"It's bad, whatever it is. I could tell that by the look in her eyes."

The look in Jess's eyes wasn't so good either.

"She's a little more comfortable now," Lauren assured. "Most of the time fat emboli absorb on their own. If it's a blood clot instead, they'll have to make a decision about tPA — the clot-busting drug. It's riskier because she's had bleeding in her brain. She's young and otherwise physically healthy, so that's on her side. But this is a very serious complication."

She touched her sister's arm. "You were a help, Jess. Letting me know immediately that she was having trouble. Working with me to get the oxygen going and holding her down when she got so agitated. That wasn't easy."

"I tried," she said, hugging her arms around herself. "But I'm not a nurse — not even close."

"You're moving closer all the time." Lauren caught her gaze, nodded. "I'm proud of you."

"I suppose I should get downstairs."

"Right. I just wanted to ask you about — oh, my phone's ringing. Hang on a second. I'm going to grab this."

Lauren took a few steps away before connecting to Eli's call. "Your timing's perfect. My relief is here, and I'll be leaving for —"

"I can't get ahold of Jessica." Eli sounded breathless, almost panicked. "She's not answering her phone. The clerks say she's not in the ER. I have to get ahold of her."

"Eli, what's wrong?" She waved to Jess, beckoning her over.

"My parents called me. Emma's not there. She never arrived. I've tried calling Emma's cell phone a dozen times. There's no answer."

"But . . ." Lauren's heart froze. "That's not possible. It must be a misunderstanding. Wait, I'll get Jess. She's right here." Lauren cradled the phone to her chest, anxiety making her mouth go dry. "It's Eli. He's worried sick. You didn't take Emma to his parents' house?"

"I . . ." Jess's face went pale. "No. I was going to tell you about that. I was. And call Eli too. Then all this happened with Darcee."

Eli was shouting through the phone, his voice unintelligible but frantic.

"Jess —" Lauren grabbed her sister's arm — "where is she? Where's Emma?"

"At our house. The traffic was awful toward River Oaks. The dog was howling at the storm, and Emma said she'd be fine at the house till one of us got back."

Lord, please . . .

"Eli . . ." Lauren paced across the floor, the phone trembling at her ear. "Emma's at my parents' house. Jess said something about the traffic and Shrek being scared of the storm."

"In that house — alone? I told you there was damage on those streets, tornadoes maybe. Why did I take a chance she could be responsible?" His groan was half-curse. "Call 911 right now; tell them there's a child alone in your house. I'll be . . . fast . . . I can." His phone was cutting out. "Never mind . . . call 911 myself . . . should know better . . . to trust anybody."

36

"No, sir. It's a bad idea." Cyril planted himself beside Eli's car, the look on his face saying he'd like nothing better than to wrestle the keys from his hand. He glanced down Mimaw's drive. Even in the deepening shadows, the mud and tire ruts were clearly visible. "There's no way this car's going to make it through that low-water crossing. I understand you're —"

"You've got a child, Cyril?" Eli demanded, frustration making his temples throb. " 'Cause if you don't, there's no way on earth you can understand!" He jabbed a finger toward the road. "My daughter's out there. Scared, alone . . . maybe hurt, maybe even . . ." Bile rose, bitter as the terrifying possibilities. "My phone's going out; the emergency phone lines are jammed. I can't wait around not knowing. I've got to go to her. Don't get in my way."

"I can't stop you, Elijah. I don't have a

child, but I've seen far too many folks torn from their children, their family . . . I've seen that pain. And I've seen some terrible things happen when good folks, desperate folks, try their best to save someone." He laid his beefy palm on the hood. "You won't make it through the water in this car."

"Then . . ." Eli whirled around. "I'll take the dump truck. Give me the keys. If you don't, I'll hot-wire it or —"

Cyril's hand clapped onto Eli's shoulder, heavy as a sandbag. "I'll drive. All the roads round here are flooded. The only one worth considering is the one you came in on. Creek's high over the low-water crossing. I have my doubts even that big truck can get through, but I'll take you there, man. We'll give it a try."

"Thank —" Eli couldn't get the words out, but there wasn't time anyway.

"I'm not criticizing you or 'piling on the blame,' " Lauren told her sister, wishing that were completely true. There was no way she could rationalize what Jess had done. "Jess . . . ?" Lauren leaned closer, struggling to make eye contact with her in the otherwise-vacant hospital chapel. She swore she could hear the wall clock ticking, each second making her more anxious and frustrated. "I'm only trying to understand."

"It sure doesn't sound like it." Jess glowered. "It sounds more like you agree with Eli — about this and maybe all his judgmental opinions about me. Now that he's your new *boyfriend,* you're taking his side."

Sides? Lauren wanted to scream that this wasn't a game; this was about a child whose life was in danger.

She'd never felt so torn. Part of her wanted to be here for Jess the way she'd always been; but at the same time she ached to run as fast as she could to her Beetle, floor the pedal, and race to the house. Find Emma. She'd tried to call several times, but it just rang and rang. She clung to the fact that Eli had called 911. Lauren had too.

God, please, keep her safe.

"She's eight, almost nine." Jess finally met Lauren's gaze. Her expression was equal parts petulance and quaking fear. "Mom and Dad left us alone when I was nine."

Because I was fifteen. This wasn't the time to argue that point. "You couldn't get through the traffic to River Oaks?"

"Maybe. If I was willing to crawl bumper to bumper for an hour or more. With Shrek howling and shaking. He's afraid of storms. I swear, it was Emma's idea to go back. She was worried about the dog. She kept saying

441

her friend's old dog had died and Shrek has diabetes. She thought he was having a heart attack." Jess's brows bunched. "She had her arms around that big dog, whispering and singing to him; it looked like she was going to start crying any minute."

Lauren had no problem believing that. "Then after you got back to the house, you found out your class was canceled."

"Yeah. I would have hung around, except I got that call from the hospital. And then a message asking me to phone Darcee's mother." Jess chewed at the edge of her nail again. "I knew you were due back. And I thought it would look good if I went in to the hospital. Make me look responsible, you know?"

Responsible? The irony made Lauren queasy.

"She said she'd be fine. I shut Hannah in my room with a bunch of toys and told Emma not to let her out. I showed her the pantry. I told her to help herself to any snacks she liked. Healthy snacks — I made a point of that. We got Shrek settled in the weather room — Emma loved all of Mom's stupid equipment and all those maps. I pulled out a stack of Disney DVDs and got her a blanket." Jess sighed. "I told her to lock the doors. Not to let anyone in. I said

I'd call her father so he could let her grandparents know. . . . But I didn't get a chance to do that."

Lauren's mouth went dry with dread. "Eli said Emma's not answering her cell phone."

"It's in the Beetle. I noticed it on the backseat when I got here. She was so busy hanging on to Shrek that I think she must have forgotten it. The party favors are in there too." Jess's defensiveness was gone, her expression pinched with worry now. "Should we call Fletcher?"

"I did. It went to voice mail."

"Eli called 911?"

Lauren nodded. "I did too. And I tried to call Earl and Marion — next door to Mom and Dad's — but there wasn't an answer. They might have decided to evacuate. And the Stobs are out of state, visiting that new grandbaby. I don't have numbers for the other neighbors. It's possible that the lines are jammed with calls . . . or down altogether now."

Jess hugged her arms around herself, tears brimming. "You think the power's out at the house?"

"Probably."

"Hannah will be howling."

"Yes." For the first time ever, Lauren hoped that was true. She glanced at the

443

chapel's mosaic. Jesus calming the storm. She tried not to imagine a little girl alone in the dark. With tornadoes brewing. Lauren breathed a silent prayer for Emma. And her father.

"Try it," Eli insisted, leaning out the open passenger door. Muddy water from the overflowing creek raced by with alarming speed, carrying branches and debris and obliterating any glimpse of the road. "It's only a third of the way up the tires. Try a little farther. See how it feels."

Cyril turned to him, hands on the wheel. "It feels like we're far as we can go. Before the engine cuts out." As if to prove it, the big truck shuddered. "That's it. I'm sorry, but I'm backing this rig up."

"No. Wait. We can make it — I'm sure of it."

"Shut that door; I can't have you fallin' out." Cyril shoved the truck into reverse and it shuddered again, then began slowly moving backward, tires spinning as they hit a mud slick before gripping finally. He backed more, and they came to a stop.

"Well, I can't sit here and do nothing!" Eli barked, holding his nearly useless cell phone in a death grip. He must have tried thirty times to get through to emergency operators, to find out something. Anything. "Switch places with me; I'll drive. I think if I angle it toward —"

"No." Cyril's expression was as determined as a linebacker's. "Not doing that. Look, Eli, you're going to have to —"

Eli flung open the door, jumped to the road, boots sinking immediately. He lumbered forward, mud sucking his feet, toward the low-water crossing. He'd get to Emma or die trying. There had to be a way. . . .

"Hey . . ." Cyril caught up with him at the water's edge, raising his voice over the sound of the once-peaceful creek that was now a raging river. He laid a hand on Eli's shoulder. "Don't. You've done all you can."

"I . . . can't. I can't accept that," Eli told him, his voice breaking. "I'm her father. I'm supposed to protect her."

"I get it. I'm all for stepping up, doing something — it's why I've got all those sandbags around that house back there. Why I spent so much time on that roof, made sure those generators were ready. And why I'm sleeping in the loft tonight. I'm looking out for my family. I'm right with you on that, Eli. I can only imagine how much more I'd feel if I had a child who needed my help."

Eli stared at the water, unable to speak.

"But there comes a time," Cyril continued, his voice gentle and deep, "when you have to trust in bigger hands . . . when you go by faith. That little daughter of yours has a pure, believing soul. And our God is bigger than any storm. You've done what you can do. Emergency services are working on it. We'll keep calling for a report." He pointed to the dump truck. "Let's get back. Your brother's waiting for you."

Fletcher contacted dispatch, put himself back in service.

He shook his head. In his experience, most neighbors found ways to pull together in a crisis, help each other. These two couples had come close to a fistfight over a couple of rain tarps and a case of Lone Star beer — obviously the most vital of the "storm supplies." But he'd settled it or at least managed to get the warring parties to agree to stay within their own soggy property lines. Thank heaven power wasn't out in this neighborhood. If ever there was a need for the numbing effect of reality TV or back-to-back Netflix movies, it was tonight. One of the wives had even suggested renting *Twister* in honor of the tornado advisory. Add a couple of beers to that and the next call would be to paramedics for heart palpitations. Fortunately not Fletcher's area of expertise.

He glanced at the time display on his car's computer. He'd do that drive-by on his parents' street, then maybe head over and see how Houston Grace was faring under emergency power.

His gaze moved back to the computer screen as a call came in. His parents' street? Yes, and the house address was . . . the Barclays'. A call for a welfare check on an eight-year-old child "in residence alone." His eyes widened at the ID info.

Emma Landry.

37

The streets were dark. Not because rain clouds hid the setting sun, but unnaturally dark because there were no lights in the majority of the homes. No universal bluish glow from TV after TV. No porch or garage floodlights. Some of the homes had storm shutters in place; only scattered residences appeared to have generator backup — slits of light through shutters or uncovered windows. There were a dozen streets in this community, and from what Fletcher could see already, he'd bet most of them had considerable storm debris in the yards. Porch swings upended, basketball standards flattened, bushes pulled up and tossed, and —

Fletcher cranked the wheel to avoid a large bough, along with what looked like someone's patio umbrella. He drove on, past several completely uprooted trees, noting countless others tipped precariously.

High winds alone could do that, but . . .

There were a few people walking in yards, shining flashlights to survey damage now that the wind had stilled. Ordinarily he'd stop to check with them, but not now. He grimaced at his first sight of significant home damage. A porch overhang — hanging way too far over because one of the posts had snapped. A memory intruded of Jessica on a ladder, trying to patch her parents' leaky roof.

Eli must be beside himself with worry.

Fletcher picked up speed as best he could, dodging branches and debris. A few more homes, and . . . there, his parents' place. No damage that he could see. It was all so dark at this end of the street.

He slowed, pulling as close as he could to the curb while he continued on, using his spotlight to pick out the houses. The Barclays were four houses down. Fletcher spotted a bicycle in a tree and a detached gate tossed like a Tinkertoy. His pulse kicked up; it was looking more and more like a twister had hopped through. Just a few yards farther . . .

Fletcher's spotlight hit the darkened Barclay house . . . leaning fence, uprooted shrubs, and —

His breath caught. The roof . . . *No.* The

roof was completely missing on one end, beams exposed like a skeleton.

He swerved to miss a garbage can. Then rolled up onto the sidewalk and hit his brakes, his gaze riveted to the roof. A quick calculation said the severe damage was over the family room — the weather room.

How on earth did the little girl end up here alone? Please, Lord . . .

He radioed for backup and then bolted from the car.

Lauren glanced through the registration office window into the waiting room. It was only lightly populated. Folks were staying home unless severe pain or injury forced them to navigate the flooded streets. Obviously the reason she hadn't been asked to stay over in the ER. She turned to Jess. "I'm going."

"I'm staying." Jess's eyes connected with hers. "Maybe another hour or so. Until I can finish these computer entries. Mrs. Grafton is up in the waiting area now; she said she'd give me an update."

"Good."

"And —" Jess lowered her voice so the other clerks wouldn't hear — "you'll call me when you hear something about Emma? From Eli or . . . ?"

Lauren wasn't sure she'd hear from Eli. Emma was his priority, of course. But the way he'd told her not to call 911, that he'd do it himself because he couldn't trust anyone . . . She had a horrible feeling he no longer trusted her, either. "I'll call you," she promised. "As soon as I know."

The parking lot was awash with debris. Maintenance workers from all shifts were more than earning their overtime. Someone had managed to run into the stockpile of sandbags, making the pavement look like Galveston beach. If that beach was still there.

Emma's phone was indeed in the Beetle's backseat. Lauren moved a paper crown and sack of gummy bears and picked up the cell, thinking of Eli's desperate unanswered calls. Someone you love, missing — she knew that horrible feeling.

Lauren checked her own phone again: no messages from Eli. Or from Fletcher. Surely a first responder from fire or police had been to the house, found her. But Lauren wasn't going to wait to find out.

The front door was locked.

"Emma?" Fletcher tried the bell, pounded against the door. Then flashed his light beam through the side window into the dark foyer. "Emma? Open the door, please. It's Officer Holt — Fletcher. I'm here to help you."

Nothing. He shone the light on the dining room windows to the right of the porch. One of them had been broken by the wind or a branch and . . . He winced. The space had been plugged with a bed pillow. A little girl protecting herself.

He pounded again before jogging to the back gate. It was ripped from its hinges. Glorietta's tornado spawn — had to be. He stumbled, aimed his light downward to find the mermaid weather vane that had saved his neck all those years ago, now lying on the walkway. He yanked aside a flowering bush, stepped around the igloo doghouse Hannah had never once deigned to use. Fletcher's heart stalled. Why wasn't the dog barking?

The back door was locked too. The screen door lying twisted on the patio.

"Emma?" He banged on the door with his flashlight. "Open the door. I'm here to help you." In the distance he heard a siren. Hopefully a rescue rig. He might need to break a door down. Unless . . .

He bent low, pushed on the dog door . . . and it opened. Not latched. He breathed a sigh of relief. Carl Barclay had installed the oversize, malpositioned pet door himself in a rare fit of handyman fervor. The Landrys' Newfoundland could have moved through with room to spare. Fletcher had tried to explain the security risk of an opening in an exterior door in such close proximity to —

He reached through again, cheek flattened against the back door, felt around for the doorknob, and turned the lock.

Fletcher stepped into a puddle on the kitchen floor. He aimed the light at the ceiling, saw dark sky through a hole. "Emma?"

Where would she hide? *Please be hiding . . . only hiding, not . . .*

As Fletcher walked past the open pantry, he shone his flashlight inside, its beam hitting Mrs. Barclay's huge disaster-preparedness list.

No Emma.

He made a quick circuit of the bedrooms, then skirted hallway debris — framed photos, broken glass — to the weather room. And stopped. He'd been right. The roof was gone here. The room in staggering upheaval.

"Emma? Are you there?" *Please don't be . . .*

He stepped over a pile of shingles and a piece of splintered plywood. Scanned the room with his flashlight. Broken glass, maps, and weather instruments scattered over the carpet. Couch covered with dry-wall debris . . . and a blanket. His heart climbed toward his throat. "Emma?"

Fletcher waded farther into the room with his light focused on the couch, then heard sounds from the hallway. A radio? Music? He hadn't heard it before . . .

He retraced his steps, breaking into a trot along the hall. He stopped. Listened. There it was again . . . from the guest bath.

"Emma?"

Singing. *Oh . . . God, yes!*

She was singing, angel sweet:

"The sun'll come out
Tomorrow.
Bet your bottom dollar that tomorrow . . ."

Fletcher opened the door as slowly as he could, careful not to frighten her. He kept his voice low. "Emma, it's Officer Holt. I'm a friend of Lauren and Jessica — and your daddy."

"I'm here . . . in the tub."

He shone the beam, careful to keep the light indirect and not blind her. His chest squeezed at the sight. The little girl was huddled in the bathtub, sharing the space with the huge Newfoundland. Hannah, amazingly, was asleep in her arms. Emma's hair was dusty with drywall, but her eyes were bright. And her smile melted his heart.

"Are you okay?"

"Yes," she whispered. "Except I think I've got a charley horse in my throat. Or a frog — I always forget which. Anyway, it's from singing so long. That's the only way to keep these two from being scared."

38

"You talked with her?" Eli asked.

"Only for a minute." Lauren cradled the phone, glancing from her little balcony to the city lights beyond. Dark spots showed where power outages continued. Her parents' neighborhood among them. "And then I went into the house to get some things. When I got back, she was asleep in the back of Fletcher's patrol car. Otherwise I would have volunteered to drive her to your folks' house myself."

"I gave Fletcher permission."

"He told me that." Was she imagining Eli's cool distance?

"She was fine," Lauren assured him. "The medics looked her over. She didn't have any problems. Not even a nip from Hannah — they seem to have become friends. Bonding through the storm, I guess." She fought a shudder, thinking of the destruction to her family's home. A few other homes in the neighborhood had sustained similar damage. "Apparently Emma heard the tornado warning on TV. She'd seen the instruction list my mom posted in the pantry. It says to take refuge in the guest bath — safest because there aren't any windows. So Emma took the dogs with her and climbed into the tub. She kept singing to them. Show tunes and worship songs and —"

"I know. I talked to Fletcher. And I just got off the phone with Emma."

She wasn't imagining it. There was so much distance in Eli's voice that Lauren could have been phoning from Austin. Right now, she almost wished she'd stayed there.

"I'm sorry, Eli," she whispered, tears choking her. "I'm so sorry this happened."

There was a long silence.

"She tried to use the kitchen phone, but the lines were down." He sighed. "I shouldn't have let something between us influence my caution regarding Emma. I never would have said yes to Jessica's offer if . . ."

"If it weren't for me?" She hated where this was going.

"I don't know. Maybe. I told you at the beginning that I don't share my daughter. This proves why. It was my fault for forgetting that I can't trust anyone."

"Even me?"

"Look . . . Jessica is who she is. You're who you are. And I'm me — for better or worse. I get it that you want to believe your sister doesn't have serious problems. Potentially dangerous problems. I get that your family will hire a therapist for the dog, but pointing their daughter in the direction of real help is some sort of . . . taboo."

Lauren stiffened.

"I even accept that you want to place everything in God's hands. Trust completely in that kind of hope. My daughter does. Drew too, I suspect. But she's eight. He's brain damaged. And I . . ." Eli's voice broke, ragged, raw. "I can't believe what I don't see, Lauren. I have to do what I can. Me, myself. In real time. Now."

"Okay . . ." Lauren brushed a tear from her cheek, torn between sadness and anger. "But how's that working for you? Living without trust? Without hope? From what I see, it's making you anything but happy, Eli. And it's tearing your family apart. I'd say your restraining order is proof of that." She was sure she heard him groan, but she kept going. "Yes, I believe my sister can get past her problems, change her life for the better. Yes, I trust God to make that happen. And that's an amazing gift. A relief.

You should try it sometime. Instead of stepping in and firing from the hip whenever
trouble comes. Like a one-man army. I think
you must be pretty tired by now."

Eli was quiet so long that Lauren was sure
he'd disconnected.

"I am tired," he said finally. "But I'm used
to that. I can handle it. I appreciate your
checking on Emma. And calling to tell me.
But I need to go. Drew's not so good right
now. I'm going to stay here tonight, do what
I can to help him."

"Oh, Eli . . ." Lauren pressed a hand to
her chest. "I'm sorry."

"You said that already. I should go."

Eli disconnected without saying good-bye.

How had this all gone so terribly wrong?
Lauren looked toward the lights of Hermann Park, where Fletcher had found Darcee. The same day Drew was brought into
the ER. An ache crowded her throat. It
seemed like it had begun with those two
things — a sunburned young woman dancing in a park and a disabled man struggling
to breathe. Separate tragedies. Yet somehow
they'd combined like the air masses that
sent that freak tornado. It had affected them
all: Fletcher, Jess, Emma . . . and most
certainly Eli and Lauren.

She squeezed her eyes shut, turned away

459

from the cityscape. But she couldn't stop the memory of Eli's eyes in the candlelight. Or his voice telling her that she was his music. Only last night they'd held each other, shared, talked, laughed — looked forward to much more of that. She'd heard Eli pray with his daughter, felt her heart tug toward something solid and wonderful. And now, not even a full day later, that hope felt as ravaged as her parents' home. How on earth could this be?

Lauren walked back inside and sank onto the couch, hugging a pillow against her. Hannah snored softly, curled up on an old beach towel on the hardwood floor. She'd become amazingly docile and compliant after her brush with the storm and the forced evacuation to Lauren's apartment. No toys here, no bribe treats; the firefighters had allowed Lauren only a moment to take a few items from her parents' house. The home she'd felt secure in all her life was now a safety hazard. Her parents were expecting her to call again. She'd promised to do that after she checked on the temporary measures taken to secure the property. Jess would be coming here as soon as she left Houston Grace. That much, at least, was settled, but . . .

Lauren's gaze fell on her Bible. She'd

begged a firefighter to let her into the weather room to search for it. He'd found it on the floor beside her mother's shattered Galileo thermometer. Its worn cover had been splattered with soggy drywall, but the pages remained dry, the purple ribbon marker still in place. She'd opened it last night after she'd come home from dinner with Eli and Emma. Reread her favorite verse, underlined so long ago: Jeremiah 29:11.

"For I know the plans I have for you . . . plans to prosper you and not to harm you, plans to give you hope and a future."

Last night she'd been certain of those plans. Tonight she had nothing but doubts.

Lauren closed her eyes, the ache in her throat spreading to her chest, stealing her breath. "Why?" she whispered. "I've always trusted you. You promised. And now nothing is right. My sister, our home . . . and with Eli. Aren't you hearing me, Lord? I've always put everything in your hands. What more do you want?"

"He's worse." Eli held the misting treatment mask to his brother's face, seeing his eyes flicker open for a moment, then roll upward ominously. "Breathing too shallowly to pull the albuterol into his lungs. And he's more tachypneic. Taking about —"

"Thirty-six breaths per minute," Florine reported, concern on her face. And fatigue, though she'd probably refuse to admit it.

It was nearing 3 a.m., and the rest of the residents were long asleep. Only Vee, Florine, and Eli were awake. Maybe Cyril, too; Eli knew him well enough now to believe he'd be quietly watching things from the window of the loft above. Watching and praying.

Eli had made a nest of blankets in the room's overstuffed recliner, pulled it close to his brother's bed, thinking it was almost like the twin beds they'd had for years. Except now the roles felt wrongly reversed — he was the big brother.

"What's the pulse oximeter reading?" He glanced toward the probe taped to Drew's finger. "Any better?"

"Still at 90 to 91 percent. He's had three doses of the antibiotic now. The two by mouth and that last one IV." Florine glanced at the normal saline IV she'd started by phone order just after midnight. For the meds and hydration. Drew was no longer able to drink. "I put a call out to his physician to see if he wants to change it or add another. Or if he wants us to try to arrange transport to the hospital." She frowned.

"Roads are still closed. Only way out of here is by helicopter."

No. There's one other way. . . . Florine knew it as well as he did — probably the reason she'd lit the candles in the small makeshift chapel. And left the Bible on the table next to his brother's iPod and the fishing photo.

"Does Drew's doctor know I'm here?"

"Yes. He's glad of it. Regardless. Not only because of your training, but because you're family," Florine said. "It's a blessing you got here before the storm closed the roads."

Eli was certain the judge wouldn't agree. He'd likely dismiss that physician from his brother's case. Eli wasn't going to ask Florine if she'd talked with their father. He didn't want to know.

"If you bring me a pan of tepid water and some washcloths, I'll sponge him." Eli rested his hand gently on Drew's flushed forehead. "It may help with the fever, but mostly it will feel soothing, I think." His thumb traced Drew's dark brow. "Our mother used to do that when we were sick."

"I'll bring it." She glanced toward the table. "And maybe you could turn that music up a hair? I think some soul soothing would go nicely with that sponging."

Eli was surprised by the sting of tears.

"Right . . . I'll do that."

It was Vee who brought the water basin and the compresses. And then a mug of herbal tea for Eli. She'd shed her storm gear and was dressed in her usual festive work garb: a flowered skirt, tie-dyed tee, and a polka-dot scrub cap pulled over her braids. Her crystal earrings were like that rainbow maker Emma had hanging from the window in her bedroom. Eli wished his brother could see her.

"Call me if you need me to spell you," she said gently as Eli dipped a terry cloth into the barely warm water. "It's still several hours till dawn. You might want to catch some sleep."

"I'm fine."

"I'd say you're much more than that. And I have no doubt your brother would agree." Her amber eyes held his for a moment. "I'll be praying for you both."

Eli swallowed. "Thank you."

He squeezed water from the cloth and pressed it to Drew's forehead, sweeping his hair gently back and getting it damp too. Evaporation — Eli knew the science. But at this moment, he cared more about easing his brother's discomfort. Bringing some kind of peace to him — without a helicopter. He dipped the cloth again, wrung it out, and pressed it over and over against Drew's forehead, face, and neck. A few minutes later, he realized he was sponging in rhythm with the music.

Lauren jerked upright in bed, stared at the clock, confused. Four in the morning and she was . . . at the apartment. Yes. Because a storm tore off the roof, trapped Emma . . . and took Eli away. The painful reality returned, pulling at her sleep-dulled senses like gauze stuck to a wound. She'd fallen asleep praying, with no clearer understanding of why her world had been tossed upside down. The only miracle in this mess was Hannah Leigh. Her parents should have hired Emma and Shrek in place of that pricey dog therapist. The scrappy little dog had been transformed; she'd even climbed into Lauren's lap last night, burrowing close in what appeared to be a sweet attempt to offer comfort.

Lauren grabbed her scrub jacket in place of the robe still at her parents' house and walked barefoot toward the living room. She'd check on Hannah, get a drink of water. Try to catch more sleep, if that was at all possible. She squinted around the living room, dark except for the electric glow from the stove-top light in the adjacent kitchen. The black-and-white bump on the floor was undoubtedly shih tzu in origin; the sofa bed had been pulled out, meaning Jess had arrived at some point after calling to say she was going to hang around with Darcee's mother.

Lauren's breath snagged as she saw the open balcony door.

"Jess!"

She jogged toward the glass doors, her pulse hammering and eyes on her sister. She was leaning too far over the —

"Jess! What are you doing?"

39

Jess whirled around, hand on her chest. "You scared me." Her eyes flooded with tears. "Oh, Lauren . . ."

"Here." She took hold of Jess's hand. "Come in. Please."

Lauren led her to the sofa bed, went back, and closed the door. Halfway to the sofa, she retraced her steps and locked it. She switched on a single small lamp, just enough that they could see each other. The pain in her sister's expression made Lauren want to turn it off again.

"What is it?" She settled cross-legged on the mattress across from Jess, took hold of her hands. "The house? Emma? Darcee?"

Jess shrugged, her bare arms looking scarecrow thin in the baggy tank top Lauren had snatched on her foray into the wrecked house. "All of it, I guess. Darcee's doing better, though. Her mother said they think the danger is past. I just . . ." A tear slid down her cheek. "I feel . . . bad. About everything. Like I'm drowning in it. I can't make it go away this time."

This time. Because there had been other times. Lauren knew that, but hearing Jess admit it was —

"That night," Jess continued, "when I went up to check on Darcee . . . That first time, when Gayle chewed me out for disappearing?"

Lauren nodded.

"We did talk about her baby. She was worried that her daughter would be taken away." Jess swallowed. "Because she has that chemical imbalance — bipolar disorder. I googled it."

Oh, honey, so have I. . . .

"I think . . ." Jess's voice broke. "I think maybe it was my fault."

"What?"

"The roof. That night before, Darcee was telling me about how it feels to have that disorder. The highs — she loves the highs — and the lows. How awful the lows are." Jess took a slow breath. "I told her I understand all that. That I've felt it — that I still feel it. Then Darcee said she's tried to kill herself before. I said I understand that, too."

Lauren's throat closed.

"She said if they took her baby away, she

couldn't go on. That the only thing worse was if her 'crazy' made her a truly bad mother, caused harm to her daughter. She said she'd rather step in front of a bus than let that happen. Or . . ." A sob tore free from Jess's lips. "Or jump off a building. She said that. I should have told somebody."

"Jess . . . ," Lauren breathed, still rocked by what her sister had revealed about herself. "You didn't cause that. We don't even know if —"

"If it was the wind that blew her off." Jess sighed. "Darcee doesn't remember, either. She told me that yesterday. She still can't believe it happened. She can't even remember being up there. If there really is such a thing as God's mercy, maybe that's it." Her lips twisted into the saddest smile Lauren had ever seen. Jess slid her hands from Lauren's, swiped at her eyes, then dragged her fingers through her hair. The dim light played over a cluster of dark lines on her inner forearm. A tattoo?

"What's that?" Lauren reached for her sister's arm, held on to it as Jess tried to pull away. "Hold still. What are those?" Her eyes widened. "Scars?"

"They're old."

Dear Lord . . . Lauren stared at what could be a dozen gray-pink scars, almost parallel to each other, marring the skin on Jess's forearm. She fought a sickening wave of dizziness. "You . . . did that to yourself? That spring when you ran away?"

"Then. And other times."

"But . . ."

"Why?" Jess supplied the word. Then crossed her arms, the scars hidden as effectively as they had been under the long sleeves she wore regardless of the season. "I don't know. Maybe it's the same reason they did those things to Darcee when she was in the coma — the pinches, pressing on her fingernails, all that. Because pain can be good. Something physical you can bandage . . . and heal up. Maybe that's why."

"That . . . cutting . . . was easier than the pain you were feeling inside?"

"I guess so. Sometimes." Jess shook her head slowly. Her breath shuddered. "I don't want to be like her. Like Darcee. I don't want to ever feel as bad as I did that time I ran away. I can't stand hearing some of the things I say to people . . . wanting them to notice me and then hating when they get too close. Hating everybody sometimes — mostly myself." Fresh tears came. "I don't want to make you and Mom and Dad worry all the time. I can't stand hurting you that way. I can't keep making the kind of mistakes like I did yesterday with Emma. And I don't want the kind of joy that makes me run till my feet blister . . . until I vomit or believe I can actually fly. I don't want to try to do that someday."

"What *do* you want, Jess?" Lauren realized she'd never asked that before.

"I'm not sure. Except that it's not this." Jess spread her palms, and the scars on her arm showed again. "I can't do this. Nothing makes me feel better anymore. Not food, not exercise, not alcohol, not —"

"Drugs?" The truth hit Lauren like a fist to the gut. "You took them. Those painkillers from Mrs. Humphries."

Jess's lips tensed, a bare hint of defensiveness coming and going as fast as a blink. And a look of misery replaced it. "I swallowed a couple of them right there at work. Then I freaked out about what I'd done, ran to the bathroom, and stuck my fingers down my throat. I flushed the rest of the meds down the toilet — except for the hair ball junk. Whether you believe me or not, it's the truth. I threw those pills away." Her shoulders sagged. "What are you going to do? Now that I told you?"

"I don't know." Lauren didn't have a clue what to do. How did she protect Jess? From any of this? "I only know that right now . . .

I just need to hug my sister. Please."

"I think . . . I can deal with that." Jess's chin trembled.

"Come here."

Lauren pulled Jess close, hugging her like she hadn't done in years. She petted her hair, rocked her as if she were that Camelot princess again. Held her so close that she had no idea whose tears she felt, her own or her sister's. She only knew that when this long-overdue moment ended, she was going to need to lean on God harder than she ever had in her life.

Please tell me how to help her.

It wasn't so hard to breathe now. It felt like he really didn't need to; it was more like swimming. Going down deep. Like when Drew wore his fins in their grandmother's pool, and his brother had to stay on top because he had those blow-up things on his arms. Drew would dive down and pretend he was a shark. Shoot up top and make Eli laugh. Yank on his swimsuit and make him shout, "Quit! I'm gonna tell!" He never did, though. They never tattled. They were a team. And they made a promise that they'd always stick together.

Drew shivered, and his teeth made noises like Grandma's poodle on the tile floor when its toenails were too long. He was cold. Not because of the swimming. The swimming felt warm. He was cold because Eli had washed his hair with those towels. But now . . . Drew turned his head as best he could. The mask poked against his eye. He could still see his brother anyway. Asleep right next to him. Right underneath Emma's drawing . . . and the cross. Jesus liked water too. He didn't need blow-up arm things or fins. He could walk on water. Maybe Drew could learn that.

The shivers were gone. He was swimming again in the warm water. It was funny — he could use both of his arms and legs. Like they were new. Nothing hurt. And his music was there, right in the water. All around him. Maybe even inside him, sweet . . . warm. Better than blueberry pancakes. He didn't need to breathe, but he could sing . . . all the words about lambs and love and glory.

There was light now. So much light. And — Drew smiled — rainbows, rainbows everywhere. Emma would love it. . . .

Eli thrashed, fought the blankets, and then jerked to a sitting position in the chair. Awake, drenched in sweat, and confused. He'd dreamed he was drowning and —

No.

"Drew!"

Eli freed himself from the recliner and hunched over the bed. "Breathe, Champ — take a breath!" He grasped his brother's shoulder, shook him, holding his own breath. The mask was delivering oxygen, but there was no fogging from respirations, no movement of Drew's chest.

"Florine, Vee!" he shouted, pressing his fingers under his brother's jaw. *Please, let me find a pulse. Please* . . . "Breathe, Drew. Breathe for me!"

They were there in seconds, and in half that time he sent Vee to get the portable suction and the Ambu bag. Eli's knees went weak when Drew's eyelids flickered and he drew a raspy breath at last. He'd looked peaceful, like he was sleeping, but the flush from the fever had been replaced by a waxy pallor.

"I checked on him not fifteen minutes ago," Florine said, attaching the blood pressure cuff to Drew's arm. "His temp was down to 100, and he looked comfortable. His pulse ox reading hadn't changed. I didn't want to disturb him for anything more."

"It's okay," Eli assured her quickly. "He's done this before. Gone down the tubes really fast. Respiratory acidosis. It's what happened last Christmas." Saying it, he expected the familiar rush of anger and frustration. Images of Drew tied to the bed with an ET tube shoved down his throat. But all that came to mind was Emma . . . the Nativity picture she'd had that janitor tape over Drew's bed. Her prayers. And her hope that her uncle would live.

"Here." Vee handed him the Ambu bag, moved to connect it to the portable oxygen tank.

"I've got the suction ready," Florine reported. Her gaze rose to Emma's Palm Sunday cross, her lips moving. Eli had no doubt she was praying.

"I'm here too," Cyril reported from the doorway. His rumpled appearance said he'd slept even less than Eli. "I'm not medical, but I've got two good hands. Tell me what you need and I'll give it my best."

"Thanks," Eli told them. "I'm going to prime his breathing with this bag. Try to blow off some of that CO_2. Then see if we can get him going enough to pull in another respiratory —"

"I'm getting the albuterol," Florine anticipated, already moving to the doorway.

Eli fitted the Ambu mask over Drew's face, gave the bag a first oxygen-rich squeeze. His brother's dark eyes opened, searching for his. "I'm helping you breathe, Champ. The same way you helped me . . . with so many things. I'm here. I'm not going anywhere. And neither are you. We'll play your music and I'll squeeze this bag. You'll feel better . . . and so will I."

He did as he promised, the rhythm of the Ambu bag matching the music beat for beat, in the same strange way the fever sponging had. Eli watched his brother's face and remembered the time the roles had been reversed. When, like in his nightmare, he'd been drowning in the Gulf of Mexico. And Drew dived in. Dived deep and pushed him to the surface of the water. Allowing him to breathe while putting himself at risk. And then Eli thought of last night's desperate moment, when he'd stood beside that raging water, feeling helpless to save his child. Knowing he'd failed to keep her safe. His father must have felt exactly the same way when his sons were in that storm-swept ocean.

"Thank you," Eli told Florine as she handed him the aerosol treatment. "I'm going to bag him a little longer, and then I'll see if we can get this medication into his lungs." Eli drew a slow breath, watching his brother's face. "Meanwhile, call 911. Tell them to get that chopper here, stat."

"Yes, sir."

They hurried away, Cyril to secure a landing spot, Vee and Florine to make the arrangements for transport. Eli was left squeezing oxygen into his brother's lungs. And feeling a need he'd denied for far too long.

"Please, God," he prayed in a thick whisper. "You know I've doubted you. Blamed you, even. But I need your help now. For my brother. And for me. I'm tired, and I need this long storm to end. I need peace. I know you're the only one who can do that. I'm putting this in your hands now."

40

Lauren checked the coffeepot, then glanced around the living room, satisfied it was reasonably tidy. Morning sun filtered through the balcony doors, a narrow shaft of light landing square on the sleeping Hannah Leigh's furry behind. Sun and just enough rain in the clouds to make . . . Lauren smiled. She'd seen it when she carried her coffee onto the balcony half an hour ago: a rainbow among the remaining clouds. Pale, like a watercolor painted with a too-soggy brush, but there it was. A hopeful banner of color. She'd take that.

The sound of the hair dryer in the distance stopped. She'd insisted Jess take the bedroom for the rest of the night, telling her it would be more comfortable — telling herself it wasn't so that she could guard the balcony door. Lauren took the sofa bed, but she hadn't slept. She'd spent the hours before dawn petting Hannah and praying for answers. Then certainty finally came, like that pale rainbow. *Thank you, Lord.*

Her pulse quickened as Jess ambled into the room, yawning.

"I smell coffee," she said, hiking up the waistband of Lauren's old jogging capris. The matching hoodie's long sleeves reached her fingertips.

"Full pot. Powdered creamer on the counter," Lauren offered and watched her sister move toward the kitchen. She looked at least somewhat rested. "Fridge is pretty bare, so I ordered some breakfast."

"Delivered breakfast?" Jess blew on her coffee. "I didn't think you could do that."

Lauren smiled. "I have my ways." She patted the couch. "Bring your coffee over here. I've been doing some thinking about those things we talked about."

"Me too." Jess sat beside her, took a long sip of her coffee, and groaned with pleasure. "Ah, caffeine. I needed you."

"You were thinking?" Lauren prompted.

"Right. About that problem with Mrs. Humphries's meds. First, the point is that they were outdated. *Expired* prescriptions. The pharmacy had already been called to come get them for disposal." She shrugged. "Basically, when you look at it, you might say I was doing a kind of service."

Lauren told herself that pointing out the flawed logic would be counterproductive.

"And," Jess continued, "everyone already thinks that Gayle took them. I mean, it's the least of her worries now, considering. Everything's probably going to be blamed on her thyroid condition anyway. So I thought, why not leave it like that? It seems like a perfect solution."

Ah, Jess . . . Lauren's heart lugged as she remembered the ICU conversation with Gayle about Mrs. Humphries's meds. Gayle told her not to worry, that she'd *"never do something like that."* She hadn't.

"Because," Jess finished, "I've got to keep my job if I ever hope to get my own apartment again. And —"

"You told me you don't want to feel the way you've been feeling," Lauren interrupted. It was time to do what she had to do. "You said you'd talked to Darcee about bipolar disorder, that you understood those highs and lows. You said . . . you said you understood thoughts of suicide. You've cut yourself because it's less painful than how you're feeling inside. You said you feel like you're drowning, and you can't make it go away this time."

"I was tired, that's all."

"You need help, Jess."

480

"Don't." Jess set her coffee down. "Don't get all preachy on me. I really can't handle that today. I'm fine. Storm's over; we all survived. End of story." Her eyes met Lauren's. "All I'm asking is that you help me out. Like you always have. Cover for me on that one stupid mistake. You want Mom and Dad to find out? Do you really want to wreck my chances of getting into nursing — ?"

"You're not ready."

"What?"

Lauren forced herself to imagine twelve-year-old Vee raising a gun in that foul, hellish darkness. And Cyril's wise words: *"I don't expect God to fill the sandbags."*

"You're not ready for nursing school, Jess. Not yet. You need to get healthy first. I'll handle things with our parents; don't worry about that. This is the way I'm going to help you now. Because . . ." Lauren's voice cracked. "I love you with all my heart. I can't stand by and watch you suffer. Yes, I'm praying for you. But I'm also going to see to it that we tackle these problems on all fronts."

The doorbell rang. Followed by a knock.

"Breakfast." Lauren managed to stand despite her weak knees.

"I'm not hungry."

"I am."

Stay with us, Lord. . . .

Lauren opened the door, and Fletcher stepped in. Street clothes, shadow of a beard, food boxes in both hands.

"Somebody order breakfast burritos?"

"I told her I wasn't hungry." Jess crossed her arms. "Just tell my sister to butt out, Fletcher."

"No can do." Fletcher stepped aside so that Angela could come in.

"Good morning, Jessica."

"Oh, for pete's sake, what is this?" Jess shot Lauren a look.

"Breakfast. With people who care about you." Lauren walked back, settled on the ottoman, and reached for her hand. "We only want to talk, to toss some ideas around. See what we can come up with — all four of us — to help you start feeling better. Will you do that?"

"I . . . I can't believe this. . . ."

Lauren squeezed her sister's fingers. "It's time, honey."

Jess shut her eyes for a moment, as if by doing it she could make them all go away. Her shoulders rose and fell with her deep sigh. She opened her eyes. Then lifted one brow. "You have bacon in there, Fletcher?"

"Yes, ma'am. Enough for five — including

Hannah Leigh."

"Good." Tears filled Jess's eyes. "I think this is going to take more than a cupcake."

Lauren leaned forward, wrapped her arms around her sister. Then raised her gaze toward the ceiling. There might have been bacon for five, but Lauren had no doubt there were six at this meal. And hope enough for all.

"Come here." Eli gathered Emma into his arms in the Memorial Hospital intensive care waiting room. "I can't get enough of you, my brave little girl." She smelled of shampoo, Cheerios, and blind Newfoundland. He'd never inhaled anything so wonderful.

"Did you really come here in a helicopter?"

"I did."

The enormity of it all, especially the peace Eli felt now, struck him again as his daughter's arms circled his neck. "Your uncle and I were up there in the clouds like a couple of action-movie heroes. He wanted to fly the chopper himself, but I said I knew he'd hijack us to Disneyland. I told him that Mickey Mouse would have to wait until he was rested up."

Emma's giggle tickled his ear; then she

leaned back, her expression serious now. "He's going to be okay, Daddy."

"I hope so." The word rolled off Eli's tongue with surprising ease.

"We've been praying. Grams and me and Shrek." Her eyes could have been a poster for the word *hope*. "God's hands are big. He's got it covered."

"I believe that," Eli managed around the rising lump in his throat. He touched a fingertip to her nose. "Wise on top of brave; that's my girl."

"You betcha." She tilted her head. "I heard Yonner tell Grams that you saved Uncle Drew's life at Mimaw's. I think he was crying when he said it. Is it true?"

The lump was threatening to choke him. "Well . . . I had lots of help."

"Emma?" Eli's mother beckoned from the doorway; she was smiling, though her eyes were still puffy from crying. "Let's go find some juice. Yonner wants to talk with your daddy for a minute."

Here we go. . . . Eli took a deep breath, reminded himself that he was prepared for anything. He was going to trust for the best and keep a grip on this new sense of peace, no matter what.

"Hello, sir."

"Elijah." His father looked like he'd been

awake half the night too. Beat, far beyond any fatigue. "Your brother is opening his eyes more now," he reported, glancing toward the hallway and then back at Eli. "They think maybe they can turn things around with that Bi . . ."

"BiPAP."

"Yes. And maybe not have to do the tube." His father cleared his throat. "I told them we'd feel better if that didn't happen again. Not unless it was a short-term measure and the outcome looked promising." He met Eli's gaze. "I told the doctors in charge of your brother's care that we would all sit down and talk about making the advance directive more specific."

Emma had been right, because tears were gathering in the judge's eyes now.

"I said we want comfort and mercy for Drew," he continued. "And for all of us."

"Dad . . ." Eli's voice caught.

"Let me get this out, please." His father took a breath. "After we got Emma back last night, I couldn't sleep. I poured myself a stiff drink. And then I poured it out. I thought about my grand-daughter, curled up in that bathtub with a tornado tearing the roof off. It wouldn't have happened if you'd trusted me to pick her up from that party — if I hadn't made it blasted impossible to trust me." He rested his hand on Eli's shoulder, steadying himself as though his knees might buckle. "And then I thought about that day when I took you and your brother fishing."

Eli wasn't so sure about his own knees.

"I thought about your mother telling me not to take a chance in the storm. I asked myself, what kind of father does that? Takes a risk with his children's lives?" He shook his head. "And then . . . after all these painful years, bars one son from seeing the other. What kind of man chases his son down the driveway with a shotgun?"

Eli closed his eyes. *Please, God . . . be here.*

"And I answered myself, Eli." A tear coursed down his father's cheek. "An irresponsible, arrogant fool of a man. A judge playing God. I've been hanging on to Drew any way I could, no matter how he or your mother or you or Emma suffered for it. I've held on because letting him die would prove the truth once and for all: I killed my boy."

"Dad . . ." Eli swallowed against a rush of tears.

"I *am* proud of you, Son," his father continued, his hand beginning to tremble on Eli's shoulder. "I always have been. I have no excuses for the way I've treated you. I guess I was afraid you could see through me, see everything I wouldn't let myself see all these years. You've been the responsible one, Eli. You've been the man, the father, I never was."

"Not always, sir. I've made more than my fair share of mistakes."

His father smiled, squeezed Eli's shoulder. "This is where your mother would pop in and say something about grace. She does that."

"Emma too." He smiled back at his father. "We get it in stereo."

"That we do. And more." The judge shook his head. "Your mother read me the riot act this morning. All but pointed my bird gun to get me to sit down and listen. She made me promise I'd extend my sabbatical into a medical leave of absence. Get some problems straightened out."

Relief washed over Eli. "Go, Mom Landry."

"So . . ." His father sighed.

"So you'll have more time for Emma. She misses having all of us together, and . . . I do too." Eli's voice fell to a whisper. "I love you, Dad."

"Eli . . ." His father clapped him on the shoulder, then pulled him into a tight bear hug for the first time in far too long. "I love you too, Son."

41

Lauren stared upward. The new roof was under way. Or would be, once the last of the shingles were pulled off. Those that hadn't blown across the neighborhood, into swimming pools, and onto the playground of her grammar school. One had apparently been wedged in the top of the monkey bars like a flag. She'd heard countless stories of Barclay shingle sightings. Glorietta's baby tornado had been confirmed. Their house had been the worst hit — but then, the roof had been easy pickings.

Her father decided to go with a standing-seam metal variety this time. More resistant to hail, wind, fire, and freezing — not that he was expecting many frozen days in Houston. But post-tornado, he wasn't taking any chances. He wasn't willing to put bolt holes in that new roof either. So Pamela Barclay intended to make a weather vane wall display once the family room remodel was complete. She'd also decided that pink was passé and was leaning toward a cocoa-brown-and-turquoise color scheme. And she wasn't entirely sure she was going to replace all the weather equipment. She'd been a little embarrassed that she'd boasted about all those alerts and preparedness supplies . . . under a roof the contractor said could have fallen in from the vibration of her Zumba DVD. Mom was rethinking things. And of course, much of their time — and Lauren's — was spent supporting Jess.

At Angela's suggestion, Jess had decided to start outpatient therapy. After a thorough medical workup. Counseling — private and group — would begin to address her interpersonal problems, the substance abuse, and her eating issues. The team was also carefully evaluating Jess for the most effective prescription medicine to treat the chemical imbalance at the root of her mood disorder. It was all voluntary and too early to tell for sure, but so far things were going well. Even if, according to Jess, "Nobody's going to let me wear my princess crown in this place. That's been made more than obvious."

Lauren smiled. She'd never been more proud of anyone than she was of Jess. It had been incredibly hard to admit to the Houston Grace administration that she'd taken the missing drugs. And a huge relief when the hospital decided to be lenient in light of her decision to pursue treatment. Nursing school was put on hold for now. Their parents were finally accepting all of that and slowly becoming less concerned with what other people thought. In fact, Mom seemed determined to educate herself about bipolar illness with the same zeal she had given to meteorology. Their parents' enlightenment would go a long way toward encouraging Jess. Lauren was proud of them, too. But she hadn't told them about Eli. There hadn't seemed much point.

She stopped in the foyer, catching sight of the flying pig weather vane lying against the hall tree. It had been there since the day Eli arrived on her porch holding it in his hands. That day he kissed her. It had only been nine days since the storm, but it seemed like a lifetime ago. She'd heard Eli was taking family leave to be at Drew's side as much as possible while he was hospitalized. She'd communicated with him through a few short texts. It sounded like he was on better terms with his father. He was glad Jess was getting treatment. Lauren said she was happy to hear Drew's condition had improved. Sporadic messages. Nothing too personal. They hadn't actually talked since that stormy night when they'd both said such difficult things to each other. The truth — both sides of it — had driven a wedge between them. Which was why Lauren was a little nervous today. Since he'd texted that he was going to —

"Hey."

"Eli." Her heart sailed like a Barclay shingle.

He was dressed in a black polo shirt and faded Levi's and looked far more handsome than Lauren even remembered. "Come in. The mess is cleaned up. No dog. Hannah's living the good life at my folks' rented high-rise condo. There's a dog walker."

Eli's brows rose. "How's that going?"

"Fine, actually." She smiled despite the fact that her insides had begun to tremble. "She's like a new dog. Mom thinks it had something to do with barometric pressure. Attitude adjustment in the eye of a tornado. I think it had everything to do with Emma and Shrek." Unexpected tears rose. "I'm so very sorry about what happened. It's my fault."

Somehow he'd closed the distance between them. It only made her heart ache all the more.

"I don't blame you for not trusting me," she continued. "I waited far too long to do something about Jess's problems. You were right. And so were Fletcher and Angela. I did everything wrong."

"Lauren . . ."

"It's true," she insisted, her shakiness even worse now that he'd lightly grasped her elbow. "I kept saying I was leaving it all in God's hands, trusting him to fix it. But I ignored all his whispers about what needed to be done. I grabbed on to his promise of hope as an excuse not to take any kind of action . . . to do nothing."

"No. No one could ever accuse you of doing nothing." His eyes held hers. "You love your sister. That's huge, Lauren."

"And I 'helped' her by lying for her, tiptoeing around her moods, monitoring her eating, going through her trash . . ." Lauren grimaced. "You said it yourself. Enabling only makes things worse. I knew that. I aced my nursing school psych exams — I'm a trained peer counselor, for goodness' sake. But I couldn't see it, didn't want to see it. Not when it came to my sister."

"But you did it, Lauren. You made her treatment happen. You stepped up." He smiled at the surprise on her face. "Fletcher told me you called a breakfast meeting."

Lauren rubbed a tear away. "I shouldn't have let Jess drive Emma. I'll never stop being thankful she's okay."

"Me neither." Eli glanced toward the kitchen. "Let's sit down."

She followed him into the room, caught sight of the open pantry door. Her mother's list. *Run from Water. Hide from the Wind.* It felt like they weren't hiding anymore.

"Actually, I came over here to apologize too," he told her as they settled into chairs. "I never should have said those things to you on the phone after Emma was found. There's no excuse for that. It wasn't your fault; it wasn't even Jess's. Emma ending up here . . ." He glanced toward the ceiling, and sunlight shone on his face through the holes in the roof. "It was my fault. I was furious with my father about that restraining order, and I took off without thinking. I knew there was a storm coming. I saw the sandbags. But I was halfway to Mimaw's before I even remembered I had to pick Emma up from that party. I forgot my own daughter. And I wasn't even going there out of concern for Drew. Not really. I was going there to stick it to my father, to best him. Show him how much of a man I was."

Lauren had a strong sense that something had changed in Eli. Something big.

"Since that night, I've been doing a lot of thinking." His lips tugged upward. "Frightening, right? But I know now that I waged the whole ugly battle with my father because I couldn't deal with what happened to Drew last Christmas. I was protecting myself as much as I was protecting Drew — maybe more. You were right, Lauren. I gave up hope." Eli's smile was gone. "My brother dove into that sea trying to save me. He didn't give up. I'm alive because Drew kept hope. I owe him at least that much. I think . . . God agrees."

Lauren was afraid to breathe.

"Yes. God. We've been talking, he and I. That night at Mimaw's and a lot since. At church this morning too — Emma's pretty happy about that." Eli sighed. "Apparently God wasn't going to let me drown, either."

She smiled at him, tears brimming. "I shouldn't say I told you so."

"That's all right. As long as you say something else, too." He traced his fingertips along her cheek. "Tell me I haven't ruined things between us. Say you're willing to still see me. I care about you, Lauren. I need you. You're . . ."

"I'm your music? Is that what you were going to say?"

"It worked last time, right?"

"It did."

"Well then . . ." Eli leaned close enough that she could feel the warmth of his skin. "You'll give me another chance — is that a yes?"

"More than yes." She slid her arms around his neck. "That's an 'Aye, captain.' "

They were both still laughing a little when their lips met. But the laughs didn't last long. Because in a heartbeat Eli's arms were around her too. And then he was kissing her throat, her cheek, her nose, before capturing her lips again. And again. Eli Landry, healer, pirate, father to her favorite little girl, wonderful hero, and —

"Excuse me, folks."

They drew apart, inspected the ceiling. And saw the grinning roofer peering down at them.

"Sorry to interrupt. But I need to get these shingles off if I'm going to get your roof going." His grin widened. "Personally, I understand your priority too. But we never know when these things will hit — hurricanes, tornadoes. You know what they say: 'Get a kit. Make a plan. Be informed.' I think a roof fits in there somewhere."

"Good point," Eli told him. "We agree. Let's get this thing covered as soon as possible. But . . . maybe check those shingles on the north side for one more minute? Just one?"

"Gotcha." The roofer winked. Boots thunked in the other direction.

"Where were we?" Eli murmured.

"Here, I think." She kissed his lips lightly, then stretched her arms around him as he pulled her close in a hug. Warm, strong, like he'd never let her go. His lips brushed Lauren's temple, and her heart thudded in her ears. Or maybe it was his heart; it was impossible to tell the difference.

"For the record, I only agreed with that guy so he'd give us a break," Eli confessed. "I'm not really worried about the next storm."

"Me neither," she whispered back, nestling closer. "Not now."

Or ever.

Whatever happened, Lauren knew where to find the truest shelter.

Thank you, Father, for always being there.

EPILOGUE

DECEMBER

"Your brother," Darcee teased, lifting Drew's earbud away from her tinsel-embellished red hair, "has been trying to make me a Christian music fan. Or save my soul — I suspect that's his real plan. All those weeks I spent here at Mimaw's, this guy made sure I had something to listen to. Drew Landry never quits."

"No, he doesn't." Eli raised his voice over another round of carols — with a splash of washboard — starting up somewhere beyond the huge Christmas tree. "He can be pretty persuasive. Right, Bro?"

"Ye-eah." Drew nodded. "Betcha."

"Especially with my mother encouraging him." Darcee winked. "That's spiritual persuasion on steroids. Lucky me."

Eli smiled. More than lucky . . .

He watched as Darcee shifted her weight onto her tripod cane and raised her hand to meet Drew's enthusiastic knuckle bump. His brother's wheelchair was strung with battery-operated twinkle lights and plastic holly. Eli would bet that Drew's crooked grin could power Cyril's entire string of emergency generators. He must have told everyone a dozen times that Darcee was coming back for the Mimaw's Christmas party. The only thing that made him smile more was that he'd be spending Christmas in River Oaks. With his family and Florine in attendance. It would be the official start of his weekends at home.

Eli drew in a breath of air scented by pine garland, spiced cider, and Cajun meatballs, thinking a completely corny thought: right now, he and Drew could be a pair of poster kids for happiness because —

His chest warmed as Lauren arrived beside them with a plate of cookies.

"Here you go." She held it out for Drew and Darcee. "Careful; the gingerbread boys are still pretty warm. Emma and Vee are in a baking frenzy. Dough, frosting, raisins, and peppermints piled up everywhere. Hannah's not complaining; she's had a couple of broken cookie legs tossed her way. Shrek has a new rawhide bone. They're hoping this party never ends." She laughed. "Whew, time for a break. I've been running like a reindeer."

"Hey there, Prancer." Eli tugged at the sleeve of Lauren's candy-striped shirt, then slipped an arm around her waist, drawing her close. "Come here."

Her face was flushed from the warmth of the kitchen, blue eyes lit with happiness. She'd tucked a sprig of mistletoe in her wavy mane of hair. Eli thought it was a great idea.

She smiled. "Cookie?"

"No. Just you."

Lauren set the cookie plate on a chair, then returned to his side. "In case you didn't notice —" she nodded toward the sound of carolers — "that's your mother and Florine singing the duet. Jess has the kazoo. And on the washboard . . . that's the judge." She laughed at the look on Eli's face. "Seriously. Your dad. I'll bet you never thought it was possible."

"No way." Eli chuckled. He wouldn't have believed that of his father. But a lot of things had changed. Including the Barclays' reservations about him — perhaps the greatest when-pigs-fly miracle of all. It hadn't been easy. But once they accepted that so much had been colored by Jessica's illness, everything was different. It helped that Emma was a huge hit. And old Shrek was always a slobbering charmer. But in the end it was about what Lauren and Eli felt for each other; there was no denying it. In these past months, he had thought it wasn't possible to love her more than he already did. Every day proved Eli wrong. Today especially.

"I talked with Gayle for a few minutes," she told him. "She was calling from Alamo Grace. She thinks she's going to like living in San Antonio. It feels like a new start. She thanked me again for organizing the drive to pay off her car loan. And she said to tell you again how much she appreciated your father's help with the attorney. And your deposition explaining the thyroid condition."

Eli nodded. The grand jury had dismissed the case after considering the combination of self-defense and the medical condition escalating Gayle's response. Leo was still in jail; much of his time would be spent in therapy. Gayle hadn't filed for divorce. Maybe hope was whispering to her, too. "I'm glad things are going better for Gayle."

There was a chorus of oohs and aahs in the distance as Darcee's parents arrived, their granddaughter toddling beside them in a glittery holiday dress and white tights. They'd been helping with child care while Darcee continued her physical therapy.

"There's my mama cue." Darcee ruffled Drew's hair and limped forward, the cane helping with her still-healing leg. She met Emma coming their way, each greeting the other with a high five.

"I'm all finished baking," Emma reported, climbing into Drew's lap and twining an arm around his neck.

Eli's heart tugged at his brother's happy smile as his niece kissed his cheek. Lauren slid her arm through Eli's, watching them too.

"It's nice outside," Emma reported, tipping her head in that coy way she'd learned for her critically acclaimed role as Annie. "Really nice. No clouds, no rain. Practically perfect."

Drew nodded. "Yeah. Perrr . . . fect."

"Uh . . ." Eli shot them a knowing look. "You haven't been out there."

"Cyril said," Emma informed him.

"Yeah." Drew's lopsided smile reappeared. "Cyril. He knows."

Lauren laughed around a bite of gingerbread. "What's up with you two?"

"Conspiring," Eli said, his pulse picking up speed. "To get rid of us, probably. Make us go outside so they can eat our cookies, maybe?"

"We'll behave. Cross our hearts." Emma

did the Annie head tip again, subtle as a truck full of sandbags. "But maybe you two *should* go out for a walk. You know, hang out, talk about stuff?"

Drew nodded, cookie crumbs on his chin. "Talk and . . . stuff."

Lauren laughed again. "I don't care what they're up to. I'm game — let's go."

"I . . ." Eli's nervousness returned. Then Lauren secured the mistletoe in her hair. It was all he needed. "Sure. Let's go for a walk."

Drew and Emma beamed, did a thumbs-up duet.

He and Lauren had gotten as far as the door when Jessica found them.

"What's up?" she asked, catching Lauren's hand.

Eli thought once again how much better Jessica looked — more rested, softer. And healthier with the benefit of those few extra pounds. She smiled more. She was doing well on the trial meds, though she complained they made her feel spacey sometimes. But then that was Jessica; it wouldn't be normal if she didn't grouch now and then. On the plus side, she was able to go back to work part-time and had signed up for limited classes last fall — in psychology. She thought she might like to be a counselor someday. Maybe help troubled adolescent girls. Angela had made an impression, clearly. And Jessica had recently started coming to church with Eli and Lauren. Not every Sunday, but most. And not always inspired. But listening . . .

"No," Lauren was telling her, "we're not leaving yet. We thought we'd take a walk. We've been booted out by popular demand." She laughed at the look on her sister's face. "I'm kidding. We're going to get some fresh air and then help the Viettes clean up after the party." She tapped Jessica's purse. "You're taking off?"

"Have to. I wanted to say hi to Darcee, but I can't stay longer. Fletcher's picking me up at six. The Tacky Country Christmas Cotillion. I told you, remember? With a costume contest."

Lauren grinned. "Princess and astronaut."

"Do you believe it?" Jessica rolled her eyes. "I could die. But Fletcher thought it would be funny, and I thought . . . why not."

"When is he flying out to California?" Lauren asked, concern in her tone. Fletcher's mother was having health problems.

"Tuesday. Charly's scheduled for more testing at the end of the week. Fletcher wants to be there for her — and for his dad." Jessica's brows scrunched. "Mr. Holt's pretty stressed."

"I can imagine." Lauren sighed, then found her smile again. "You'd better go get ready for the party, princess."

There was a flurry of hugs and they parted ways, Jessica toward her car and Eli and Lauren down the gravel road.

"Tacky Country?" Eli asked, taking Lauren's hand.

"Cotillion. It's a charity benefit for the Make-A-Wish foundation."

"Ah . . ." Eli smiled; he had a wish of his own. "Do you think Fletcher will ever tell your sister how he feels about her?"

"I think he's taking things slowly. Jess has made a lot of changes — and so much progress. Fletcher would never pressure her. You know how patient he is. Fifteen years' worth." Lauren smiled. "Besides, flak jacket or not, it's probably a little scary to risk putting your heart out there like that."

Eli couldn't agree more.

"Somehow," Lauren laughed, scooting closer to him on the bench, "we always manage to end up in this chicken coop place."

Eli shrugged. "The only private spot around here, unless you want to talk to the tune of a washboard. Or be ogled by a pack of Landrys."

"I can think of worse things. Like a man in steel-toed boots staring down at us from a hole in the roof."

Lauren noticed how the sun, dipping behind the trees, warmed the color of Eli's skin. It wasn't nearly as warm as his generous heart. Six months after the storm and she couldn't imagine life without loving this man.

"Besides . . ." Eli touched the mistletoe in her hair, kissed her forehead lightly. "I don't think of this spot as the 'chicken coop place.' I think of it as the place I first got the nerve to tell you that I wanted there to be an 'us.' And I think of it as the site where the helicopter landed after the storm, to carry Drew and me to the hospital. The morning I took a chance on hope."

Lauren reached up to stroke his face. "I'm so grateful that you did."

"It started with you, Lauren." Eli grasped her hand and kissed her fingertips. "You are more than my music. You're the woman who pointed the way out of the storm. Back to my faith. My family. You're part of my heart now. My life . . ."

Lauren nodded, happy tears welling. "I love you, Eli."

"I love you. More than I can say . . . in

the company of chickens." He smiled. "I made a reservation for dinner tonight. The Rainbow Lodge — I'm finally getting us there. It's supposed to be one of the most romantic restaurants in Houston."

Lauren smiled. "I've heard that."

"But I wanted to tell you how I feel right here first. And I want to . . ." He leaned away, reached into his jacket pocket. "Okay, imagine yourself at the Rainbow Lodge."

Lauren's heart stalled as he pulled out a small blue box. When he opened the lid, the setting sun caught the facets on the diamonds like . . . a rainbow.

"Oh, Eli, it's beautiful."

"I love you, Lauren. I want us to be married." Eli's eyes held hers. "It's a little complicated, I know. I come with a ready-made family. There's Emma. And Shrek. I have a brother who —"

"I know." Lauren pressed her finger to his lips. "I know all of that. It's a big part of why I love you, Eli. And yes . . . I want to marry you. I want to be a mother to Emma — and Shrek. A sister to Drew. I love that you'll be a big brother to Jess. And —"

Eli didn't let her finish. His arms were around her, his lips finding hers, sealing their promise, their future.

To the soft cluck of Mimaw's chickens.

As Jess said . . . why not?

Life, after all, was messy, filled with unexpected complications. Quirky. But hopeful, too. Oh, so very hopeful.

Lauren loved that.

DISCUSSION GUIDE

Use these questions for individual reflection or for discussion within your book club or small group.

Note: If you would like me to "attend" your book club's gathering, please e-mail me at Candace@candacecalvert.com. I'll try to arrange a speakerphone or Skype visit to join your discussion.

1. In the opening chapter of *Life Support,* we meet Lauren Barclay and Eli Landry. Both have a deep sense of responsibility toward their siblings, but each acts quite differently on that feeling. Eli takes a strong stance, isn't afraid of conflict or controversy when protecting his brother. Lauren is more prone to worry, hover, and even accept the blame when her sister is late for work. Which approach were you

more comfortable with? Why?

2. Eli is a single father, and his daughter, Emma, impacts the story in important ways from beginning to end. Did the father-child relationship shape how you felt about Eli? How so?

3. Darcee Grafton is a dramatic example of someone struggling with a mental health disorder. As the story evolves, we learn that Lauren's sister, Jessica, may have a similar problem. When the hospital chaplain broaches the subject of help — a medical workup, counseling, possibly medication — Lauren is uncomfortable. She insists her parents would consider treatment a failure on their part — proof their daughter is flawed, that perhaps their faith isn't strong enough. In your own experience, have you seen people hesitate to seek help because of the stigma of mental health treatment? Discuss.

4. The Barclay family's feisty shih tzu, Hannah Leigh, sashays into the

story and makes her presence known throughout. What similarities do you see in the way Lauren and her family deal with their "capricious" dog and their troubled younger daughter?

5. Though Eli's brain-injured brother, Drew, is mostly silent, we see the other characters through his eyes and even have a chance to witness his deep faith. Did Drew's point of view enhance the story for you? Look back at the storm scene in chapter 39. How did experiencing Drew's health crisis from his perspective make you feel?

6. After surviving the horrors of Hurricane Katrina, the Viette family trusts God in all things, yet their experiences have taught them to "step up" and take action when necessary. As Cyril tells Lauren when he's preparing for the coming storm, "I believe God listens to every prayer, but I don't expect him to fill the sandbags." In contrast, Lauren believes that her faith requires her to leave her sister's prob-

lems entirely in God's hands. Have you ever struggled with that conflict? What guides you in deciding when to step up and take action?

7. *Life Support* depicts storms on many levels — emotional, relational, medical, and spiritual, all against the background of an impending hurricane. Have you experienced a severe weather event? Does your family have a plan, a disaster kit? What significance is there in the fact that the Barclays have an elaborate storm plan yet live under a roof that is leaky and unsafe?

8. At one point, a frustrated Eli compares storm preparation to his brother's medical situation, saying, "We stock up on batteries and candles. But an advance medical directive that offers mercy and dignity and peace? That's too much planning, too uncomfortable to talk about." Do you agree with him? Why or why not? Have you had family members or friends struggle with similar medical or end-of-life decisions?

9. Early in the story, we see Emma Landry with a rainbow painted on her cheek. Later, rainbows appear in Emma's drawing, in Drew's music, and finally Lauren sees a pale "watercolor" rainbow from her apartment balcony the morning after the storm. What do you think these rainbows symbolize?

10. The actions of ER manager Gayle Garner serve to heighten Lauren's confusing doubts about her sister. Especially about the missing drugs. Lauren finds herself torn, uncertain of whom to believe. Which of them did you believe? Why? Were you surprised by the outcome of this subplot?

11. Despite some decidedly serious themes in this story, humor plays a part as well. Was there a favorite scene, character, conversation, or image in *Life Support* that brought a chuckle or two? Share.

12. In *Life Support*'s epilogue, we see the key characters moving forward with their lives, but some of the

secondary characters' futures are left to readers' imaginations. What do you envision for Gayle Garner? Darcee? Fletcher Holt? Does the ending tie up enough story threads to satisfy?

Thank you for reading *Life Support*. Please visit my website at www.candacecalvert.com for information on upcoming books. And do drop me a note; I'd love to hear from you.

Warmly,
Candace Calvert

ABOUT THE AUTHOR

Candace Calvert is a former ER nurse and author of the Mercy Hospital series — *Critical Care, Disaster Status,* and *Code Triage* — and the Grace Medical series — *Trauma Plan, Rescue Team,* and *Life Support.* Her medical dramas offer readers a chance to "scrub in" on the exciting world of emergency medicine. Wife, mother, and very proud grandmother, Candace makes her home in northern California. Visit her website at www.candacecalvert.com.